ISLAND OF EXILES

I. J. PARKER, winner of a Shamus Award for the short story "Akitada's First Case," is the author of *The Dragon Scroll*, *Rashomon Gate*, *Black Arrow*, and *The Hell Screen*, and lives in Virginia Beach, Virginia.

ISLAND OF EXILES

A MYSTERY OF EARLY JAPAN

I. J. PARKER

PENGUIN BOOKS

PENGUIN BOOKS
Published by the Penguin Group
Penguin Group (USA) Inc., 375 Hudson Street, New York, New York 10014, U.S.A.
Penguin Group (Canada), 90 Eglinton Avenue East, Suite 700, Toronto, Ontario,
Canada M4P 2Y3 (a division of Pearson Penguin Canada Inc.)
Penguin Books Ltd, 80 Strand, London WC2R 0RL, England
Penguin Ireland, 25 St Stephen's Green, Dublin 2, Ireland
(a division of Penguin Books Ltd)
Penguin Group (Australia), 250 Camberwell Road, Camberwell, Victoria 3124,
Australia (a division of Pearson Australia Group Pty Ltd)
Penguin Books India Pvt Ltd, 11 Community Centre,
Panchsheel Park, New Delhi-110 017, India
Penguin Group (NZ), 67 Apollo Drive, Rosedale, North Shore 0745, Auckland,
New Zealand (a division of Pearson New Zealand Ltd.)
Penguin Books (South Africa) (Pty) Ltd, 24 Sturdee Avenue, Rosebank,
Johannesburg 2196, South Africa

Penguin Books Ltd, Registered Offices:
80 Strand, London WC2R 0RL, England

First published in Penguin Books 2007

3 5 7 9 10 8 6 4

Publisher's Note
This is a work of fiction. Names, characters, places, and incidents either are the product of the author's imagination or are used fictitiously, and any resemblance to actual persons, living or dead, business establishments, events, or locales is entirely coincidental.

LIBRARY OF CONGRESS CATALOGING IN PUBLICATION DATA
Parker, I. J. (Ingrid J.)
Island of exiles / I.J. Parker
p. cm.
ISBN 978-0-14-311259-4
1. Japan—History—Heian period, 794–1185—Fiction.
2. Sugawara Akitada (Fictitious character)
3. Penal colonies—Fiction. 4. Exiles—Fiction. I. Title.
PS3616.A745I85 2007
813'.6—dc22 2007012078

Printed in the United States of America
Set in Minion

For Hannah and Tony,

in hopes that they may grow up to love books

ACKNOWLEDGMENTS

I am indebted to my readers John Rosenman, Jacqueline Falkenhan, Richard Rowand, Bob Stein, and John Bushore for their comments and encouragement. My editor, Ali Bothwell Mancini, deserves credit for making decisions at the production stage. And, as always, I am deeply grateful to my agents, Jean Naggar and Jennifer Weltz, for their unstinting efforts in promoting this series as well as for their unfailing and enthusiastic support of its author.

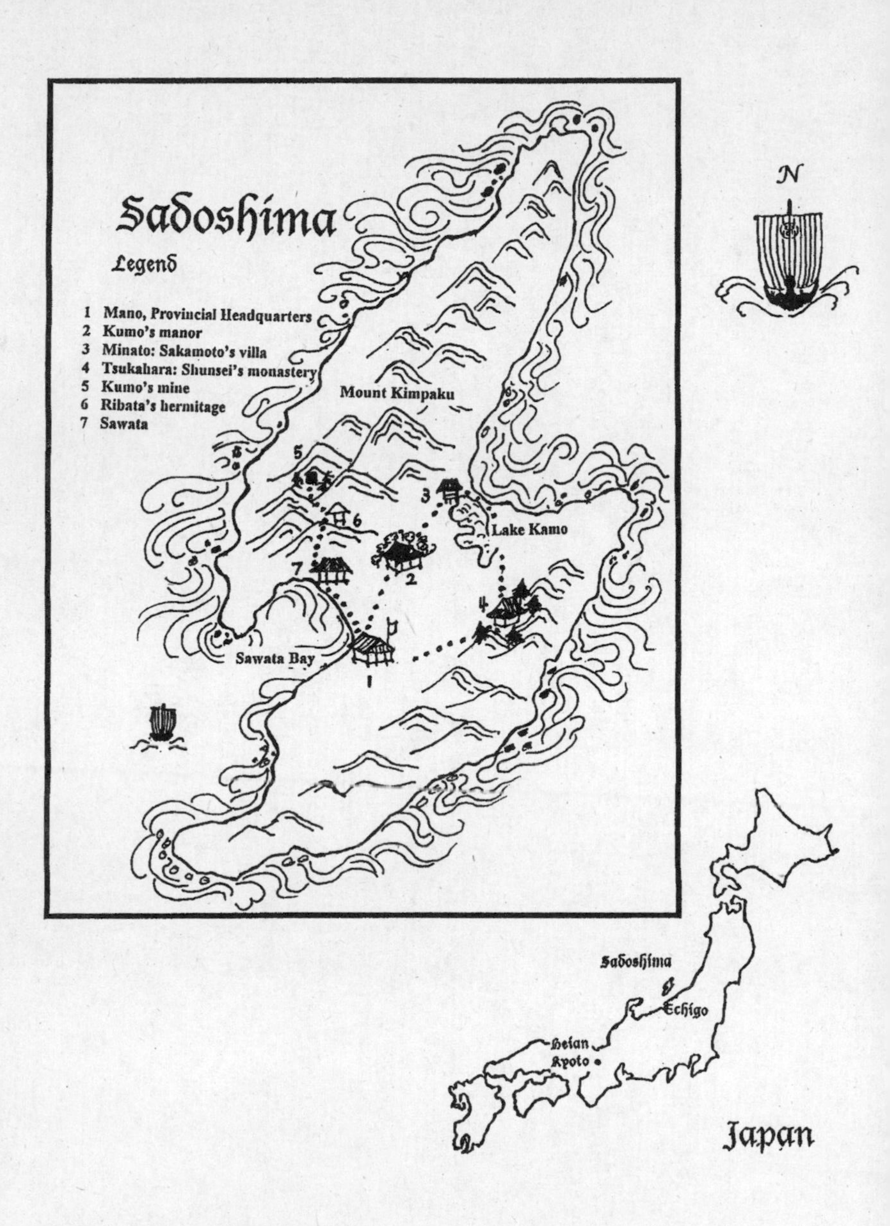
Sadoshima
Legend
1 Mano, Provincial Headquarters
2 Kumo's manor
3 Minato: Sakamoto's villa
4 Tsukahara: Shunsei's monastery
5 Kumo's mine
6 Ribata's hermitage
7 Sawata
Mount Kimpaku
Lake Kamo
Sawata Bay
1
2
3
4
5
6
7
N
Sadoshima
Echigo
Heian
Kyoto
Japan

CHARACTERS AND PLACES

Place Names:

Sadoshima	Sado Island in the Sea of Japan
Mano	Main port city and provincial headquarters on Sawata Bay
Minato	Village between Lake Kamo and the northeast coast (modern Ryotsu)
Tsukahara	Village near the southern mountains
Sawata	Town on Sawata Bay
Echigo	Northern province of Japan, known as "snow country" (modern Niigata)

Characters in Echigo:

Sugawara Akitada	Minor government official, deputy governor in Echigo
Tora	One of his retainers, presently lieutenant of the provincial guard
Seimei	His aged secretary
Tamako	His wife, the mother of his baby son, Yori

Characters in Sadoshima:

Prince Okisada	Aka the "Second Prince," oldest son of the previous emperor. Exiled for plotting the current emperor's overthrow
Taira Takamune	His former tutor and fellow exile
Professor Sakamoto	Retired professor of classics, writing a history of Sado Island
Mutobe Toshikata	Governor of Sadoshima
Mutobe Toshito	His son and assistant
Shunsei	Young Buddhist monk and the prince's lover
Yoshimine Taketsuna	Newly arrived exile with a secret
Jisei	Prisoner recently released from digging "badger holes"
Haseo	Taciturn prisoner with a scarred back
Doctor Ogata	Alcoholic physician and coroner
Lieutenant Wada	The local police authority
Superintendent Yamada	In charge of the prison and the "Valuables Office"
Masako	His daughter
Shijo Yutaka	Head of the provincial archives
Genzo	One of his scribes
Ribata	Nun with a past
Osawa	Tax inspector in search of a wife
Kumo Sanetomo	Local landowner and high constable of Sadoshima
Kita	Kumo's mine foreman

Takao	Landlady of the Minato inn and Osawa's friend
Haru	Owner of lake restaurant Bamboo Grove
Doctor Nakatomi	The prince's physician
Taimai (Turtle)	Crippled porter
Oyoshi	His sister, hostel keeper, and mother of many children
Little Flower	Childlike prostitute
Ikugoro	Wada's sergeant of constables

Also: two unnamed but high-ranking officials from the emperor's private office, cooks, guards, servants, fishermen, monks, elderly gentlewomen, constables, scribes, and an antique flute.

ISLAND OF EXILES

PROLOGUE

The orange sun disappeared behind the top of the mountain range, and a gradual gloom settled over the garden. At the lake's edge, a crane emerged cautiously from the reeds and froze, its small black eye on the five humans in the lakeside pavilion. The brilliant red patch on its head and the elegant black and white plumage were clearly visible in spite of the white mist that was beginning to rise from the darkening surface of the water. The air chilled quickly on Sado Island.

The crane was hungry for a mouthful of fish before seeking its roost. The humans, replete with good food and wine, let their conversation lag in the approaching darkness.

Advancing two slow, considered steps, the crane turned its attention to the lake bottom.

Professor Sakamoto and his four guests watched the bird idly. The professor had retired from the imperial university in the capital and settled here to write a history of the island and its famous exiles. This evening his guest of honor was Prince Okisada, a half-brother of the current sovereign and uncle of a future emperor. A frail man in his late forties, the Second Prince was by far the island's most exalted political exile.

Reaching for his wine cup, the prince raised his eyes from the crane to the mountaintop. Gilded by the last ray of sun, it looked as if a line of pure gold had been drawn between earth and heaven. He drank deeply and murmured, "It is time. The light is almost gone." His tone and expression were filled with deep emotion, but he slurred his words a little. Grimacing, he pressed a hand to his stomach. "What did you put in that prawn stew, Toshito?" he asked the young man on his left.

"Nothing, Your Highness. The woman uses just prawns, a bit of seaweed, and herbs. I was told it is your favorite." Mutobe Toshito looked annoyed. He was the governor's son and filling in for his father tonight.

The professor said peaceably, "It smelled delicious, Toshito. I am sure His Highness enjoyed the local specialty. What a thoughtful gesture. We were all pleased to see him eat with a good appetite for a change."

"There is nothing wrong with my appetite, Sakamoto," said the Second Prince irritably, and belched.

"Is Your Highness feeling unwell?" The other elderly man, on the prince's right, touched his arm solicitously. Taira Takamoto had been the prince's tutor and shared his exile now.

The Second Prince shook off Taira's hand, his face white and drawn. He kept massaging his stomach. "Shunsei," he murmured querulously to the handsome young monk sitting silently across from him, "come closer and massage my neck.

You are the only one who gives me pleasure these days. Will you stay the night?"

The young monk flushed and bowed deeply. "I am expected at the temple tonight, Highness," he said apologetically. His voice was soft and his eyes moist with adoration. He got up and went to kneel behind the prince.

The Second Prince fidgeted. "Never mind! Go, if you prefer their company. Is my room ready, Sakamoto?"

The professor got to his feet. "I'll see to it immediately, Highness."

Lord Taira emptied his cup and rose also. "I shall make sure that His Highness has all he needs. Good night, all." The two older men walked away toward the house. After a moment, the handsome monk bowed and followed them.

Only young Toshito remained with the prince. He looked after Shunsei with an expression of distaste.

"You d-don't approve of my lover?" the Second Prince said with some difficulty.

The young man flushed. "I . . . I beg your pardon, Highness?"

"D-don't bother to pretend. I've been aware that you and the governor disapprove of my t-tastes as much as my politics. It could not matter less to me. We shall prevail against the tyranny of an unlawful regime at l-last."

The governor's son stiffened and said uneasily, "I must remind you, Highness, that you were sent here as a prisoner. You are not likely to leave, certainly not as long as you voice treasonable intentions. And I'm afraid I shall have to report your words to my father, who will, in turn, report them to the emperor."

The Second Prince did not answer. He turned to look after the others, who had almost reached the house. Suddenly he groaned and bent forward, clutching his belly with both hands.

Toshito jumped to his feet. "What is it? Are you ill?"

"Help me, please!" The prince's voice rose to a shout of agony. Sweat beaded his face. He reached convulsively for his throat, choking out the words, "Loosen my collar! I cannot breathe."

The young man approached and leaned down to tug at the prince's collar, but the brocade robe fit tightly and he had to use both hands. To his horror, the prince began to scream again. His arms flailed wildly, delivering weak blows to Toshito's face and chest.

Down at the lakeshore, the startled crane had raised its head at the first shout. Now it spread its huge wings and flew off, a flapping fish in its long bill.

The others came running back to the pavilion.

Young Mutobe was still trying to restrain the wildly jerking prince. "Calm down, Highness," he gasped, and then shouted to Shunsei, "Run for the doctor!" But it was too late. The prince went first rigid and then limp in Toshito's arms and sagged heavily against him. He lowered the body to the ground.

Shunsei fell to his knees next to the prince and wailed, "Beloved, do not leave me yet."

Lord Taira was still out of breath, but his face contorted, and he struck the governor's son so violently in the chest that the young man went tumbling backward and fell against the railing.

The professor knelt to check the prince's breathing. "He's dead," he said.

"Murderer!" Taira pointed a shaking finger at Toshito, who lay where he had fallen, stunned with surprise. "You and your father did this. Did you think we would not hear his scream for help? We all saw you choke him. You killed a son of heaven. Not even the present government will countenance such sacrilege."

In the shocked silence which followed Taira's words, the first frog croaked in the reeds of the darkening lake.

CHAPTER ONE

VISITORS

The two high-ranking officials from the capital arrived in the tribunal of Echigo on a late summer afternoon.

When Seimei brought the news, Akitada was sitting on the remnants of the veranda in his private courtyard. He had been practicing his flute, while his young wife played with their baby son in the small enclosed area between their living quarters and the ramshackle assortment of halls and stables which made up the official headquarters of the province. It was no elegant courtyard with stones, lanterns, clipped trees, and raked gravel streams, but just a small square of dirt with a few weeds growing in the corners of the broken fence and under the veranda. They had been quite happy that afternoon. Tamako had swung the baby high up toward the limpid summer sky and laughed at the child's delighted gurgling. And Akitada had smiled as he practiced "Dewdrops on the Autumn Grasses." But he had felt a small pang of guilt when her sleeves slipped back and he saw how thin her arms had become.

He should not have brought her here to this inhospitable place where the rain and snow blew into their rooms, and the winters were as cold as their reception had been. But she had come eagerly, putting aside her old life to be a good and loyal wife to a struggling government official.

Sometimes he wished Tamako were a little less correct about her duties. Before the birth of his son there had been intimacy between them. In their nights together she had begun to open up to him, to share her secret thoughts after sharing her body. Because he was quite deeply in love with this slender, intelligent woman, he wanted her to be more to him than a dutiful wife and mother of his children. He loved his new son dearly but was jealous of the attention she lavished on him. It seemed that she had little time left for her husband now, that all her love and devotion were given to the child. But these feelings he kept to himself.

When old Seimei shuffled out on the veranda with his news, Akitada laid down his flute with a regretful glance toward his young family. "More messengers from Heian-kyo?" he asked, looking up at the thin white-haired man, who was servant, secretary, healer, and teacher to all of them. "I'm running out of reasons why we cannot increase the rice taxes and corvee at the same time. You would think they would know that the men are needed to work the fields if there is to be a harvest."

Seimei looked mysterious. "Not this time, sir. These are really important visitors."

Tamako's face lit up. "Important visitors?" Cradling the baby to her chest, she joined them. "Really? From the capital? Oh, it must be good news at last."

"Well, who are they?" Akitada asked, getting to his feet and brushing the wrinkles out of his second-best silk trousers.

"They did not give me their names, sir. I hope it is good news. It's been six months since you finished your tour of duty. A dreadful winter, especially for your lady."

"It has not been so bad," Tamako said quickly, but she hugged the child a little closer and looked at the broken shutters of their house.

It had been dreadfully hard for them all. Akitada had feared for their lives, his young wife's because she was with child, and Seimei's because he was old. What had started as a temporary assignment to take care of legal matters and paperwork for an absent governor had quickly turned into a nightmare. Akitada had been only a junior clerk in the ministry of justice when his stubborn pursuit of a murderer brought him to the notice of a powerful noble. When his name was put forward for the job in Echigo, Akitada had been flattered and excited by the distinction. He had taken his young and pregnant wife to this snow country, expecting to serve for a few months and then return to a better position in the capital.

But they had spent a long and bitter winter fighting the climate and hostility against imperial authority without support from Heian-kyo, and now they were apparently forgotten. Another winter loomed, though Akitada had written many letters to ask for his replacement and his back salary, for they were also nearly destitute by now.

Perhaps, he thought hopefully, his letters had borne result and they could finally leave this godforsaken place behind forever. Perhaps a duly appointed governor was about to arrive with his own staff and take over the duties that had overburdened Akitada. But even as he clung to this thought, he doubted it. It was very strange that the visitors had not given Seimei their names. Akitada glanced at his wife and saw the naked hope in her eyes.

"Oh, Akitada," she breathed. "Oh, I do hope it is the recall. Your mother's letters have been so worrying. She says her health is poor and that she will die before she sees her grandson."

Actually, the older Lady Sugawara was an ill-tempered tyrant who demanded total obedience from her son and everyone else in her household. She was at least part of the reason Akitada had welcomed this assignment. He had thought it would get them away from his mother long enough to give his marriage a chance.

He said diplomatically, "Yes. It will be good to return to the old home."

Seimei cleared his throat. "Sir, the gentlemen seemed very anxious to speak to you."

"Such haste after all this time?" Akitada mocked, but he adjusted his collar, touched his neatly tied topknot, and followed Seimei to the tribunal.

"I seated them in your office and served them some herbal tea," Seimei told him on the way. "Mint and ginger root to refresh the mind after a long journey, and a bit of ground-up iris root to purify the sluggish blood. They seemed out of sorts."

Seimei's herbal teas, changed according to the season and the recipient's needs, were not the best way to put important visitors at ease. They tended to be malodorous and bitter to the tongue, but since the old man believed they promoted good health and a long life, Akitada and his family submitted to his concoctions to make him happy.

The tribunal hall was the main building in the provincial compound. Here the provincial governor held his receptions, heard court cases, maintained the provincial archives, and conducted the business of the province. Today the hall was empty and the corridors lay silent. Such peace was a welcome change after the hectic days of the past winter. Akitada glanced around the cavernous hall critically. The floors were swept and the worst holes in the rafters had been closed with new boards, the repairs paid for from Akitada's private funds. In the archives his three clerks were bent over their desks, studiously copying documents. And in the main courtyard outside he could hear the voices of his two lieutenants drilling the constables. He hoped this orderly regimen had impressed his visitors favorably.

Seimei flung back the door to his office and announced proudly, "Lord Sugawara."

The title was his due, for Akitada was a direct descendant of the great Sugawara Michizane, but the Sugawaras had fallen on hard times after his famous ancestor's exile and death, and his present status in the world was more than modest. Not only was he poor and without influence, two serious shortcomings for which he tried to make up by carrying out his duties to the letter, but he had managed to irritate his superiors.

Two middle-aged men in ordinary dark travel robes and black caps sat on the threadbare cushions near Akitada's scratched and dented desk. They had to be of considerable rank, for neither rose at his entrance, merely turning their heads to stare at him curiously.

One of the men was tall and thin, with a long, yellow-tinged face which looked vaguely disapproving. His shorter companion had an unnaturally ruddy complexion and glowered. Akitada's heart sank, but he reminded himself that they had come a long way. Exposure to sun and wind during long journeys had unfortunate effects on the normally pale features of noblemen and probably also on their temper. And, to judge by their rudeness, these two must possess considerable rank and irritability.

Their rank was a problem. Etiquette prescribed that Akitada adjust his greeting to bridge the distance between his own rank and theirs precisely, but they were complete strangers to him and neither wore the colors of his rank on his plain black cap. His heart beating uncomfortably, he decided on a modest bow to each before taking his seat behind his desk. His visitors' cool response boded ill.

The shorter man made a face. "Well, you took your time, Sugawara," he complained, then waved his hand impatiently at the waiting Seimei. "What are you standing about for? Leave us alone."

Seimei bowed deeply and backed from the room.

When the door had closed, Akitada said, "Allow me to bid you both welcome," and faltered, looking from one forbidding face to the other. Apparently they resented his casual greeting, but he was at a loss how to address them.

"Not much of a welcome," grumbled the short one. "This tribunal looks a disgrace. The walls are falling down, your constables look like scarecrows, and your stable is unfit for horses. And what is this poison your senile servant tried to palm off on us?"

Akitada flushed. "Just some herbal tea. It is considered very healthful. No doubt Seimei—who is my secretary, by the way—felt that you might need a restorative after your long journey."

The short stranger turned down the corners of his mouth. "He must be demented. Do you drink this stuff?"

Akitada assured him that both he and his family had found Seimei's teas most helpful in the past.

"Then you must be demented also." He turned to the thin man. "I think we are wasting our time here."

Akitada was beginning to hope so, too, but the tall man shook his head. "No. I think not." His voice was dry and he barely moved his thin lips when he spoke. "And keep in mind that we have no choice." The other man subsided with a frown.

Somehow this was not encouraging. Akitada offered, "Shall I send for some wine instead?"

"By all means," said the thin man, with a smile that was almost jovial. He looked at Akitada with an interest which reminded him uncomfortably of a cat eyeing a fat sparrow.

Akitada clapped his hands for Seimei. "Some wine please, Seimei."

Seimei removed the full teacups with a little sniff but mercifully did not argue the point. When they were alone again, Akitada searched for polite words to ask who his visitors were.

"I am afraid," he began, "that I have not had the pleasure of meeting . . . Your Excellencies in the capital." He paused.

His visitors exchanged glances.

The short man said, "It is not necessary for you to know who we are."

Stranger and stranger. Akitada decided that this could not have anything to do with his inadequate administration of the chaotic affairs in Echigo. Neither, sadly, did it sound as though they were bringing his release. He cleared his throat nervously. "May I ask, then, what brings you here?"

The short man said, "In due time. First we have some questions ourselves. And we have yet to be offered adequate refreshments."

Akitada flushed. He was becoming annoyed with their rudeness and wished they would get to the point and leave.

They sat in silence until Seimei appeared with a large tray holding three small pitchers of wine and three cups. They were unmatched, badly chipped, and of the cheapest clayware. Bowing to each gentleman in turn, Seimei poured wine into a cup, presented it, and placed the small pitcher before him.

Akitada asked if there were any plum pickles left.

Shaking his head, Seimei offered, "I could slice some fresh radish from my garden."

The short man, who had made a face when he tasted his wine, muttered, "Fresh radish? What does the fool take us for?"

Akitada bit his lip. Considering their probable rank, their rudeness to him was one thing, but he was fond of Seimei, who had been like a father to him and served him still with unfailing love and devotion. On the other hand, these men were potentially powerful and he could not afford to offend them. He said, "I regret extremely the poor hospitality. Had we known of your arrival, we might have prepared more suitable refreshments, though this poor province has little with which to please someone like yourselves."

The short man grunted, but the thin one raised his brows, and Akitada realized that he had not sounded at all deferential. He fell silent again and waited.

"We have had worse wine on our journey here, Mototsune," said the thin man thoughtfully.

The short man smirked. "Once, *To*."

Akitada stared at the thin man. He was not certain he had heard right. *To* was the title of the emperor's two first secretaries, the highest position in the sovereign's private office. Each held the fourth rank. How could a man of such illustrious status be sitting in his office in the ramshackle tribunal of a remote province like Echigo?

"Are you acquainted with the Second Prince?" the thin man asked him.

The question was unexpected and flustered Akitada even more, but he managed to nod. The Second Prince was really the eldest son of the late emperor and had once been crown prince and emperor-designate. But when he had been in his twenties, his father had suddenly decided to make another son by a secondary empress his heir, and Okisada had become the Second Prince. Angered, he started an intrigue against his much younger half-brother, and the emperor had punished him by sending him to Kyushu. Okisada had apologized and been allowed to return to the capital to live there in powerless comfort and luxury for the next ten years. Then his father, worried about his health, had abdicated in favor of Okisada's half-brother. One of the court nobles, a Lord Miyoshi, discovered that Okisada was involved in a plot to kill his half-brother and seize the throne. This time his punishment had been permanent exile to Sadoshima, where he had remained for the past decade.

"Well? Have you lost your voice?" the thin man demanded.

"I beg your pardon, Excellency. I was waiting for you to explain further. I know something of Prince Okisada and once, when I was a boy, I saw him in passing. He is at present living in exile on Sadoshima."

The thin man shook his head. "Incorrect. The prince is dead. He has been murdered."

Akitada sat up. This was extraordinary news. A murder of an imperial prince on the island of exiles? What could be going on there? Sadoshima was in the Sea of Japan, about twenty miles north of the coast of Echigo. Exile to Sadoshima was the most severe form of punishment short of execution. Only very violent or politically dangerous criminals were sent there. But what did this have to do with him?

The thin man smiled. "Ah," he said. "I see we finally have your attention. You have the reputation of being clever at solving murders. We want you to go to Sado Island and find out what happened."

Akitada's eyes widened, but he shook his head. "I am sorry, Excellency, but I have no authority to leave my post. Neither do I have the power to meddle in the affairs of another province. I expect Sadoshima's governor has already begun an investigation into the crime."

"Pah! The investigation is tainted. The murderer is Governor Mutobe's son."

"What?" Akitada stared at his mysterious visitor. "Are you certain, Excellency? Or do you mean that he has only been accused of the crime?"

The thin man made an impatient gesture. "Accused, arrested, and up for trial. Apparently the prince was poisoned by some food the young man provided. The facts are not disputed."

That was a tricky situation, and Akitada was thoroughly intrigued, but he said again, "Even so, I regret that I am not able to accede to your request."

The short man turned a deeper shade and blustered, "Must I remind you that you are nothing but a clerk in the ministry of justice on temporary assignment here?"

Akitada bowed. "That is very true and I regret extremely not to be able to do as you wish. But my instructions state precisely that I am to take my orders only from my superior or a representative of the emperor."

They looked at each other. Then the lean gentleman took some rolled-up documents from his sleeve. As he sorted through these, Akitada saw the yellow silk ribbons used for imperial documents and felt his skin crawl. The thin man looked up, saw Akitada's expression, and smiled. He unrolled one of the yellow-ribboned papers partially and displayed the large crimson seal of the sovereign's private office. "Do you recognize the seal?"

"Yes, Excellency." Akitada bowed to touch his forehead to the desk. Perhaps, he thought, he should prostrate himself, but he did not quite know how to move from behind the desk and stretch out on the floor without getting up first. An imperial seal represented His Majesty, and one never stood before such an object.

"Good," commented the thin man. "I assume you are satisfied that I have the power to send you to Sado Island?"

Akitada sat back on his heels. "I am afraid not, Excellency. I do not know you or how you may have come by imperial documents or what the documents pertain to."

"Are you calling him a thief and a liar?" cried the short man. "How dare you?" He turned to his colleague. "You see? That is what comes of sending unsuitable persons to fill crucial posts in the provinces. I shall certainly report this impudent fellow's lack of cooperation to the great council of state."

Akitada turned cold. Such a thing would surely end his career.

The thin man cleared his throat, then leaned closer to whisper something to his companion. The other man still glowered but nodded reluctantly.

Akitada watched them and wished that this day had never happened. Nothing good could come from this meeting, no matter how diplomatic he was with these men. He had no idea what he was getting into, except that it involved the emperor, high treason, and murder.

The thin man sorted through his papers again, then passed a letter to Akitada, who recognized the handwriting. It was from Soga Ietada, minister of justice and Akitada's immediate superior. The letter appeared to answer some question about Akitada's background. Soga had written, "Sugawara, a junior clerk in our archives, performed his simple duties adequately, though without enthusiasm. He has a regrettable and obstinate tendency to become involved in investigations of low crime in his spare time, a situation which often strains relations between the capital police and our ministry."

When Akitada looked up, the thin man smiled his thin smile. "When I knew we would pass through Echigo, I contacted Soga. You see, we know of your interest in murder from an unimpeachable source."

Akitada handed back the letter. "This bears no superscription. I still do not know who you are, sir."

The short man made an impatient noise, but his companion raised his hand. He looked at Akitada, who looked back and compressed his lips stubbornly.

"So. You still do not trust me. But how can I trust you?"

"If you came to me knowing only what Minister Soga told you, you cannot," Akitada said bitterly.

The thin man chuckled. "Oh, Soga was not my only source. Let me see. I also heard that you placed first in your university examination. An uncommon distinction which means you have above-normal intelligence and learning."

"I was fortunate."

"Hmm. I believe you received your present appointment because you solved a complicated crime affecting another member of the imperial family?"

That was only known to a very few people. Akitada said cautiously, "It is true that my humble efforts may have brought me my present assignment," adding silently that, if he had known better, he would have refused it.

"Whose side are you on, Sugawara?"

"I beg your pardon?"

"In the matter of Prince Okisada."

Akitada was an imperial official and thought the answer should have been obvious. "Oh. His Majesty was duly chosen by the previous emperor. There can be no question about the legality of the succession. The ruling sovereign designates his successor from among his brothers or sons, provided that his choice is capable of carrying out the duties of an emperor. There is a precedent for this case. In 438, another crown prince was considered unfit and passed over in favor of his younger brother. May His Majesty's reign last a thousand years." Akitada bowed.

"Spoken like a legal scholar. Very well, I suppose I have no choice but to trust you. I cannot reveal details, but you may have a look at our original commission. I hope you will treat the information with the utmost secrecy. No one must know our purpose."

His companion objected. "I am opposed. Sugawara's character is dubious from all we have heard. He has disobeyed orders and taken matters into his own hands before. If he persists in refusing an order, I say we go back and investigate the case ourselves."

"Neither you nor I have the expertise to investigate a murder, nor sufficient background in the law, nor in the details of provincial administration. Sugawara does and he is close enough to reach Sado Island quickly." The thin man selected one of the imperial documents and passed it across to Akitada.

Akitada sat lost in amazement at what these two officials expected of him. The thin man raised his brows and gave a meaningful nod at the document roll in his hand. Belatedly, Akitada extended both hands to receive it and raised the imperial seal respectfully above his head, before undoing the silk ribbon with trembling fingers. The emperor's private office used heavy, cream-colored mulberry paper of the finest quality, and Akitada's hands were sweating. He wiped them surreptitiously on his robe, and then read. The handwriting of the imperial scribe was most elegant, so elegant in fact that he had trouble deciphering it. But flowery language and floating brushstrokes aside, he saw that his visitors were both advisors to the emperor. He recognized their names and knew that they held the fourth and fifth ranks, respectively, but they worked in too exalted an office to have come in contact with a mere junior clerk in the ministry of justice. The letter instructed them to travel to Sadoshima in order to visit Prince Okisada and discuss "certain matters" with him on behalf of His Majesty. The faint signature at the end was the sovereign's. Akitada again raised the document above his head, before rolling it up carefully and retying the silk ribbon with clumsy fingers. He returned it with a deep bow. "Please forgive my earlier lack of courtesy, Your Excellencies," he said humbly.

The short man grunted, but his thin colleague smiled. "Never mind. I like a cautious man. You will need to be wary in Sadoshima. We suspect a great deal of trouble is brewing there."

"Trouble? Forgive me, Excellency, but when did the prince die?"

"Last week. We were greeted by the news when we arrived."

"Only last week?" Akitada rearranged his thoughts rapidly. They had not been sent to him from the capital. The government was still pleased to ignore him. They—or rather the thin man (though he knew their names, Akitada preferred to think in anonymous terms), had come to him on his own initiative. He felt mildly flattered but also worried. "Then why did His Majesty send you there?" he asked.

"We cannot talk about matters which concern the sovereign," protested the short man.

The thin man sighed. "Can you not simply go and find out if the governor's son, a young man called Toshito, is truly guilty?"

Akitada hesitated. Sometimes it is better not to know too much, and he got a distinct feeling that this was one of those times. But he could not help himself. "You mentioned trouble and the need to be wary. I cannot be wary if I don't know what the trouble is. Your visit to Sadoshima suggests that there was serious concern about another plot against His Imperial Majesty. I think that is what the letter alludes to when it speaks of 'certain matters' and why you undertook such a long journey in the first place. But when you arrived you found that Prince Okisada had been poisoned by the son of the governor. Some might wonder if this Toshito had acted on behalf of His Majesty."

The short man sucked in his breath sharply. They both stared at him as if he had suddenly been transformed into something alien, as if a field mouse had turned into a fox before their eyes.

Then the thin man chuckled softly and said, "Bravo! That was quite clever of you. You will do very well."

The short man made a face. "Let us be careful," he warned.

"Never mind. Sugawara is quite right. He will need to know a little more. The danger of an insurrection may be over now that the prince is dead, but what if it is not?" He paused to pour himself another cup of wine and drank.

"It all began three months ago when we—I refer to the private office of the emperor—heard rumors of some trouble between the governor of Sado Island and its chief constable. As you may imagine, His Majesty is vitally interested in anything which pertains to the tragic situation of his brother. It is a pity that we are not kept better informed." He harrumphed. "But that is neither here nor there. We checked into the matter and found that the quarrel was unrelated to the prince. Apparently Mutobe, the governor, in a bout of ill-advised zeal, overstepped his powers and interfered with law enforcement on Sadoshima."

"Forgive me, Excellency, but I do not understand what this has to do with the prince's murder."

The thin man bit his lip and exchanged a glance with his friend. "We traveled to Sado to verify the facts."

Akitada shook his head. "I do not think so. The journey to Sado Island from the capital is long and dangerous. In this instance, Your Excellencies appear to have undertaken the journey without escort and incognito. Would a minor squabble between two provincial administrators really cause His Majesty to send his most trusted advisors on such an assignment?"

"Look here, young man," blustered the short visitor, "you ask too many questions. We have explained as much as you need to know. Now it is up to you to find out who killed the prince and why."

Akitada bowed. Nobody said anything for a while.

Finally the thin man sighed again. "As you know, Sadoshima is a notorious haven for pirates who ply the ocean up and down the coast. Not far to the north from here, our armies are fighting the Ezo warlords again. With the prince on Sadoshima, you can see what our enemies might do."

"You were afraid that the prince might become a hostage to the Ezo?"

"That was *one* possibility," agreed the thin man.

Akitada suddenly saw the real danger and the full dilemma faced by his two noble visitors. The other, unspoken and unspeakable, scenario was that Okisada himself had been negotiating with the Ezo in another attempt to seize the throne. Akitada felt a cold shiver run down his spine. The bloodshed along the path of such an army led southward by a claimant to the throne would be unimaginable. The people of Echigo and his own small family would certainly be victims in such a war.

The Ezo, their hostile barbarian neighbors to the north, had threatened the peaceful life of Japanese peasants for hundreds of years. Recently their chieftains had submitted to the emperor in Dewa and Mutsu Provinces, but the military strength and expertise of these warlords had grown. They rebelled often, and still posed a continuous threat to the nation.

"Will you accept the assignment?" asked the thin man.

Akitada bowed. "Yes, Your Excellency, provided that my doing so is properly authorized by you in His Majesty's name."

"It is not likely that you will be told anything if you go there in an official capacity. Much better that you travel incognito."

Akitada said, "Perhaps I could travel as a peddler or peasant, carrying my papers sewn into my clothing. Nobody pays attention to common people. But I must have properly authorized documents."

They did not like it, but the thin man finally agreed. "Let us sleep over it. We are tired and you will wish to make preparations." He looked at Akitada. "May I suggest that you stop shaving? Otherwise you will hardly convince anyone that you are a peasant or vagrant."

"There is one other small problem," Akitada said nervously. "I have not received my salary since I arrived here with my family. My retainers have not been paid, though they have carried out the duties of secretary of the tribunal and constabulary officers. I have exhausted my own funds making repairs and cannot leave my people destitute."

They looked at him in amazement. It occurred to Akitada that they were probably so wealthy that they would never find themselves in his desperate situation.

The short man said, "But why did you not draw on the provincial treasury for salaries and expenses? Everybody does."

"I had no authorization, Excellency."

The short man blurted, "That old law? Nobody follows that any longer. Don't you know anything? It boggles the mind that—" The thin man put a restraining hand on his sleeve, and he concluded, "Hmph. Well, do so immediately. Collect what is owed you and enough to see your family and staff through the next week or two. You should be back by then."

The thin man said more gently, "These days provincial administrators are expected to draw funds from the local treasury, Sugawara. That is why they send an examining official to settle accounts when you leave your post." He nodded to his companion, and they got to their feet.

"Thank you." Akitada was not sure whether he felt more ashamed of his ignorance or happy that his financial woes were solved. He decided on the latter. "Allow me to offer you my quarters," he said in a spirit of wanting to share his good fortune. "They are not much, but my wife and I will do our best to make you comfortable."

The short man cast a glance at the patched ceiling and broken shutters of Akitada's office. "Thank you, but we have already taken rooms at the local inn."

Akitada accompanied them to the front of the tribunal hall. From the height of its veranda, they could see across the tribunal walls and the roofs of the provincial capital all the way to the sea. On this clear day, it was just possible to make out the long hazy outline of Sadoshima on the horizon. It seemed another world.

In the courtyard, the constables were just finishing their drill. When Tora, one of Akitada's own men and their temporary lieutenant, looked up and saw them, he called the constables to attention. Arranging his cheerful face into sterner lines, he saluted stiffly as the two noble gentlemen descended the steps to the courtyard and passed on their way to their horses.

Akitada breathed a sigh of relief. The constables had actually looked pretty sharp, in spite of their lack of proper uniforms, a matter he would remedy immediately. But Tora spoiled the good impression he had made by shouting up to Akitada, "Well, sir, are we going home at last?"

The short visitor, almost at the gate, froze in his tracks for a moment before continuing.

"Report to my office, Tora," snapped Akitada, and walked back inside.

Time was when Tora had been a mere peasant and foot soldier. Then he had fallen on even worse times and was hunted by the authorities as a deserter and bandit. He owed his change in fortunes to the day Akitada had offered to take him on as a servant.

Tora had almost turned down the offer. In those days, he had hated officials almost as much as the injustices his family had suffered. But his master had been as intolerant of injustice as Tora, and they had built a strong friendship, one in which Tora expressed his opinions freely. They had saved each other's lives repeatedly and risen in each other's esteem through mutual tolerance of the other's shortcomings, namely Tora's womanizing and Akitada's rigidity about the law.

Now Tora ran after him, boots pounding on the wooden planks and startling the clerks in the archives. "Well?" he demanded again.

"Why did you shout at me?"

"Because you were too far away." Tora grinned with his usual impudence.

Akitada sighed. Tora was incorrigible, but the fault was his. He had treated him from the start more like a brother than a servant. "I shall have to leave for a week or two," he said. "There is some trouble in Sadoshima. The former crown prince was murdered. I am to investigate the murder charge against the governor's son."

Tora whistled. "The governor's son? What's the world coming to? Shall I start packing my things?"

"No. I am going alone. You and Genba will look after things here. I should be back in a week."

Tora looked disappointed, but he accepted the decision, especially when Akitada promised to pay his back wages before he departed.

After Tora left, Akitada walked back to his residence. He did not like to leave Tamako and his son but had no choice in the matter. Even if he could have refused such an order, doing so would have ended his career for good. On the other hand, if he managed to solve the problem, he hoped the two imperial secretaries would put in a good word for him in the capital.

Seimei and Tamako were waiting anxiously. Their faces fell when they saw him. Akitada hated to see the hope drain from Tamako's eyes.

"We are to stay here?" she asked.

"For the time being. I am to go to Sadoshima to investigate a murder."

"That place?" she cried. "Where they send all the worst criminals?"

"Don't worry. I shall not be gone long, and perhaps something good may come of it."

◆

But when the two noble visitors returned the following morning, his optimism vanished. They proposed an extraordinary plan which struck Akitada as both dangerous and uncertain.

CHAPTER TWO

THE PRISONER

The ship had been at sea for two days. Blown off course by a sudden violent summer storm, it had become lost in the open ocean shortly after departing from the coast south of Echigo.

The prisoner was in the back of the ship, unchained since they had left land behind and there was no longer any risk of escape. He lay against the side, as he had for days, suffering from the rough seas and the seasickness they brought.

When he had been taken on board, they had put him below deck, into a tiny black hole. Later, when they were well out at sea, one of the guards had taken off his shackles and left an oil lamp which swung from the low ceiling, putting out little light but a horrible stench. The small area had become hot and so smoky it had been hard to breathe.

But the real misery started with the storm. He had woken from a fitful sleep when the ship began to roll and plunge amid horrendous noise. Outside, dull crashing and roaring sounds of wind and water bore down on the small ship. The sail snapped loudly in the wind and sailors shouted urgent orders to each other. The prisoner had worried about the creaking timbers, which seemed hardly strong enough to withstand the combined onslaught of wind and water. And he had thought of his family.

The stench of the oil lamp, its violent swinging back and forth, the roll and pitch of the flimsy planks underneath him had sickened him until he could not control the heaving in his belly. By nature fastidious, he had crawled out of his hole and up a short bamboo ladder to the pitching deck. Nobody paid attention to him, and he had at first welcomed the icy spray of water, the sharp tearing gusts of wind, until the pitching and rolling of the ship had sent him slipping and scrabbling to the side, where he had vomited into a heaving black sea.

The vomiting was unremitting from then on, keeping pace with the storm, abating as the wind abated a little, but recommencing with the next onslaught. He was conscious of little difference between day and night, though the pitch-blackness which must have been the first night, did make way for a dense dark gray world in which water and sky were of a uniform murkiness. It was then that it had dawned on him that they were lost. He swallowed neither food nor water for what seemed like days, nor felt any desire for them, and in time he became too weak and listless to raise himself enough to bring up the bile from his stomach while leaning over the side.

So now he lay in his own filth, only half conscious and soaked to the skin.

The ship was still soaring and pitching, the wind still howled, and spray burst across the deck, but there was a subtle change in the atmosphere. Frantic activity ceased, and it became almost quiet. Somewhere someone prayed to Amida, but he was giving thanks for being spared.

The prisoner had neither the strength nor the inclination to give thanks. His journey to the island of exiles had already proven horrible beyond his wildest imaginings, and he had little expectation that what lay ahead would be much easier.

However, sea and weather calmed, the captain changed course, and a brisk wind carried them finally to their destination. A call from the lookout came early the following morning, just as the prisoner was drinking greedily from a flask of water one of the guards offered. It was snatched back quickly, too quickly, for never had water tasted so delicious. There was land westward, and the sailors and guards all rushed to that side of the boat, causing it to lean and the captain to curse them. The prisoner raised himself and peered into a pearly dawn without seeing anything. Below, the green sea slid past like translucent gossamer in a lady's train, and he leaned down to dip his hand and sleeve into it and washed his face and beard.

Before noon they steered into Sawata Bay and crossed the limpid waters under a clear summer sky toward a green shore dotted with small brown roofs huddled about a temple. Slightly above the low-lying coast a larger compound of broad roofs dominated the town. This was Mano, the provincial capital of Sadoshima.

Having been fed a small amount of millet gruel to give him enough strength to stand and walk, the prisoner was on his feet, but the transfer to the rowboat and stepping on solid land had proved a shameful affair punctuated by several falls and a drunken stagger.

On shore, a reception committee of sorts awaited. Six rough-looking constables, chains wrapped around their middles and whips in their hands, stood behind a red-coated police officer in his official black cap. The short, squat, sharp-faced man in his forties with a scanty mustache and a stiff-legged stance received the papers the captain passed to him and glanced through them. He looked the swaying prisoner up and down before snapping, "He looks disgusting. Is he sick?"

Unimpressed by the officer's manner, much less by his high, nasal voice, the captain spat, crooked a finger over his shoulder at the tattered sails, and said, "We got lost in a spell of bad weather. Spewed his guts out. He'll be all right in a day or so."

Reassured that the human cargo suffered from nothing worse, the officer addressed the prisoner next. "You are called Yoshimine Taketsuna?"

The prisoner croaked, "Yes."

Instantly one of the guards stepped forward and back-handed him. He cried out in protest, staggered, and fell.

"On your knees!" snarled the guard, kicking him in the ribs.

His nose bleeding, the prisoner slowly knelt.

"You will address me as 'sir' and bow when you speak," snapped the police officer.

The prisoner staggered up, squaring his shoulders. He looked at the officer's cap rank insignia and said contemptuously, "I have never bowed to mere lieutenants."

Punishment was instant again. This time the guard used his fists. The prisoner managed to turn his head just a fraction, but he was struck on the side of his jaw and flung again into the dirt, this time too stunned to rise. His nose gushed blood, and more blood trickled from between his lips.

The police lieutenant, his eyes cold, bent down to him. "Your past rank, whatever it may have been, is immaterial here. By imperial order you are to be imprisoned on this island for the rest of your life. You are a nobody and will be assigned to work details to earn your food and clothes. You are not to attempt escape or rebellion on pain of death." He paused, then added, "We consider lack of respect, disobedience to orders, lack of cooperation, and complaints as indicative of the rebellious character of a prisoner. You have escaped lightly this time." He straightened up and snapped, "Take him away."

Two of the guards took hold of the prisoner's arms and jerked him upright. Half walking, half being dragged, he was taken from the dockside to a nearby stockade, where he was pushed into the middle of a group of other wretches huddling in the shadow of the wall. The heavy gates clanked shut, and most of the guards withdrew to a small guardhouse, except for the four or five on duty. These gathered in a shady corner near the gates, their long bows propped against the palisade, and chatted idly.

It was hot in the courtyard. The midday sun baked the gravel, and the tall stockade blocked the breeze from the ocean. The prisoners huddled miserably around a wooden bucket. For a while no one said anything. The others looked at the newcomer with mild interest.

Taketsuna lay motionless for a few moments. Then he spat out a mouthful of blood. His eyes closed, he explored the inside of his mouth with his tongue. Thankful that no teeth seemed to be broken, he settled for a bitten tongue and split lip, opened his eyes, and struggled into a sitting position.

His eyes went slowly around, studying his fellow prisoners one by one: three huge muscular men and one little shrimp of a fellow, all as filthy and more ragged than he. Then he touched his face and winced. The side where the guard had punched him was swollen and tender to the touch, and his nose still bled a little. He dabbed at it with a sleeve and swallowed more blood.

The shrimp, who had bandaged knees and elbows, reached for the water bucket and pushed it toward him. Taketsuna nodded his thanks, dipped both hands into the warm water, and drank deeply. He was about to dip in one of his full sleeves when one of the other prisoners snatched the bucket away.

"Damn you," he snarled, "for dirtying our drinking water with your stinking rags."

"Sorry. I didn't know." The newcomer glanced across the courtyard to the well. Another bucket hung ready to be lowered. He staggered to his feet and started toward it.

"Hey," cried the shrimp. "Don't do that. They'll shoot you."

The prisoner stopped and glanced at the lounging gate guards, who seemed engrossed in a dice game. He continued to the well, when another "Hey!" louder than the first sounded behind him. Ignoring it, he lowered the bucket, filled it, and brought it up. There was a loud plonk, followed by a whirring sound. It drew his eyes to the crossbeam supporting the bucket. An arrow stuck deep in the wood, vibrating softly. The prisoner set the bucket on the coping and began to splash the water over his face, hair, and neck. Then he washed his hands, the bloody sleeve, and the front of his robe.

A rough hand grabbed his shoulder and spun him around. "Are you deaf?" the guard growled. "Washing is not allowed. Walking around is not allowed. Talking, shouting, and singing are not allowed. Get back with the others." He gave the prisoner a vicious shove. Taketsuna staggered, then returned to his assigned spot, where he sat down and wrung out his sleeve.

The others were whispering together. One of the big men missed an eye. He said, "Don't bother. He must be deaf. You saw what happened."

"I'm not deaf," said the new prisoner.

They gaped at him. The man with the crippled leg asked, "Then why did you go to the well? Jisei warned you. You're lucky the guard didn't shoot you."

"I wished to wash."

Silence, as they looked at each other. "He wished to wash," said the cripple, and laughed.

"Aren't you afraid to die?" the small man with the bandaged knees and arms wanted to know.

"Very much. But I didn't think they would shoot a man for washing his face."

"Hah!" muttered the one-eyed fellow. They all shared a bitter laugh at the newcomer's innocence. "What's your name?" the small man asked.

"Yoshimine Taketsuna."

The shrimp's eyes grew round. "Two names. A gentleman. No wonder you act like you own the place. How come they sent you here?"

"I killed someone."

"Ah!" They looked at each other and nodded understanding.

Introductions followed. The small man with the bandages was Jisei; he had just returned from a work detail digging tunnels deep into the earth and bringing out rocks. His knees and elbows had become infected after a year's crawling on all fours. "I'll be reassigned now," he told Taketsuna importantly. "Maybe I'll even get to go home." He looked away, across the top of the stockade, a dreamy smile on his lined face.

Haseo, a huge burly man, spat. The others introduced him; apparently he rarely spoke himself and appeared to take little interest in the conversation. They only knew his name and imagined that he, too, must be a convicted killer. Haseo did not correct them.

They passed the long hot afternoon in desultory conversation interspersed with naps.

The two big fellows, one crippled with a badly set leg, the other one-eyed, were pirates, Kumaso and Yoshi. They passed the time telling of adventure at sea, of stolen treasure, monsters of the deep, and apparitions of floating fairies. According to Jisei, they also had an uncanny talent for predicting the weather.

Jisei, the shrimp, had been on Sadoshima longest, having been sent here for stealing a golden scepter from the hand of a temple statue.

All of them awaited reassignment, though none was as optimistic as Jisei. They expected to be put to work building roads, digging irrigation canals, building stockades, or repairing public buildings.

Taketsuna wanted to ask about Jisei's strange tunneling when shouts sounded outside the gate. The guards rushed to throw open both sides of the double gate and stood to attention. A contingent of uniformed runners entered at a trot, carrying the banner of the governor of Sado. His Excellency followed on a fine horse, and more runners brought up the rear. "Make room for the governor!" shouted the frontrunners in unison, and the prisoners immediately prostrated themselves.

All but one, that is. Taketsuna wanted a good look at the man who ruled this island in the emperor's name. The governor was an elderly man with a clean-shaven, intelligent face and eyes which roamed around the yard until they found the prisoners. For a moment he locked eyes with Taketsuna, then the new prisoner quickly prostrated himself with the rest. He had seen the expression on the other man's face and wondered if he looked worse than he felt.

The governor's visit was short and did not seem to concern the prisoners. The great man and his escort left after only the briefest stop in the guardhouse.

This was not the only excitement of the day, for an hour later there was another shout outside the gate. This time the guards were in no rush to admit the visitor. They exchanged some unintelligible words with someone outside and finally cracked the gate grudgingly to admit a fat man in the black robe of a minor official. He was followed by a ragged youngster with a bamboo case.

The fat man also cast a glance toward the prisoners and then waddled to the guardhouse.

"That's the doctor," Jisei informed Taketsuna. "Hope he looks at my knees. They been getting worse. What do you think?" Jisei lifted one of the stained rags around his knees.

Taketsuna looked and averted his eyes. A huge area of swollen, dirt-encrusted flesh, ringed by angry purplish red skin, oozed a bloody liquid and yellow pus. If Jisei did not get some medical attention soon, he would get a fever and die from the infection.

Moments later, one of the guards emerged from the guardhouse and strode briskly toward the prisoners. Jisei scrambled to his feet.

But the guard's eye was on Taketsuna. "You," he barked. "Get up. You're to see the doctor."

Taketsuna rose and followed him into the building, past disinterested guards, and into the far corner of the open space, where two screens of woven bamboo had been set up to create some privacy. The arrangement astonished the prisoner, but he was grateful for it. His present condition was still so novel that he found it difficult to put aside past habits of modesty.

The doctor proved, on closer inspection, less confidence-inspiring. The black gown was covered with stains, his fingernails were dirt-rimmed, and his eyes bleary and bloodshot.

"Harrumph," said the doctor. "I'm Ogata, physician and medical officer for the prisoners. Was told to have a look at you. You're Taketsuna? No family names here, I'm afraid. Strictly forbidden. You don't look too good. What happened?"

"I'm all right. We ran into a storm coming over, and I'm not used to sailing. But there's a man outside whose wounds have become infected."

The doctor nodded, then stepped closer to peer at Taketsuna's face. A strong smell of sour breath and wine assailed the prisoner's nose and made him flinch.

"Hmm. I suppose the welcoming committee issued its usual warning," the physician said, probing Taketsuna's cheekbone and jaw with surprisingly gentle fingers. "Open your mouth." He pursed his lips and shook his head. "Eating will be a bit painful for a while, but you should get over that."

Taketsuna smiled a little, painfully. "So far there has been no food. Only water. I could eat raw greens at this point." He wondered if the physician had heard his comment about little Jisei.

The physician cocked his head. "When did they feed you last?"

"A bowl of gruel on the ship after the storm. It was all the food I've had in three days. I was seasick."

"No wonder you're swaying on your feet. Never mind. You'll get fed. And, as soon as I've checked the rest of you, you can sit down. Take off those filthy rags."

The prisoner glanced at the doctor's stained gown and smiled again, but he complied without protest.

"Heavens," muttered the physician, stepping back and walking around the patient. "You've got muscles. Ever do any wrestling?"

"Just for exercise."

"They'll put you to hard labor if they see that. You'd better keep your clothes on at all times and slouch a bit when you walk."

"What sort of labor?"

The physician was feeling the bruised ribs. "Roads. Dikes. Mines. Lifting and carrying rocks. Not healthy unless you're used to it." He moved around to the prisoner's back and pressed near the lower spine. "Does this hurt?"

The prisoner shook his head, and the physician came around to face him again, prodding about the abdomen, asking about pain. Again the prisoner shook his head.

"You can get dressed now," the doctor said, digging about in his medicine case and pulling forth a stoppered flask. "My guess is . . ." he said, pausing to take a long swig from the bottle before extending it to Taketsuna, "that you have never done a day's hard physical work in your life, and the sort of forced labor the stronger prisoners do here will cripple or kill a man like you. Have you any skills?"

Taketsuna was holding the flask dubiously. The contents smelled like wine, and he wondered what it would do to his empty and painful stomach. "I can read and write," he said. "I could do secretarial work or bookkeeping, I suppose."

"If you're not going to drink, give it back," the doctor snapped crossly, extending his hand.

Taketsuna took a deep swallow and doubled over, coughing. The wine, if that was what it was, packed an incredible punch.

"Hmph," commented the doctor, "not much of a stomach, either. Can't imagine why they put someone with your background on the hard labor detail. I'll see what I can do for you." He raised the flask to his mouth and drank deeply, waving the prisoner out.

◆

An hour later, when Taketsuna was sitting with the others in the shade of the wooden palisade again, the doctor emerged from the guardhouse in the company of the officer. The doctor's gait was unsteady and his path less than straight, but he made his way over to them.

"That doctor's as drunk as a frog in a sake barrel," muttered one of the pirates.

Jisei smiled. "That's never stopped him before. He'll look at me now. And maybe he'll get us better food, like last time."

The physician ignored Jisei's eager greeting and merely looked at each man blearily, had them open their mouths and perform some simple actions, before moving on to the next man. When it was Jisei's turn, he frowned at the wounds on his knees and arms and pursed his lips. But even here, he made no comment, merely digging a small earthenware jar from his medicine chest. Turning to the guard officer, he said, "All these men look filthy. Have them bathe, and then put this ointment on this man's wounds."

The officer stepped back, affronted. "What, me? You're drunk! They're prisoners, not honored guests."

The doctor handed the ointment to Taketsuna. "Here, you do it." To the guard, he said, "If you don't keep these men clean and well fed, they'll sicken and die, and nobody will get any work out of them. Do you want me to report you to the governor?"

"My men won't like it," grumbled the officer. Seeing the doctor's implacable silence, he relented. "Oh, very well. They can have a bath if they heat the water and clean the bath afterwards."

"And food!"

"Of course, Master Ogata. We'll sauté some kisu fish for them, with ginger shoots and sesame seeds," the officer sneered. "Perhaps you can spare some of your wine for their banquet?"

The fat physician hunched his shoulders, then turned his back on them and staggered off.

◆

But they got their bath and a hot dinner. Taketsuna appreciated both far more than the others and was grateful for the drunken physician's visit. From snatches of conversation among the prisoners, he gathered that forced labor could be brutal and hoped he might be spared that. Not only Jisei, whose wounds he had tended after the bath, bore the scars of his toils. There was also Yoshi's missing eye, lost when a guard's whip caught him across the face instead of the back, and Kumaso's crooked ankle, broken and badly set after a rock fell on it. And the bath had revealed that the silent Haseo's back was so heavily scarred by crisscrossing stripes and welts that he must have been near death after his punishment.

With darkness they drew closer together against the night chill. Kumaso and Yoshi engaged in a game of "rock, scissors, paper" like two carefree children. Taketsuna thought with longing of his distant family.

The stars above were particularly clear tonight. He lay back, his arms folded under his head against the sharp bits of gravel, and wondered if he would get used to his new life, used to sleeping on the hard, cold ground without cover and under the open sky, used to humiliation and rough physical labor, used to beatings. The last was the most difficult, a disgrace impossible to be borne without retaliation. He wished for the warmth of silken quilts, but being tired, he dozed off.

The discomfort of the cold night and the hard soil beneath him woke him somewhat later. Two of his companions were whispering softly.

"Forget it. It's too dangerous. They might find out."

The other man made some inaudible protest.

"Lot of good that'll do you, when you're dead. You know what they say about the Second Prince's murder."

Startled, Taketsuna sat up. The whispering stopped. "Who was that?" he asked softly. "Who was talking?"

Silence.

He reached over and shook the shoulder of the sleeper next to him. The man grunted and sat up with a curse. "What the devil d'you want? Can't a man have a little peace at night?" he complained sleepily.

At the gate the dozing guards came awake. "Quiet over there," one of them shouted, "or we'll give you what for, you lousy pieces of dung."

Taketsuna whispered an apology, lay back down, and closed his eyes. He did not have much chance to sleep, because a short time later someone arrived to pick up the new prisoner.

The sleepy guards grumbled but seemed resigned to comings and goings all day and night. Taketsuna was chained again and walked off behind a burly guard. This time they entered the city. The streets were silent, and the shops shuttered. Moonlight lit their way. The prisoner shivered in the cool night breeze and tried to suppress his nervousness. Mano extended from the flat shore of the bay halfway up the encircling hills, and the provincial headquarters rose well above the rest of the city, with a commanding view of its many roofs and the shimmering silver of the bay and ocean beyond. Taketsuna risked a glance backward, as they climbed the wide stairs to the gate leading into the government compound, and was struck by the extraordinary beauty of a scene in such sharp contrast to the misery of certain of Sadoshima's inhabitants.

The government compound was smaller than those Taketsuna had known in his former life, but it seemed in good repair and had the usual separate courtyards surrounding buildings of various sizes. The governor's residence occupied a tree-shaded section just beyond the tribunal and archives. Except for the guards on night duty at the main gate and at the gate to the governor's quarters, the compound lay deserted. Their arrival was barely noted. Taketsuna's guard saluted the guards at the gate and led his prisoner past the tribunal to a smaller building just behind it. Here another pair of guards nodded them through the doorway. They walked down a long hallway lit by flickering oil lamps and stopped in front of a pair of wide doors. The guard knocked. Someone called out, "Enter!" and they stepped into a large room which was bare except for a desk and the seated figure of the governor.

The guard stood to attention, and Taketsuna knelt, touching his face to the polished floor.

"Take his chains off!" The governor's voice sounded remote. His tone was clipped and his speech cultured, but there was an abruptness and tension in his voice that made Taketsuna uneasy.

He felt the guard's hands remove his chains but did not change his position.

"You may leave. Tell the guards outside that I do not wish to be disturbed."

They must think the governor either a very brave man or a foolish one, thought Taketsuna. A desperate and violent criminal could easily make a hostage of him and bargain his way to freedom.

The door slammed behind the guard, and they were alone. A rustle of silk; then soft steps approached and passed Taketsuna. There was the click of a latch falling into place, then the stockinged steps returned and paused next to the kneeling Taketsuna. A hand fell on his shoulder.

"My dear fellow, please rise. It is quite safe now. We are alone."

CHAPTER THREE

A CANDLE IN THE WIND

The governor was nearly as tall as the prisoner, but age had bent his back a little. The black cap did not hide the gray of his hair, or his robe of office the weariness on his lined face. In the candlelight his eyes looked deeply sunken as they searched the convict's features anxiously. "You are the person who has been sent . . . I mean, you are the man known as Yoshimine Taketsuna?"

Thinking the governor's tone and manner odd, the prisoner said cautiously, "Yes."

"I was informed of your coming. The captain of your ship brought me a letter from . . . someone of very high rank. It told me that you were to help me in my present difficulties."

The prisoner sighed. "May I see the letter, please?" he asked.

The governor fished it from his sash and passed it over. "My dear Sugawara," he said earnestly, "I cannot tell you how sorry I am to see you like this."

Akitada, who had been accustoming himself to the role of the convict Taketsuna, was angry. He looked around the room, bare except for the desk, a tall candle, two silk cushions, and four large lacquer trunks, and then went to throw open one panel of the sliding doors to the outside. A tiny landscape of rock, pebbles, lantern, and a few shrubs had been squeezed between the governor's room and a high, blank wall. It was too small for anyone to hide in. He closed the door again and faced the governor.

"You should have destroyed this," he said, after glancing at the short letter. "Please do it now." He waited as the other man held the letter into the candle flame until it grayed, shriveled, and became dust. "Our meeting," Akitada continued, "is dangerous. But since I am here, and you are informed of my purpose, I suppose you had better tell me what you know." Reaching up to the collar of his stained robe, he picked at a seam. After a moment, he eased a thinly folded sheet of paper from between the layers of fabric and extended it to the governor, who unfolded it and read quickly before raising it reverently to his forehead.

With a deep bow, he returned the document. "Yes, quite in order. The vermilion seal and the seals of His Majesty's private office. I am deeply honored. As you saw, my letter instructed me to assist you in investigating the murder of the Second Prince. But my son—" He broke off and looked away. His thin hands, folded across his chest, clenched and unclenched convulsively.

Akitada said more gently, "Let us sit down."

Mutobe looked flustered. "Yes, of course. Please forgive me. The past week has been terrible, terrible." After they had seated themselves on the cushions—they were of good quality and not at all worn like those in Echigo—he looked at Akitada with deep concern. "Your face . . . I blame myself, but I could not prevent it."

Akitada waved the apology away. "It is nothing."

"Welcome to Sado, such as it is," the governor said, still dubiously, "though, of course, you may not wish to continue with this dangerous impersonation now."

"Why? Has the situation changed?"

"No. If anything . . . but heavens, sir . . ."

Akitada raised a hand in warning. "No names and no honorifics. I am a convict called Yoshimine Taketsuna."

The governor swallowed and continued, "I cannot protect you. Not only is my administration compromised by the murder charge against my son, but now my son's life is in danger. I dare not take any actions against my enemies." He smiled bitterly. "It was my fault for attempting to curb Kumo and his minions. Now they are planning to get rid of me. The central government considers this island no more than a prison colony. The law here is enforced by the police, whose commander is a government appointee but works for Kumo, and by the high constable, who thinks he is responsible to no one but himself. So you see, your scheme is much too dangerous. A matter of life and death."

"The murder of the Second Prince may well hide something far more dangerous. You suspect the high constable of plotting to remove you from office by linking you to the crime? Why would he do this all of a sudden?"

The governor blinked. "Isn't it obvious? The man is a megalomaniac. He wants to rule this island. He already controls most of its wealth. Now he wants absolute power. In the years that I have been governor here, I have seen him seize more and more control. I have tried to stop him, but all it got me was a reprimand from the capital, and now my son is accused of a murder he did not commit."

Akitada knew that local overlords could become very powerful and that the government often made use of their power by appointing them high constables, thus saving the cost of maintaining troops in the distant provinces. But surely Kumo would not kill the Second Prince to seize a province? He said, "The emperor is concerned. I am here to learn the truth about the murder and to verify your suspicions."

Mutobe brightened a little. "Yes. Perhaps Kumo will think you are one of them. Your disguise was a real stroke of genius."

Akitada was not so sure. He said dryly, "Let's hope the matter is settled before they find out that the real Yoshimine is in jail in Heian-kyo."

Mutobe fidgeted. "I must warn you. No matter how hard we try to intercept messages, Okisada's people always hear of news in the capital. Pirate ships carry their letters. I am afraid this is going to be very dangerous indeed. Of course, you must do as you wish, only don't count on me to save you. Kumo's people don't stop at murder, and with my son's life at stake . . ." His voice trailed off. He looked at Akitada's face again and shook his head. Reaching for a slender porcelain flask, he poured wine into two fine porcelain cups and extended one to his visitor. "I was told you almost died at sea and then were beaten by Wada's constables."

Akitada emptied his cup thirstily, nodded in appreciation, and passed it back for a refill. "Wada is the police official who greeted me at the dock? If he treats all arriving prisoners that way, something should be done about him, but for the present it does not matter. The incident lent a certain realism."

Mutobe shook his head again. "I don't want to belabor the point, but I wonder if you realize that even under the best circumstances an ordinary prisoner's life is worthless here. Wada is a brutal beast and his constables act as he wishes. The high constable has made a special pet of Wada. Between them, they claim to keep the peace on Sado, reminding me that my function here is purely judicial and administrative. And it seems the prince, whom I have had to remind of his status many times, still has friends in the government."

Akitada was becoming impatient with Mutobe's whining. His ill-considered actions against the high constable and his dilatoriness in reporting the trouble to the council of state had provoked the situation. He suspected that the governor had let a personal power struggle get out of hand. He changed the subject. "Did you send that very drunk physician to me?"

Mutobe looked embarrassed. "Ogata is my coroner and tends to the prisoners. When I got the captain's letter, I went to take a look at you. I was shocked by your wounds and thought you needed medical attention. Ogata drinks, but he is a perfectly capable physician. In fact, if it had not been for his drinking and slovenly appearance, he would have treated the late prince. The prince's doctor, Nakatomi, is more interested in wealth than healing. Ogata can be trusted. He is absolutely unbribable because he has neither ambition nor greed."

"A rare man indeed. I was not complaining but wanted to thank you."

The governor relaxed and smiled for the first time. "Apparently Ogata liked you, too. He told me that I had to find you a place here because you might not survive the hardships of roadwork or mining. When I pretended lack of interest, he offered to make you his assistant because he was getting too old for his work. He put on quite a good performance, gasping and pressing a hand to his heart. He even groaned as he bowed."

Akitada laughed. "He must think me a weakling. I thought I was in excellent physical condition."

"Working on roads or breaking rock is not the same as a bout with the sword or some hard riding. In any case, I will find you a place in the archives where I can keep in touch with you."

"I am not sure that is a good idea. Any close contact between us will cause suspicion. Also I must be able to travel."

"But I thought . . ." The governor looked upset and said in an almost pleading tone, "Surely you will want to meet my son? To get his story? Then I'll do my best to send you away."

Akitada weakened. "Well, perhaps. If it is only for a day or two. Do you have a map of Sadoshima?"

Mutobe rose and delved into one of the lacquered trunks. He produced a large rolled-up scroll and spread this out on the desk between them.

The island's shape resembled a large butterfly flying northeast, its body flat heartland, the wings mountainous. The governor pointed to the southwestern opening between the two wings. "We are here, on Sawata Bay. The murder happened in Minato, a small town on Lake Kamo near the opposite coast. Okisada was the guest of honor at the villa of a retired professor there. Okisada's own manor is in Tsukahara, not far from the lake. The central plain northeast of us is full of rice farms. Kumo's estate is there." Mutobe pointed to the center of the island. "Most of the farmed land belongs to the descendants of earlier exiles. I mention this because some families still bear a grudge against the government. Kumo and Okisada may have formed allies there."

Akitada nodded. "Tell me about Kumo."

"He is thirty-eight years old. His great-grandfather was sent here on trumped-up charges. The family has been cleared, but since the descendants had become wealthy on Sadoshima, they stayed here. Kumo now controls one-third of the rice land in the province. He also owns two silver mines. Kumo's father was appointed high constable, either because of his wealth and influence on the island, or because of the emperor's guilty conscience. His son inherited the office."

"What sort of man is he?"

Mutobe made a face. "Handsome, arrogant, and fiercely possessive of the island. He regards imperial appointees as a form of harassment for the natives and claims that the non-political prisoners are responsible for all the crime. Hence his support for Wada."

Akitada thought about this. "Who really controls Sado?"

Mutobe flinched. "There is no need to be so blunt," he said stiffly. "I am fully aware that you were dispatched here because it is thought that I have failed in my duties."

"No, that was not the reason," Akitada said quickly. "You are in no position to investigate this murder. But let's not waste time. I cannot remain in conference with you indefinitely before someone will take notice."

Mutobe took a deep breath. "Yes. Sorry. It is just that I have not slept much since . . . the murder. Briefly, then: nominally, I have administrative authority over the whole province; however, the special nature of Sado as a prison for exiles of different types gives extraordinary powers to the *kebiishicho*, that is Wada, and the high constable, namely, Kumo."

The provincial *kebiishicho* was the police department run by an officer from the capital. Their original purpose had been to assist the governors in curbing the power of provincial strongmen. In Sadoshima, this seemed to have backfired. Evidently Lieutenant Wada had allied himself with Kumo and ignored Mutobe's wishes.

Mutobe explained, "Political exiles are generally well-behaved, but men who are sent here for piracy, robbery, and other violent crimes are another matter. There is a small garrison to protect provincial headquarters, but the soldiers are all local men and the commandant is an elderly captain for whom the assignment was tantamount to retirement. And, of course, Kumo controls the landowners and most of the farmers."

"Farmers are generally a peaceable lot."

"Yes, but large landowners like Kumo are not, properly speaking, farmers. They own most of the land and therefore the wealth of Sado. Since we must maintain ourselves and the prisoners and exiles with their families, we need their rice, and the emperor needs their silver."

"I see. Where is your son?"

Again Mutobe's hands twisted. "My son is in jail," he said bitterly.

Akitada sat up. "In jail? You mean here in the provincial jail? Is that not somewhat unusual?"

"Yes. Well, there was some thought of putting him in the stockade, but I managed to avert that. He could have given his word and been put under house arrest, but they insisted on jailing him like a common criminal." Mutobe buried his face in his hands. "Every day I fear for his life. In a jail cell it is so simple to fake a suicide."

Akitada softened toward the man. No wonder he lived in fear of upsetting his enemies. "Would it be possible for me to speak with him without causing comment?"

Mutobe lowered his hands. "Yes. I think I can arrange that."

"Tell me about the people who were present when the prince died."

"Okisada died after a dinner at the home of Professor Sakamoto. Sakamoto used to teach at the Imperial University in the capital, but after a visit here he decided to stay and write a history of Sado Island. He is a well-respected man, but I have wondered if he was sent to spy on the prince. If he was, Okisada made it easy. He and his companion, Lord Taira, were regular visitors at his house. Okisada enjoyed boating and seafood, both of which are excellent on Lake Kamo." Mutobe paused. When he continued, his voice was curiously flat. "On this occasion, there were two other guests, a young monk called Shunsei, and my son. Originally I had been invited, but I begged off. My son represented me." Passing a weary hand over his face, he sighed. "Forgive me. This is a painful matter for me. Besides being my son, Toshito has been my official assistant."

Akitada was startled. "Your assistant?"

"Sadoshima is not like other provinces. I came here almost twenty years ago and married a local woman. She died when Toshito was only a baby. I could have returned to the capital, but a man of my background has no future there. I decided to stay and raise my son, and the government was happy with the arrangement. Few capable officials are willing to serve on the island of exiles. When Toshito showed promise, I sent him to the capital to study law, and after he returned he became so useful to me that I requested official status for him. My request was granted last year."

Akitada thought of his own young family. He had not yet achieved Mutobe's status. Would he, too, be condemned to spend the rest of his career in Echigo, far from the capital and with no chance at promotion? What if he lost Tamako and found himself raising his son alone? He suddenly felt great sympathy for the pale, elderly man across from him. He said, "I see. Please continue."

"The witnesses were all in agreement about what happened . . . well, Taira, of course, cannot be trusted, but the others had no reason to lie. Sakamoto lives quietly, except for visits by the prince. Apparently the prince took an interest in the history Sakamoto is writing. And Shunsei is just a young monk the prince has befriended. Kumo, of course, did not attend because I was to be there. Anyway, they all claim that after dinner Toshito was left alone with the prince in the lake pavilion. They were walking back to the house when they heard Okisada shout for help. Toshito was bent over the seated prince with both hands at his throat. They ran back and found the prince dead. Toshito denied having attacked Okisada, but he was not believed."

"Strange. What did the coroner say?"

"His report shows that Okisada died of poison."

Akitada stared at him. "Poison? I do not understand. Why is your son in jail?"

"Unfortunately, Toshito had taken a favorite dish to the prince. There was not enough for the others, so Okisada alone ate it. The prince complained about the taste and a pain in his belly before he died. Later, when someone let a dog lick the bowl which had contained the stew, the animal died in convulsions."

Akitada shook his head. "I can hardly believe it. I assume, of course, that your son also denies poisoning the dish."

"Of course."

"Why was the monk there? Was the prince religious?"

"I have been told that he had become so lately. I'm afraid the prince led a very private life. I don't know anything about the monk."

"Do *you* have any idea how and why this murder happened?"

The governor compressed his lips. "I am convinced Kumo had a hand in it. My son was set up. I would be in his place if I had accepted the invitation."

Akitada thought about this. He still did not like it. "Have you made any public threats against Okisada?"

Mutobe flushed. "Yes. Okisada made outrageous public comments charging me with dishonest practices. A month ago I sent him a letter warning him that I would take steps to stop his libelous attacks on me and my administration. When he apologized, I put the matter from my mind."

"I see. It seems an incredible story. If you can arrange it, I'd like to meet your son first, but then I must try to see Kumo and the men who attended the dinner. Do you send inspectors to outlying districts?"

"Yes. One is to leave soon." Mutobe clapped his hands together. "Of course. That's it. You can go along as a scribe. Both Kumo's manor and Shunsei's monastery are on his regular circuit."

"Perfect." Akitada rose and smiled. "I pride myself on my calligraphy."

Mutobe also stood. "In that case," he said eagerly, "you might start by working in the archives. I will have a pass prepared for you. It gives you a limited amount of freedom. While you are in this compound, you won't be locked up, but you cannot leave it alone. I'm afraid I can only offer you quarters with the prison superintendent."

"A jail cell would be more convincing, but perhaps it is better not to keep such very close contact with your son."

They walked out together, Akitada falling several steps behind when the governor clapped his hands for the guard outside.

"Take him back," Mutobe told the man. "Tomorrow he is to report to the *shijo*. Pick him up at dawn. I want reports on his behavior as soon as possible." He turned on his heel and walked back to his office without another glance at Akitada.

Akitada followed the guard meekly back across town. His return raised no interest. Only the silent Haseo was still there, curled up in his corner, apparently fast asleep. When Akitada asked one of the sleepy guards, "What happened to the others?" he got a grunted "None of your business" in reply. He decided that the prisoners had been moved at night and hoped that little Jisei had been released. Then he lay down and tried to catch a few hours' sleep before dawn.

◆

The guard reappeared early and took Akitada back to the tribunal before he had a chance to eat his morning gruel. At this time of day, the merchants were opening shutters, and the first farmers were bringing their vegetables to market. Nobody paid much attention to a guard with a chained prisoner.

In the government compound there were also signs of life. The guard removed the chains, and Akitada looked about curiously. Soldiers passed back and forth, a clerk or scribe with papers and document boxes under his arm rushed between buildings, and a few civilian petitioners hung about in deferential groups.

They crossed the graveled compound to a small building with deep eaves. Its interior was cool and smelled pleasantly of wood, paper, and ink. A gaunt man, bent from years of poring over manuscripts, came toward them.

The *shijo*, or head scribe, was nearsighted and hard of hearing. He had the guard repeat the governor's instructions. "Good, good," he finally said. "We're very short-handed. Very much so." Peering up at Akitada, he said dubiously, "You are tall for a scribe. How many characters do you know?"

"I'm afraid I never counted them."

"Counting? There's no counting required. You are to write. Can you use the brush?"

Akitada raised his voice. "Yes. I studied Chinese as a boy and young man. I believe you will be satisfied with my calligraphy."

"Don't shout. Hmph. We'll see. They all brag. The fools think copying work is easier than carrying rocks or digging tunnels. Never mind. I'll know soon enough. Soon enough, yes. What's your name?"

"Yoshimine Taketsuna."

"What? Which is it?"

Raising his voice again, Akitada repeated the double name, adding that the first was his family name.

The old man stared at him. "If you're one of the 'good people,' where are your servants? Yes, where are your servants, eh? And why were you sent to me? Only common criminals work."

"I killed a man," shouted Akitada.

The *shijo* jumped back, suddenly pale. "I hope you don't have a violent disposition."

Akitada lowered his voice a little. "Not at all, sir. It was a personal matter, a matter of loyalty."

"Oh. Loyalty." The other man seemed only partly reassured but said, "I'm called Yutaka and you will be plain Taketsuna here. Come along, Taketsuna."

Sado's provincial archives were neat and orderly. Akitada looked about with interest. Rows of shelves with document boxes divided the open interior of the hall into convenient smaller spaces. In each was a low table for making entries or searching through records. There were altogether six of these work areas, but only two were occupied by clerks copying documents. The largest space was Yutaka's own, and he took his new clerk there.

"Sit down," he said, peering up at one of the shelves. He stretched for a document box, and Akitada jumped up again to get it down for him. "Hmm," muttered the old man. "You'll be useful for something, at any rate. Yes, useful."

Akitada suppressed a smile and sat down again. Yutaka opened the box and extracted a thin roll of paper. This he unrolled partially before Akitada. Then he moved a sheet of clean paper, brushes, water, and an inkstone toward him. "Can you read this?" he asked, pointing to the document.

The document began with the usual formalities, and Akitada quickly ran his eye over these, unrolling it further to get to the text. "It appears to be a report on the flooding of Lake Kamo and the damage done to rice fields there."

"Harrumph," grunted Yutaka and poked a thin, bent finger at one of the characters. "What's that?"

Suppressing another smile, Akitada pronounced the character in Chinese.

"What? Oh, well. I suppose that one's too hard. It signifies 'forced labor.' The high constable is requesting His Excellency to supply him with more prisoners to help dam the lake waters. Let's see you write that character."

Akitada poured a little water into the ink dish and rubbed the ink stone in it. When the ink was the proper thickness, he selected a brush, dipped it, and with a flourish wrote the character on the paper.

"Too big! Too big!" cried Yutaka. "You wasted the whole sheet. Make it very small."

Akitada selected another brush and wrote it again on an unused corner, this time as small as he could.

Yutaka picked up the paper and brought it close to his eyes. Without comment, he laid it down. "Come with me," he said and took Akitada to meet the other two clerks, neither of whom was a prisoner and therefore regarded the new clerk with disdain. Yutaka assigned Akitada to one of the empty desks, with instructions to copy a set of tax accounts from one of the districts. For the rest of the day, as Akitada labored, he appeared on silent feet, peered over the prisoner's shoulder, muttered, "Harrumph," and disappeared again.

Akitada made good progress, but after several hours the unaccustomed work caused his back to ache and his wrist to cramp. His stomach growled. After more time passed, his feet had gone to sleep, and his belly ached with hunger. Apparently he was not entitled to a midday rice break.

Or rice, either. That was reserved for better people. Near sunset, a gong sounded somewhere in the compound. Akitada heard his fellow scribes rustling papers and shuffling off rapidly. He continued until he had finished the final page of a document he was working on and stretched. Suddenly Yutaka appeared.

"You didn't hear the gong," he said accusingly.

"I heard it. Why?"

"Time for the prisoners' evening meal."

Akitada said, "Oh." He started to wash out his brush.

"Never mind," said Yutaka irritably. "Give it to me and run, or you'll be too late. Masako doesn't tolerate stragglers. No. Doesn't tolerate them at all."

"Run where?" asked Akitada, rising.

"The jail. Where else?" Yutaka pointed vaguely. "I think you'll be too late," he added glumly.

Akitada bowed. "Thank you. I look forward to seeing you tomorrow."

When he found the jail, or more precisely the jail kitchen, it was empty except for a very shapely young maid who was stacking dirty bowls into a basket.

"I was told that the prisoners eat somewhere around here," said Akitada.

She swung around, and he saw that she was very pretty, with a round face and sparkling eyes. At the moment they sparkled with anger. "Well, you're too late," she snapped. "The gong sounded an hour ago." A threadbare cotton robe, much too big and too short for her, was firmly tied around her small waist, its sleeves rolled up to reveal work-reddened hands and arms, and her hair was pinned up under a kerchief. Surprisingly, the skirts of a pale blue silk gown peeked forth underneath the rough covering.

"I didn't know. I am new," he offered hopefully, staring at the silken hem.

She relented a little. "The fire's out. You'll have to eat the soup cold."

He smiled at her with relief. "I don't mind." Her speech was more refined than he had expected in a kitchen maid, and his eyes went again to the pale silk hem. As she moved, a dainty bare foot, dirty but white and slender, appeared for a moment.

She scooped something from a large iron kettle into a bowl and handed it to him. Whatever it was, it looked and smelled unappetizing—some kind of millet mush with a few wilted greens. Akitada held the dripping bowl gingerly away from his clothes and looked about for a place to sit. Finding none, he leaned against the kitchen wall and raised the bowl to his lips. But the mush had thickened, and he had trouble drinking it.

"Would you happen to have some chopsticks?" he asked the girl, who was sweeping the floor in a haphazard fashion.

She stopped and stared at him. "Chopsticks? For a prisoner?"

"A little joke." He chuckled. "I suppose there's not much hope in asking for wine, so maybe I'd better settle for water, right?"

"Right!" She pointed to a large bucket in the corner.

He did not dare ask for a cup. Instead he used the dipper to pour some water into his food, stirred it with his finger, and then drank it down in several hungry gulps. It had little taste, but he gladly accepted the refill she offered. This, too, he mixed with water, and when he was done, he poured more water in the bowl, took it outside to rinse it, and refilled it to drink.

The girl had watched him surreptitiously. When he returned the bowl to her with a bow and a smile, he said, "Thank you. My name is Taketsuna. You're very kind. And very pretty. May I ask your name?"

Her eyes narrowed. "I'm Masako," she snapped. "And my father's the superintendent, so you'd better watch yourself."

He was so astonished, he was speechless. The superintendent of a provincial jail, though of low rank, was still an official. How could such a man allow his daughter to work in the prison's kitchen? It occurred to him that she might be the result of an affair with a native woman, and he said, "Certainly. I'm to report to him. Can you show me the way?"

"You'll have to wait. I have to finish cleaning up first." She put his bowl into the basket and bent to pick it up.

"Allow me to carry that for you. Perhaps I could help you wash up?"

She regarded his tall figure thoughtfully for a moment. Her lip twitched. "All right. You can do with a wash yourself. Come along, then, Taketsuna."

He followed her across the courtyard to the well and hauled buckets of water, while she washed the bowls and restacked them in the basket. "Now take off your robe," she told him. "You won't get a bath tonight, so you'd better wash here."

He glanced around. The courtyard was empty, so he obeyed, draping his stained gown carefully over the rim of the well while he stood in his loincloth, sluicing himself down with the cold well water, uncomfortably aware of her eyes on his body. When he reached for his robe, she snatched it away. "It's filthy. I'll wash it for you later. Get the basket and come with me."

"B-but," he stammered, looking down at his wet self, "I can't go like this. I have nothing to wear."

She was walking away. "Nonsense. Nobody cares what a prisoner wears," she snapped over her shoulder.

He picked up the basket and followed. The guards outside the gate threw it open as they passed, and two constables appeared, carrying a litter between them. Behind them waddled Ogata, the fat physician.

Masako stopped, and Akitada quickly hid behind her, clutching the basket to his body.

As the litter passed, he saw that the slight shape on it was hidden under a woven grass cover. A dead child? He recalled that Ogata was also the local coroner. The child's death must have been suspicious, or Ogata would hardly take this kind of interest in the corpse.

For once Ogata's eyes were alert and sharp. He recognized the prisoner instantly and halted, letting his eyes move from the girl to Akitada and back again. "Are you keeping company with half-naked men now, Masako?" he drawled. "In broad daylight, too. Must have a talk with your father."

Akitada saw the color rise in Masako's pale neck. "If you go worrying Father, Uncle," she cried, raising a clenched fist, "I'll . . ."

"Oho! Is that the way the wind blows? A secret affair." Ogata raised his brows comically.

Masako dropped Akitada's robe and picked up her skirts to rush at Ogata. The doctor held her away easily, laughing while she shouted at him.

The constables stopped and put down their litter to watch. They, too, began to laugh, looking from the half-naked Akitada to the angry girl. Guards peered in at the gate and people came from buildings to stare.

Akitada put down the basket and snatched up his robe. Slipping it on, he joined the doctor and the girl. "Is a suspicious death an occasion for mirth on Sadoshima?" he asked.

Masako dropped her arms, looked at the stretcher, and stepped away from Ogata, who continued to chuckle helplessly. After a moment the doctor choked back another peal and wiped his face. "Sorry," he gasped, looking mildly shamefaced. "The sight of you with our lovely Masako here drove this other matter from my mind for a moment. Masako's my goddaughter, by the way, which accounts for my teasing her." His eyes narrowed speculatively. "As a man like you knows how to use a brush, come along. I'm to do a postmortem on this man. You can take notes." With a wave of the hand, he set the constables and their litter in motion and they moved off.

Akitada looked at Masako and the basket.

"Never mind," she said crossly, still rosy with embarrassment. "You go along. I can manage. Come to the house when you're done." She pointed out a modest building which huddled under some trees behind a bamboo fence.

Akitada followed the litter into another low building not far from the kitchen. It contained only a long table, raised to waist height, a low desk with writing implements and paper, and several rough shelves with lanterns, oil lamps, and assorted medical instruments.

Ogata directed the constables to place the body on the table, and then to light the lanterns. He placed these himself so that the still-covered body was brightly illuminated. When all was arranged to his satisfaction, he turned to Akitada.

"Squeamish?" he asked.

"I've seen death before."

"This man you know," said Ogata and whipped aside the cover.

The corpse was nude and very small. Yellowish gray in death, his ribs and bones unnaturally prominent, his face contorted as if in pain, and his eyes mere slits, he lay childlike on his side with his knees drawn up and his arms wrapped about his belly. The only wounds apparent were on both knees and elbows. It was little Jisei, the prisoner.

Akitada stifled an exclamation. "What happened?" he asked, stepping closer. "He was well yesterday. He said the ointment you had me apply eased the inflammation in his wounds. He looked forward to being released. How could he have died so quickly?"

"Not sure. That's why we're here." Ogata told the constables to turn the body on its back and straighten the limbs. When one of them was careless and broke an arm, he snarled at the man, "I'll make sure to deal roughly with your carcass when your time comes. Which may be sooner than you think." The constable blanched.

There were faint marks on the poor thin body in addition to the gruesome wounds on his knees and arms. Ogata said, "He got those crawling in and out of badger holes. When a prisoner's as small as this one, that's the work they make him do."

"Badger holes? Why?"

"Mines. There's silver in the mountains. The men tunnel in and bring it out. It's grueling work. But that's not what killed him."

He began to study every inch of the naked body, taking special note of the sunken area just below the rib cage, ordering the constables to turn Jisei on his stomach and then back again. He pursed his lips and next gave his attention to the skull, feeling all over it carefully. Lifting the lids, he peered at Jisei's eyes. Finally, he pried open the dead man's mouth with a thin ivory implement. When he straightened up, his face was filled with angry disgust. The sudden movement caused the flames in the lanterns to flicker, and for a moment it seemed as though Jisei smiled.

"What is it?" asked Akitada. But Ogata did not answer. He stared at the dead man, then looked at the constables. "You can go," he said harshly. "It seems to be a natural death after all."

They trooped out.

Akitada stepped forward and bent to peer at Jisei's mouth. It was filled with blood. He straightened. "I think this man has been tortured," he said flatly. "I don't know how, but he's bitten through his tongue."

Ogata was still angry. "No. He was beaten to death. Hit in the stomach where the marks don't show. He may have bitten his tongue also, but he would have died from the ruptured organs inside. The fools thought I wouldn't notice." Suddenly he looked old and defeated. Pulling the mat back over the pathetic corpse, he muttered, "Not that it makes any difference. Let's go."

Akitada said, "But the man was murdered."

"It will be reported as a fight between prisoners."

"A fight? This man would never fight. Look at him."

Ogata laid a finger on his lips. "Ssh. You know it and I know it, but knowledge can kill. Forget it and watch your step, young man."

"You mean you won't do anything about this?" Akitada was outraged. "How can you allow the murder of a human being to go unpunished?"

Ogata sighed. Blowing out the flame in one of the lanterns, he said sadly, "Here a human being is nothing but a candle in the wind. Remember it well, Taketsuna."

CHAPTER FOUR

THE NUN

Akitada's awakening was much more pleasant than the previous ones. He woke to the chatter of birds and the brightness of sunshine outside the shutters of a small, neat room, comfortable in soft bedding and aware of the good smell of food.

For just a moment, he imagined himself home, but instantly the ugly image of the emaciated and abused body of the prisoner Jisei superimposed itself on his fantasy. He sat up. Where he had dropped his own filthy robe the night before lay, neatly folded, a new blue cotton robe and a white loincloth. He unfolded the clothes in wonder, then looked about for his own things. They were gone, and he was seized by a sudden fear for his documents. Day by day, events proved his undertaking more foolhardy and impossible. It should have occurred to him that his clothes might get lost or stolen.

Dressing quickly in the new robe, he pushed back the shutter. Outside was a vegetable plot, its plantings of radish, cabbage, onions, and melons stretching higgledy-piggedly in all directions. The sun was fully up; he would be late for his duties in the archives. This puzzled him as much as the new clothes. Someone should have come for him—some guard with a whip for the lazy prisoner.

Stepping down into the garden, he looked around. Never mind the mouthwatering smells and the gnawing emptiness in his stomach. He must find out what happened to his clothes and then run across to the archives where Yutaka, no doubt, had already raised an alarm.

He turned the corner of the house quickly and halted in dismay before a private family scene. On a small veranda sat a balding man with pendulous cheeks and a small paunch, his host, no doubt. To judge by the sloping shoulders and downcast expression, the superintendent was in very low spirits. Across from him knelt Masako. She wore her blue silk gown today, and her shining hair hung loose. The difference from the girl in the prison kitchen was startling. She looked charming and entirely ladylike as she urged her father to sample a dish she was filling from several bowls on a small tray.

Akitada attempted to withdraw, but a scraping of the gravel beneath his feet caused both to turn their heads simultaneously. Akitada bowed, thought better of it, and knelt instead, bending his head to the ground.

"Ah," said the superintendent. "Is that our guest, daughter? Good morning to you, sir. Please join us."

Akitada sat back on his heels and looked at the superintendent in astonishment, wondering if whatever weighed on the man's mind had unbalanced his reason. "Good morning, sir," he said. "Please forgive the intrusion. I lost my way. I am not a guest, only a prisoner. Having overslept, I was on my way to the archives to report for work."

Masako now said very pleasantly, "Please take some gruel first."

He stood up slowly, not understanding. "Thank you, but there is no time. Allow me to express my thanks for your hospitality and for lending me these new clothes."

The superintendent cleared his throat and looked at his daughter. "Er, don't mention it," he said. "Please accept our food, such as it is. It's only some millet gruel and fruit from the plum tree in the backyard. But my daughter is a fine cook as well as a good judge of men."

"It would not be proper. I'm a prisoner, sir," Akitada protested and became suspicious about his lost papers.

The superintendent waved the objection away. "Masako says that you are of good background. Whatever brought you here was, no doubt, due to some careless association, or even perhaps a noble act. These are politically troubled times, and many a good man is deprived of home, office, income, and happiness." He gave his daughter a sad nod.

Akitada was faced with a dilemma. He looked at Masako, who kept her eyes lowered, blushing modestly. This certainly was not the fiery, sharp-tongued girl he had met in the prison kitchen. "I am deeply honored by the young lady's good opinion," he said, "but I was sent here because I murdered a man. Under the circumstances, I fear that both you and I will suffer if I accept your generosity. And I am already late for work."

Masako now said softly, "Please do not worry. You need not report to Yutaka until later today. Come, there is plenty for both of you. Father's appetite has been poor lately."

Bemused, Akitada obeyed and took his place on the veranda, accepting a bowl of millet gruel, and feeling uneasy about this change of attitude. The success of his assignment depended on his being taken for an exile and a dangerous individual. He tried to think of a way to introduce the subject of his missing clothes, but Masako spoke first.

"Were you of some use to the doctor last night?"

He suppressed a grimace. "There was little enough to do and no postmortem. The doctor seemed to think the prisoner died as a result of a fight." He stared unhappily at the gruel his hostess had passed to him.

"I am sorry it is only millet," she said.

"Oh, the gruel? No, no. It's delicious," he said. "No. It's the dead man. I knew him, you see. He was kind to me when I first arrived."

"Ah," she murmured. "I am very sorry the man died, but life is hard for the prisoners here." She shivered a little.

Akitada set the gruel down half eaten. There seemed to be different rules for different men. He was sitting here, at his ease and in the company of a gentleman of rank and his charming daughter, taking his morning gruel in new clothes, after spending a night in fine bedding in a room of his own. And only one night ago he had slept under the open sky along with the crippled wretches who were beaten regularly by cruel men and suffered from the festering wounds they got by crawling in and out of mine tunnels. Was this justice? He said angrily, "The prisoners are abused until they die, and the authorities permit this, if they don't actively encourage it."

There was a brief silence in which father and daughter looked at each other. Then the superintendent said, "You speak very frankly but not wisely. In this house you are safe, but not so elsewhere. As you may spend the rest of your life on this island, you can hardly wish to make it a life of torment and suffering."

This was said in a tone of sad finality, and Akitada recalled himself. "Of course not," he said humbly. "I was merely struck by the contrast between my condition and theirs."

Yamada nodded and fell into another bout of melancholy.

Akitada looked at the daughter. "I wondered what had become of my clothes," he said, giving up any effort at diplomacy.

"Oh. I mean to clean them. You'll have them back tonight."

Relief made him smile. "Thank you, but there is no need. If I may borrow a brush, I can do it myself."

"Very well."

Picking up his bowl, Akitada finished his gruel quickly, then rose to bid father and daughter goodbye.

"Yes, ah," said Yamada vaguely without raising his head, "delightful to meet you, young man."

"Father," said Masako sharply. "Remember the governor's message!"

"Ah," said the superintendent after a moment's puzzlement, "yes, of course. How silly of me to forget! I shall need your skills for an hour or so. You see, I have no clerk, and a prisoner is to be questioned again. It is quite beyond Masako, who has other duties anyway, I'm afraid. So will you take notes?"

"I'll gladly do whatever you require of me, but is it permitted?"

"Oh, yes. The governor himself said so."

So Mutobe had wasted no time to have him hear about the murder from his son's lips. And that also explained his accommodations. Akitada suppressed his excitement and bowed again. "I'm quite ready to accompany you, sir."

As they walked across the courtyard toward the low building that served as jail, the superintendent muttered, "It's so difficult. One doesn't know how to behave."

"I beg your pardon?" asked Akitada catching up a bit.

"Young Mutobe. As assistant to the governor he was my superior, but now . . . well, he's a prisoner charged with a capital crime. A crime against the imperial family." He sighed heavily. "I'm fond of that young man. He and my daughter grew up together, and I had hopes . . . but never mind."

Akitada said, "That is difficult." He was beginning to like Yamada. His moral sense was stronger than his self-interest. But why did such a man force his daughter to perform the most menial tasks for depraved criminals?

When they stepped into the small jail building, they startled two drowsy guards, who sprang to attention. The guardroom was bare except for an old desk and a small shelf of papers, but its walls were liberally decorated with whips, chains, and other devices meant to put obstinate prisoners in the proper frame of mind.

"We're here to see young Mutobe," announced the superintendent.

"He's got his usual visitor with him," said one of the guards. He reached for a lantern and led the way down a narrow, dark hallway.

Yamada followed without comment, and Akitada trailed behind. Apparently the visitor had raised no eyebrows. Akitada wondered if the governor was with his son.

Most of the cells appeared to be empty. Prisoners from the mainland were put to hard labor upon arrival. Mutobe Toshito's cell was toward the back. To Akitada's surprise, the sound of a woman's voice came from it.

There was little light in the cell. A pale glimmer of sunshine fell through a single small window so thickly barred that it seemed the bottom of a basket. In the murky gloom, Akitada made out two seated figures. One was that of a young man of middle size, dressed in a pale silk robe; the other was an elderly nun in white hemp robe and veil.

At their entrance, the nun rose awkwardly with the assistance of the young man, and turned to face them. As the guard raised his lantern, Akitada saw a thin figure with a narrow face that was darkened by sun and weather and dominated by enormous eyes like pools of ink. She looked frail, like a sliver of discarded wood, as if exposure and illness had destroyed a former great beauty by consuming what once gave it life.

"Madam." The superintendent bowed deeply. "Your visit honors this dismal place. You bring spiritual riches to those who have nothing else left in this life."

She shuddered at his words. "Let us hope for a better outcome in this instance, Yamada, but thank you. I shall leave now." Her voice was beautiful, and the elegance of her diction reminded the startled Akitada of the faraway court at Heian-kyo.

Turning back to the prisoner, she said, "Do not forget what I told you." Then she slipped past them so gently that she seemed no more than a wraith on a breath of air.

Akitada stared after her. "Who was that?" he burst out, forgetting for a moment his own position.

Fortunately, Yamada was preoccupied. He was greeting the prisoner with a friendly courtesy which the young man seemed to return. Over his shoulder, Yamada said, "They call her Ribata. She's a hermit nun who lives on a mountain not far from here. Sometimes she visits prisoners in need of spiritual counsel."

The guard added helpfully, "She's been visiting him every day."

The young man with the pale, intelligent face smiled bitterly. "I suppose that means my case is desperate. We pray together. She is very holy." His tone was casual, but Akitada did not quite believe it. Mutobe Toshito glanced at him and asked, "Who is that with you, Yamada?"

"His name is Taketsuna, a new prisoner. He's here to take notes." Pulling a sheaf of papers from his sleeve, Yamada said apologetically, "I am to ask you some more questions. The answers are needed to prepare your case."

"You mean, the case against me," the prisoner corrected him.

Yamada fidgeted uneasily. "Let us sit down," he said, seating himself on the dirt floor. When the young man reluctantly sat, he added soothingly, "You mustn't be so downcast. Your father will speak for you, as will many others." But he did not sound as if he believed it, and the prisoner gave a harsh laugh.

"The governor is no longer my father. How could he be, when I have been charged with such a hideous crime?"

"Now, now," mumbled Yamada again. "Sit down, sit down," he told Akitada, then turned to the guard. "Paper and ink for the clerk."

An uncomfortable silence fell as they waited. After a moment, Toshito addressed Akitada. "I would bid you welcome, but this prison and the island are a special kind of hell for people like you and me. So you have my pity instead. What did you do to have been sent here?"

Akitada glanced at Yamada for permission to answer, but the superintendent was again lost in his own thoughts, his chin sunk into his chest. "I killed a political enemy," he said.

"Really? Much the same crime of which I stand accused. With, of course, the major difference that I'm supposed to have murdered an imperial prince and will not live to see exile."

Akitada could not think of an appropriate response, so merely murmured, "I'm sorry."

Another silence fell, and then the guard reappeared to hand Akitada a lap desk, paper, and writing utensils. Akitada rubbed the ink, then glanced at Yamada, who still brooded. "Ready, sir."

"What? Oh. Oh, yes." Yamada focused his eyes on the sheaf of questions in his hand. "Very well. Write: Interview between the prisoner Mutobe Toshito and Yamada Tsubura, superintendent of Sado Provincial Prison. The fourteenth day of the eighth month of the third year of Chogen."

Akitada wrote.

"Now write down all the questions I ask and the answers the prisoner gives." Yamada consulted his papers and addressed the young man. "Mutobe Toshito, how did you come to attend the banquet during which the Second Prince died?"

The prisoner made a face. "I have already answered that several times. My fa . . . the governor often received invitations to dinners given for the Second Prince. Because of Prince Okisada's illustrious rank, it was his habit to accept these, but on this occasion the governor was not well and did not wish to make the journey. So I went instead and carried his apologies."

Yamada frowned. "Ah, yes. You are right. These questions seem to have been asked before," he muttered, scanning the list in his hands. "Feel free to add any information you may not have given earlier. Perhaps it will reveal something to your benefit."

Akitada knew very well why there were no new questions. They were meant to give him access to the evidence from young Mutobe's own recollections.

"Now, about that prawn stew you brought for the prince. Why did you bring food to the dinner?"

A good question that had puzzled Akitada.

The prisoner compressed his lips. "I know that is against me. It was customary to bring the prince a small gift. I never liked this custom and used to argue against it, but my fa . . . the governor insisted that it would offend certain people in the capital if we did not show such courtesy. When it was a matter of my going by myself, I decided to take something simple. I knew that the prince was particularly fond of the prawn stew a woman in Minato made, so I decided to take him this instead."

Ah! A second unplanned event.

"This woman, did she know the stew was for the prince?"

"I mentioned my purpose when I picked it up, I think. She lives not far from Professor Sakamoto's villa and knows about the prince's tastes."

"Could she have poisoned the stew intentionally?"

Young Mutobe shook his head. "No. She's just a simple fisherman's wife who runs a small restaurant. She would never do such a thing."

That was naïve, but then the governor's son seemed rather naïve in other ways, too.

"Could the stew have become poisoned by accident?"

"I don't know. I expect the police have investigated."

The superintendent nodded. "They have. Apparently the woman served the same stew to her customers without ill effects. It seems you are the only one who could have added something to the dish after it left her premises."

Toshito said sharply, "What about Professor Sakamoto, his servants, or his other guests?"

Akitada shot a glance at the prisoner. So the young man was not completely resigned to his fate.

Yamada sighed. "The guests and servants testified that you arrived late and presented the dish to His Highness, who placed it on the tray before him. The servants had already served the prince and neither of his neighbors was close enough to add anything to the stew without being seen. I'm afraid the burden of the charge does fall on you . . . unless you can account for some other instance in which someone might have tampered with the food?"

The superintendent was trying to help, but the prisoner shook his head. "I've had weeks to think about it, and I cannot understand what happened. Perhaps the stew was fine and the poison was in something else."

Yamada shook his head. "You forget the dog died."

"Perhaps the dog died from some other cause."

Yamada moved restlessly. "Too much of a coincidence. And such speculations are remote indeed when motive is considered. Who in that house that night would have had a reason to kill Prince Okisada?"

"I don't know," cried young Mutobe, his voice rising in frustration. "How could I know? That is for the authorities to discover. Why ask me what I cannot speak to?"

The superintendent cleared his throat. "I am sorry. You're quite right. Let us return to the questions. You are accused of attempting to strangle His Highness the moment the other guests left the pavilion. You have testified that you were merely loosening the prince's collar as he had asked you to do. Why then did he scream for help?"

Toshito raised his hands helplessly. "I cannot say, except that he was in distress. He seemed to be gasping for breath."

"A man who is choking cannot call out," Yamada pointed out. "And according to the physician, the poison caused pains in the belly and later convulsions."

The prisoner shook his head. "All I know is that it happened. I have no explanation."

With a sigh, the superintendent folded his papers and put them back in his sleeve. "Is there anything you can say in your defense?" he asked. "For example, do you know of anyone at all who might have wanted to kill the prince?"

Toshito cried, "I did not want to kill him, but they arrested me. He was not a likable man, but why would anyone kill him for that?"

There. It was out. The motive was not his, but his father's. The charge would be that Governor Mutobe had prevailed upon his son to poison Okisada because the prince had become a threat to Mutobe's career.

Yamada rose abruptly. "That is all. We'll leave you in peace now." He looked distressed at his choice of words and muttered something.

Akitada cleared his throat. "Your pardon, sir," he said, "but being new at this kind of thing, I'm concerned about accuracy because my notes might be used in court. Could I clear up a small matter to make sure I wrote it correctly?"

"What is it?"

"Whose idea was the prawn stew? It seemed to me the accused said the prince had asked for it, and that was why he thought to bring it."

The superintendent turned to the prisoner. "Well, was it your idea or the prince's request?"

The young man looked confused. "I cannot recall. Surely it was mine. I believe the prince had talked about his fondness of stewed prawns on a previous occasion, but I was the one who decided that day to stop at the restaurant. The owner's prawn stew is well known in the area."

Yamada pressed him, "Perhaps your father suggested it? I assume he was the one who told you of the prince's taste for prawns?"

The prisoner sprang to his feet. "He may have heard him talk about it," he cried, his eyes flashing. "The prince was always talking about food. But no, he never made such a suggestion. It would never have occurred to him to take such a humble gift. He had nothing to do with the stew. The stew was my idea, no one else's, do you hear?"

With a sigh, Yamada nodded. Akitada, whose eyes had hung on the prisoner during his outburst, hurriedly wrote down the final questions and responses, then bundled up his notes. Bowing to the prisoner, he followed the superintendent out of the jail.

Yamada looked dejected. "Poor young man," he said. "It will go hard with him. And with the governor, too. He loves the boy dearly." He heaved a deep sigh and added with a breaking voice, "Life is full of suffering, but nothing compares to a father's pain when he causes misery for his child." He stretched out his hand for the notes of the interview and said in a more normal tone, "Thank you, young man. Better report to Yutaka now." Then he turned and walked away.

◆

Akitada spent the rest of the day in the archives, wielding his brush and thinking over what Yamada had said. Apparently he believed the governor had used his son to carry out the murder of the prince. That was shocking enough, but Akitada could not rid himself of the conviction that Yamada had also spoken of himself. If so, he must have been thinking about the drudgery, which the lovely Masako accepted so readily, but which seemed shockingly cruel to Akitada. What would make a father demand such a sacrifice from his daughter?

He decided to ask Yutaka.

Taking one of the documents as a pretext, he left his cubicle and sought out the superintendent of archives.

Yutaka was at his desk, bent over some papers, with his thin back to the entrance. Apparently the shortage of scribes kept him as busy as his clerks.

"I beg your pardon, sir," Akitada said, raising his voice a little, "but I have a question about this."

There was no answer, and Akitada saw that the brush had fallen from Yutaka's hand. With a sudden sense of foreboding, he stepped quickly around Yutaka. The elderly man's chin had sunk into his chest and his eyes were closed. The brush had left a jagged line on the paper, and his lifeless hand hung limp. Fearing that the man was dead, Akitada put his hand on his head to raise it.

"Wh . . . what?" Yutaka, coming awake, jerked away, stared up at Akitada, and shrieked for help.

"Sir! Sir!" cried Akitada, dismayed. "Please calm down. I did not realize you were asleep. I thought . . ." He did not get any further, because at that moment the other two clerks burst in and flung themselves upon him so violently that he crashed to the floor. Though he offered no resistance, they belabored him with whatever they could lay their hands on, a water container filled with inky liquid, Yutaka's wooden armrest, and a document rolled around a wooden dowel.

Akitada suffered a number of crushing blows to his skull, particularly from the armrest and the document scroll, before

Yutaka, perhaps out of concern for his precious scroll, put a stop to the beating.

It took a while to clear up the misunderstanding, because Akitada was too dizzy and nauseated to be able to say much. But eventually Yutaka grudgingly apologized, taking his embarrassment out in a tongue-lashing of the two clerks, who slunk away silently. Akitada staggered to his feet, wiping dazedly at some blood which was running down his cheek.

Seeing his condition, Yutaka sent him home.

Later Akitada had little recollection of how he had crossed the yard and collapsed on the bare floor of his small room. He passed out or fell asleep, and did not return to full consciousness until a touch on his bruised head made him jerk away. This movement caused such a jangling and ringing in his head that he sucked in his breath and closed his eyes again.

But not before he had caught a glimpse of Masako's face, bent over him with an intense look of concern on her pretty features.

"What happened to you, Taketsuna?" she asked, her voice trembling and cool fingertips touching his cheek. The gentle caress almost brought tears to his eyes, and he snatched at her hand. After a moment, she pulled it from his grasp. "Can you speak?" she asked.

"I . . . yes. It was all a misunderstanding. Yutaka was asleep at his desk and thought I meant him harm. He called for help and his clerks gave me a beating."

"Oh." She looked at him from her large, soft eyes, a spot of color in her cheeks. "We should have warned you. You see, he really was attacked last year. One of the prisoners went mad, and Yutaka got cut pretty badly. But that he should have set the clerks on you is outrageous. We must report it to the governor. And you need a doctor." She rose with a rustle of silk.

"No!" Akitada snatched at her hem and begged, "Please don't mention this to Dr. Ogata or the governor. It was nothing, and Yutaka apologized. Please! I don't want to lose my job in the archives."

She stood, frowning in indecision. Then she nodded. "Very well. I'll get some water and salve and see what I can do."

When the door had closed behind her, Akitada stared at it in confusion. Something had just happened between them, something that had made his heart beat faster and heated his blood. When she had touched him, he had felt a powerful attraction to her, a desire that was more than physical. Only two women in his life had moved him this way. He had lost the first one and been wretched. The second he had taken for his wife. Perhaps the beating had robbed him of his sanity. He loved Tamako. His reaction to this girl seemed like a betrayal, and he was suddenly afraid of being alone with her, of letting her touch him again. Sitting up, he saw his own robe lying neatly folded on the trunk in which his bedding was kept. He tried to rise, but a blinding pain shot through his skull.

He tensed at the sound of returning steps in the corridor and was ridiculously relieved when the door opened and he saw that Masako was not alone. The white-robed nun he had seen that morning in young Toshito's cell followed her into the room.

"This is the reverend Ribata," Masako announced, setting down a bowl of water next to Akitada. "I found her at the well and brought her because she has great skill with wounds."

Intensely aware of the girl, Akitada kept his eyes on the nun. "Th-there was no need," he stammered, staring into the strange black eyes, which regarded him fixedly.

"We have met," Ribata said, in that beautiful, cultured voice of hers. "You are the new prisoner from the capital who has made himself useful to the governor."

She was well informed for an ordinary nun. But then this was no ordinary nun. She came from a background as good as his own, perhaps better. What had brought her to this godforsaken outpost in the Northern Sea?

She came forward and crouched on the floor next to him to examine his head. Her hands were so thin from age and deprivation that they looked more like the claws of some huge bird of prey. But her touch was not ungentle, though certainly more businesslike than Masako's. The comparison was unfortunate, because it made him glance at the younger woman's anxious face on his other side. She was leaning forward a little, and the collar of her robe revealed a smooth white neck. The soft silk hid the rest, but as she bent toward him, it was easy enough to imagine her full breasts where the fabric strained against them. The effort to control his desire brought a frown to his face.

"Oh, you are hurting him," cried Masako, bending over him more closely so that he could smell the scent of her hair and skin and feel the warmth from her body. "Is it serious?"

Ribata sat back, her eyes resting thoughtfully first on Akitada, then on her. "No," she said. Reaching into her sleeve, she pulled out a handful of bundled herbs. Selecting one, she said, "He has a bad headache and feels slightly feverish. Take a few of these leaves of purple violet and pour boiling water over them. Let them steep as long as it takes to recite the preamble of the lotus sutra, and then bring the infusion back."

Masako left, and Akitada said, "Thank you. It is most kind of you to trouble. I shall be well again shortly, I'm sure."

She nodded and reached for a cloth, which was soaking in the water bowl. Squeezing it out, she began to clean the dried blood from his face and scalp. "They say you killed a political enemy."

"Yes." He was glad the story was beginning to circulate. In the abstract it was no lie. He had killed, and killed for the same reasons as the real Taketsuna.

"What did you think of Toshito's story?"

This was strange questioning, but he decided that a nun's life was of necessity dull. No doubt she took an avid interest in the people she met. He said cautiously, "I liked him and felt sorry for him."

She paused in her ministrations. "You avoid an answer, so you think his case is hopeless?" Her gaze was intent, as if she willed him to deny it.

"I don't know much about it," he said evasively.

She nodded. "You will. You're not a man to rest until you have the truth."

He stared at this strange remark, but she resumed her work, firmly turning his head to the side to dab at a particularly sore area. He gritted his teeth and winced at the sharp pain.

"The girl likes you."

"What?"

"Masako likes you. I could see it in her face and hear it in her voice. Don't hurt her."

"Of course not. I hardly know her." He was glad his face was averted, for he could feel the heat of his embarrassment along with the beginnings of anger. "If you are so concerned about the young lady," he said, "why don't you speak to her father? Making his daughter labor like an outcast among rough criminals is cruel and wrong."

She clicked her tongue. "All human beings have the lotus of Buddhahood within. It flourishes even in foul water." She had finished what she was doing, and he turned to glance up at her, catching a speculative gleam in those deep-set eyes. A tiny smile formed at the corner of her thin lips and disappeared instantly. "There may be reasons," she said, folding away the wet cloth and putting the bowl of dirty water aside. "For example, they may be very poor and need the extra money."

"Poor?" he scoffed. "Yamada is a man of rank and good family. He has his salary and probably also family income. How could he be poor enough to treat his only child this way?"

"Masako is not his only child. Yamada has a son in the northern army. He is very proud of him. The boy has distinguished himself and has hopes of a fine military career."

"Then he cares more about his son than his daughter," Akitada charged. "As if it were not enough that she is confined to this island where suitable husbands must be singularly lacking—" He stopped abruptly and flushed.

Ribata gave him a sharp glance, and he felt angrier than ever. Closing his mouth firmly before his temper caused him to say too much, he glared at the ceiling.

When she spoke, her voice was sad. "Sometimes events happen which force us to make cruel choices."

Masako returned with a steaming bowl. He drank the pungent, vile-tasting brew and was reminded of Seimei and home. Ribata's ministrations had turned the steady pain in his head to vicious pounding.

They left him after a while, and he lay there, miserable in a confusion of pain and puzzlement. After a while, he forced himself to check his robe. The stains were gone, but his papers still stiffened the lining of the collar. With a sigh of relief, he crawled back and tried to think.

He had suffered humiliation, abuse, and repeated beatings without having made the slightest progress. And now, as if this were not enough, he had allowed himself to become distracted by a girl who was of no concern to him and threatened to interfere with his task and peace of mind.

CHAPTER FIVE

THE UNPOLISHED JEWEL

In the morning, Akitada had only a slight headache and a few swellings and lacerations which his hair hid well enough. He verified these matters by peering at himself in the courtyard well. Unfortunately, his appearance was marred by the unkempt state of his beard. Since he had no razor, he decided to ask Yamada for the use of his.

Father and daughter were at breakfast as before. It was millet gruel again, this time with a bit of radish thrown in. It was poor food indeed for a family of Yamada's status. Akitada cast furtive glances at his hosts. Masako wore the same silk dress, not new because the blue had faded in the folds, and Yamada's dark robe was mended at the sleeve and collar. Could they indeed be abjectly poor? Perhaps the son in the northern army required hefty sums. Many young men in the military gambled.

Yamada politely inquired about Akitada's injuries and repeated the story of Yutaka being attacked by the prisoner. Masako said nothing and, beyond a bow and a muttered thanks for her ministrations the day before, Akitada avoided speaking to or looking at her. When they were done, he begged the loan of the razor. An awkward silence met his request. Then Yamada said, "Forgive me, but it is not permissible to provide prisoners with such things."

"Oh," said Akitada. "Of course. In your house I tend to forget that I am a prisoner." He touched his beard with a rueful smile. "I do not like to appear in front of you so unkempt, but I suppose I must."

"But," said Masako quickly, "I could trim it for you. I always shave Father."

"No," cried Akitada, rising quickly, "I would not dream of asking such a thing of a lady."

"Well," put in her father, "I suppose it is out of the ordinary, but we can hardly expect to live by the old rules, any of us. Masako is quite skilled with a razor. You may trust her completely."

"Of course I trust her," said Akitada, reddening, "but it is surely not seemly for her to trim my beard. A servant, perhaps . . ."

"We have no servants," Masako said practically. "But if it embarrasses you, I would rather not."

It was an impossible situation which ended, predictably, after reassurances and apologies from Akitada, with him sitting on the edge of the veranda, while she knelt beside him and trimmed his beard. Yamada had withdrawn into his room, where he was bent over some paperwork and out of earshot.

Masako's closeness was as disturbing to Akitada as her featherlight touch on his skin. He could not avoid looking at her face, so close to his that he felt the warmth of her breath. She had unusually long lashes, as silken and thick as her hair, and her full lips quirked now and then with concentration. Once they parted, and the tip of her pink tongue appeared between her teeth. White teeth. She did not blacken them as other women of her class did. Neither did his wife, for that matter, unless she had to appear in public. The memory of Tamako shook him enough to avert his eyes from Masako's pretty features. But there was little escape, for they next fell on her wrist, slender and white where the sleeve of her gown had slipped back, in contrast to the rough redness of her hands.

He remembered the first time he had met her, how she had been barefoot, and how dirty her pretty feet had been. How could such a beautiful and wellborn young girl lead the life of a rough serving woman? Had her education been as neglected as her manners? He felt a perverse desire to protect her.

In his confusion, he blurted out, "Why are you and your father so poor?"

She dropped the razor in her lap and stared at him. "What do you mean?"

Oh, dear. He could hardly refer to the millet gruel and their mended clothes. But there were always her menial tasks. "You know very well," he said severely, "that a young lady of your class should not engage in the kind of work I have seen you perform. That is for slaves or outcasts to do. Only utter penury could have caused your father to care so little about his daughter's behavior."

She reddened and her eyes flashed. "My behavior is not your concern," she hissed, waving the razor at him to make her point. "If I wish to shave men, it is my business. And if I want to work in the prison kitchen, it is also my business. Let me tell you that I find such a life more entertaining than spending all my days and nights in some dark room reading poetry like the fine ladies you are familiar with. I am fed up with people telling me how improper I am and how no gentleman will want me for a wife. There are only farmers, soldiers, and prisoners in Sadoshima. The few officials are either too old or too settled to look for another wife. The best I can do is to marry some penniless exile like you, and he would surely appreciate the fact that I can cook a meal, clean the kitchen, and trim his beard when it needs it."

They stared at each other, dismayed at opening the floodgates of so much suppressed frustration. The deep color which touched her translucent skin reminded Akitada of the blushing of a rose.

"Forgive me," he said, taking her hand.

"I didn't mean that," she cried at the same moment. They both laughed a little in mutual embarrassment.

He took the razor from her hand and laid it aside. "You have been very good to me, Masako, you and your father. I have been wondering if you are in some sort of trouble. Perhaps I can help."

She did not point out to him that he was hardly in a position to help anybody. Instead she shook her head and smiled tremulously. "Thank you. You are very kind. It is a temporary situation and involves my father's honor. I'm afraid I cannot tell you more than that."

"Something to do with the prison or the prisoners?" he persisted, wondering if Yamada had become involved in some way in Toshito's predicament.

"No. Not the prison. Another duty. Please don't ask any more questions." She took up the razor again and finished trimming his beard, while he sat, puzzling over her remarks. What other assignment did Yamada have? Whatever it was, it probably involved money somehow, for the deprivation they suffered must be due to the fact that he must make restitution. Had Yamada mismanaged government funds?

She laid aside the razor and smiled at him. "There. You look very handsome," she said. "And you could easily have slashed my throat and made your escape."

He smiled back. "Your throat is much too pretty for that, and there is little chance of my getting off the island. That is why exiles are sent here in the first place."

"As to that, there have been escapes. At least, people have disappeared mysteriously. They say fishermen from the mainland used to do a lucrative business ferrying off exiles. Of course, it takes a great deal of gold, but some of the noblemen here have wealthy families back in the capital or in one of the provinces." She stopped and put a hand over her mouth. "Oh, dear. I talk too much. Do you have a family?"

Akitada laughed out loud. "We are very poor." It was the truth. He could hardly have raised the money for the passage to Sadoshima, let alone the sum involved in an escape attempt. But the topic was an interesting one. "I assume Prince Okisada could have availed himself of such a method if he had wished to do so. Why did he remain?"

"Oh, the prince was too famous. He would have been caught quickly. And they say he was too soft to be a hunted man." She regarded Akitada affectionately. "You, on the other hand, look able to take on any danger. Where did you get the scar on your shoulder?"

Akitada saw the admiration in her eyes and smiled. "A sword cut. And it wasn't proper of you to stare at a man washing himself."

She blushed. For a moment they sat looking at each other, then she turned her face away. "I told you that my life is more entertaining than that of proper young ladies," she said lightly. "I could not help noticing that the scar is recent, and there were others. Are you a famous swordsman?"

"Not at all." Her sudden warm regard made him uncomfortable, and he started to rise. "It is time to go to the archives."

She snatched at his hand. "Not even a thank-you, when I have made you look so handsome?"

Akitada looked down into her laughing eyes. The invitation in them was unmistakable and unnerving. There was a part of him which disapproved of such forwardness. She was the most improper young lady he had ever met. Yet his heart melted and he felt his hand tremble in hers. She managed to make him feel as awkward as a young boy. Detaching his hand gently, he bowed. "I am deeply in your debt, Masako. Perhaps I could do some of your chores for you after work tonight?"

She stood also, twisting the razor in her hands. There was still color in her cheeks and her eyes sparkled as she returned the bow. "Thank you. I would be honored, Taketsuna."

One of the clerks was peering out of the door to the archives but disappeared instantly when he saw Akitada. No one was in the dim hall. Akitada looked about nervously, wondering what to expect after yesterday's attack. Suddenly Yutaka appeared. He was all smiles. The two clerks followed him, looking glum. Yutaka gestured and they knelt, bowing deeply.

For a moment, Akitada feared his identity was known, but then Yutaka said, "These stupid louts wish to express their humble apologies for their mistake. They hope you will forgive them this time."

"Please," Akitada said to the two clerks, "get up, both of you. *Shijo-san*, there was no need for this. The mistake has been explained to me, and I assure you I am much better."

"That is good," cried Yutaka. "Good and generous. Yes. Well, then." He looked at the two clerks, who were still on their knees, and cried, "You heard, you lazy oafs. Up! Up! Back to work! And don't make such a foolish mistake again or I'll see that you get another beating."

Akitada winced. Yutaka had been rather unfair. They had merely responded to his cries for help. No wonder the big one, Genzo, gave Akitada a rather nasty look before he scurried out. They blamed him for their punishment.

The day passed quietly. As a rule the documents Akitada worked on were of little interest to him, and he had fallen into a habit of copying mechanically while turning over in his mind the many puzzling events of the past days. Foremost among these was the death of Jisei. Who had beaten him to death? Ogata had mentioned a fight, but surely the prisoners would have been caught. Had it been done by the guards? Why? He was such a weak, inoffensive creature, and much too timid to make an escape attempt. Besides, he had counted on being released shortly. And that fat drunkard Ogata had almost certainly covered up the murder out of fear. That suggested that Jisei had been killed on someone's orders. Had he seen something he should not have? Akitada remembered with a shiver how certain Jisei had been that he would be sent home. Who had promised him an early release? Akitada had taken it for a sort of merciful practicality because Jisei's festering knees and arms made him useless for crawling about in silver mines, but there were laws against releasing prisoners before their sentences were served. And that left only an empty promise, a lie, which was never intended to be kept. The real intention all along must have been to kill him. Akitada decided that Jisei had known something with which he had bargained for his release and which had cost him his life.

He was so preoccupied with Jisei's murder that he almost overlooked an interesting item in the document he was working on. It concerned an institution called a "Public Valuables Office." Apparently one of the earlier governors of Sadoshima had established a storehouse where people could deposit family treasures in exchange for ready money or rice. Later, say after a good harvest, they could redeem the items. Such places existed elsewhere in the country, but they were usually run by the larger temples and helped farmers buy their seed rice in the spring. He skimmed the pages for an explanation of government oversight in Sadoshima and found it in the fact that much of what was left in safekeeping seemed to be silver. Akitada recalled that some of the silver mining was in the hands of private families, Kumo's for example. But most intriguing was the fact that the official currently in charge of the "Public Valuables Office" was none other than Yamada.

◆

After work that evening, Akitada went directly to the prison kitchen. Steam rose from one of the cookers in the large earthen stove, and the smell of food hung in the hot air. Masako, her back to him and dressed in her rough cotton cover and kerchief, was filling a bamboo carrier with steaming soup. A basket of empty bowls stood beside her. Except for her slender waist and a certain grace in her movements, she looked exactly like a peasant girl.

"I came to help," said Akitada.

She turned, her face red and moist from the fire and the steam, and brushed away a strand of hair that had escaped from the scarf. Flashing him a smile, she pointed to the basket of bowls. "I'm about to take food to the guards and prisoners. You can help if you want."

He accepted with alacrity, taking the handle of the full soup container in one hand and the basket of bowls in the other and following her across the yard to the low jail building.

They met with a rude reception in the guardroom.

"What? Bean stew again?" complained one big, burly fellow, sniffing disdainfully. "It's been a week since we've had a bit of fish. I suppose you're saving up for a new silk gown."

His smaller companion lifted her skirts and eyed her leg. "We don't mind if you wear a bit less," he said, and guffawed.

Masako slapped his hand away and snapped, "If you don't want the soup, the prisoners will be glad of an extra helping. The food is supposed to be for them anyway. You get paid enough to buy your own. If you want delicacies, go to the market. We've been feeding you lazy louts long enough."

This was received with shocked surprise. "But," whined the first guard, "it's been the custom. And you know we can't leave our post to go to the market."

She put her hands on her hips and glared. "Then bring your food from home. Now open up! I don't have all day."

The larger man muttered under his breath, but he got the keys and his lantern. As he passed Akitada, who was carrying the heavy food container in one hand and balancing the basket of bowls with the other, he sniffed. "It smells good for bean stew," he said in an ingratiating tone.

"Open up!" snapped Masako.

Muttering some more, he preceded them down the hallway, stopping to unlock each cell door to let Masako fill a bowl and hand it to an inmate. They finally reached young Mutobe, who stood waiting and bowed politely to Masako before receiving his bowl.

"How are you today, Toshito?" she asked the prisoner.

"Well. Thank you, Masako." He looked at her with concern. "And how is it with you and your father? Any news?"

"No. Nothing. And you?"

"No talking allowed," growled the guard.

Masako sighed and filled another bowl. "Here," she said, handing it to the guard. "Hunger makes you irritable. Go away and eat."

"What about Kintsu? I can't go back without taking him something."

Akitada handed Masako a second bowl with a wink. She chuckled softly, filled this also, and gave it to the waiting guard. He nodded and departed with the food.

"Well, that got rid of him," said Masako, giving Akitada a conspiratorial smile. "They're becoming unbearable. Even the outcast sweepers ignore my orders. As Father's daughter I used to get some respect, but now they think of me as one of their own. What a difference poverty makes." She turned and saw that young Mutobe was still holding his full bowl, worried eyes moving between her and Akitada. "Sit down, Toshito, and eat, please."

He bowed and started eating, but would not sit in her presence. After a few mouthfuls he said, "You cannot continue this, you know. They are savages. One of them might get ideas." He glanced at Akitada again.

"I'm not afraid. Besides, Taketsuna can come along to protect me."

"Taketsuna?" His eyes narrowed. "Oh, it's you. You were here yesterday with Masako's father, taking notes. I wasn't paying attention."

His tone had become arrogant and faintly hostile. When Akitada nodded, he turned back to Masako with a frown. "How do you come to know this prisoner?"

"Taketsuna is no criminal. He is a political exile who works in the archives during the day and stays at our house."

"You mean like a houseguest? Why the special treatment? He should be locked up here or sent inland to work."

Masako stared at him. "Oh, Toshito, how can *you* of all people say such a thing?"

Young Mutobe flushed and said angrily, "It is not safe to take a criminal into your house. You know nothing about him. What can your father be thinking of?"

"Don't be ridiculous," she cried, moving closer to Akitada and putting her hand on his arm. "For all you know he's of better birth than you."

Young Mutobe paled and pushed the half-empty bowl her way. "No doubt. I can see how the wind blows. Here. I've lost my appetite."

"Oh, Toshito," she cried, "I'm sorry. I did not mean to insult you. Please forgive me." But the young man folded his arms across his chest and turned his back to them. She pleaded, "Come, you insulted Taketsuna. That was not well done, either. As for his staying with us: it was the governor's wish, and he pays for Taketsuna's lodging and food."

"I see. It's the infernal money again!" Toshito said bitterly to the wall.

Akitada wished himself elsewhere. He did not like being talked about as if he were not present, especially with the hostility displayed by this man. But the news that Mutobe had made elaborate arrangements for him after all was more disconcerting. Word had probably already got out that the was being treated like a guest in the provincial headquarters. He cleared his throat. "Forgive me for interrupting," he said, "but as I am to leave Mano shortly, the arrangement is strictly temporary. My being given special lodging has more to do with my ability to take dictation and write well. I understand there is a great shortage of scribes here. Of course, I am most grateful to Superintendent Yamada. I assure you, his daughter is quite safe from me."

Akitada's polite speech was a reproach to the other man's manners, and he turned around. "I am sorry for my rudeness. My situation is frustrating to me because I cannot help my friends."

Akitada bowed. "I understand."

But there was resentment in the air, and Masako called the guard. When she picked up their empty bowls in the guardroom, the little guard remarked with a grin, "Found yourself a new fellow, eh? He'll give better service than that little sprout Toshito and he'll live longer, too."

Masako gasped, and Akitada took a threatening step toward the man, but she caught his arm and pulled him away.

Outside, she stopped. "Oh, Taketsuna, you must never do that again. Fighting with a guard will get you nothing but a vicious flogging and chains."

She was right, of course, and he could not afford to make a scene in any case. When he muttered an apology, she reached up to touch his face. "Thank you, Taketsuna. It was kind of you to want to protect me." She was looking up at him with a little smile, her eyes suddenly moist. "I would put up with a great deal more than a few silly words to spare you pain," she said softly. When he said nothing, she asked, "Are you really leaving so soon?"

He saw the tears in her eyes, and his heart started beating faster. Feeling like a brute, he said, "Yes. I'm to travel inland with one of the governor's inspectors."

"Oh, Taketsuna. So little time." She looked dejected, then brightened. "But you'll come back soon?"

He said nothing and they walked back to the kitchen courtyard. At the well he helped her wash the bowls. She was deep in thought and said little. He was relieved. Her words and expression had touched him deeply. He wondered what the relationship was between her and Mutobe's son and knew he did not like it. Ashamed of his jealousy, he forced his mind to more important matters.

Regardless of Mutobe's assertion that his son had been framed by his own political enemies, Akitada was by no means convinced of the son's innocence. Toshito had attended the university in the capital and might have come in contact with Prince Okisada's enemies. He might, in fact, have been their tool to eliminate a troublesome claimant to the throne.

Back in the kitchen, Akitada took up the broom and began to sweep while Masako busied herself about the stove, laying the fire for the morning meal and gathering the remnants of bean soup for their own supper. The Yamadas' provisions seemed scarce and of the plainest sort, but Masako had managed to prepare decent meals with what she had. Such extreme poverty was still a great puzzle to Akitada.

"You seem to be on very familiar terms with young Mutobe," he began after a while.

She stopped, a bamboo dipper with bean soup in her hand, and stared at him. "What do you mean?" she asked, color rising to her cheeks.

"That was badly put." He leaned on the broom and smiled at her. "Nothing insulting, I assure you. You speak to each other like brother and sister."

She finished emptying the soup kettle. "We are friends, because we grew up together."

"You must know him very well, then. Well enough to share secrets, as children do. Would you tell each other things you might not mention to your fathers?" He tried to make it sound like gentle teasing.

But she was too sharp for that. "Why do you want to know?" she demanded suspiciously.

He retreated. "No reason. Or rather, there are so many mysteries about you that I . . . Never mind! It was just idle conversation."

She came then and looked up at him searchingly. "Was it, Taketsuna?" she asked, her voice suddenly husky. Akitada started to back away, but she put her hand on his arm to stop him. "Who are you really?"

This startled him. "You know who I am. Yoshimine Taketsuna."

"No. I mean, who are you inside? You ask about me, but what are your thoughts? What is your family like? What did you wish for before you came here? What sort of life will you make in the future?"

He moved away from her and started sweeping again. "What I was does not matter here," he said, "and I have no future."

She followed him. "Your past matters to me, and so does your future. Many exiles have settled to a comfortable life here. They have taken wives and raised families."

Appalled by where this conversation seemed to be leading, he kept his back to her. "I will never rest until I return to my home and family," he said firmly.

"Tell me about your family."

He turned then. "I have a wife and a young son."

She flinched a little at his fierceness. "Oh," she murmured. "I should have thought of that. I'm sorry. You must love them very much." Tears rose to her eyes, making him sorry for his cruel frankness. "Taketsuna," she whispered, "you may not see them again for many, many years, or perhaps never. What will you do meanwhile?"

"Nothing. Hope. What else can a man do?"

Her eyes pleaded. "He can make another life."

He put away the broom then. "I have no life," he said in a tone of finality. "And now, if you have no other chores for me, I think I'll go clean up before the evening meal."

Outside, at the well, he started to strip off his gown, but a strong sense of being watched made him stop and look over his shoulder. Masako stood in the kitchen doorway, a small, secretive smile on her pretty face. When their eyes met, she turned abruptly, took up the container of bean soup, and walked away humming a song.

They took their evening meal—the leftover bean soup with some pickled radish—as always on the veranda in front of Yamada's study. For Akitada it was a difficult meal. Masako had appeared a little late. She was again in her faded blue silk gown, but she had put a new ribbon in her shining hair.

Her father was in his usual abstracted mood, and she attempted to make conversation with Akitada, making sure he had enough soup, that it was to his liking, that the setting sun was not in his eyes. All of these overtures Akitada met with a monosyllabic "Yes" or "No," and she finally turned to her father.

"When will you get paid again, Father?" she asked, startling Yamada, who cast an embarrassed glance toward Akitada.

"Not for another five days, child," he said. "I am very sorry. It must be difficult for you."

"Not at all," she said lightly. "I'm a very good manager. But the guards were demanding fish today, and it has been days since we've had any. I expect you would like some, too."

"Fish?" He seemed surprised. "You have no money left? I am very sorry, my dear. You shall have some tomorrow. The truth is I had not noticed the absence of fish." He added with a smile to Akitada, "Masako makes even the plainest dish taste like something fit for the emperor. Isn't that so?"

The meals had been adequate but hardly fit for an emperor, or even one of their own class. A farmer or a monk might have approved, though, of the vegetarian dishes. Millet and beans were their main staples. The flavor was due to herbs, fruit, or vegetables, all things which were raised in their garden or gathered in the woods. However, Akitada agreed politely, then changed the subject.

"I noticed a document in the archives today which refers to a rather peculiar institution of which you seem to be the overseer, sir. It's called a Valuables Office. Apparently it pays out rice against securities like silver? I thought such operations are usually carried out by temples."

Masako dropped her bowl with a crash and stared at him wide-eyed. Her father turned rather pale. His hands shook as he put down his own bowl. After a moment, he took a deep breath and said, "Clean that up, child." He waited until Masako had scooped up the shards and food bits and left the room. Then he asked, "What is your interest in this matter, young man?"

Akitada knew now that he was on the right track but said only, "Curiosity, mainly. Sadoshima is a strange place to me. There are private silver mines here, when I thought all the mined silver belonged to the emperor. Why is so much silver in private hands, and what is the reason for the valuables office?"

Yamada relaxed a little. "Some of the mines belong to the emperor, and the silver from them goes into storage in the garrison until it is shipped to the mainland. But the landowners do their own mining under special permits. This created a problem in the past. There is very little minted currency in Sado, and people began to barter in silver, which caused it to become devalued, even the silver coins minted by the emperor, and so it was thought best to control the matter by allowing people to trade their silver for rice from the government storehouses. Now the value of the silver is fixed. In addition, many people are leaving their valuables in our hands for security. There are, after all, many criminals on this island."

Akitada thought he had a pretty good idea what had plunged Yamada into sudden but temporary poverty. The man was trying to make restitution before the next inspection. For the time being Akitada had to let the matter rest. There were far more urgent worries on his mind.

After the evening meal, Akitada made his way in the dark to a storage shed and climbed on its roof. From here he could see over the tribunal walls down to the city and the peaceful bay. The moon was nearly full and shone very brightly on the shimmering water. Below him huddled the dark roofs of the houses of the city, and beyond rose the dusky headlands which stood between him and his home and loved ones. The bay looked like molten silver where the moonlight touched it. The distant coast of Echigo was hidden behind the dark mountains, but he fixed his eyes on the faint silver line which marked the separation of land and sky and thought of Tamako and their son.

He had almost died on the way here, and he might die in the attempt to carry out his orders. The possibility of never seeing his wife or child again threw him into a stomach-twisting panic, and he was tempted to give up this mad assignment and go home.

Oh, how he longed for safety from the tangled and deadly schemes of men, and from the tear-drenched eyes of a brave and lovely girl.

CHAPTER SIX

TWISTING A STRAW ROPE

Midmorning of the following day the governor paid a surprise visit to the archives. He came accompanied by a small, round-bellied man who walked with short, quick steps and cast a curious glance into Akitada's cubicle. The governor passed by without a nod and made straight for Yutaka's office. A murmur of voices told Akitada nothing, but after a few minutes Yutaka, his face stiff with disapproval, put his head in and told him the governor wished to see him.

"This," said Mutobe, when Akitada had knelt and bowed, "is Inspector Osawa. He is leaving on an inspection tour, and you are to accompany him as his secretary. One of Yutaka's scribes will also go along."

Akitada bowed again, suppressing his amusement. A promotion from scribe to secretary? Mutobe must really be uncomfortable with his lowly status. He bowed also to Osawa, who merely stared back. Primly attired in brown robe and black cap, the inspector was in his late forties, and looked like a typical midlevel provincial official. Such men were born and trained in their own provinces, where they made themselves indispensable to the governors with their knowledge of local conditions. Here on Sadoshima, such a man might have allegiances with the wrong factions, and Akitada decided not to trust him.

Mutobe told Osawa, "Perhaps you had better just look into the matter of the Valuables Office before you leave. I will send word to Yamada to have the books ready tomorrow morning."

Akitada cleared his throat.

"Yes?" asked Mutobe. "Is there a problem?"

"No, Your Excellency. Superintendent Yamada mentioned that he had some copying work for me to do in my spare time. Since I am indebted to him for my lodging, may I take your message and offer my assistance in getting the accounts ready for Inspector Osawa's visit?"

Mutobe looked momentarily confused, no doubt wondering what possible interest Akitada might have in an inspection of the Valuables Office, but he said only, "Good idea. Why don't you go now?"

Akitada bowed to Mutobe and Osawa and went to tell Yutaka that the governor had dispatched him to Yamada.

"Oh, all right," muttered the *shijo*, pursing his lips. "But it is very disappointing. First he sends you here, then he sends you away. Yes. Very disappointing." He shook his head, sighed, and bent to his copying work.

Akitada found Yamada in the small garden behind his house. He was digging radishes and putting them in a basket which already contained some leafy vegetables. When he saw Akitada, he looked embarrassed. "Ah, hmm," he said. "Back already? You find me at my hobby. Gardening is very good for health and useful, too." He pointed to the basket. "For our evening meal. I wish the radishes were bigger, but I don't seem to have the touch. And caterpillars have been in the cabbages. Do you happen to know about such matters?"

Akitada had no time to discuss gardening. He said brusquely, "I'm afraid not. The governor sent me to tell you that Osawa will inspect the books of the Valuables Office tomorrow."

Yamada was too shocked to take note of Akitada's abruptness or his lack of courtesy titles for Mutobe and Osawa. He dropped his spade, turned perfectly white, and began to sway on his feet. Akitada caught his arm and helped him to the veranda steps.

"All is lost," groaned Yamada, putting his head into his muddy hands. "All the hard work in vain. Poor Masako. Poor child. And what will become of my son when his father's disgrace is known?" He ran his fingers through his hair and shook his head in hopeless despair.

Akitada sat down beside him. "What precisely is wrong in the Valuables Office?" he asked.

Yamada raised his head. His mud-streaked face and disordered hair would have looked comical, if it had not been for his tears. "I discovered a month ago that two bars of silver were not what they were supposed to be. Masako and I have been trying ever since to save the money to replace them. One has already been purchased, but we shall not be in time to replace the second one. Osawa was not supposed to visit until the end of the month, and I would have received my salary by then, as well as Masako's pay for prison maintenance. It was enough to make up another bar. Now it is all for nothing."

"What do you mean, 'two bars were not what they were supposed to be'?"

"I accidentally dropped one of them and it broke. It was only clay covered with a thin layer of silver foil. I frantically checked and found another one. Now it will be thought that I made the substitution. They will say I stole the silver to equip my son, who is an officer with the northern army. But that is not so. I sold everything we owned to do that. Then I started this garden and dismissed all my servants. We were so poor when I discovered what had happened to the silver that I could not make good the loss. I was desperate, but Masako thought we might save and earn some extra money and put the silver back before the annual inspection. She took over the duties of the kitchen staff for the prison. I was against it, because it would ruin her reputation. But she argued that my disgrace would also ruin her, and this way we might salvage a great deal, particularly my son's career. And now, poor child, she has suffered to no purpose." Yamada fell to weeping again, the tears leaving wet tracks on his dirt-smudged cheeks. Akitada's heart went out to him and to the girl who had borne her hardship without complaint.

"But," he said, still mystified, "why didn't you arrest the person who deposited the fake bars?"

Yamada's misery deepened. "I couldn't," he whispered. "No record."

"The thief gave a false name?"

"I wouldn't know. There was a small fire. It destroyed a ledger."

"Good heavens! Are you the only one who takes care of the Valuables Office?"

"I used to have a clerk, but had to let him go. I discovered the clay bars when I checked the stored goods against my own records after the fire. I was trying to piece together some sort of documentation from the charred remnants of the ledgers."

Akitada mentally raised his brows that Yamada had not checked deposits regularly before but only said, "The governor has given me permission to help you get ready for the inspection."

"Very kind of him," muttered Yamada, "but it won't do any good. I might as well go to him now and confess the whole thing. I will be dismissed, of course, but the worst part is the dishonor. It will ruin my son's career and Masako's prospects of marriage." He brushed fresh tears from his face and rose.

Akitada caught his sleeve. "Wait!"

"Oh, I forgot." Yamada turned, his expression, if anything, more dismal than before. "Masako must be told. Would you do it?" He raised his hands in a pathetic gesture of entreaty. "I don't have the belly for it."

The thought of facing Masako with this bit of news daunted Akitada also. "Don't give up yet," he urged. "Perhaps we can buy some time. Could I have a look at the Valuables Office?"

In spite of Yamada's distress, he looked shocked. "There are rules against allowing people into the storage area," he said. "And you being a prisoner—well, I don't think—"

"In that case," said Akitada, "I don't see how I can help you. But surely if you are with me, an exception might be made?"

Yamada hesitated. "Why do you want to see it?"

"To get an idea how the theft was done and perhaps find the thief."

"It could be anyone. I told you, the records are gone."

But Yamada's fear was so great that he took Akitada across the compound to a small building in the far corner.

The Valuables Office had been fitted into the outer wall so that its front faced out into the main street, where it was accessible to merchants and farmers, while the rest of the building was within the walls of the guarded compound. Apart from the front, its plaster walls were windowless and it had only one rear door.

Yamada and Akitada entered through this back door, which Yamada unlocked with a set of keys he carried. He lit a lantern that stood on a shelf beside the doorway. By its light, Akitada could make out rows of shelving filled with all sorts of objects. In one corner was an iron-bound chest for money and many bags of rice. Silver and copper coins were a more practical form of tender, but less common than the ubiquitous rice as a medium of exchange.

Yamada passed through this room and unlocked a second door, which led into the front area where business was transacted. Here some light filtered in through high and narrow paper-covered windows. The walls still bore traces of smoke damage. From outside they could hear the voices of passersby and the sounds of wheels and horses' hooves.

"We only open for business on the first and tenth day of each month," explained Yamada.

Against the back wall stood shelves which held scales for weighing precious metals, an abacus, various writing tools, candle holders, and ledgers. Both the front door and the heavy door they had just passed through were protected by metal locks and a series of iron bands and studs.

"Who, besides you, has keys to this place?" asked Akitada, walking over to the new-looking ledgers and turning the pages idly.

"Nobody."

"Not even the clerk who used to work here?"

"Certainly not. I did not trust him. He drank and made careless mistakes."

"And where do you keep your keys when you don't carry them?

Yamada frowned at this interrogation. "With me at all times. Why? The torch was thrown in from the street. Nobody broke in or unlocked any doors."

Akitada turned to look at Yamada in surprise. "A torch was thrown from the street? Why?"

Yamada shook his head. "Who knows? There are too many criminals on this island. The fire was put out quickly, and we did not pursue the matter when we found the deposits safe behind their locked doors. The only loss was one ledger and a broken window screen. We moved the shelves against the back wall after that, and I copied what information I could gather from the charred ledger."

Akitada nodded and studied the entries. "You wrote all this? I see you loaned five strings of cash on five bars of silver. Is that the going rate?"

"It's generous but not unusual. If the person is known to us and reliable, as much as a thousand copper cash or fifty *sho* of rice are advanced for one bar of silver. About half its value."

Akitada whistled. "So two bars would have got a man enough to feed himself for a year. Let's have a look at your treasures."

"Is this really necessary? If someone found out—"

"You would be no worse off."

Yamada sighed and turned back into the storage room, taking the keys from his sash again to relock the door. Holding up the lantern, he led the way to the shelves which filled an area two or three times the size of the front room.

Akitada saw that the shelves bore numbers, each number corresponding with a deposit. He walked along picking up this or that, while Yamada followed, watching nervously to make sure he replaced it in its assigned spot. The goods consisted of rolls of silk and brocade, lengths of cotton, various art objects, books, musical instruments, swords, elegant utensils in lacquer and inlaid metals, and numerous stacks of silver bars. He thought of the death of the Second Prince and the murder of little Jisei. Silver figured in both instances. The prince's plot, if indeed there had been one, would have been financed with local silver, and the little convict had worked in one of the mines.

"Here," said Yamada, pointing to three silver bars in a corner of one of the shelves. "These are the two clay ones. The third one is the silver bar I purchased."

Akitada took them up one by one. The first two seemed a little lighter than the third, and he saw that a piece had broken off one of these, revealing the red clay underneath. The second bar showed clay beneath some scratches, no doubt made by Yamada to verify that it, too, was counterfeit. Whoever had accepted these bars was criminally negligent. The scales in the other room would have revealed the problem instantly. "You said you checked all the rest?" Akitada asked, looking around at the many small piles of silver.

"Yes, I checked them all."

"Hmm. Only two out of all of these. When did your clerk leave?"

Yamada frowned. "It was before the fire. A very unreliable person. I had to speak to him repeatedly about sleeping during working hours, but after the fire I wished I had kept him on."

Akitada looked at another deposit. It was a large one, consisting of some fifteen silver bars and various boxes. Noting a small silk pouch, he picked it up. It was astonishingly heavy.

"That is raw gold," Yamada said.

"Gold?" The contents felt lumpy. Akitada opened the bag and saw small irregular chunks of the yellow metal inside. None was larger than the average pebble. "Where did this come from?" he asked.

"Sometimes a farmer or some youngster finds a piece in a stream. Often they don't know what it is and take it to a temple."

"And you don't know its owner either?"

"But I do. It belongs to the Kokubunji Temple. I remember the little bag of gold. Silver bars are more common."

"Yes. Hmm." Akitada fell into deep thought, and Yamada began to fidget with the keys and shuffle his feet. "Yes," said Akitada again, coming out of his reverie, "it might work. Here is what we'll do to catch our thief."

Yamada's eyes grew round as he listened, and he shook his head violently at first. But the more Akitada explained, the more he came around, and finally he nodded reluctantly.

"Mind you," warned Akitada, "you must tell the governor what happened. Throw yourself on his mercy. I believe he is an understanding man and will forgive you if you get the loan back and arrest the thief."

"But what about Masako? Do we tell her or not?"

Akitada wanted to say no, but the girl deserved to be told. She had proven her devotion to her family and could be trusted with the secret. Akitada feared that she might feel some obligation to him. "Tell her, but don't mention me," he advised.

Yamada shook his head. "No. I'm going to the governor now before I lose my courage. You should know that I am a very bad liar. Perhaps I may manage to claim credit for your idea with him, but Masako would have the truth out of me in a minute. You had better speak to her. Oh, dear! She's at home, waiting for the vegetables. Would you mind taking them? I suppose people must eat."

"You had better wash before you see the governor."

Yamada looked at his hands and touched the drying mud on his face. "Oh, dear!" he muttered and made for the door. Outside he stopped and came back to pull Akitada out with him and relock the Valuables Office. Then he rushed off again.

Akitada followed more slowly, amused to see Yamada washing himself at the kitchen well in order to avoid his daughter. He went through the garden to pick up the basket of vegetables. In the entrance he set down the basket and kicked off his sandals before stepping up on the wooden floor. There was no sign of Masako.

"Anyone home?" he called out.

"Yes." Her voice came from the back, and he followed the sound.

"It's me," he said loudly, faced with a hallway of closed doors. One of the doors flew open, and Masako looked out.

"Taketsuna?"

She was wearing the old scarf around her head, but her hair had escaped and was slipping down her back and across one cheek. Her face was hot and flushed, and she appeared to be wearing a man's cotton shirt over an old pair of trousers. There was a smudge of dirt on her nose and one cheek. With her eyes wide and her lips half opened, she had never looked more desirable to Akitada, who stood transfixed.

"I did not expect you at this time of day. Is anything wrong?"

"No. I had a message for your father."

"Oh." She became aware of his eyes on her, brushed helplessly at her hair and then wrapped her arms about her middle, looking at the floor in mortification. "I'm ashamed you caught me like this," she murmured. "I was cleaning the floor and—"

"You look beautiful," he said hoarsely.

"Oh, no. Oh, I wish I were more like other women, with their beautiful gowns and their elegant manners. I wish you . . ." And she burst into tears.

Later he would find all sorts of excuses for what happened next: having embarrassed her so deeply, he had to reassure her—he merely wished to calm her so he could give her the news—he was only offering her brotherly support.

None of these was true, of course. Akitada took the three steps separating them and opened his arms because he had wanted to hold her for a long time now, had wanted to feel that lithe body against his, had wanted to comfort her with his caresses and be caressed in turn.

Masako came to him with a small cry of joy, nestling against him, murmuring endearments, and responding with a passion which startled him into partial sanity. He loosened his embrace and caught her hands on his bare chest where she had slipped them under his robe.

"No, Masako," he pleaded. "Please don't tempt me. Your circumstances are sufficiently improper without this."

"I don't care," she cried. "I have wanted you to love me since I first saw you. I don't care about me. I don't care about anything but you." She pulled him into the room, closed the door behind them, and drew him down onto the matting, tugging feverishly at his sash.

Kneeling above her, he caught her hands again. "No, Masako," he said, "I cannot take a wife, and you must save yourself for a husband."

She gave a bitter laugh. "Save myself? Don't be ridiculous. I'm not a woman of your class." She flushed. "Besides, it's too late to worry about that." When he still hesitated, her eyes filled with tears. "Oh. You do find me disgusting."

"No," he cried. "You are beautiful. I want you. More than anything, but . . ." Weakening, filled with desire, he released her hands.

She reached for his face, bringing it so close to her own that he could taste her breath as she whispered, "Prove it, then." Her breath was so sweet that he tasted her lips with his own and was lost.

Afterward, as they lay together, he cradling her nude body in his arms, she with her eyes closed and a smile curving her lips, he said in wonder, "I came to speak to you about your father's problem and now I do not know how to face him."

"Father's problem?" She sat up and looked at him through narrowed eyes. "Tell me."

It was difficult to concentrate. She had a lovely and utterly desirable body. "I am sorry, Masako," he said, touching a long tress of hair and following it across one breast and down her small, flat belly. "I should not have done that."

She shivered at his touch, but caught his hand with hers. "What problem?" she demanded.

He told her about the inspection. She paled and reached for her trousers. Putting them on and then slipping on the shirt, she asked, "Does this mean that the shortage is known?"

He marveled at her. One moment she was all passionate seductive female, and the next as levelheaded and businesslike as any man. He said, "No, your father has a plan and, with the governor's approval, we shall put it into operation tonight."

Reaching for her scarf, she cried, "Oh, no. The governor must not know. I hope Father has not had another urge to bare his soul." She twisted her hair up and tied it quickly under the scarf. Akitada admired the way her breasts strained against the thin fabric of her shirt. Starting toward the door, she said, "I must talk to him immediately."

"Too late. He has already left to discuss the matter with His Excellency."

She turned with a wail. "Oh, no. Then all is lost. How could you let him do such a stupid thing?"

"Because," he said, getting to his feet and rearranging his own clothes, "I will not take part in an illegal act even if it is to catch a thief. And what we plan is against the law unless it has the approval of the governor."

"What?" She suddenly looked furiously angry. "So! I see it was your idea. To catch a thief according to the letter of the law, you will ruin my family. And you a convict yourself! What sort of man are you? Did you trade my father's honor for your freedom?"

He flinched and tried to mend things. "You misunderstand. What we have in mind will clear your father and allow you to return to a normal life. And your father will receive the credit for the capture of the thief."

After a moment, she asked suspiciously, "What is this plan?"

He told her and watched her face begin to relax and her eyes to shine with excitement. "It might work. Very well, let's get started right away. You and I can move the goods here, and then, after dark, we'll make a hole in the outside wall."

"That will not be necessary, Masako. A torn paper covering on one of the windows, a broken lock, and an abandoned iron bar, and it will look convincing enough."

She nodded after a moment. "Yes. You're right. Less damage is easier to fix." That settled, she became suspicious again. "How did you find out about the silver bars?"

"It's a bit complicated."

Her eyes narrowed. She folded her arms across her chest. "Never mind! I want to know."

"Well, I wondered what would cast a family like yours into such abject poverty that you had to work like this." He gestured at her clothing. She blushed, ripping off the unflattering cotton scarf so that her glossy long hair fell freely about her shoulders again. His fingers yearned to touch it, but he continued, "At first I wondered if either your father or your brother was a gambler, but then you said the hard times would soon be over. Since gamblers don't change their habits, it occurred to me that some other costly mishap had befallen your father. Then I found out about his stewardship of the Valuables Office. Your reaction when I asked you about it proved that I had guessed correctly. Your father admitted the rest a short while ago when I told him about the inspection. That was all."

"Very clever. Do you always pry into other people's affairs?"

"Yes," he said quite seriously.

She chuckled, thinking he had joked. "Oh, very well. But don't try to tell me that this was Father's idea. He is a dear man and a most honest official, but he has never been devious."

◆

The trap was set during the night. Having made the necessary arrangements, Akitada returned to his room for a few hours' rest. Masako had laid out his bedding, and he took off his robe and got under the quilts. A moment later, his door opened quietly, and she slipped in and joined him. He wished she had not come, but when he felt her naked body searching with eager passion for his embrace, he gave in.

Very early the following morning, notices appeared all over town. The notices read:

To the people of Sadoshima

Robbers and thieves have broken into the Valuables Office. I, the governor, order all those who have made deposits to appear in person with their receipts to identify their property or receive compensation for their loss. It is the duty of all citizens to report any knowledge of the criminals.

These orders must be obeyed.

A noisy crowd gathered in front of the message board outside the gates to the tribunal, and within minutes a short line had formed at the door to the Valuables Office. Two guards stood watch outside. People chattered excitedly, pointing up at the broken window. Inside Yamada and Akitada had been joined by the governor.

Yamada stood on a small cask and peered through the torn paper down at the waiting people.

"Do you recognize anyone?" the governor asked.

"No, but it's still early."

"Yes," said Akitada, "if he isn't here yet, he will be. He's a greedy man who expects to collect two bars of real silver in exchange for two of clay, and without having to worry that the theft will ever be laid at his door."

The governor muttered, "Perhaps. But this is most inconvenient. You were supposed to leave right after the inspection today. Now we have to wait another day. I cannot imagine what made you so careless, Yamada. You should have inspected all the silver daily."

Yamada stepped down from his cask and hung his head. "I am most sorry, Excellency. I wish you would accept my resignation."

Mutobe waved the offer away irritably. "I told you, I cannot spare you. At least you thought of a way to rectify your carelessness—even if, as the saying goes, we are twisting a straw rope after the thief has escaped. Still, if you catch the man, we will say no more about it. Well, I must be off. Taketsuna can help you interview the claimants. If nothing else, you will be able to confirm ownership that way."

When the governor had left, Akitada said encouragingly, "There. I told you it would be all right. Now let us get busy twisting that rope. We'll tie that thief up yet." He opened the door and admitted the first claimant.

By midday they had interviewed nearly fifty people and produced two hundred bars of silver and assorted other items of value demanded by their nervous owners. Seeing their property safe, most claimants decided to leave it on deposit. Yamada was able to update and correct his ledgers. Of course, no one had any information about the robbers, although one old man attempted to trade information for wine. The old-timer told a rambling story about a man in his quarter who had been bragging only that morning about a sudden windfall. The windfall turned out to be no more than some fifty or a hundred coppers, and they more than likely had been earned by his wife, who was a potter. They refused the old-timer's offer and sent him away in disgust.

Yamada fell to brooding, and Akitada did not feel much more cheerful. Why had the thief not come or sent an associate? From the beginning, Akitada had suspected the former clerk. The clay bars differed in weight from the real thing and anyone accustomed to handling silver bars would have known they were a sham. In fact, they should have been weighed. Short of Yamada himself, the clerk was the only other person who could have accomplished the fraud. But there was no proof until he claimed the two bars of silver, and this he would hardly do in person. No, he would send someone else. As Akitada considered the matter of a likely accomplice, a memory stirred, and he turned to Yamada. "Do you suppose the man whose wife makes pottery could be involved after all?"

Yamada shook his head despondently. Outside a cart rumbled past. The guard posted at the door yawned loudly. It was almost closing time.

"We have failed," Yamada said.

"Perhaps our man is out of town and did not hear of the notice," Akitada offered, but he did not really believe it himself.

"It was kind of you to try to help," Yamada muttered glumly, "but I'm afraid it's no good. I shall tender my resignation in the morning."

There was nothing Akitada could say. He was racked by guilt over his affair with Masako, and his failure to solve Yamada's problem made him feel worse. It struck him that this matter was trivial by comparison with his true assignment. If he could not even catch a petty thief, how was he to succeed in his much more complex and dangerous undertaking?

And now there was a new complication in his life. In a moment of weakness, he had made Masako and her family his responsibility. Many men of his class had several wives or concubines, but he had hardly sufficient income for one wife and small son. How could he maintain additional families? And he shuddered at the prospect of bringing Masako home with him. Quite apart from the fact that such an act so soon after their marriage and the birth of his son was a profound insult to his wife, the two women had little in common. Feeling wretched, he got up to put away the ledgers and clean out his brush.

But just then the guard outside hailed someone, then ushered in a thin, dirty-looking man in his thirties.

The scrawny individual clutched a token and a bag of coins. With a nervous glance at the guard, he sidled up to Yamada's desk. "It's about my silver," he said. "I'm a bit late, but I'm just back from a trip. The minute I got home, my neighbor comes running and tells me to hurry over here. He says there was a robbery and to bring my claim token. A poor man like me can't afford to lose his hard-earned savings. Two bars, it was." He extended the wooden token. "I brought the two strings of cash." He lifted the bag of coins.

Akitada took the token, recorded the name in his ledger, and checked the date. Then he passed it to Yamada.

Yamada stared at the characters, then at the man. "Your name, profession, and place of residence?"

"Tobe, Your Honor. I'm a vegetable farmer. Me and my wife live in Takase."

"Takase? Where is that?" asked Akitada, looking up from the entries.

"It's a village down the coast," explained Yamada.

"When did you bring in the silver bars?" Akitada asked.

"I forget. It says on the token, doesn't it?"

Yamada glanced again at the token. "I might have known the drunken sot was too careless to weigh them," he muttered in a tone of outrage.

"What?" The thin man blinked. "It's all proper and right, isn't it?"

"Oh, yes," Akitada said quickly. "But we have to check these things. Anyone could claim two bars of silver with a stolen token. How did you come by that much silver as a farmer?"

The man shuffled and tried an ingratiating grin. "I work hard and save my earnings."

Yamada frowned. "Surely that is an extraordinary amount to have saved at your age. I think we had better check to make sure your claim is legitimate."

The man paled. "It's the truth," he whined. "My wife and me, we both work hard."

Akitada said, "Hmm," and gave him a sharp look. "Can you bring any witnesses who saw you depositing two bars of silver here?"

Tobe looked panic-stricken. "I . . . I'll be back tomorrow. Give me back my token."

"No. We're getting to the bottom of this now," said Yamada with uncharacteristic firmness.

The man gasped a little. "It's not urgent. I can wait," he cried, bowing and backing toward the door while clutching his coins to his chest.

Yamada rose and called the guard when another man ran in and collided with the retreating Tobe. It was the old drunk, considerably more unsteady on his feet than earlier. He clutched at Tobe for support, and for a moment the two swayed together like an odd pair of lovers.

The drunk cried, "It's you. Now I get my reward." He wrapped both arms around Tobe's thin figure and announced, "He's your robber. Arrest him quick."

The other man cursed and pushed the drunk away viciously. The beggar hit the wall with a thud, and Tobe made a dash for the door, where the guard caught him in mid-flight.

Akitada bent over the old drunk to help him up. "Are you hurt, old man?" he asked.

The beggar felt his shoulder and ribs, started to shake his head, then croaked, "I'm a bit dizzy. Could I have a drop of wine?"

"No more wine," Akitada said firmly. "What's this about a reward?"

"I was here before. Don't you remember? That fellow's called Shiro. He's the mat mender. He's the one robbed the Valuables Office. I want my reward."

"You say his name's Shiro and he lives right here in town? Are you sure, old man?"

"Of course I'm sure. He lives in my quarter. His wife makes clay pots and sells them on the market."

"Aha!" Yamada eyed their claimant, still in the clutches of the grinning guard, with grim satisfaction.

The man's haggard face was covered with sweat. His eyes moved about the room like a cornered animal's. "I'm no robber. I'm a respectable tradesman," he protested. "And he's only a drunken beggar and he lies."

"Tradesman? I thought you said you are a farmer," Akitada reminded him.

"Yes, and you also claimed to live in Takase," Yamada put in. When the man said nothing, Yamada told the guard, "Put him down. Then close the door and wait outside. We may need you."

The guard released his captive, saluted, and left, slamming the door behind him. The sound caused their captive to start trembling.

"Well, what *is* your name?" Yamada snapped.

"Shiro. I . . . I go by both names." Their suspect started to inch toward the door again. "If it's too much trouble, I can come back tomorrow," he offered.

Akitada laughed. "Don't worry. It's no trouble at all. It must be a great thing for a man to have a wife who helps him earn a living. I suppose, being appreciative, you lend her a hand every now and then, do you, Shiro?"

The man thought about this and decided to agree. "Of course. I'm a considerate husband. I'm always carrying clay for the little woman and taking her pots to the market."

"And you help her fire her pots, no doubt? Perhaps even shape a simple clay object yourself?"

The other man gulped. "N-no, n-not that. No."

"Oh, well. Just a guess," said Akitada. Picking up the token, he disappeared into the storage area. When he reappeared, he carried two silver bars. "Here you are." He tossed the bars to Shiro, who was so astonished that he was a bit slow catching them. One bar fell and broke.

The man put the other one down on the desk as if it burned his fingers. Perspiration beaded his face again. "There's been some m-mistake," he mumbled. "These are not mine."

The old drunk staggered over to stare at the broken pieces. Picking up a shard, he squinted at the red clay inside the silver foil. "Looks like your wife made this one," he told Shiro. "Why did you rob the place when you've been making your own silver bars?" He burped loudly.

"I didn't." Shiro clutched his bag of coins. "It doesn't matter. I'll go now. Thank you very much. So sorry for the inconvenience."

But Yamada had lost his patience. He rose, glowered at Shiro, and snapped, "Not so fast. This man has accused you of a crime. You are under arrest pending a full investigation. Guard!"

Shiro fell to his knees and began to weep. "I didn't want to do it. Tosan made me do it, your honor. And I gave him most of the money. I only got thirty coppers for my trouble."

"Tosan? Who's Tosan?" Akitada asked.

"He's Shiro's neighbor," volunteered the old drunk.

"Tosan used to work here," muttered Shiro.

Yamada was dumbfounded. "You mean my own clerk planned this?" he asked. Both the beggar and Shiro nodded their heads. Yamada looked at the waiting guard. "Send someone to bring Tosan here this instant!" The guard saluted and left.

Akitada said, "You made the clay bars from your wife's clay and fired them in her kiln, didn't you, Shiro?" The man nodded miserably. "Then you covered them with foil and brought them to the Valuables Office, and the clerk Tosan paid you two strings of cash for them, and you and Tosan divided the money later?" Again the man nodded. "Did Tosan help you set fire to the office, too?"

"Oh, the evil creature!" Yamada cried, his eyes round with shock.

"I didn't set the fire," whimpered the thin man.

"Never mind," said Akitada. "The judge will have the whole story out of both of you with a good flogging. And then, you dog, it will be the mines for a skinny fellow like you."

It was an inspired threat.

"No! Not the mines. I'll talk, but not the mines." Prostrating himself before them, Shiro knocked his head on the ground.

"Let's hear the whole story, then," demanded Akitada. "We've been wondering how an ordinary thief could pull such a trick, but as you had clay handy and a clay oven hot enough to bake it and melt a bit of silver, that part is clear as water. How did you get involved?"

"Tosan made me do it because I owed him money."

Yamada said disgustedly, "I should have fired that crook a long time ago."

At this the man calmed down a little—thinking perhaps that he had two sympathetic listeners—and poured out his story.

Leaving aside the fact that he cast himself as the helpless victim of Tosan, the mastermind, it had a strong element of truth. As neighbors, Tosan and Shiro had spent their evenings together, drinking as they watched Shiro's wife making her pottery. Tosan complained about his work, his low wages, and his master's unfair reprimands, while Shiro blamed his misfortunes on ill luck. Tosan often described the stored wealth in glowing terms to Shiro, and the two men would discuss the pleasures that could be had with just one bar of silver. Once Tosan picked up some fresh clay to shape into an approximation of a silver bar. That moment the idea was born. Shiro shaped the clay, glazed and baked it, wrapped it in a few sheets of silver foil, and thus produced two replicas of silver bars which met with Tosan's approval. The next day, Shiro deposited the bars and took away two strings of a thousand cash each. They split the proceeds that very night. Soon after, Yamada dismissed Tosan for laziness.

On Tosan's instruction, Shiro had given a false name and place of residence, but as the entry was in Tosan's handwriting, the ex-clerk decided that a bit of arson might serve to destroy the evidence and also be a nice revenge, since Yamada would have to replace the ledgers or suffer severe reprimands himself. Shiro claimed his part in this had merely been to carry the ladder Tosan used to break the high window panel and toss the torch down on the ledgers.

At this opportune moment, two constables arrived with Tosan. He was a fat man with the red, puffy face of a habitual drinker, and he took in the situation at a glance.

Yamada greeted him with a shout of fury. "You miserable dog! Not enough that you spent half your time here drunk out of your head or asleep; you had the ingratitude to reward my trust and patience by stealing and setting fire to the Valuables Office."

"What?" cried Tosan. "Who told lies about me?" He looked at the old drunk, who grinned back impudently. "Him? A beggar? He's a piece of dung who makes up stories to get wine." He turned to Shiro, who still knelt weeping in front of Yamada's desk. "Or him? He's owed me money for months and is probably trying to weasel out of paying me."

For a moment, Yamada looked dangerously close to having a fit. He opened and closed his mouth a few times before finding his voice. "We'll see who speaks the truth," he finally said, his eyes flashing. "You are both under arrest. And the charge is plotting to overthrow His Majesty's government. You, Tosan, have misused your official position to steal goods placed into the government's safekeeping for the express purpose of stirring up popular unrest against the emperor."

Akitada's jaw dropped. The charge was as ridiculous as it was brilliant. Treason on a penal colony warranted the death penalty. The clerk knew it, too. He uttered a strangled croak and fainted.

Yamada stood beside Akitada outside the Valuables Office when they took away their two thieves. "Thank heaven it's over," he said with a deep sigh of relief. "I had given up all hope, but now all is well. And I even have my silver back."

"Well, yes," said Akitada, "though you might express your appreciation to the drunk. He did identify the thief."

◆

That night, Tosan and Shiro signed their confessions, and Masako came to Akitada for the third time.

Her eyes shone as she slipped under Akitada's blanket. "Thank you, Taketsuna," she whispered, reaching for him. "Father could never have done it without your help."

Akitada put her hands from his body and sat up. "No, Masako," he said, "not tonight or any other night. You are beautiful and you know quite well that I find you most desirable, but I cannot take you to wife. What has happened between us was a mistake, my mistake, which I regret deeply. I'm already married, and there can be no formal relationship between us. Because I value your father's good opinion, I will not make love to you again."

Making this speech had been extraordinarily hard. He had lain awake wondering what to say to her. Having spent every moment since their first encounter in self-recriminations, he had added self-disgust after he succumbed to his desire for her a second time. A third time would, by custom, formalize their relationship, and he could not bring himself to take that step. But he did not like hurting her and watched her face anxiously, expecting a torrent of grief and arguments.

But Masako neither wept nor argued. She said calmly, "I did not expect you to marry me. But I thought we might be lovers. I like to pay my debts."

He flinched a little. "You owe me nothing. You and your father have offered me hospitality and I have done little enough in return. I am in your debt."

"As you wish." She got up then and bent for her discarded undergown. Turning away a little, she slipped it back on. The flickering candlelight made the thin silk transparent, and in her modesty she was more seductive than she had been when she had pressed her warm naked body to his. "When you leave us, will you remember me?" she asked without looking at him.

He felt ashamed. "I will never forget you, Masako," he said and caught her hand to his cheek. "I am half in love with you."

She smiled a little then, and left.

The following morning, after Osawa approved Yamada's books, Akitada departed on his journey to find Prince Okisada's killer.

CHAPTER SEVEN

THE UGLY BUDDHA

Akitada welcomed the journey. Masako had slipped too deeply under his skin, and he was torn by feelings of shame and guilt.

And then there was the fact that he had put his assignment from his mind in order to satisfy his curiosity about the girl and her father. It was high time he did what he had come to do and went home to his family.

The day began inauspiciously in Yutaka's office. The governor had sent the *shijo* on an errand so that he and Akitada would have a private moment to discuss the upcoming journey.

"I know that you want to meet Kumo for yourself. Osawa always calls at his manor to go over the tax rolls with him and discuss the upcoming harvest and the mine production. After that you will travel on to Minato. Osawa has a letter from me to Professor Sakamoto, just a pretext to get you into his house. The return journey is to take you through Tsukahara. The prince's manor is there and Taira still lives in it. Okisada also had many friends among the Buddhist clergy at the Konponji Temple nearby. The temple happens to be the district tax collector. You will probably find the monk Shunsei there. If word has reached Kumo, he may approach you first, but if he does not, then you will no doubt find a way to talk to him."

That was perhaps overly optimistic, but Akitada thanked him and asked, "Can you provide me with some signed paper in case I have to overrule your good Inspector Osawa?"

Mutobe's face fell. "Oh, dear. Yes, of course. I should have thought of that. Better not tell him anything yet, right? Osawa is all right, really. A bit lazy, but he's unmarried and can travel whenever I need him. Besides, he is my only inspector and known to Kumo and Sakamoto and the others." He helped himself to Yutaka's ink, brush, and paper and dashed off a short letter, then gave it to Akitada, who read it and nodded. Mutobe took his seal from his sleeve, inked it with red ink, and impressed it next to his signature. Then he handed the folded note to Akitada, who was trying to tuck it away with his other papers when he made a disturbing discovery.

He was wearing his own clothes again, having packed his blue cotton clerk's robe in his saddlebag. When he touched his neck where the fabric was doubled over and stitched into the stiff collar, he felt the papers inside, but the seam he had opened to pass the imperial document to Mutobe the day they met had been resewn. Masako must have discovered the loose stitches when she had cleaned his robe. Surely she had found the papers. He felt beads of perspiration on his brow.

"What is the matter?" asked the governor, seeing his face.

"Nothing. Just wondering where to put this," Akitada said, holding up the governor's note. He quickly tucked it in his sash as footsteps approached and Yutaka entered with Osawa and one of the scribes, the big fellow called Genzo.

They knelt and bowed, the scribe looking sullen and giving Akitada a hate-filled look. Of the two who had been punished by Yutaka for the vicious beating they had given him, he was the one who had continued to bear Akitada a powerful grudge.

"Ah, yes, Yutaka," said Mutobe. "Is this the man who is to go along?"

"Yes, Your Excellency. His name is Genzo."

Akitada was dismayed but could hardly object.

The governor continued, "I realize you cannot easily spare both Taketsuna and him, but it will only be for a few days, four at the most. They will take horses to make better speed. I have sent instructions to the stables to have them ready in two hours."

"Horses?" gasped Osawa, then bowed immediately. "I beg your pardon, Excellency, but I did not expect . . . a great honor, of course . . . but I usually travel on foot. Perhaps a sedan chair? Surely good bearers can move as quickly as a horse. And the two young men can run alongside."

The big scribe's jaw dropped.

"No," said the governor brusquely, getting to his feet. "You will make all the speed you can. Oh. I am dispensing with a guard. Taketsuna has given his word not to escape." He departed, leaving consternation behind.

Osawa stared at Akitada as if he were measuring his potential for unexpected violence.

"I can't ride," the scribe announced. "You'll have to take Minoru instead."

Osawa looked down his nose at him. "If you are referring to the other scribe in the archives, I am told he is nearly illiterate and it takes him forever to copy a page."

"Well, then just take the prisoner. Master Yutaka always brags about how fast and elegant his brushstrokes are."

"I need you both," snapped Osawa. "He is to act as my secretary and you'll do the copying. You are both under my orders now and will do as you are told." He looked hard at Akitada, who bowed.

The problems multiplied at the stables. The horses were lively and pranced about the stable yard, making it hard for the grooms to control them.

Osawa saw this with an expression of horror. "These horses are half wild," he protested. "We want something tamer."

The head groom shook his head. "Governor's orders."

Akitada took the bridle of the calmest horse and led it to Osawa. "Please take this one, Inspector," he said with a bow. "He has a soft mouth and will be manageable." He turned to the scribe. Although Genzo was big-boned and heavy, he cringed from the horses. "And you, of course, will want the black?" The black was so big that two grooms hung on to his bridle.

Genzo shot Akitada a venomous look. "You take him," he said. "I have no desire to kill myself."

"As you wish." Akitada swung himself into the saddle, taking pleasure in being on horseback again, while Genzo had to be helped onto the third horse and instantly fell back down. "Are there any mules?" Akitada asked the grinning head groom.

A sturdy mule was substituted for the horse, and Genzo managed to get in its saddle. They rode out of the stable yard accompanied by half-suppressed laughter from the grooms, passing the prison and Yamada's house without seeing either father or daughter.

And so they left Mano and headed inland. The narrow road wound northeast through a wide plain of rice paddies stretching into the distance. On both sides wooded mountains rose, and ahead lay Mount Kimpoku, a dark cone against the blue sky. It marked the other side of Sadoshima and overlooked Lake Kamo and Minato.

The two horses and the mule trotted along smoothly. Lush green rice paddies promised a good harvest, a soft wind rustled through the pines lining the way, and small birds twittered in the branches. The sky was clear except for a few cloudlets, and the sun had not yet brought the midday heat. Now and then a hawk circled above, looking for field mice or a careless dove.

It would have been altogether pleasant, except for Akitada's assignment and his companions' ill humor. The former he could do nothing about; the latter he tried to ignore. Osawa was becoming used to his horse and did not do too badly, but he clearly disliked riding and was in a foul humor, which he took out on Genzo. The scribe kept slipping off his mule, causing delays while Akitada dismounted to help him back in the saddle. Genzo maintained a sullen silence under the barrage of ridicule and reproof heaped upon him by Osawa, and Akitada's assistance made his antagonism worse instead of better.

They reached the hamlet of Hatano by midday and stopped at a small temple. In the grove of cedars surrounding the temple hall, they ate a light repast of cold rice wrapped in oak leaves and drank water from a well bubbling among mossy rocks. Osawa, still in a bad mood, maintained distance between himself and his helpers, choosing to sit on a large rock near the well while making Akitada and Genzo squat on the ground next to their mounts.

Akitada was glad not to have to engage in chitchat with either of his companions. As soon as feasible, he left to relieve himself and inspected the collar of his robe by unpicking some threads. Both the imperial documents that commanded him to investigate Prince Okisada's death and Governor Mutobe's safe conduct were still there and in good condition. But he cursed himself for his carelessness; he should have foreseen his robe might need cleaning, though he had not expected to bleed quite so copiously over it. Masako must have washed out the bloodstains. But had she removed the documents first and later reinserted them and sewn up the collar?

If so, had she recognized the imperial seal? Could she read? Her rough manners and the fact that she was a girl suggested that Yamada probably had not bothered to teach her, concentrating his efforts on his son instead. He had certainly not called on her to help him with his bookkeeping. But wouldn't she have taken the documents to her father, who would have recognized them immediately? She had not done so, or Yamada would have mentioned it. It was puzzling and worrisome.

They remounted and continued the journey for another mile when Akitada's horse shied and unseated him. He landed hard on his hip and right shoulder and stared in surprise at his saddle, which lay beside him in the road. The big black had jumped off the roadway into a rice paddy, where the deep mud prevented him from galloping off. Akitada picked himself up to a snicker from Genzo. Osawa frowned but said nothing. When he looked at his saddle, Akitada saw that both saddle band and back strap had broken because someone had partially cut them. Genzo's work, he thought, but he said nothing. Instead he caught the black and, slinging the saddle and saddle packs over his shoulder, rode the rest of the way bareback.

They reached the manor of Kumo Sanetomo, high constable of Sadoshima, before sunset. They had passed through rich rice lands, dotted here and there by small farms and modest manors, but Kumo's estate was very large even by mainland standards. The walled and gated manor house was surrounded by a cluster of service buildings and an extensive garden. The whole looked more like a small village than a single residence. Deep, thatched roofs covered the main hall and attached pavilions. The garden stretched beyond. A separate enclosure contained stables, kitchens, storage buildings, and servants' quarters.

Akitada was intrigued by these signs of wealth. "The high constable's manor looks more like a nobleman's seat than a farm," he said to Osawa, who was saddle sore and glowered. "All those stables must contain many horses, and he probably employs and houses a hundred servants. If the place were better fortified, it might be a military stronghold."

Osawa grunted. "Kumo, as his father before him, is very wealthy. Horses are his particular fancy. Being a descendant of an old noble family, he carries on its traditions of hunting, swordsmanship, and archery from the back of a horse. Wait till you see the residence. I doubt there are many better in the capital."

The big double gate opened promptly at their approach. Kumo's servants were well-dressed and healthy-looking men who took the animals and directed the travelers to the main hall of the residence. There an elderly house servant in a black silk robe received them and led them into a small but elegant room. Sliding doors were open to the garden, panels covering storage areas had landscape paintings pasted on them, the rice mats underfoot were thick and new, and on the large black desk rested lacquered and painted writing boxes, jade water containers, bamboo brush holders, and a small, delicate ivory carving of a fox.

Osawa took one of the cushions near the desk, leaving Akitada and Genzo standing. After a minute, a young woman in a pretty green silk robe entered and placed a tray with refreshments before Osawa. She bowed and informed him that her master would come immediately.

He did. They could hear his firm steps and deep voice in the corridor outside before he flung back the sliding door and ducked in. The doorway was not particularly low, but Kumo was one of the tallest men Akitada had seen. He guessed him to be about his own age and in excellent physical condition. Dressed in a copper-colored brocade hunting jacket and brown silk trousers, Kumo wore his hair loose to just above his broad shoulders and had a full mustache and short, well-trimmed chin beard. Perhaps he meant to combine the costly costume of the court noble with the manly appearance of the military leader. His eyes, strangely light in the deeply tanned face, passed indifferently over Akitada and Genzo, who had knelt and bowed their heads at his entrance.

"Ah, it's my good friend Osawa," Kumo said, his voice filling the small room, much as his large figure dominated it.

Osawa bowed deeply. "It is my very great pleasure to call on Your Honor again."

Kumo laughed, seating himself on the other cushion and pouring wine from a flask into the two cups on the tray. Both flask and matching cups were of Chinese porcelain. He passed one of the cups to Osawa. "Never mind all the respectful phrases, my friend. I'm just a simple farmer who is honored by the visit of our governor's most trusted advisor. Please, eat and drink. You must be quite exhausted from your long journey. How is His Excellency these days?"

Osawa blushed with pleasure at the attention. "Not so well, I'm afraid," he confided. He drank, he nibbled, and he became expansive. "In fact, he's quite distraught. His son is awaiting trial, you know. The governor paid him a visit just the other day. I expect he was trying to elicit some shred of evidence in his favor."

"Ah." Kumo shook his head. "A dreadful tragedy. Was he successful? The trial is set for the end of this month, is it not?"

"Yes. It's only a week away. And he was not successful, I think. His spirits were quite low when he came back, and his servants say he does not sleep at night."

Akitada was surprised how well informed Osawa was about Mutobe's private life, but he was even more intent on watching the high constable, hoping to get the measure of the man who might have played a part in the late prince's life and death. Suddenly he found himself the object of Kumo's interest and quickly lowered his eyes again. Too late.

"You have a new assistant, I see," drawled Kumo. "Usually you bring only one scribe with you. This signifies some new honor, I assume?"

Osawa flushed and laughed a little. "You are too kind, sir. No, no. The fellow is a prisoner who happens to write well. The governor is desperately short-handed and wished us to return quickly." He added in an aggrieved tone, "He even insisted we ride horses on this occasion."

"What? No bearers, and you not used to riding? My dear Osawa, you must have a hot bath immediately and rest before we talk business. Perhaps your assistants can start on the work with the help of my secretary. Come," he said, getting to his feet, "I have just returned from hunting myself. We shall enjoy a nice soaking together and you can fill me in on all the news from Mano."

To do Osawa justice, he hesitated. But then he rose. "You are most kind, Your Honor," he said. "I am a little fatigued. If your secretary will be good enough to give the documents in question to Taketsuna—the new fellow—he will show the scribe what should be copied for our files. This Taketsuna has a good education. I shall inspect their work in the morning." Turning to his companions, he said, "You heard me?"

Akitada nodded and bowed. Kumo and Osawa disappeared, and a servant took him and Genzo into a large office where several scribes were bent over writing desks or getting books and boxes from the shelves which covered three sides of the room.

Kumo's secretary was a small, pleasant man in his mid-fifties. He took one look at Genzo's broad face and dull eyes and addressed Akitada. "I started gathering the relevant tax documents the moment I heard of Inspector Osawa's arrival," he said, with a gesture to a desk covered with bulging document boxes. "My name is Shiba. Please feel free to ask for anything. My staff will see to it immediately."

Kumo's scribes, all pretending to be busy while casting curious glances at the visitors, were a far cry from the pitiful staff of the governor's archives, and Akitada, encouraged by Shiba's courteous manner, said, "I am Taketsuna, an exile from the mainland and still a stranger here. Forgive my curiosity, but I was told that capable scribes and clerks are extremely rare. How is it that your master seems so well supplied with them?"

Shiba chuckled. "We are part of his household. The master and his father before him saved likely boys from work in the mines by training them in different skills," he said. "I, for example, was sixteen when my mother died in poverty. Like you, my father came here as a prisoner. My mother followed him when I was four. My father died soon after our arrival, and my poor mother worked in the fields to support us. She tried to teach me a little, but when she succumbed also, I—being a boy and small of stature—was sent to the mines. The master's father found me there and took me into his household, where he had me taught by his son's tutor. My master continues his father's legacy."

Shiba's image of Kumo differed diametrically from Mutobe's. The governor had called young Kumo "haughty and overbearing," but Akitada had seen no sign of it in the man who had greeted a mere inspector like Osawa as a valued guest.

Turning with new interest to the documents, he saw quickly that Shiba and his scribes had indeed been well trained. The system of accounting was efficient and the brushwork of the scribes far superior to Genzo's. He quickly identified the relevant reports and handed some of them to Genzo with instructions to begin copying.

Genzo folded his arms. "Do it yourself," he growled. "I'm not your servant."

The man needed a good beating, but Akitada said peaceably, "Very well. Then you will have to read through those and summarize them for the governor." He pointed to a stack of documents he had set aside for himself.

Genzo went to look at the top document, frowned, then said, "Dull stuff, this. I prefer the copying." Having got his way, he settled down and started to rub ink. Akitada smiled.

Shiba had watched with interest. He said in a low voice, "Forgive me, Taketsuna, but I see that you are a man not only of superior education but also of wisdom. Perhaps, before your trouble, you had the good fortune to live in the capital?"

"That is so."

Shiba pressed his hands together and said fervently, "Truly, how very blessed your life must have been. And by chance, have you ever visited the imperial palace?"

Akitada smiled. "I used to work there and once I even saw His Majesty from a distance. He rode in a gilded palanquin and was accompanied by the empress and her ladies in their own palanquins, a very beautiful sight."

"Oh!" breathed Shiba. "I imagine it must have been like a glimpse of the Western Paradise." He was rapt with pleasure for a moment, then remembered his duty. "Forgive my chatter. You will want to get started. Perhaps tonight, after your work, you might join me for a cup of wine?"

Akitada said regretfully, "You are most kind, but I do not think Inspector Osawa will permit it."

"Ah. Well, I think that may be managed. You are now in the Kumo mansion. All men are treated with respect here. I'll send someone for you after your evening rice."

Akitada spent an hour checking the tax statements and writing brief summaries of the salient points, a chore he was abundantly familiar with. At sundown, a gong sounded somewhere nearby. Genzo dropped his brush noisily in the water container, yawned, and stretched. "About time they fed us," he muttered.

Akitada rose and went to look over Genzo's shoulders. The sheet of paper the man had been copying was splotched with ink, and the characters were barely legible. Worse, a few were missing so that whole phrases made no sense.

"You'll have to do better," he said. "We want clean copies, and you left out words and characters. Do that one over again more carefully." He leaned forward to reach for the other sheets, pathetically few for an hour's work. "Is that all you've—" he started to say, when Genzo suddenly lashed out, pushing Akitada back so hard that he sat down on the floor.

The scribe was up quickly for someone of his size and general lack of energy. "I'll teach you to tell me what to do, filthy scum," he ground out and threw himself on Akitada.

Irritated past reason, Akitada met the attack by leaning back and kicking him with both legs in the stomach. Genzo sucked in his breath sharply as he flew back against the table, scattering papers and ink. Akitada stood and pulled him up by the front of his robe. He said through gritted teeth, "I have had enough of you. Don't think I don't know you cut my saddle bands. One more outburst from you, and I'll make sure you never walk again. Do you understand?"

Eyes bulging, Genzo nodded. He looked green and held his stomach.

"Clean up this mess," Akitada snapped, dropping him back on the floor. "I don't think you will feel much like food, so you may as well spend the time copying those papers over neatly. I'll let the secretary know that you are finishing some work before retiring." He strolled out of the room and left the building.

The evening was delightfully cool after the heat of the day. If the high constable did, in fact, practice common courtesy toward even the lowliest prisoner on the island, then his staff might share his philosophy and allow him the privileges accorded a guest. He decided to test this theory by exploring and found that, wherever he strayed, servants smiled and bobbed their heads. One or two stopped to ask if he was lost, but when he told them he was just stretching his legs and admiring the residence, they left him alone. He did not, of course, enter the private quarters but wandered all around them by way of the gardens.

These were extensive and quite as well designed as any he had visited in the noble mansions and villas of the capital. Paths snaked through trees, shrubs, and rockeries, crossing miniature streams over curved bridges to lead to various garden pavilions. Patches of tawny lilies bloomed everywhere and birds flitted from branch to branch.

One of the pavilions turned out to be a miniature temple. Akitada was enchanted by its dainty size, which nevertheless duplicated the ornate carvings, blue-tiled roofs, and gilded ornamentation of large temples. Someone had taken great pains and spent a considerable amount of money on this little building. He climbed the steps to a tiny veranda surrounded by a red-lacquered balustrade and entered through the carved doors. Inside, every surface seemed carved and painted in glorious reds, greens, blacks, oranges, and golds. Even the floor was painted, and in its center stood a gilded altar table on its own carved and lacquered dais. A wooden Buddha statue rested on the altar, and a number of gilded vessels with offerings stood before it. Behind the Buddha figure, a richly embroidered silk cloth was suspended, depicting swirling golden clouds, emblems of Kumo's family name, on a deep blue background. A faint haze of intensely fragrant incense curled and spiraled lazily from a golden censer, perfuming the air and veiling the gilded tablets inscribed with the names and titles of Kumo ancestors. This was the Kumo family's ancestral altar.

Akitada read some of the tablets and saw the names of two emperors among the distant forebears of the present Kumo.

Only the most recent tablets lacked titles. Kumo's great-grandfather had been stripped of his rank and sent here into exile. Akitada reflected that few families survived such punishment in the style of this one. His own family, though they had retained their titles, barely subsisted since his famous ancestor had died in exile.

He made a perfunctory bow to the Buddha. No larger than a child of three or four, the figure was an unskilled carving from some dull wood. It seemed out of place among all the gold and lacquer work, yet somehow for that reason more numinous, as if it somehow symbolized what the Kumos had become. Perhaps a local artisan had carved it or, more likely, the first Kumo exile had done so in order to find solace in religious devotion.

Stepping closer, Akitada found that the surface was astonishingly smooth for an artless carving, but the Buddha's face repelled him. It was quite ugly and the god's expression was more like a demon's snarl than the gentle, peaceful smile of ordinary representations. The figure had golden eyes, but they shone almost shockingly bright from that dark, distorted visage. Odd. The Buddha's shining eyes reminded Akitada of Kumo's pale eyes and he wondered about his ancestry.

A faint and unearthly music came from the garden. Akitada stepped out on the veranda to listen. Somewhere someone was playing a flute, and he felt a great longing for his own instrument. The melody was both entrancing and beautifully played. Like a bee scenting nectar, Akitada followed the music on paths which wound and twisted, leading him away as soon as he seemed to get closer until he lost all sense of direction. Shrubbery and trees hid and revealed views. He heard the splash of running water and passed a miniature waterfall somewhere along the way; he heard the cries of birds and waterfowl, then caught a glimpse of a pond, or miniature lake with its own small island. The flute seemed to parody the sounds of the garden until he wondered which was real.

The artist was playing a very old tune with consummate skill. It was called "Land of the Rice Ears," and Akitada stopped, following each sequence of notes, paying particular attention to the second part, for it contained a passage he had never mastered himself. There! So that was the way it was supposed to be. He smiled, raising his hands to finger imaginary stops, wishing he could play as well.

Just after the last note faded, he reached the lake. The sky above was still faintly rosy, almost iridescent, like the inside of a shell. All was silent. A butterfly rose from one of the lilies that nodded at the water's rim. Then a pair of ducks paddled around the island and lifted into the evening air with a soft flapping of wings and a shower of sparkling drops. Akitada wondered if he had strayed into a dream.

With a sigh, he followed the lakeshore. His stomach growled, reminding him that food was more useful than this longing for a flute he had been forced to leave behind. Then his eye caught a movement on the small island. He could see the curved roof of another small pavilion rising behind the trees. Two spots of color shimmered through a gap between the trees, a patch of white and another of deep lilac.

A dainty bridge connected the island to the path he was on. He crossed it and heard the sound of women's voices. Two ladies in white and wisteria blue sat behind the brilliant red balustrade and under the gilded bells that hung from the eaves of the pavilion. Thinking them Kumo's wives, Akitada stopped and prepared to retreat. But then he saw that both women were quite old. The one in purple silk had very long white hair which she wore loose, like young noblewomen, so that it draped over her shoulders and back and spread across the wide skirts of her gown. She was tiny, seemingly shrunken with age, but her skin was as white as her hair, and the rich purple silk of her outer robe was lined with many layers of other gowns in four or five different costly colors. Such a costume might have been worn by a young princess in times gone by. On this frail old woman it mocked the vanity of youth.

It was the other woman who had been playing the flute—the other woman who, in sharp contrast to her companion, wore a plain white robe and veil, and whose face and hands were darkened from exposure to the sun. The nun Ribata.

CHAPTER EIGHT

FLUTE MUSIC FROM ANOTHER LIFE

"Approach, my lord!"

The old lady's voice was cracked and dissonant, sharply at odds with the lovely sound of the flute which still spun and wove through Akitada's memory.

He felt a moment's panic. Was she someone who had known him in another place and recognized him in spite of his beard? Surely not.

The old lady in the gorgeous robes waved a painted fan at him. Gold dust sparkled like stars on its delicate blue paper. "Come, come!" she invited him impatiently. "Do not be shy. You were never shy with me before."

He felt completely out of his depth and glanced back at the small bridge he had just crossed as if it had led him into an otherworldly place, like the Tokutaro of the fairy tale who had ended up among fox spirits.

The nun Ribata put down her flute and gave him an amused smile.

"I beg your pardon," he said, bowing to both women. "I heard the music and came to meet the artist."

"Silly man." The old lady snickered coquettishly behind her fan. "You thought it was I and hoped to find me alone. Come sit beside me. Naka no Kimi won't give old lovers away."

Old lovers? And Naka no Kimi surely referred to an imperial princess? It dawned on him that the old lady must be demented. Akitada heaved a sigh of relief and walked up the steps of the pavilion.

Ribata gestured toward the cushion beside her companion. "Please be seated," she said, her own voice as warm and resonant as a temple bell. "Lady Saisho is the high constable's grandmother. We are old friends."

Whatever her official status, the Lady Saisho had survived the harsh years of early exile to live in luxury again. But to what avail? Close up, she looked incredibly frail, withered, and wrinkled. He saw now that her skin was not abnormally white, but that she had painted her face with white lead. Rouged lips and soot-ringed eyes parodied former beauty, and heavy perfume mingled with the sour smell of old age and rotting gums. Yet she eyed Akitada flirtatiously and batted her eyes at him.

Feeling an overwhelming pity, he bowed deeply and said, "I hope I see your ladyship in good spirits on this lovely evening."

"Lovely indeed. A poem, Lord Yoriyoshi," she cried gaily, waving her fan with the studied grace of a court lady. "Make me a poem about the evening so I can respond."

"A poem?" Apparently she took him for a poet called Yoriyoshi. Poetry was not one of Akitada's skills. "Er," he stammered, looking to the nun for help.

"She lives in a happier past," said Ribata softly. "Humor her, please."

Hardly helpful. His eyes roamed around for inspiration and fell on the bridge. The last of the sunlight was gone and the brilliant red of its balustrade had turned to a dull brown of withered maple leaves. Akitada recited, "The evening sheds a lonely light upon the bridge suspended between two arms of land."

The old lady hissed behind her fan. "Prince Okisada could have done better, even when his illness was upon him. However, let me see." She tapped her chin with the fan. "'Evening,' 'lonely,' 'suspended,' 'arms.' " She cackled triumphantly, and cried, in a grating singsong, "Waiting, I cradle loneliness in my arms, hoping you will cross the bridge."

Akitada and Ribata applauded politely, their eyes on the ridiculous old creature who simpered behind her fan and sent inviting glances toward Akitada.

They were unaware that someone had joined them until Kumo spoke.

"I think my honored grandmother must feel the chill of the air. I have come to escort her back to her quarters."

Akitada knelt quickly, his head bowed, hoping he had not broken some rule, but Kumo took no notice of him. He went to his grandmother and bent to lift her to her feet.

"No!" She scrambled back like a small, stubborn child. "I don't want to go. Lord Yoriyoshi and I are exchanging poems. His are not as good as the prince's, but . . ." She screwed up her face and began to cry. "The prince died," she wailed. "All of my friends die. It's your fault." And she lashed out with a frail hand like a bird's claw and slapped her grandson's face. He stepped back, his expression grim, as she staggered to her feet and faced him with glittering eyes. "I hate you," she shrieked. "You are a monster! I wish you would die, too." Then she burst into violent tears and the mask of the court beauty disintegrated into a grotesque mingling of black and white paint. Her thin frame shook in its voluminous, many-colored silks, and she began to sway alarmingly.

Both Ribata and Kumo went to her aid. "She is overtired," muttered Ribata, while he said, "I hate to see her like this."

Lady Saisho clung to the nun, but her tears diminished, and after a moment she allowed her grandson to lift her in his arms and carry her away with tender care. The nun walked with them a little ways, then returned.

Akitada had got to his feet. "What was she talking about?" he asked, puzzled by Lady Saisho's references to Prince Okisada.

Ribata sighed. "Old age may take away the mind, yet leave the pain behind. She has seen much grief and many horrors in her long life."

He gave her a sharp look. "I have heard that, in spite of the favor shown the high constable by the government in the capital, her grandson still bears a grudge for what happened three generations ago."

Ribata looked into the distance, her arms folded into her wide sleeves, and murmured, "They are a proud family."

Following her glance, Akitada said, "Look around you." His sweeping gesture encompassed the elegant garden with its pavilion, shrine, lake, and lacquered bridge. "The Kumos have not fared badly here. I see power, wealth, and luxury all about me where I least expected it."

She gazed silently at the scene. The last light was fading in the sky and already the darkness of night seeped forth from the trees and ground. Fireflies glimmered faintly. Only the lake still shimmered, reflecting, like a lady's polished silver mirror, the dying lavender of the sky. "You play the flute?" Ribata asked softly.

The question startled Akitada. "I used to, poorly, in another life."

She went back into the pavilion. Picking up her flute, she offered it. "Come. Play for me."

Ribata was a woman of extraordinary culture, one of the mysteries of this island, and part of him did not want to play, fearing her censure, even if it remained unspoken. But his desire overcame his shyness. He took up the flute with a bow. They seated themselves, and he put the mouthpiece to his lips and blew gently. The sound the instrument produced was strong and very beautiful. It told him that this flute was of extraordinary, perhaps legendary quality. He looked at it in wonder. At first glance very plain and ordinary, it consisted of a piece of bamboo with seven holes and a mouthpiece—called a cicada because it resembled the carapace of that insect—the whole wrapped in paper-thin cherry bark of a lustrous deep red and then lacquered with the sap of the sumac tree until its patina shimmered like layered gossamer.

The flute was old and must be very precious, a family heirloom. "What is its name?" he asked reverently.

"Plover's Cry."

"Ah." He raised the flute to his lips again. The name was apt. High, clear, and full of longing, the notes resembled the melancholy cry of the male bird on the seashore calling for its lost mate. His hands shook a little with awe and pleasure, and he closed his eyes before playing in earnest.

The song he chose was one he knew well, but still he was nervous. He knew he could not do justice to such a flute, even if he tried his best. "Rolling Waves and Flying Clouds" was not his favorite, but it contained a passage he had never quite mastered, and he hoped Ribata would correct him. So he concentrated, paying attention to his fingering, and thought he did not do too badly. But when he opened his eyes and lowered the flute, he saw that the nun had fallen asleep.

It was almost dark. As if to respond to the call of the flute, a cicada began its song nearby, and gradually others joined. He listened for a while, feeling mournful and unhappy.

Then he raised the flute to his lips again and played to the cicadas. He played "Twilight Cicadas" for them, and as they seemed to like that, he also played "Walking Among Cherry Blossoms," and "Wild Geese Departing," and "Rain Falling on my Hut." As he played, he thought of his wife Tamako dancing about the courtyard with their infant son. He had a sudden fear that he might not survive this journey to see them again and resolved if he did, he would try to be a better husband and father.

As always, the music eased his black thoughts, and when the last song was done, he sighed and with a bow, he laid the precious flute on the mat before the sleeping nun. Then he rose.

Ribata's voice startled him. "You are troubled."

He stood in the dark, waiting.

"I think you play the flute to find the way out of your troubles," she told him.

"Yes," he admitted, awed by her perception. "I'm not very good, because I don't concentrate on technique but only on the sounds and my thoughts. How did you know?"

In the faint light remaining, he could see that her eyes were open now and rested on him. "The flute told me."

"I want to do better," he said humbly, and, saying it, he knew he meant more than flute playing.

He waited a long time, but she made no other comment. Finally he bowed. "I have been a nuisance," he said. "Please forgive me. Thank you for allowing me to play this magnificent flute. I shall always remember it." He turned to go.

"Take it with you," she said.

He stopped, appalled. "No. I couldn't. Not that flute. I'm not worthy and—"

"Take it," she said again.

"You don't understand. I could not care for it properly. It might get lost or broken. Where I am going there is . . . unrest, perhaps danger."

"I know. Take it. You can return it to me when you have done what you came to do." And silently, she rose and slipped past him with a mere whisper of her robe.

He looked after her, dazed with wonder, until she passed across the bridge, her white robe a brief glimmer against the black mass of trees—a pale insubstantial ghost returning to the darkness. Only the flute remained, a tangible link to the mystery of her past, and perhaps to that of Kumo, and his grandmother, and of Prince Okisada who had died, or been murdered, for his own past.

Akitada went back, took up the flute, and put it tenderly into his sleeve. Then he left the garden in search of food and a place to sleep.

◆

Wherever Inspector Osawa would be bedding down, the convict Taketsuna could only hope for a dry corner among the servants and horses. It was fully dark now, and no one seemed about. Lights glimmered from the residence, and torches spread a reddish glow over the stable yard.

As Akitada approached the stockade enclosing the stables, kitchens, storehouses, and servants' quarters, he heard the crunch of hooves on gravel and the creaking of leather. A moment later a horseman passed him. Even in the dark, Akitada could see that both animal and man drooped with fatigue. For a moment, he thought the governor had sent someone after them, but when he had followed the rider through the open gate, he found him talking to one of the grooms. Apparently the rider had come from some other Kumo holding with a report for his master.

"Rough journey, Kita?" asked the groom.

The other man slid off his horse wearily. His voice was indistinct with exhaustion, but Akitada caught the phrases "pack train to the coast," "bad mountain roads," and a place name: "Aikawa."

"Why not rest first?" offered the groom.

The rider shook his head and mumbled something Akitada could not hear.

"A fire? What a turn-up!" the groom commented. "The master'll be up to check for certain now."

They parted, the new arrival in direction of the residence, and the groom with the horse toward the stables. Akitada followed the groom.

Perhaps because of preoccupation or the noise of the horse's hooves on the gravel, the groom took no notice of Akitada. He led the tired animal into a fenced pen next to the stable and began to feed and water it and rub it down. The enclosure already held their mounts and others. As the groom seemed occupied for a while, Akitada decided to take a look in the stable.

He opened the heavy double door just enough to slip in—and stopped in amazement. It was a large, open hall, very clean and well lit by torches attached to the support beams. One whole length of the stable was taken up by a raised dais, the other by fodder, saddles, bridles, and assorted armor—helmets and breastplates, bows and arrows and swords. On the dais stood ten or twelve superb horses, dozing, feeding, drinking, or being brushed by an attendant. Each animal was of a different color or marking, each was held only by a thick straw rope which passed under its belly and was tied to a large metal ring on a ceiling beam to allow it maximum comfort of movement within its space, and each seemed to have its own attendant sitting close by or tending to his chores.

Akitada loved horses and had never seen so many superb ones in one stable. The grooms smiled and nodded as he passed slowly, admiring their charges. Several of the great men in the capital were also horse fanciers, but few could claim such a collection. It must be worth a fortune.

He was about to speak to one of the grooms when a heavy hand fell on his shoulder. A squat, burly fellow, wearing an old hunting jacket and plain trousers pushed into boots, stood behind him. The head groom?

He eyed Akitada suspiciously. "Who are you and what do you want?"

Akitada gave him an apologetic smile. "Sorry to trouble anyone. I am Taketsuna and came today with Inspector Osawa. We have been working late in the main house, and I can't seem to find my way about. I thought perhaps I was supposed to sleep here."

"In the stable?" The head groom looked him up and down. What he saw seemed to reassure him a little, but he remained hostile. "We don't like strangers snooping. The guest quarters are over there." He pointed in the direction of a low dark building Akitada had passed near the gate.

Akitada hung his head humbly. "I'm not a guest. I'm a convict."

Surprisingly, this information improved the groom's attitude. "Well, why didn't you say so?" he cried. "All of us here are convicts, or former convicts, or the sons and daughters of convicts."

Akitada's eyes widened. "You don't mean it!"

The groom grinned and slapped his shoulder. "Just arrived on Sadoshima? Cheer up! Life's not over. You can live quite well here if you serve the right master. Now, our master only employs convicts. Says they're grateful to be treated like humans and work twice as hard. And he's right. We'd all die for him."

"He must be a good master," Akitada said in a wistful tone. He was surprised by the constant praise heaped on Kumo. In his experience, wealthy and powerful men rarely earned such veneration from their servants.

"He's a saint. Better than anyone you'd find on the mainland or in the capital."

Akitada hung his head again. "You're lucky. I've had nothing but beatings and little to eat since I set foot on this island six days ago."

The groom narrowed his eyes and stepped closer to peer at Akitada's head, where the scabs and bruises from the beating Genzo and his partner had given him were still visible. "Is that how you got those?"

Akitada nodded. When he lifted his sleeve to show the purplish bruises left by his fall from the horse that day, the groom sucked in his breath. "You poor bastard." He patted Akitada's back sympathetically. "Well, at least we can look after you while you're here. I'm Yume, the head groom, by the way." They bowed to each other. "How about sharing my quarters while you're here?"

"That's very good of you, Yume. Are you sure it's permitted?"

"Of course. Have you had your evening rice?"

"Well, no. I missed it. Working late."

"Bastards!" growled the groom. "Come along. We'll get you something in the kitchen."

The kitchen was a place of good smells, and Akitada was ravenously hungry by now. The groom had eaten earlier, but to be companionable he joined his new acquaintance in a bowl of noodle soup.

"Good, isn't it?" he said.

Drinking the last drop, Akitada nodded, smacked his lips, and looked hungrily toward the large iron kettle suspended over the fire. The soup had been thick with succulent noodles and tasty bits of fish and vegetables. Kumo's people ate well.

Yume laughed and got up to get him a refill. The cook, a fat man who had lost a leg but moved with surprising agility about the kitchen on his crutch, was pleased and gave Akitada a nod. It was a comfortable place to live and work. Akitada thought that Seimei would have had a saying for it: In a rich man's house there are no lean dogs.

"You look strong," Yume said. "Maybe you could work for the master, too. Trouble is, there's no opening here, but the master always needs good men at the mines. If you don't mind roughing it a bit, it'd be worth a try."

Akitada shook his head. "I met a little guy with running sores on his arms and knees from working the mines. They say lots of prisoners die or come out crippled for life."

"See the cook? He lost his leg in a rock slide. The difference is the master looks after his people."

"Really? Where exactly are your master's mines?"

"Near Aikawa. Why don't you talk to Kita? He's the mine foreman. Maybe he'll take you on to keep records."

Akitada shook his head and sighed. "It sounds tempting, but I'd never be allowed to leave my present place. Especially not now when we're just starting an inspection tour."

The talk turned to horses. Kumo's had been brought over from the mainland about a year ago. The high constable had sent an agent to purchase the finest animals anywhere at whatever cost. He planned to breed superior horses in Sadoshima. "He loves hunting and fighting on the back of a horse. We often have races," Yume informed Akitada proudly.

When the cook finished his chores, he came to join them, bearing a flask of warm wine. Though he had suffered his crippling injury in one of Kumo's silver mines, he also spoke of his master with great affection. Urged by Akitada, he talked about working conditions for miners. He seemed to take the hardships lightly, stressing instead the master's kindness and certain amenities. "There's foreign women there. Rough-looking bitches and not much to talk to, but brother, do they give you a good time. In fact, there was one . . ." A dreamy look came to his face and his voice trailed off.

When Akitada raised the subject of the murder of the Second Prince, Yume and the cook looked at each other. "That was a funny thing," said the cook. "Why would the governor's son go kill the prince? You would've thought he'd poison the master instead."

"Why?" asked Akitada, who could guess the answer.

"Because that stuck-up tyrant hates our master. Why, they had such a fight we thought he'd show up with his soldiers and arrest him. We were ready, but somebody must've warned Mutobe off and he's minded his manners since. And now his own son's in jail. We'll soon be rid of him for good." He grinned with satisfaction.

That confirmed what Mutobe had told Akitada. He asked, "Were your master and the prince close?"

Yume said, "Of course. The Second Prince used to come here all the time. He and the old master were friends. After the old master died, the prince and the young master'd ride out hunting with kites. People said they were like father and son. Some even said the prince would be recalled and become emperor, and then he'd make the master his chancellor. But that's just silly talk, I think."

The cook smirked. "That's because the fools think the prince was sleeping with the master's mother."

Yume said, "Don't go spreading those lies. Besides, you and I know better, don't we?"

They cook guffawed and nodded.

"Oh, come," urged Akitada, raising his cup. "I love a good story, even if there's no truth to it."

But Yume shook his head. "It's just silly talk. Nothing in it, believe me."

And then the cook made the most puzzling remark of the evening. "You know, the way the prince died reminds me of that time they thought I'd poisoned him."

Akitada was so taken aback that he stared at the cook. "How was that?"

The cook grinned. "Oh, he had this hobby. Liked to fix his own dishes. Well, one day he got really ill at a banquet. I was frightened out of my wits, I tell you, but it turned out he'd eaten something before the banquet."

Yume nodded. "One of the house servants saw it. The prince started choking, and then his chopsticks dropped from his fingers and he fell down like dead. His eyes were open, but he couldn't talk or move his limbs. They thought he was dying, but after a while he came around and acted as if nothing had happened."

The cook said, "Everybody blamed me till it turned out he'd cooked up something for himself. Probably poisonous mushrooms."

That night Akitada retired more confused than ever.

Before slipping under Yume's redolent quilts, he took the flute from his sleeve, wrapped it carefully into his outer robe, and placed the roll under his head.

◆

It was not until the following morning that Akitada recalled his appointment with Kumo's secretary. Shiba had promised to send someone for him the night before. Nobody had come, but perhaps Akitada had missed the summons—as he had missed his evening rice—by playing the flute in the garden. He dressed quickly in his blue scribe's robe and packed his own gown and the flute into his saddlebag.

The secretary greeted him with reserve and did not mention their appointment.

"I hope," Akitada told him, "that we did not miss each other last night. I was late returning to the servants' quarters."

"No, no," Shiba said quickly. "Do not concern yourself. I had urgent business to attend to. This is a rather busy time for me. Regrettable. Especially since you are to leave today. Perhaps next time?"

It did not sound very convincing, but Akitada nodded and went to his desk. Genzo had not arrived yet but left a stack of last night's copies.

Akitada had little interest in Genzo's work, or his own, for that matter. All of it was just a subterfuge to meet Kumo. If Kumo had been informed about the prisoner Taketsuna and his background, he had given no indication of it. But Akitada had learned enough. Kumo's leading an uprising seemed less likely than he had feared. The governor had painted a villainous image of the high constable, but the man who rescued convicts from unbearable working conditions, trained them, and then treated them with generosity and respect was surely no villain. In Akitada's view such goodness could hardly coexist with a desire for bloody vengeance against the emperor. In fact, Akitada began to doubt Mutobe, an unpleasant state of mind comparable to feeling the earth shift during an earthquake. Kumo seemed to have done his best to ease suffering, while Mutobe apparently turned a blind eye to the abuse of prisoners by guards and police alike.

But he was puzzled by the change in Shiba's manner. Last night the secretary had been friendly and eager for news of the capital, yet today his greeting had been cool, distant, and nervous, as if Akitada had suddenly become an undesirable acquaintance. What had happened? Akitada briefly considered his meeting with Kumo's senile grandmother, but what was in that? Perhaps the change had nothing to do with him, but instead with the man from Aikawa bringing some bad news. A fire?

Akitada sighed and looked at Genzo's copies. They were better than the first batch, but one or two pages had to be rewritten, and he settled down to the chore. He was just bundling up the finished document when Genzo made his sullen appearance.

"Any more instructions, boss?" he demanded. His tone was hostile and impudent—or it would have been impudent, had he not been speaking to a convict.

Akitada sorted through the stack of records, looking for something to occupy Genzo's time. He came across an account of the silver production of a mine called Two Rocks. As he glanced at some of the figures, he was struck by the modest yields for what was, according to Yume, one of the best silver deposits on the island. But then, he knew nothing about silver mines. Passing the sheaf of papers to Genzo, he asked him to make copies.

Toward midday, Inspector Osawa arrived, clearly suffering from the effects of too much wine. He listened with half an ear to Akitada's report, glanced at the copies and notes, and said, "Good. Finish up, will you? We are leaving for the coast as soon as you can be ready. I'm going to lie down a bit. I don't feel at all well today."

Akitada wished him a speedy recovery. There was little more work to be done. At one point, he sought out the secretary again to ask a question, but more to gauge the man's changed manner than to gain useful answers.

Shiba answered freely until Akitada mentioned the Two Rocks mine, saying, "I noticed some papers relating to it, and wondered where it might be located."

Shiba blinked and fidgeted. "Mine?" he asked. "In the mountains, I suppose." Seeing Akitada's astonishment at this vague reply, he added, "I know nothing about that part of the master's business, but all the mines are in the mountains of

Greater Sadoshima, that is, the northern half. Our mines must be there also."

Well, it was hardly a satisfactory answer, but Akitada knew from the governor's map that the closest coast to the mountainous areas was the one facing away from the mainland, a particularly rocky area not used by regular shipping, but familiar to local fishermen and pirates. He wondered about the "pack trains to the coast" mentioned by the supervisor from the Kumo mine. But perhaps he had said "coast" when he had meant Sawata Bay and the harbor at Mano where all the silver was loaded for the trip to the mainland.

The secretary busied himself with paperwork, muttering, "Forgive me, but there is much work. If there's nothing else . . . ?" Akitada gave up.

Osawa eventually reappeared in traveling costume. Under his direction, Akitada and Genzo carried the documents out to the waiting horses and packed them in the saddlebags.

Kumo came to bid Osawa farewell. "All ready to leave?" he boomed cheerfully. Turning to Akitada, he said, "I hope my people gave you all the assistance you needed?" Mildly astonished by such belated attention, Akitada bowed and praised the secretarial staff.

"And you have been made quite at home here, I trust?" Kumo continued, his light eyes boring into Akitada's.

Was the man hinting at Akitada's trespassing in his garden? Meeting the high constable's sharp eyes, Akitada said, "Yes, thank you. I have been treated with unusual kindness and respect. A man in my position learns not to expect such courtesy. And your beautiful garden brought memories of a happier past. I shall always remember my stay here with pleasure."

"In that case you must return often," Kumo said, then turned to Osawa, putting a friendly hand on his shoulder. "And where are you off to next, my friend?"

Osawa glowered at his horse. "All the way to Minato on that miserable animal. At least the weather is dry." He put his foot in the stirrup and swung himself up with a grunt.

Kumo stood transfixed. "Minato?" he asked, his voice suddenly tense. "Why Minato? I thought you were on an inspection tour."

"Governor's orders. I'm to deliver a letter to Professor Sakamoto there."

"I see." Kumo's eyes left Osawa's face and went to Akitada's instead, and this time Akitada thought he caught a flicker of some smoldering, hidden violence which might erupt at any moment. The shift was so sudden and brief that he doubted his eyes.

CHAPTER NINE

MINATO

The road to Minato continued through the rich plain between the two mountain ranges. This was the "inside country," the most populated area of the island, where the rice paddies extended on both sides to the mountains, their green rectangles swaying and rippling in the breeze like waves in an emerald sea. Peasants moved about their daily chores among them, bare-legged and the women often bare-chested, and half-naked children stopped their play to watch round-eyed as the riders passed.

In all their journey that day, they saw only one other horseman. The rider stayed far behind, traveling at the same moderate speed. Osawa, who started to feel better as time passed, was eager to reach Minato before dark, and they made better time than the day before. Halfway, they took a brief rest at a shrine to water their horses and eat some of the rice dumplings provided by Kumo's cook. They had just dismounted and led their horses under the shrine gates into the shady grove when they heard the other rider. A moment later he passed, hunched in his saddle, incurious about the shrine, his eyes fixed on the road ahead. The man looked vaguely familiar. Akitada searched his memory as to where he might have come across a short fellow with a large nose but failed.

The sky clouded over after that, and in another hour the wind picked up. Osawa grumbled to himself, but Akitada breathed the moisture-laden air with pleasure. He caught the first hint of the sea and knew they were close to the coast. Soon after, the rain began to fall.

"I have no rain cape," complained Osawa. "The weather was so fine when we left that I refused the offer of one. And now there won't be another village till we reach Minato." A gust of wind drove the heavy drizzle into their faces, and he added irritably, "If we reach it today."

They reached Lake Kamo in spite of the rain and muddy road, but the heavily overcast sky had caused dusk to fall early, and there was still half the lake to skirt to reach Minato on the opposite shore.

Minato turned out to be a large village between the lake and the ocean. Its inhabitants were mostly fishermen who fished both the open sea and the lake. Minato was well known for its excellent seafood, and its houses and shrines looked more substantial than those of other villages.

But the travelers were by then too miserable to be interested in anything but shelter, a change of clothes, and some hot food and wine. The rain had soaked their robes until they clung heavily to their cold skin, and Osawa and Genzo were so exhausted that they were in danger of falling from the saddle.

On the deserted village street, Akitada stopped a barefoot old woman under a tattered straw rain cape to ask directions to Professor Sakamoto's house. She pointed across the lake to the shore on the outskirts of Minato where several villas and summerhouses overlooked the water. When they had wearily plodded there, Sakamoto's residence turned out to be walled and gated. Unfortunately, the servant who answered Osawa's knocking claimed his master was absent and he had no authority to admit strangers. He seemed in a hurry to get out of the rain.

Osawa started to berate the man but was too exhausted to make much of a job of it. The servant merely played dumb and refused to admit them or provide any information.

"Perhaps an inn for tonight?" Akitada suggested to the desperate and shivering Osawa. "We passed a nice one on our way here."

Osawa just nodded.

An hour later, Osawa, dry, bathed, and fed with an excellent fish soup provided by the proprietress, took to his bed in the inn's best room, and Genzo went to sleep over his warmed wine in the reception room of the inn. Akitada, more used to riding than the others, had washed at the well and then borrowed some old clothes from the inn's owner. His own robe and trousers were draped over a beam in the kitchen, and he now sat by the fire, dressed in a patched shirt and short cotton pants held by a rope about his middle, devouring a large bowl of millet and vegetables. Not for him the delights of the local seafood or warmed wine, or even of decent rice, but he was hungry.

Their hostess was a plain, thin woman in her thirties. His borrowed clothes had belonged to her dead husband. She was not unkind, but too busy with Osawa to pay attention to him. Besides, Genzo had informed her immediately that the fellow Taketsuna was only a convict. After that it had taken all of Akitada's charm to beg a change of clothes. She drew the line at feeding him a meal like the one she had prepared for Osawa. Instead she busied herself with starting the rice for the next morning and grinding some dumpling flour with a large stone mortar and pestle.

When he was done with his millet, Akitada went into the scullery and washed his bowl, drying it with a hemp cloth. Then he took a broom and swept the kitchen. That chore done, he headed outside to bring in more firewood, and looked around for other work.

She had watched him—at first suspiciously in case he might steal something, then with increasing astonishment. Now she asked, "Aren't you tired?"

"A little," he said with a smile. "I noticed that you don't have much help, so I thought I'd lend a hand before I rest."

A smile cracked her dour face, and she wiped her hands on her apron. "I lost my husband, but I'm strong." Then she went to a small bamboo cabinet and took out a flask and a cup. "Here," she said. "Sit down and talk to me while I make the dumplings. How do you like your master?"

He sat and thanked her. "Mr. Osawa? He's fair enough, I guess. A good official, but he claims he's overworked." The wine was decent. Akitada sipped it slowly, savoring its sweetness and warmth, wondering if she had saved it for a special occasion.

"Is he married?"

"I don't believe so."

"Ah. Poor man. And you? Where are you from?"

He gave her a heavily altered story of his life. Only what he told about his family was the truth, because he suspected that she, being a woman, would catch him in a lie most easily there. As it was, talking about Tamako and his baby son caused a painfully intense longing for them, and his feelings must have shown, for when he paused, she shook her head and muttered, "What a pity! What a pity! It's terrible to be alone in this life."

Perhaps this small comment more than anything he had seen or heard brought close what exile to this island meant to the men who were condemned to spend their lives here, working under intolerable conditions if they were ordinary criminals, or just measuring out their days in enforced idleness if high-ranking court nobles.

"Will you play a song for me?" she asked with a glance at the flute, which he had laid beside him.

He obliged, gladly. She was inordinately pleased when he was done. Perhaps he had touched a long-since-abandoned chord of romance in her. In any case, she unbent some more.

"I hear you were turned away at the professor's place," she said, her nimble fingers shaping perfect white spheres. When Akitada mentioned Osawa's disappointment, she said with a sniff, "The professor's getting drunk in the Bamboo Grove as usual."

"In this rain?" he asked, misunderstanding.

She laughed and became almost attractive. "The Bamboo Grove is a restaurant. Haru's place. Besides, it's stopped raining."

"I heard the professor keeps company with the good people. Glad to hear that he's friendly with the common folk, too."

"Only when he's drinking. The rest of the time he stays to himself in that fine house of his. He's writing a great history book about Sadoshima. Sometimes the good people visit him and then he has dinner parties. You know the Second Prince was murdered at his house? You should have seen all the fuss to get ready for that party. We were all put to work cooking and carrying. The professor's a bit of a skinflint, but he spent his money then. The best wine, the finest delicacies, the best dishes, whatever the prince wanted."

"You prepared some of the food?"

"Yes. Rice cakes filled with vegetables, salted mushrooms, pickled eggplant, and tofu in sweet bean sauce."

"You must be a fine cook. I hope they didn't blame you for the death?"

"No. They arrested the governor's son. Some people say he didn't do it."

Akitada waited for more, but the landlady took her time. She finished her dumplings, wiped her hands on her apron, and carried the large wooden tray to a shelf. Then she took off the apron, shook it out, and put it away. He was about to remind her of her last words when she came to join him in a cup of wine.

"People talk," she said, sipping. "And they talk mostly about the good people. Some people say the governor's son's been set up. Others think he killed the prince because the prince wrote to His Majesty about the governor stealing the government's silver. And some—" She broke off and shook her head.

"And some? Go on!" urged Akitada.

She leaned forward and whispered, "Don't tell anybody, but some say the governor made his son do it. Can you imagine?"

Akitada could and felt grim. "The ones who think he's been framed, do they mention names?"

She shook her head. "It's only gossip. Good deeds won't step outside your gate, they say, but evil will spread a thousand leagues." She refilled their cups. "Some of the good people here would like to get back at the governor. He's not very popular."

"It's a great puzzle," Akitada said, shaking his head. He was beginning to feel pleasantly warm and sleepy and had a hard time concentrating. "How was the Second Prince killed, do you think?"

"Oh, it was poison, but nobody knows for sure what kind. I thank the gods they didn't suspect me." She smirked a little. "They say Haru made the special prawn stew the governor's son took to the prince. A dog died from licking the bowl."

"Is this the same Haru who owns the restaurant where the professor is drinking?"

"Yes. The Bamboo Grove." She sniffed. "Haru's husband is just a fisherman, but she thinks she's something special because the good people buy their fish from them and stop at her place for a meal after one of their boating or hunting parties. She's nothing special that I can see, but men like her. All that bragging, and now look at the trouble she's made for herself."

"But they did not accuse her of anything?"

"No. Seems like some of her customers said they ate the same stew and it was fine."

"Maybe it was an accident. Say some poisonous mushrooms . . . or . . . I don't suppose blowfish could have got in the stew?"

She sat up and stared at him. "Blowfish? Funny you should say that. The prince used to buy that from her. Serve her right if she made a bad mistake with blowfish. But the poison was in the dish the governor's son brought, and that was prawn stew."

"Well, I was just wondering. Do many of the good people live around here?"

"Oh, yes. It's the lake. They came and built their villas here. You know already about the professor. And the prince's doctor has a place here, and some of the lords, like Iga and Kumo, have summerhouses here."

"I thought the exiles were forbidden to use their former titles."

She yawned and stretched. "They may have had their titles taken away, but to us they're still great men." She got to her feet. "Well, it's bedtime for me. I've got to be up early to start the fire. There's bedding in that trunk. It'll be warm near the fire pit."

Akitada rose and thanked her. He, too, was very tired. As soon as she had left, he took out the bedding and spread it before the fire. It looked inviting, but he did not lie down. Instead he tucked the flute into it and then slipped outside, closing the kitchen door softly behind him.

Though the rain had stopped, it was still cloudy and very dark. The rain-cooled air had caused a thick mist to rise from the surface of the lake, and this crept over the low roofs of the silent houses and filled the streets and narrow alleys between them. Akitada stood still for a moment and listened. He thought he had heard a stealthy sound somewhere, but the silence was broken only by the soft dripping of moisture from the roof behind him. The mist muffled noises; he could no longer hear the sound of the surf on the nearby coast. Cautiously he started down the road. He planned to pay a quick visit to Haru's restaurant before retiring.

Minato, though considered a village, was almost a small town. No doubt this was due in equal parts to the lake's attractions and to the fishing off the Sadoshima coast. Nighttime entertainment, totally lacking in ordinary villages, could be found here in a wine shop or two and in the Bamboo Grove.

The street passed between the single-storied houses, mostly dark now and built so close together that the alleyways between them were too narrow for more than one person. Now and then there was a small break to allow for a roadway to the lake or to accommodate a temple or shrine. Akitada had paid little attention to these details earlier, being too preoccupied with the condition of his companions. Now he took note that the Buddhist temple, though small, was in excellent repair, its pillars painted and gilded, and its double doors studded with ornamental nails. It was closed now, but a little farther on the houses made room for a small shrine surrounded by pines and a stand of tall bamboo.

Akitada had always had a strong affinity for shrines. Though he was not a superstitious man, he had found them a source of peace during troubling times in his life. On an impulse he decided to pay his respects to the local god. Turning in under the *torii*, two upright beams spanned by two horizontal ones, marking the threshold between the unquiet world of men and the sacred precinct of the god, he found amid the dripping trees a small building of unpainted logs with a roof of rain-darkened cedar shingles. It brooded silently in the gloom. The smell of wet earth and pine needles was all around. Ahead the almost-darkness was broken by one small, eerie point of light. As Akitada approached, he found that it was an oil lamp flickering in a niche of the shrine building. It illuminated a grotesque birdlike creature which seemed to crouch there watchfully. The bird was the size of a four-year-old child and seemed to ruffle its brown feathers and fix him with a malevolent and predatory eye. Akitada stopped, then relaxed. A trick of the flickering light had given momentary life to the wooden carving of a *tengu*, a demonic creature believed to inhabit remote places and play very nasty tricks on unsuspecting humans. A few crumbs of rice cakes, now soggy from the rain, still lay near the oil lamp, and someone had placed a wooden plaque against the image, inscribed with the words: "Eat and rest, then go away!"

This shrine was no restful place, and Akitada retraced his steps without addressing the god. He was about to emerge into the street again when he heard footsteps. Since he had no desire to explain what he was doing wandering around Minato in the middle of the night, he ducked under some bamboo which, heavy with rain, drooped low and screened him from the road. A man was walking past. The bamboo's slight rustle drenched Akitada in a cold shower and caused the passerby to swing around and stare suspiciously at the shrine entrance.

It was difficult to see clearly in the murk, but for a moment Akitada thought the *tengu* had flown off its perch to look for victims. The man was small, his shoulders hunched against the cold mist. He had a nose like a beak, and his clothing also was as dark brown as the carved plumage of the *tengu*. Perhaps the sculptor had found his model in this local man. Akitada smiled to himself. The passerby was probably himself nervous about the demon bird of this shrine, for he stared long and hard before continuing on his way.

It was late and Akitada was tired. He was glad when he found the Bamboo Grove by following one of the narrow roads down to the lake. A sign hung by its door and a dim glow and the sound of male voices raised in song came from inside. Haru's restaurant was still open, and among its late revelers was, perhaps, their elusive host, the professor.

But Akitada could hardly walk in as a customer. Besides, he carried only a few copper coins, hardly enough for an evening's carousing and too precious to be wasted on wine. For once he felt a sympathetic concern for the plight of the poor workingman.

He peered into the Bamboo Grove's interior through one of the bamboo grilles which covered the windows.

The large room contained the ubiquitous central fire pit, where a handsome buxom female stirred a pot with a small ladle. Her guests were neither poor nor working class, to judge by their clothes. From time to time, they would extend an empty cup which the hostess filled with warm, spiced wine. Its aroma drifted tantalizingly through the grille.

The four men reclined or sat cross-legged around the fire, their faces flushed with wine and warmth, their hands gesticulating as they sang, or chatted, or recited poetry. The quality of their performances varied sharply and there were both loud laughter and applause. A corpulent elderly man with thin white hair and beard dominated the entertainment. He was quite drunk and his speech slurred, but he recited well and from a memory that revealed an excellent education. Akitada guessed that this was Sakamoto.

The exchanges were mildly entertaining, but Akitada heard nothing of interest and was glad when the gathering broke up. Somewhere in the fog a temple or monastery bell was marking the hours of devotion. Inside, the hostess cocked her head, then laid down her ladle and clapped her hands. "Closing time, gentlemen!"

Akitada watched from the corner as the guests departed, then followed them.

The four men stayed together for a little, chatting and breaking into snatches of song, and then, one by one, turned off toward their homes. Eventually only the professor was left. He seemed to have difficulty walking and was talking to himself as if he were still carrying on a conversation with his friends. For some reason, the cool night air turned what had seemed mild inebriation into staggering, falling-down drunkenness, and Sakamoto proceeded homeward by starts and stops, with Akitada following behind.

In this manner they passed through the village and were still a distance from his villa when the professor suddenly rolled into a ditch and stayed there.

The rain had filled the ditches with water, and when Akitada caught up, he found Sakamoto face down and blowing bubbles while his hands scrabbled at the sides of the muddy gully. Jumping in, he hauled him out, a strenuous job since the man was heavy and his water-soaked robe added more weight. Once he sat on the side of the road, Sakamoto looked considerably the worse for wear, his face and beard covered with mud, and wet leaves and weeds sticking out of his topknot. He gagged, coughed up water and wine, then vomited copiously, holding his belly. Akitada helped the process along by slapping his back smartly.

"Wha . . . mph," croaked the professor. "S-stop it. Oarghh. Dear heaven, I f-feel awful. I'm all wet. Wh-what happened?"

"You fell into a ditch and almost drowned," said Akitada, and delivered another unsympathetic smack for good measure.

"Ouch. Drowned? Ditch?" Sakamoto turned his head and peered blearily at the water, then flung both arms around Akitada's knees. "You saved my l-life. Sh-shall be rewarded. S-silver. At my house."

An invitation to Sakamoto's house was tempting, but Akitada was tired. Besides, it might raise questions when he returned with Osawa the next day. On the whole, he preferred to remain a ragged stranger encountered on a dark night. Putting his arm around Sakamoto's back, he hauled him to his feet.

Their progress was not much quicker than before because Sakamoto became talkative again and insisted on stopping every few yards to recite poetry or bits of a sutra. The realization that he could have died but for the intervention of this kind stranger put him into a maudlin mood.

"To die forgotten in a ditch somewhere, how s-sad," he muttered mournfully. "An exile in a distant land, dead on the strand of this s-sad world." He stopped and raised his face to the cloudy skies. "All dead, every one of us, not a one left to tell our tale. F-forgotten. Gone. Like dewdrops. Snowflakes. Mere wisps of s-smoke." Bursting into tears, he clutched Akitada's hand and peered up at him blearily. "You're a young man. Wh-what's your name?"

"I have no name," Akitada said, hiding a smile.

"No name?" Sakamoto pondered this, then nodded wisely. "M-much better not to have a name." Stepping away from Akitada, he flung his arms wide and recited, " 'Oh you, who now have gone to dwell among the clouds, do you still call yourself by the old name?' "

Akitada took hold of him firmly and managed to take him a little way before Sakamoto stopped again.

"He died well, you know. A warrior's death. But what good is it now? S-so sad. All of life is a road towards death." He nodded to Akitada and recited in a tragic voice, " 'I, too, am already deeply entered on the pathway of the gods and wonder what lies beyond.' Do you think I shall find him there?"

"Find whom?"

"Him. My true sovereign. Oh, never mind." He clutched at Akitada's arm. "I'm sleepy. Take me home."

Akitada shared the feeling. He was exhausted himself. Fortunately, Sakamoto was no more trouble after that, and his servant received him with the unsurprised expression of long-suffering. Hardly glancing at the muddied figure of Akitada, who wisely kept his face in the shadow, he supported his master with one arm and fished a single copper coin from his sash. Handing this to Akitada with a curt, "Thanks," he slammed the gate in his face.

So much for the promised silver, Akitada thought, adding the copper to his small supply, then turned his steps toward the inn.

But soon he stepped off the stony roadway and continued on the grassy strip next to the ditch. In the silence, he now heard it clearly: someone else's steps softly crunching on the gravel. He thought that he had been trailed for quite a while. At first he had paid no attention. Others had the same right as he to take a stroll before bedtime. And when he had followed Sakamoto, he had assumed another reveler was on his way home. But now, on this quiet street leading to the lakeside villas, he knew someone had been watching and following them, and had done so from the time they left the Bamboo Grove.

The steps ceased abruptly. Either the other man had stopped or, like Akitada, he was walking on the soft grass. Akitada stepped back into the street and resumed his walk but increased his speed. As soon as he reached the first houses of Minato, he slipped into a narrow alley between two buildings and waited.

Nothing happened.

The other man was too wily. Well, he had time, and his pursuer had two choices. He could either give up the pursuit and go home, or he could come and investigate what had become of Akitada. A long time passed. The great bell at the temple sounded again, its deep peal muffled in the mist. It was wet where Akitada crouched; cold water dripped steadily down his back from the roof of one of the houses. He moved a little, but found more drips, and his legs began to cramp. Rising to his feet, he decided to give up, when he heard the crunching of gravel again.

The small man in the brown clothes walked past. He was almost close enough to touch and scanned the houses opposite. For a moment, Akitada was tempted to jump out and force some answers from him, but he knew that the man would simply deny having followed him. The other's face was not visible, but Akitada knew he was the birdlike individual he had seen earlier at the shrine. And now he noticed also that this man had a very slight peculiarity in his gait. His right leg seemed stiffer than the left.

Keeping to the dark shadows of the houses, Akitada followed silently, but eventually he lost him to the darkness.

Somewhat uneasy, he returned to the inn and let himself quietly into the kitchen, where he took off his wet shirt and pants and reassured himself that the flute was safe. Then he slipped into the bedding, falling instantly into an exhausted sleep.

CHAPTER TEN

THE PROFESSOR

The next day Osawa had a cold.

Akitada became aware of this when their hostess, surprisingly rosy and handsome in a brightly colored cotton robe and with her hair tied up neatly, shook him awake because she had to start the fire and rush hot gruel and wine to Osawa's room. She seemed preoccupied, and he got up quickly, dressed in his dry blue robe, put away his bedding, and laid the fire for her.

Then he went outside to get water from the well. The sky had cleared overnight, and a fresh breeze blew from the ocean, reminding him of the distance, in more than one sense, between himself and his family. But he put aside the troubling thoughts; the business at hand was the murder of the Second Prince.

Drawing the water and carrying the pail into the kitchen, he pondered the ramblings of the drunken professor, but could make nothing of them.

Having finished his chores, Akitada washed himself and retied his topknot. His beard itched and he wished for a barber, but the facial hair was his best disguise in the unlikely case that someone here knew him from the capital or from Echigo. It occurred to him to check his saddlebag in the kitchen. His own robe was still inside, tightly folded as he had left it. He slid a finger inside the collar and felt the stiffness made by the documents. Satisfied, he tucked the flute inside the robe and closed the saddlebag. Then he fortified himself with the rice dumpling offered by the hostess, who was assembling a tray for Osawa, and went to have a look at Minato by daylight.

This morning Minato sparkled freshly after the rain and seemed an ordinary, pleasant place after all. Akitada saw no sign of his shadow from the night before and wondered whether fatigue and the eerie, misty evening had made him imagine things. Shops were opening, and people swept in front of their doors or walked to work. The temple doors stood wide, and a young monk was setting out trays of incense for early worshippers. Only the shrine lay as silent as the night before behind its grove of trees and thick bamboo.

Akitada turned down the street to the Bamboo Grove. Before him the lake stretched like a sheet of glistening silver. Fishermen's boats were plying their trade in the far distance, and closer in some anglers trailed their lines in the placid waters. And everywhere gulls swooped, brilliant flashes of white against the azure sky, their piercing cries a part of the freshness of the morning.

To the northwest, Mount Kimpoku loomed, its top bright in the sun. It reminded him of the tall and striking Kumo, high constable of Sadoshima, and Mutobe's choice as arch-traitor.

Kumo's status and his influence over the local people made him an obvious leader, and his wealth could finance a military campaign. And, perhaps most importantly, his family believed itself wronged.

But the Kumo he had met, while something of a mystery, did not fit Akitada's image of a ruthless avenger of family honor or of a man driven by hunger for power. According to his people, Kumo was modest and kind. The man who had alleviated the suffering of those condemned to work in the mines surely could not have ordered the murder of little Jisei.

Haru's restaurant was still dark and silent after its late hours the night before, but in an adjoining shed a man was scrubbing a large table. All around him stood empty barrels and baskets, and a strong odor of fish hung in the air. Akitada called out a "Good morning."

The man looked up. Of an indeterminate age, he had the deeply tanned, stringy physique of a fisherman. Seeing Akitada's plain blue robe and his neatly tied hair, he bowed. "Good morning to you. How can I help you?"

"You own the Bamboo Grove?"

"My wife Haru does."

"Then you must be the man whose catches are famous hereabouts."

Haru's husband grinned. "I may be, but if it's fish you came for, you're too early. The first catch won't be in until later. What did you have in mind? Eel, turtle, octopus, shrimp, abalone, clams, bream, trout, mackerel, angelfish, flying fish, or blowfish?"

Akitada smiled. "Blowfish?"

"Yes. *Fugu*. It's a great delicacy. But expensive." His eyes swept over Akitada again, estimating his wealth.

"It's for my master, who's visiting Minato," Akitada explained.

The man's face brightened. "Ah! Of course. Many gentlemen enjoy *fugu* here. I can have some for you by evening. How many? You want them prepared, don't you? My wife's an expert at removing the poison. You'd be well advised to let her do it. Otherwise . . . well, your master wouldn't live long enough to thank you for your service." He paused. "And his family might accuse you of murder."

Akitada said, "I hope not. Has that ever happened here?"

"Not with any fish we've prepared," the man said almost belligerently.

Akitada told him that he would consult with his master. As he returned to the inn, he wondered if Haru's expertise with blowfish had come in question recently.

Osawa was up and freshly shaven but complained of feeling too ill to leave his room. He handed Akitada the governor's letter and told him in a weak voice to deliver it to Sakamoto, making his apologies. "It's not as if I were a common messenger," he sniffed, "or as if there were any need to discuss anything with Sakamoto. Just hand the letter to a servant and wait for a reply. Sakamoto may, of course, rush right over here to apologize for that lout of a servant who turned us away so rudely last night, but I have no intention of moving to his house. I'm very comfortable right here."

And so he was, sitting in a nest of bedding with a brazier warming the air, a flask of wine beside him, and the remnants of his morning meal on a tray. Akitada took the letter with a bow and departed happily.

This morning there was activity at the Sakamoto house. The gates stood wide open, revealing a rather weedy courtyard and dilapidated stables. A groom was walking a handsome horse around the courtyard. Evidently another guest had arrived. The professor would be relieved to hear that Inspector Osawa preferred the inn to his villa. Akitada saw that the horse, a very fine dappled animal, had been ridden hard. Then something about it struck him as familiar. Yes, he was almost certain that this was one of the horses from Kumo's stable. Had Kumo himself followed them to Minato? But Kumo's groom had told the mine foreman that Kumo would want to inspect the fire.

"Hey, you!" One of the house servants, a fat youth who seemed to be eating something, waved to him from the house. "What do you want?" he demanded when Akitada came to him.

Akitada held up his letter and explained.

The fat youth took another bite from his rice dumpling, chewed, and thought about it. "Wait here," he finally told him, and waddled off. Akitada walked into the stone-paved entry. Scuffed wooden steps led up to a long corridor. Somewhere a door creaked and slid closed. He heard the sounds of conversation, and then the door squeaked again. The fat youth reappeared, followed by the long-faced, middle-aged servant from the night before. He still looked ill-tempered. Holding out his hand, he said in a peremptory tone, "You can give it to me. I'm in charge. I'll see the master gets it."

Akitada shook his head. "Sorry. I'm to give it to Professor Sakamoto in person. Tell him it's from the governor."

The long face lengthened. "The professor has guests. You'll have to come back later."

Akitada was intrigued by a conference which was so important that Sakamoto could not be interrupted by a messenger from the governor. Drawing himself up, he said sternly, "Do you mean to tell me that you did not inform your master of Inspector Osawa's visit yesterday?"

Recognition dawned belatedly, and the man flushed. "Oh. Well, no. There hasn't been time. The professor did not get back until quite late." And then in no condition to take in such news, thought Akitada. "And this morning we had an unexpected guest. If you would tell your master, I'm sure he'll understand. Perhaps the professor could call on him later?"

This did not suit Akitada at all. He said, "Don't be a fool, man. Inspector Osawa is still angry about being turned away yesterday. He asked me to deliver this personal message from the governor because he is ill, a fact he blames entirely on being refused shelter by you. The message is bound to be important and urgent. If you make me go back to him with another refusal, he will return to Mano and report the snub. Your master will be in trouble."

That shook the surly servant. He glared at the fat youth, who was leaning against the wall picking his nose, told Akitada to wait, and disappeared. Akitada ignored the hulking lout and sat down to remove his boots. Then he stepped up into the house.

The corridor led to a room overlooking the lake. It appeared to be empty. Sliding doors to the veranda and garden beyond had been pushed back for a lovely view across the shimmering water to Mount Kimpoku. The garden sloped down to the shore, terminating in a pavilion which appeared to project out over the water—the pavilion where the Second Prince had died.

Two men were standing at its balustrade watching the boats on the lake. One was certainly tall enough to be Kumo. They were joined by a third. The crabby servant was reporting his visit to the professor, the shorter, white-haired man. The professor said something to his tall guest and then hurried with the servant toward the house.

Akitada hoped that Kumo, if it was indeed Kumo down there in the pavilion, would stay well away from the house while he gave his message to the professor.

The professor's eyes looked slightly bloodshot, his right temple was bruised, and there was a deep scratch on one cheekbone, mementos of last night's bender and the tumble into the ditch. But this morning his beard and hair were neatly combed, and he wore a clean silk robe, somewhat threadbare but presentable. He scowled at Akitada.

"What's all this?" he said, matching a curt nod to Akitada's bow. "My servant tells me you have a letter from the governor? Can you make it quick? The high constable is here."

The irritable tone was probably due to a hangover. Akitada bowed again. "I serve as secretary to Mr. Osawa, the governor's inspector. Mr. Osawa wished to put His Excellency's letter into your hands in person. Unfortunately, we found you absent from home yesterday, and today Mr. Osawa is too ill to come himself. Rather than causing a further delay, he has asked me to deliver it." He handed over the governor's message.

Akitada's speech caused Sakamoto to narrow his eyes and look at him more sharply. Then he unfolded the letter and glanced at it. "Oh, bother!" he grumbled. "I have absolutely nothing to add to the case. Well, you'd better come along while I respond to this. I see he expects a reply."

They went to the room overlooking the lake, evidently Sakamoto's study, and comfortably though plainly furnished with well-worn mats, old bookcases, and a large desk with writing implements and a stack of paper. Two screens warded off cold drafts and a large bronze brazier the chill of winter.

Today there was no need for either. The sun shone brightly outside and no breeze stirred the trees. As Sakamoto reread the letter, Akitada watched the pavilion. Kumo still leaned on the balustrade, looking across the lake. It struck Akitada that the pavilion was perfectly suited for plotting treason. It was surrounded by open ground or water, assuring absolute privacy to anyone in the pavilion. No doubt that was why Kumo and Sakamoto had been talking there now. Akitada wished he could have heard their conversation.

Sakamoto gave a grunt, and Akitada took his eyes from the pavilion. The professor was frowning, almost glowering at him.

"Who exactly are you?" he asked. "Have we met before? Osawa never had a personal secretary on previous visits."

Apart from their belligerent tone, the questions were probably due to Kumo's visit. Kumo had shown a suspicious interest in the fact that they were headed for Minato. But Akitada had to answer and thought it best to stick to the original story. Whatever Kumo suspected, he could have no proof that Akitada was not what he pretended to be, or that Osawa's trip was somehow connected with what everyone seemed so anxious to hide.

"My name is Yoshimine Taketsuna," he began, patiently, as befitted his present status. "I am a convict. His Excellency, the governor, being short-handed in the provincial archives, heard that I have skill with the brush and employed me as a clerk. The governor told me to assist Mr. Osawa because he cannot spare the inspector for more than a few days. I doubt we can have met before. We only arrived in Minato last night."

Sakamoto was still frowning, and Akitada wondered if he had recognized his voice. "What were you convicted of?" the professor asked.

Akitada hedged a little. "That is surely not material to my errand, since both the governor and Mr. Osawa trusted me. However, I'm not ashamed of what I have done. I killed a man who got in my way. The man was a retainer of Lord Miyoshi."

"Miyoshi?" Sakamoto's eyebrows rose. A series of expressions passed across his face, surprise, curiosity, and perhaps relief. "What do you mean, he got in your way?"

Akitada looked past him. "My object was Lord Miyoshi. I consider him a traitor."

Sakamoto cried, "And so do I, though perhaps we had better not say so. I am sorry. You have my sympathy. Men like Miyoshi have few friends here." He narrowed his eyes. "But it seems rather strange that Mutobe should trust you under the circumstances."

Akitada laughed. "I doubt he knows. I arrived recently and the shortage of clerks in Mano is desperate."

"Ah." Sakamoto nodded. "It must be, and I expect you have an excellent education. Such men are very useful in Sadoshima." He glanced toward the lake. The irritation returned to his face. He held up the governor's letter. "Do you know what is in this?"

"No, but . . ."

"Well?"

"I heard that the governor's son has been arrested for murdering the Second Prince. His trial is coming up shortly. Since the crime took place in your house, it might be that the governor is asking for information which might help to clear his son."

Sakamoto made a face. "You guessed it, and it's an imposition. He should know I have nothing to tell him that he does not know already. Unfortunately, I must answer, and answer in writing. You could not have come at a worse time. The high constable dropped by and I expect other guests shortly. Could you return tomorrow for your answer?"

Akitada was instantly and overridingly curious about the other guests and decided to extend his stay as long as he could to see who else arrived. The fact that he could hardly insist on an immediate answer, nor give in too easily after creating a scene with the servants, gave him an idea. In a tone both regretful and sympathetic, he said, "I am very sorry to put you to this inconvenience, sir, but I don't have the authority to make such a decision." He paused to make a face. "The problem is aggravated by the fact that Inspector Osawa is still very unhappy about being turned away from your door last night."

Sakamoto looked vexed. "Yes, yes. I heard. Most unfortunate. Tell him the servant in question has been disciplined severely. Of course, I shall make my apologies in person. Only not today."

"If I might make a suggestion, sir? Perhaps I could compose the answer for you? All I need are a few particulars; then you can see to your guests while I write the letter for you."

Sakamoto stared at him. "Really? Could you?" he said, his face brightening. "Yes. Very generous of you to offer. I'll tell you what. Why don't you have a cup of wine while I explain matters to my guest? Then we'll discuss the letter, and you can write it out while I tend to business. How's that?"

It was precisely what Akitada had proposed. With any luck, he would be kept in Sakamoto's house long enough to see the other guests arriving, while trying to find out what the professor knew of the murder.

After Sakamoto left, the long-faced servant brought a flask of wine and a cup on a tray. The offended expression on his face announced that he was not used to serving other people's servants.

Akitada greeted him with a smile. "I'm sorry to be such trouble on a busy day. Believe me, it wasn't my idea. I gather you expect guests?"

The servant set down the wine. "Don't let it bother you," he said with a scowl.

"Your master's household is in capable hands. Please pour yourself a cup. I'm not very thirsty."

The surly fellow hesitated, torn between temptation and the need to show his resentment. The wine won. He poured and emptied the cup, licking his lips. Akitada nodded with an encouraging smile. "Thanks," muttered the servant. "I needed that. It's been a long night and a hectic day. Looks like I'm not getting any sleep tonight, either."

"That's terrible." Akitada shook his head in sympathy. "I know the feeling. The inspector's laid up with a cold, or we'd be in the saddle going to the next inspection, where he'd keep me bent over my desk all night while he sleeps. Then we start all over again the next day. Have another cup. Still having people come about the murder, are you?"

The servant thawed a little and poured himself another. "Yes. You can't imagine the trouble that has caused. First the governor and the police, now all the prince's friends, and I've got to get rooms ready and arrange for food. They expect only the best and the professor hates spending money. He employs only the three of us. Yuki takes care of the stables. That leaves Tatsuo and me. And you've seen Tatsuo. He spends all his time eating and resting his great hulk. Serving meals and refreshments in the lake pavilion is a great nuisance. We're kept running and fetching between the lake and the house the best part of the day and into the night."

Akitada followed his gaze through the open doors to the pavilion and the glistening lake beyond. Sakamoto was again in close conversation with his guest.

"That's where it happened, wasn't it?" he asked. "Were you there?"

"No. We had already served. They send us away while they're talking. And they wouldn't let us touch the body afterwards. They put him on a litter and covered him up before they let Yuki and Tatsuo carry him to the doctor's house. I guess our hands weren't fine enough to touch him, or our eyes to look on his dead face."

Akitada shook his head. "And then you had to do the cleaning up. I heard a dog got to the dish of poison?"

The servant sighed. "My dog. Poor Kuro. I was really fond of him. We always let him eat the leftovers. That dirty scoundrel of a killer!"

At the bottom of the garden the two men started toward the house.

"Uh-oh," muttered the servant. "They're coming back. I've got to run. Thanks for the wine."

For a moment Akitada was tempted to make himself scarce, too. Dealing with Sakamoto had been one thing, but Kumo was suspicious. Well, he would just have to bluff it out.

When the two men entered from the veranda, Akitada rose and bowed deeply.

"So we meet again," drawled Kumo, his eyes passing over Akitada as if he wanted to memorize his appearance. Today he wore a hunting robe of green brocade with white silk trousers, a costume suitable for riding and handsome on his tall, broad-shouldered figure. He smiled, but his eyes were cold.

Akitada smiled back. "I had not expected to meet you again so soon, sir. We left you only yesterday."

Kumo's smile disappeared. "Yesterday you were a mere scribe. Today, I understand, you claim to be the governor's emissary, empowered to gather new evidence which might clear his son in the murder of the Second Prince? You are a changeable fellow, Taketsuna."

The bluntness of that left Akitada momentarily speechless. "I . . . I beg your pardon?" he stammered. "Inspector Osawa entrusted me with a letter because he is too ill to bring it himself. I never claimed anything else."

Again that fleeting, mocking smile, and Akitada fought the uneasy feeling that he might be out of his depth with this man.

"So you kindly offered your talents to assist the professor in his response," Kumo said. "I must say I am sorry I did not take the time to chat with you at my house. Your background is interesting. How exactly did you become involved with Lord Miyoshi?"

They were still standing. Sakamoto fidgeted, clearly uncomfortable with the tone of the interrogation. Akitada controlled his nervousness and offered up the tale that had been concocted at the time of his assignment, hoping that the gentlemen from the sovereign's office had not made any glaring mistakes, for he did not doubt for a minute that the high constable had kept himself thoroughly and minutely informed about the factions in the capital.

If Kumo found fault, he did not say so. When Akitada had finished, he regarded him thoughtfully for a few moments and then said, "My sympathies are entirely with any man who would oppose Miyoshi in this dispute. But I had better leave you both to your chore."

Akitada, more puzzled than ever about Kumo, bowed and murmured his thanks.

"Well," said Sakamoto, when they were alone, "we'd better get started. Please sit down. Here at my desk. And make use of my writing things. Now, what shall I say?"

Akitada picked up the letter and scanned it. "The governor asks if you recall any odd happenings before or after the tragic event. Perhaps we can start with that."

"Tell him no."

"You want me to say that nothing out of the ordinary happened during the days preceding the prince's visit?"

Sakamoto frowned. "Nothing really strange. He sent a letter asking that the food not be too spicy. He had a delicate stomach, but I knew that. I must say I was surprised he ate the stew young Mutobe brought. I could tell it was highly spiced. That's why I didn't worry when he complained of a bellyache. Of course, now we know it was the poison." Sakamoto shook his head. "The prince always trusted too easily when it came to young men who captured his fancy."

That remark startled Akitada. But he decided the professor was merely venting his ill humor again. "And after the prince's death? Anything out of the ordinary then?"

Sakamoto snorted. "Don't be daft, young man. Everything was out of the ordinary then. We watched the prince die, Taira, Shunsei, and I. It was horrible. I was completely distraught. We were near the house when we heard him cry out and turned to see Toshito strangling him. At least that's what it looked like. We rushed back, but the prince had already expired. Taira attacked Toshito, calling him a murderer. Toshito claimed he was helping the prince breathe, but I think he didn't trust the poison and was making certain the prince would die." Sakamoto shuddered. "It was a vicious crime against a son of the gods. Anyway, we called for a litter and had His Highness taken to Nakatomi. He lives nearby and is the prince's physician. He looked at the body, and later at the dead dog who'd licked the bowl, and said the prince had been poisoned. Taira had young Toshito arrested and charged with murder."

"It must have been very upsetting to have this happen in your house and after one of your dinners. No doubt you were glad that the dog licked the bowl."

"What do you mean by that?"

Akitada met Sakamoto's frown with a bland face. "Nothing at all, sir. Since the source of the poison was quickly found, the local authorities could not suspect your kitchen staff. Or ask questions about the dishes you served. For example, was there anything with mushrooms? Or perhaps that local delicacy, blowfish?"

"There was certainly no blowfish. I cannot afford such extravagance. And all the dishes were perfectly wholesome. We all ate of them, except for Mutobe's stew."

Well, that took care of the blowfish theory. Akitada asked, "Who did the postmortem?"

"Nakatomi. There was no time to wait for Mutobe's disreputable coroner. In the summer, a body decomposes quickly. And Nakatomi is a very able man, in my opinion. He wrote out the report himself and hand-delivered it to the governor."

"And then?"

"We had a fine Buddhist funeral. No expense was spared. The prince's funeral pyre was twenty feet high."

Akitada wrote.

"The other information the governor asks for concerns those who attended the dinner. That would be Taira Takamoto and a young monk called Shunsei? Is there any chance, even a remote one, that either or both had a hand in this?"

"Certainly not. Lord Taira is a man of superior learning and of absolute loyalty to the prince. He's an old man now, older than I am. When he was appointed tutor to Crown Prince Okisada, he was the most brilliant man in the capital. He loves the prince, and the prince's death devastated him. In fact, he withdrew from all matters of this world until today."

So Taira was expected. "And Shunsei? How is he connected with the prince?"

Sakamoto frowned. "Shunsei belongs to the Konponji Monastery near Tsukahara. The prince enjoyed religious ceremonial. Being impressed with this young man's devotion, he took him under his wing." He bit his lip. "Perhaps he needed spiritual stimulation and was inspired by Shunsei's fervor."

Apparently Shunsei had been tolerated only because Okisada had insisted on his presence. In fact, Sakamoto's manner implied that Okisada had preferred men, or boys, to women. There had been gossip in the capital, and perhaps that had had something to do with Okisada's being replaced as crown prince. More to the point, such a relationship might have considerable bearing on the prince's death. Akitada asked, "Were you surprised at the attachment?"

Sakamoto met his eyes, looked uncomfortable, and shifted on his cushion. "Not surprised, really. Need you write all that to the governor? Shunsei was with us when the prince died, and none of us sat close enough to put anything in his food. All that is well-known evidence."

"Thank you. The final question concerns any friends, females, or business associates, anyone else who might have had a motive to kill the prince."

Sakamoto was becoming impatient. He said testily, "We have been over all that with that police officer, Wada. As you may imagine, Prince Okisada associated with very few people, basically those of us who attended the dinner and the Kumo family. Kumo was not here, and besides, he had no motive. There were no women in Okisada's life. And he had no interest in business. He lived on the allowance made to him by the court. And now you really must excuse me." He stood up. "I shall return after a while and sign the letter." With a nod he left the room.

Akitada started rubbing more ink, his mind weighing what Sakamoto had said. If the professor was involved in the plot, he had handled himself very well just now. But last night he had been drunk and babbled wildly. Such a man was a risky confidant. Perhaps he really knew nothing. He seemed to have a good reputation. Even Mutobe had not made any adverse comments about him. If the prince had been murdered by someone other than Mutobe's son, that only left the young monk and Taira as possible suspects. And, of course, the murder could be unrelated to the political issues. He was not really getting anywhere.

Taira, the man closest to the victim, was a complete enigma to Akitada. He must be nearly seventy by now and had once been favored by fortune. He had had a reputation at court as a superb diplomatist. Taira was in the prime of his life when he was appointed as tutor to the crown prince, a certain signal for a rapid rise in the government hierarchy. Then Okisada had been replaced by his half-brother, ending not only the prince's future, but Taira's career also. To everyone's astonishment, Taira had followed Okisada into exile, although he was never clearly implicated in the prince's rash action against his brother. Such loyalty became legendary. Would Taira murder the prince he had served so devotedly?

Akitada hoped that Taira would make his appearance soon, but the house remained silent, and he put his brush to paper to write Sakamoto's reply to Mutobe.

When he reached the reference to Shunsei, he paused. Sexual relations between men were not uncommon either at court or in the monasteries, but as a staunch follower of Confucius, Akitada held strong convictions about family and a man's duty to continue his line, and therefore he disapproved as much as Sakamoto. However, such an affair was not so different from a man's relations with a woman. It also involved lust, passion, possessiveness, and jealousy—all motives for murder. He looked forward to meeting this Shunsei.

The long-faced servant came in again. "The master asks if you're finished. He's in a hurry."

Akitada looked out into the garden. The groom was running down the path toward the pavilion with a broom and rake.

"Just finished," he said, laying down his brush and getting up. He gestured toward the garden. "After what happened, isn't your master afraid to entertain his learned friends in the pavilion again?"

"Well, you'd think so," said the servant. "It certainly gives me the chills. It's not as if it were in good repair, either. It's going to rack and ruin."

"The setting is beautiful. I suppose the view inspires poetry."

The servant grimaced. "I don't know about poetry. They always talk a lot and keep us running, but we're not allowed to stay and listen. I doubt it's poetry though, because mostly it looks more like they're arguing. Especially Lord Taira. He's got a terrible temper. I'll tell the professor you're done."

Akitada walked out on the veranda. The sweeping of the path and the pavilion completed, the fat servant was staggering down the path with a stack of cushions in his arms. Four. Kumo, Taira, Sakamoto, and one other. Shunsei? Like the disgruntled servant, Akitada doubted it would be a social gathering and wished again he could eavesdrop.

It was interesting that the servants were warned away between servings. It meant confidential matters were being discussed. It was impossible to approach the pavilion unseen.

Or was it?

Akitada was wondering if he could stroll down there for a closer look without causing undue suspicion when Sakamoto rushed in.

"Finished?" he cried. "Good." He ran to the desk, snatched up the letter, skimmed it, nodded, and signed. As he impressed his personal seal next to the signature, he said, "My compliments. An excellent hand and the style is acceptable." Letter in hand, he told Akitada, "I wish I had more time to talk to you. A man like you could be very useful. I shall speak to the high constable about you tonight."

Akitada bowed. "Thank you, sir, but the high constable is aware of my abilities."

"As you wish." Sakamoto handed the letter over. "Well, good luck to you, then, and give my compliments to the inspector. Tell him I'll ask Dr. Nakatomi to take a look at him if he is still indisposed tomorrow."

As Akitada walked back to the inn, he considered Nakatomi as the fourth guest. Nakatomi had not only been Okisada's personal physician, but it was he who had determined that the prince had been poisoned by young Mutobe's stew. Kumo, Taira, and Nakatomi. It was crucial to find out what these three men had to say to each other, and Akitada thought he knew a way to get to the pavilion unseen.

CHAPTER ELEVEN

THE LAKE

Osawa was dressed and sitting in the sun on the veranda outside his room. The veranda overlooked a narrow dusty courtyard with a small empty koi pond and a twisted pine. Osawa no longer looked ill. In fact, there was a sleek look of contentment about him which changed quickly to disappointment when he saw who had come into the room.

"Oh, it's you. I must say you took your time. That lazy slug Genzo has disappeared, too."

Akitada explained and produced the letter.

Osawa made a face. "I suppose that means we'll have to move on tomorrow. I don't understand what the big rush is, but who am I to question the governor? Well, you two have had a nice rest, anyway. You'd better both be up by dawn and have the horses saddled. It'll be a hard ride to Tsukahara."

They would start their homeward loop, spending the night in Shunsei's monastery near Tsukahara. The monastery collected the local rice taxes, and Osawa customarily visited it on his rounds. Monasteries also offered accommodations for travelers, and, apart from the strictly vegetarian and wineless meals, these were far more comfortable than sharing some farmer's hut or sleeping in the open. Osawa, Akitada knew by now, was not given to roughing it.

Asking for instructions, Akitada was told, with some hemming and hawing, to report to the landlady and make himself generally useful. This astonished him, especially since Osawa blushed and avoided his eyes.

In the kitchen a strange gray-haired woman was at work preparing a meal, while their hostess, dressed in a fetching robe with a colorful chrysanthemum pattern and with her hair neatly tied up in a silk ribbon, gave her instructions for an elaborate feast.

"And be sure that there are plenty of pine mushrooms and bamboo sprouts," she told the older woman. "Master Osawa is particularly fond of those. I'll be serving him myself, but you can bring the food and wine to the door of his room." She saw Akitada then. "Oh, you're finally back. Would you bring in more wood for the fire? There's some soup left if you're hungry, but eat it quickly. I need you to go to Haru's husband and buy some *awabi* and a sea bream for your master's dinner. His shop is next to the Bamboo Grove Restaurant. Tell him I'll pay later." Seeing Akitada admiring her costume, she smiled and added with a wink, "Your master is better and feels like a little company."

The older woman gave a snort, but Akitada grinned and bowed. "Ah! Osawa is a lucky man."

"Thank you," his hostess said, patting her hair, and walked away with a seductive wiggle of her slender hips.

Akitada whistled.

The elderly woman at the fire straightened up and glared at him. "Where's that wood?"

Akitada brought it and then helped himself to the small bit of cold broth with a few noodles, which was all that remained in the pot.

"Make yourself right at home, don't you?" sneered the old woman.

"Just trying to save you the trouble, auntie."

"Don't call me auntie," she snapped. "That's what whores call their old bawds. Maybe that's what my slut of a daughter makes of me, but I brought her up decent. Hurry up with that soup and get the fish. I have enough to do without having to wait for your convenience."

Akitada gobbled his soup meekly and departed with a basket.

He knew where Haru's husband sold his fish, but since the restaurant was open, he decided to meet the famous Haru herself.

He found her on the veranda, bent over to beat the dust out of some straw mats and presenting an interestingly voluptuous view of her figure. His landlady's rival, both as a hostess and as a woman, she was about the same age but considerably plumper.

Akitada cleared his throat. Haru swung around, broom in hand, and looked at him, her eyes widening with pleasure. "Welcome, handsome," she crooned, laughing black eyes admiring him. "And what can little Haru do to make you completely happy?"

Midday lovemaking must be in the air in Minato, thought Akitada. He returned her smile and stammered out his errand like some awkward schoolboy.

"Poor boy," she said, laying aside her broom and coming closer. "You're a little lost, but never mind. Does Takao treat you well?" She put her hand familiarly on his chest, feeling his muscles. "Where did that lucky girl find someone as young and strong as you to work for her?"

"I'm not really working there. My master's staying at the inn and asked me to lend a hand while she sees to his dinner."

"So that's the way it is." She cocked her head. "Pity she prefers your master. I could use someone like you to lend me a hand." She reached for his and placed it on her rounded hip. "How much time can you spare me?"

Akitada could feel her warm skin through the thin fabric and flushed in spite of himself. Haru was not in the least attractive to him, but her forwardness and overt sexual invitation reminded him of Masako. Suddenly their recent lovemaking struck him as no more than a coming together of two lecherous people, and he felt a sour disgust—with himself for having lost his self-control, and with Masako for being unchaste. He had not been the first man to lie with her. Women were very clever at pretending love.

But men could learn and be wary. He snatched his hand back from Haru's hot body and hid it behind his back. "I'll go see your husband. All I need is some *awabi*, and—"

She smiled. "Foolish man. You don't need *awabi.* That's what old men eat to regain their vigor. All you need is a good woman. And don't worry about my husband; he doesn't care." She stroked his shoulder and played with his sash.

Akitada retreated. There were limits to how far he was prepared to go in the interest of an investigation. He wished he had Tora here. This situation would suit his rakish lieutenant perfectly. He said, trying to look disappointed, "You are very kind, but I'm afraid I can't. They're waiting for the fish. I'd better find your husband. Goodbye." He bowed and turned to go.

She followed him, chuckling. "He's out on the lake. Never mind. I'll see you get your fish, and the best, too, even though that stupid Takao doesn't deserve it."

They passed through the restaurant, where a few locals were noisily slurping soup, and into the kitchen. A sweating girl was chopping vegetables to add to the big pot which simmered on the fire. The fish soup smelled very good, and Akitada said so.

"Would you like some?" Haru asked.

"I have no money."

"I'll add it to Takao's bill," she said, and grabbed a bowl and the ladle. Filling the bowl generously, she handed it to him. "Bring it along to the fish shack and tell me what she wants. You can eat while I get the fish."

"Some *awabi*, and a bream," he said, inhaling the smell of the soup. "Thank you for the soup. I only had a few noodles at the inn."

She snorted. "I'm a very good cook. Much better than Takao. Much better in bed, too, I'll bet."

They passed out into the sunlight and walked to the shack where Akitada had met Haru's husband that morning.

"See, he's not here," said Haru, giving him a sideways look. "And it'll be hours before he gets back."

Akitada pretended not to understand. The baskets and casks, empty this morning, were now mostly filled with the day's catch.

She busied herself gathering the fish and putting them in his basket, while he looked around with pretended interest. "Do you sell much blowfish?"

"*Fugu?*" She turned and peered into a small cask. "You want some?" she asked, lifting up a small fish by its tail. It flapped about and swelled into a ball. She laughed. "They say, '*Fugu* is sweet, but life is sweeter.' Don't worry. I know how to clean it so it's safe. I also know how to prepare it so you think you've gone to paradise because you feel so wonderful." She dropped the fish back into the water with a splash.

"Oh? Are there different ways of preparing it?"

"Yes. Many people know how to make *fugu* safe, even in the summer, but only a few know how to leave just a bit of the poison, not enough to kill you, but enough to let you visit paradise and come back."

"It sounds dangerous. Is there much call for it?"

She smiled. "You'd be surprised who likes to take such risks to reach nirvana. Of course, it's not cheap."

Akitada took a chance. "I heard the Second Prince was fond of *fugu*," he lied. "Do you suppose that's what killed him?"

Her smile disappeared instantly. "Who's been saying my fish killed the prince?" she demanded, her eyes flashing angrily. "Was it Takao? I had nothing to do with that, do you hear? It was bad enough when they thought I'd poisoned my prawn stew. There was nothing wrong with that stew when the governor's son picked it up. I served it in the restaurant and we ate it ourselves. I bet that Takao's spreading lies again because she's jealous that I'm a better cook and do a better business. I'll kill that trollop." She grabbed up a knife, her face contorted with fury.

"No, no," Akitada said, eyeing the knife uneasily in case she might force her way past by slashing at him. "Please don't get excited, Haru. It wasn't Takao. I heard the story of the poisoning in Mano. Hearing you talk about *fugu* made me think, that's all."

She stared at him, then put the knife down. "People talk too much," she said in a tired voice. "It's true the prince liked *fugu*, but I had nothing to do with his death. And that's all I've got to say."

She had lost interest in him, and Akitada was glad to make his escape so easily. In spite of her denials, he was certain that she, and her husband, knew something that was connected with the prince's death and the poisonous *fugu* fish.

Having delivered the fish to Takao's mother and fetched some water for her, he found that she wished him gone. Snatching up a rice dumpling in lieu of his evening meal, he left for the lake.

When he passed Sakamoto's house, he saw that the gates were closed again and all was quiet inside. He had to walk a long way before he found a place to get down to the water. An overgrown field, shaded by large firs and oaks, suited him perfectly. He worked his way through the undergrowth and brambles to the muddy bank, where thick reeds hid most of the lake, stirring up first a rabbit and then a pair of ducks, which protested loudly and flew off with a clatter of wings. He was fond of waterfowl, but could have done without them at this juncture. Taking off his boots and outer robe, he waded into the water, parting the reeds until they thinned enough for him to see along the shore to Sakamoto's place. He recognized it immediately because it was the only one with a pavilion on the lakeshore. The distance was shorter than he had expected, because the lake formed a small bay here, and the road he had followed had made a wide loop. There was no one in the pavilion yet.

He glanced up at the sun: at least an hour until sunset. Returning to shore, he put on his robe and boots again, found a dry and comfortable spot among the grass and buttercups, and lay down for a nap.

Whcn he awoke, the shadows had thickened and gnats had left behind itching spots on his face and hands. The sun was almost gone, and the sky had changed to a soft lavender. Akitada got up and stretched, disturbing a large ibis fishing in the shallows. It thrashed away through the reeds with a clatter, its curving red beak and pink flight feathers bright against the large white body, then took flight over the open water, followed by the scolding ducks.

Waterfowl presented an unforeseen problem. Ducks in particular always set up a loud clamor when disturbed. But he would have to risk that. He decided to do some more exploring first. This time he not only removed his boots and robe, but his pants and loincloth also, and waded naked into the muddy water, sloshing along, his bare feet sinking deep into the mud and feeling their way among sharp bits of debris and reed stubble.

When he emerged from the reeds, the water was chest-high and the bottom of the lake smoother and less soft. Some fishermen were a long way out in the middle of the lake. They would hardly see a swimmer at that distance, and as soon as the sun was gone, they would be making for home.

He swam about a little, the water cool against his hot and itchy skin, and felt quite cheerful and optimistic about his plan. Above, seagulls dipped and dove, their wingtips flashing gold in the last rays of the sun, their cries remote and mournful. He had a good view of the shoreline and saw that he would have to rely on the reeds to hide him.

And there they came, small figures moving down the hillside from Sakamoto's villa, a servant running ahead carrying a gleaming lantern. It was time.

Akitada swam back to his hiding place to rest a little and eat his rice dumpling. He did not want his empty stomach giving him away with inappropriate rumblings later.

Then he set out, cutting boldly across the small bay, swimming smoothly. The sun had disappeared behind Mount Kimpoku, and the land lay in shadow while the sky still blazed a fiery red, turning the surface of the lake the color of blood. The fishermen were headed home to their families, and up ahead, lit eerily by lanterns, waited the pavilion where an imperial prince had died of poison.

He caught glimpses of the seated men and saw servants popping up and disappearing as they brought food, knelt to serve, and then left again. The closer he got, the more chance there was that someone would glance his way and notice the head of a swimmer bobbing in the lake. And this time he would not be able to talk himself out of it with Kumo.

When he was within a hundred feet, he turned back toward the reeds and slipped into their protection. Progress became slow and difficult. Akitada moved in a crouch, using channels left by fishermen whenever possible. Once he froze after raising an egret. It flew off, awkwardly flapping its huge wings until it was airborne and soared like a silver ghost across the darkening sky.

Abruptly the reeds stopped, and an open channel of water stretched between him and the pavilion. Someone had cleared away the water grasses to make sure no boats could approach the pavilion unseen. Such precautions made his undertaking seem all the more vital.

Up in the pavilion, in the yellow light of lanterns hanging from the eaves, he could see the four men. They sat facing each other and were eating and talking quietly.

Kumo, the only one who wore his hair loose, had his back to Akitada. Next to Kumo sat the gray-haired, round-shouldered Sakamoto. Another old man, probably Taira, with white hair and improbably black brows, looking bent with age and scrawny as an old crow in his black robe, sat across from Sakamoto. The fourth man must be Nakatomi. He was partially hidden by Kumo's broad back, but wore a rich robe of patterned blue brocade. Whoever he was, fortune had treated him well.

But Akitada could not remain forever in the shelter of the reeds. He did not relish the idea of crossing open water, but decided that, being in the light, the four men would not notice a lone swimmer in the dark lake. This conviction was almost immediately put to the test when Kumo got up and stepped to the balustrade. Akitada sank down, keeping his face half submerged. But Kumo merely emptied the dregs from his wine cup and returned to the others.

Moving slowly and smoothly so he would not make any noisy splashes, Akitada half swam, half crawled through the shallow water, keeping his face down so that his dark hair would blend with the water.

When he was close enough to hear them, the water no longer covered him completely and he had to hurry. Slithering across the mud on his belly, he scraped his skin painfully on stubble, but he kept his face down until he reached cover.

He had almost made it when there was a shout above, and he stopped. Naked and defenseless, he lay in the mud, imagining an arrow in his back, though it was not likely that any of the four was armed. But nothing happened, and after a moment he peered up. The surly servant was running up the steps, and Sakamoto asked for more wine.

With a sigh of relief, Akitada crawled into the darkness under the pavilion and waited for his heart to stop pounding and his eyes to adjust. A few straggling weeds grew on the muddy bank he crouched on. If he raised himself to his knees, he could touch the boards above his head. Wide cracks between the boards let light fall through in slender ribbons which undulated on the waves slapping softly against the timbers and creeping up the shore. He could hear the conversation of the men above as perfectly as if he were sitting beside them.

The supporting beams—there were eight of them—rested on large flat rocks covered with slimy moss. The three outermost supports disappeared into the lake water. Beyond was the lake and darkness.

Someone—he did not recognize the voice—was saying in a peevish tone, "You should really maintain your property better, Taro. These boards creak alarmingly every time that fat servant steps on them."

Sakamoto sounded humble and apologetic. "I had no intention of ever using this place again after the tragedy. But the present emergency—"

There was a snort of derision.

Kumo cut in, "We all agreed that this meeting needs the privacy which only this pavilion affords."

Akitada smiled to himself and brushed off a mosquito with muddy fingers. More of the pesky insects hovered in the thin beams of light, and he considered slipping back into the water. Someone moved above, and a thin cloud of dust descended. He looked up, wondering how strong the old floor was.

They had fallen silent after Kumo's words. Someone belched loudly.

Then the first speaker—he guessed it was Taira—spoke again. "I personally saw no need for all this fuss," he said, his voice tight and bitter and the tone accusatory. "The worst possible thing you could do was to draw attention to us at this juncture. The trial is next week, and I see no reason why it should not go the way we expect. Tomo will make certain; won't you, Tomo?"

Tomo? Oh, yes. Nakatomi, the physician.

"I shall testify to nothing but the truth," a sharp, slightly nasal voice responded.

Someone muttered something.

"Yes, Tomo," drawled Kumo, "provided you can confine yourself to the cause of death."

"What else would a physician be asked about? I am not a witness or a suspect. I was not here at the time, as you recall."

"Suspect?" cried Sakamoto. "You think we are suspects? Dear heaven, has it come to that? Oh, why did this have to happen?"

"Stop that foolish whining," snapped Taira.

"What if the judge asks Nakatomi about the prince's health? What will we do then?" Sakamoto's voice was tense and worried. "He was his personal physician, after all."

"The only thing I worry about is a case of nerves like yours," Taira reproved him. "Such loss of self-control could ruin us all."

There was a gasp, then Sakamoto's trembling voice: "Forgive me, my lord. You know you can count on me. It's just that this was not in the plan."

Below, Akitada let out a soft sigh. So there had been a plan. Perhaps there still was one. But the prince's death had not been part of their scheme. What had happened?

Kumo said abruptly, "There is no need to quarrel among ourselves. It strikes me, though, that Shunsei is not here, and *him* I do worry about. He is emotional and not very bright. And he is a witness who will testify at the trial."

Taira said, "Shunsei is not here because he is no part of this and knows nothing for the reasons you have just stated. However, I have had a talk with him about his testimony."

Two people spoke up at once. Akitada could not make out their words.

Then Taira spoke slowly and clearly, as if to foolish children. "No. Shunsei is completely loyal to the prince, whom he worships even more assiduously than the Buddha. I made it clear to him that revealing any part of the prince's private life would destroy his memory. The fellow wept and swore by all that's holy that he would never besmirch the name of his beloved."

Nakatomi laughed. He said something about splitting the peach to find the Buddha, but Kumo warned, "Careful! Here comes more wine."

There was a short silence. Akitada heard the pavilion stairs groaning and creaking. Then heavy slapping steps crossed above. Apparently the fat barefooted youth had arrived to refill the wine flasks. He looked up at the black-stained boards above his head, and saw them bending. More clouds of dust descended. The thought crossed Akitada's mind that he might be crushed underneath the combined weight of the pavilion, the four conspirators, and the fat servant.

What happened was not quite that bad, but bad enough.

Sakamoto cried, "Watch out, you oaf!"

Next there was a heavy thump, and a sharp cracking sound, then a tearing and splintering. One of the wide boards split and a fat naked leg descended to the accompaniment of a terrific squeal of pain. Akitada stared at a dirty foot, dangling and twitching inches from his face. Above, all hell broke loose. Men shouted, dishes clattered, more steps caused more dust and splinters to descend. And the fat servant still wailed. He wailed steadily for more than a minute before he settled down to moaning and sobbing.

Akitada withdrew to a corner near the outer edge of the pavilion.

Upstairs, the other servant joined the fracas and shouted at the unfortunate fat youth to get his leg out of the hole. Akitada could see that the dangling limb was bleeding slightly. The fat upper thigh was held in place by a large splinter which threatened to penetrate more deeply if the leg was pulled upward. The youth explained his predicament amid loud groans and sobs.

"Well, go down there and free him," snapped Kumo.

The other servant protested shrilly that he could not swim. The lakeside balustrade creaked, and Kumo pointed out that the water was quite shallow. Kumo, and perhaps the others, were scanning the surrounding lake and shore. Akitada was trapped under the pavilion, and the surly servant was about to join him. Discovery was imminent. Keeping close to the corner support, Akitada let his body slip into the water until only his head protruded.

Sounds from the stairs suggested that some of the guests were abandoning the pavilion for safer ground from which to watch the rescue operation. Next came the telltale squelching as the servant approached through the mud from the lake side. He had to bend to squeeze under the pavilion. Akitada could see him only as a darker blob against the faintly lit grayness outside. The man muttered under his breath, then called out, "Where the devil are you? I can't see a thing."

The fat leg wiggled, and a pained voice cried, "Here. Be careful! It hurts dreadfully."

The older man found the leg and gave it an exploratory push upward, which resulted in an earsplitting scream. The rescuer abandoned the leg and splashed back to the edge of the pavilion.

"Got to cut it off," he shouted to someone on top. "I'll need a knife and a saw."

The unfortunate youth above started babbling wildly that he did not want it cut off. A lengthy discussion followed, succeeded by a tense wait during which the older servant could be heard slapping mosquitoes and muttering imprecations against gluttony and stupidity. Above, the soft sobbing and moaning continued. And Akitada waited tensely.

In time someone passed tools to the resentful rescuer below. He returned to the twitching leg and proceeded to saw and cut the boards, while the fat youth squealed and pleaded. Sakamoto added his own shouts from a safe distance, encouraging one servant while telling the other what a useless fool he was to destroy his master's property.

The time crawled for Akitada, but eventually the squealing above and cursing below stopped. The leg was free, and someone, Kumo presumably, hauled the youth out of the hole. The ill-tempered servant departed, still muttering, and silence fell.

Breathing a sigh of relief, Akitada emerged from under the pavilion. He listened and looked about. When all seemed clear, he quickly swam back into the reeds and from there to where he had left his clothes. As he dried himself with his loincloth and dressed again, the nervous tension of the past hour melted and he started shaking with laughter.

It was a while before he calmed down and realized that, for all its farcical humor, the fat youth's accident had spoiled his perfect chance to get the answers he had come for.

CHAPTER TWELVE

THE MANDALA

The following morning brought more surprises, the most disturbing of which was the disappearance of Genzo.

As instructed, Akitada had risen early. Nobody else seemed to be awake yet. After carrying wood and water into the kitchen and washing at the well, he went to the stable to saddle their horses. He wondered briefly about Genzo, but the scribe's laziness was by now so well established that he did not become suspicious until he saw Genzo's saddlebags lying empty in a corner.

He finished saddling up, then went back into the inn, where he found the sharp-tongued mother of their hostess back in charge. She merely grunted in response to his greeting. When he asked about Genzo, she gave him a blank stare. "Who's that? Another lazy layabout belonging to that piece of deadwood in there?" She jerked her head in the direction of Osawa's room.

Akitada grinned and asked if Osawa was awake.

For some reason, she flushed crimson. "If you can call it that," she snapped.

Akitada started down the corridor.

"Hey, you can't go in there now!" she shouted after him.

Ignoring her shouts, he raised his hand to open the door to Osawa's room, when he heard soft laughter inside. He smiled to himself. The middle-aged, stuffy Osawa was revealing some astonishing talents in seduction. He knocked softly and called Osawa's name. The abrupt silence inside gave way to the rustling of bedding. Osawa shouted, "What do you want?"

"I've saddled the horses, sir, but Genzo seems to have left already."

Another silence.

"Left? What do you mean, he's left? He's probably sleeping someplace, the lazy lout. Wait, Takao!"

Too late. The door opened abruptly, and Takao, looking almost pretty with her rosy flush and disordered hair, smiled up at Akitada. She clutched her loose gown to her middle, but there was little doubt that she was quite naked under it.

Osawa was sitting on his bedding and jerked up a quilt to cover his own nakedness.

When Takao stepped aside, Akitada walked in, closing the door behind himself. With a straight face he wished the inspector a very pleasant good morning and congratulated him on his amazing recovery.

"Get out!" Osawa snapped. "Can't you see I'm not . . . dressed?"

Akitada bowed to the landlady. "Your honorable mother is in the kitchen," he told her.

She rolled her eyes, then turned to Osawa and said, "Please permit me to speak to my mother, dearest heart."

He blushed and waved a languid hand.

Takao winked at Akitada, then asked Osawa coyly, "Shall I get your gruel ready, since you are in such a hurry to leave me?"

Osawa looked embarrassed. "Yes. Er, we'll talk later." When she was gone, he demanded, "Now, what is this about Genzo?"

"His saddlebags are empty. That suggests that he has left us. Perhaps he has found better employment?"

Osawa scowled. "That piece of dung?"

"I believe the last time anyone laid eyes on him was the night we arrived. He may have walked off as early as yesterday morning. If he left Minato, he is long gone, and if he stayed in town, he is keeping out of sight. What do you wish me to do?"

Osawa muttered a curse. He knew as well as Akitada that Genzo's sudden flight made it likely that someone had lured him away. True, he was not a very good scribe, but scribes were scarce. And that was not all. Working for the provincial administration, Genzo was privy to information which could be valuable to criminal gangs or pirates, and Sadoshima certainly had those. Genzo knew the size and itinerary of tax collections, the contents of granaries and the provincial treasury, and the number of guards assigned to them. That made him a valuable source of information.

"I have to bathe and eat something before we leave," Osawa grumbled. "Go into town and ask around if anyone has seen him. If you cannot find him, report him to the local warden. Make up some tale. Say he has stolen the mule."

"He hasn't stolen the mule."

"Don't be a fool," snapped Osawa. "Of course you'll have to get rid of the mule. Just let it loose someplace." He fluttered a pudgy hand in the direction of the door. "Go on! Go on!"

Osawa's manner seemed more irresponsible than usual. But then, Akitada was concerned about Genzo's whereabouts for reasons other than the security of provincial taxes. Genzo hated him and had made one attempt already to cause him harm. Akitada had expected him to retaliate before now for his humiliation at Kumo's place. Possibly Genzo's departure meant that trouble was afoot.

He walked about town for an hour or so, asking shopkeepers, monks, and market women if they had seen a big man, dressed, like Akitada, in the blue robe and black cap of a provincial clerk. No one had. Genzo had disappeared into thin air, and Akitada felt the same puzzled unease as two nights ago, when the bird-faced man had followed him through the dark streets and alleys of Minato.

Eventually he stopped at the warden's office to report him missing. He did not claim that Genzo had stolen the mule but instead suggested the possibility of foul play. The warden was unimpressed. He seemed to think that any free man working for the governor was more likely to look for better employment elsewhere.

When Akitada returned to the inn, he found Osawa and the landlady walking about the courtyard. Osawa wore his boots and traveling clothes and had the contented air of a man of means. She was dressed in another pretty gown and clung to his arm, fanning herself lightly. He was pointing at features of the inn, while she listened attentively.

"And over here an addition," he was saying, "as the family grows, you know. We wouldn't want to lose guest rooms."

She giggled, hiding her face behind the fan.

As Akitada took his puzzled gaze off the couple, he noticed the landlady's mother standing in the kitchen doorway. She waved to him, nodding her head and smiling broadly. This was so contrary to her usual behavior that he went to ask her what had happened.

"Happened?" she said vaguely, watching the couple in the courtyard. "Isn't your master a handsome figure of a man? You're lucky to be working for such a learned and dignified official."

Akitada turned to see if they were discussing the same person. The balding and round-bellied Osawa was patting the landlady's hand and whispering in her ear. Perhaps the old crone was just happy to see him depart. But there was something proprietary in the way Osawa regarded the inn, and something equally proprietary in the way its owner clutched his arm. Akitada realized that Takao had used her charms to a purpose. She needed a man, and it looked as though she had caught Osawa. Apparently he intended to give up his government job in order to run an inn and be pampered by a devoted wife. Mutobe had not only lost an undesirable scribe, but also his tax inspector.

Understandably, with a comfortable and leisurely future assured, Osawa washed his hands of Genzo and seemed to want to get through the rest of his duties as quickly as possible. He told Akitada to bring out the horses while he made his farewells to the "ladies." He probably planned to hand Mutobe his resignation as soon as they reached Mano.

Shifting their saddlebags and Genzo's empty ones to the mule, Akitada led all three animals into the courtyard. Osawa ignored the mule and climbed on his horse, waving to the women, who followed them to the gate.

It was a good day for travel. The weather continued clear and sunny, and Akitada relaxed for the first time in many days. He was glad to be rid of Genzo, whom he would have had to watch continuously. Osawa was in a pleasantly distracted mood, and Akitada felt that he had learned all he could in Minato. The rest of the puzzle would fall into place as soon as he saw Shunsei.

They headed south along the shore of the lake, the way they had come, but this time under a blue sky and with a light, refreshing wind at their backs. They trotted along easily, Osawa in front, and Akitada, leading the mule, following behind.

Osawa's riding skills had improved as much as his mood. When they had left the last houses of Minato behind and had the road to themselves, he suddenly broke into song.

> *"Ah, on Kamo beach, on Kamo beach in Sadoshima,*
> *The waves roll in and splash my love.*

Ah, on the beach, my girl, as pretty as a jewel,
As pretty as the seven precious jewels,
Beautiful from head to toe,
As we lie together on the beach,
On Kamo beach in Sadoshima."

Osawa's voice was powerful but far from melodious. He made up for this with great enthusiasm and after his rendition of "Kamo Beach" he plunged straight into "Plum Blossoms," following up with "Summer Night," "The Maiden on Mount Yoshino," and "My Recent Love Labors." Finally he rendered "Kamo Beach" a second time and turned around to ask Akitada how he liked the song.

"Very appropriate," said Akitada with a straight face, "and your voice is truly amazing."

Osawa smiled complacently. "Do you think so? Your praise is very welcome, since you are someone who has visited the capital and is bound to have heard many singers. Of course, I am strictly an amateur, but singing is a hobby of mine. Ha, ha, ha! It's very useful with the ladies sometimes."

Akitada raised his eyebrows. "I did not hear you sing to our charming hostess. Surely you made a conquest there without displaying your remarkable musical gifts."

Osawa laughed again. "I did, too. You just didn't hear me. You were at Sakamoto's. I entertained the little woman all afternoon. In fact, Takao had mentioned you playing your flute for her, so I thought I'd show her what I could do. She was impressed." He laughed again, a happy man. "How about taking out your flute now and playing along with me?"

Osawa's present good humor was an immense improvement over his previous irritability, but Akitada cringed at riding down the road while playing his flute to accompany Osawa's off-key love songs. Still, he could not offend him. He needed a free hand with Shunsei and could not hope for another distraction like a cold or an attractive landlady. So he dug the flute out of his saddlebag and played whatever suited Osawa's repertoire.

They attracted a certain amount of embarrassing notice. In one lakeside village, a group of children abandoned their games to follow them, adding their own, astonishingly rude variations to Osawa's song, and later an old woman gathering berries by the road clapped both hands over her ears as they passed. But Osawa was irrepressible.

Finally, toward noon, his throat rebelled, and they stopped for a rest at the crossroads to Tsukahara. A small grove of trees provided shade from the sun which had blazed down on them more and more fiercely as the day progressed. Osawa produced a basket of food and wine, which his betrothed and her mother had packed for him, and shared generously with Akitada while praising his bride's talents and business acumen. Then he stretched out under a pine tree for a short nap.

Akitada went to sit on a rock near the two horses and the mule, who were grazing under a large cedar. From here he had a view of the road, the lake, and the mountains embracing them from either side. Far, far in the distance lay the ocean that separated him from all that mattered to him in this world. He wished he could solve this case and return. The trouble was he seemed to be no closer to finding Okisada's murderer than before he started.

He thought about the four men in Minato and their meeting in the lake pavilion. There was no longer any doubt that they had been plotting and were still determined to rid themselves of Mutobe and son. Was Kumo planning a rebellion? Sakamoto was too weak to be more than a minor player. From the cavalier fashion in which Taira had spoken to him, it was clear that the others thought the same. Taira and Nakatomi were unknown factors. Nakatomi had sounded both sly and clever, but his relatively modest status as a mere physician made it unlikely that the others would treat him as an equal. He had probably been used only to prove that Okisada had died from young Mutobe's stew. And if so, what had Okisada really died from? And who had killed him? And why?

Akitada's thoughts turned to Taira. He had been closer to the prince than anyone else, and even the few words the man had spoken before the fat servant's accident proved that the others looked up to him. The trouble was that Taira was too old to lead a rebellion on his own account. And so Akitada came back to Kumo, a man he had come to respect, even admire. And to the prince's murder.

He shook his head, dissatisfied, and glanced up the dirt road toward Tsukahara. Buddhist monks had settled in the foothills above Tsukahara, seeking higher ground to build Konponji, their temple. Shunsei lived there. Tsukahara was close enough for Okisada's periodic visits to his friends at the lake and at least once, on his last visit, his fondness for Shunsei had caused him to bring the young monk along.

Akitada would have preferred not to probe into the details of a private love affair of two men, but Kumo had been worried that Shunsei might reveal some secret during the trial. Had the four men been talking about the fact that prince and monk had been lovers? It was possible, but given both Kumo's and Sakamoto's nervousness, Akitada suspected that there was another secret and that it had something to do with the murder.

The faint sound of rhythmic chanting caused him to look back toward the lake. He could not see who was coming, because the road disappeared around a bend. It seemed to be a day for singing, and this did not sound like a monk's chant. It grew louder, and then a strange group appeared around the trees. Two bearers, carrying a large sedan chair suspended from long poles on their shoulders, came trotting along. They were naked except for loincloths and scarves wrapped around their heads, and they chanted something that sounded like "Eisassa, eisassa." The sedan chair's grass curtains were rolled up on this warm day, and Akitada saw that it contained the hunched figure of an old man which bobbed and swung gently to the rhythm of the bearers' gait.

Sedan chairs of this size and quality were rare even in the capital, where the old and infirm preferred ox-drawn carts or carriages. But Akitada's surprise was complete when he saw who the traveler was.

The white hair and bushy black eyebrows were unmistakable. Lord Taira was on his way home from his meeting with Sakamoto and the others. Akitada got up quickly and went to busy himself with the horses, keeping his face down. The chanting stopped abruptly as the group drew level.

"Ho!" shouted Taira.

Akitada peered over his horse's crupper. The bearers had lowered their burden and were grinning. Their eyes and Taira's were on the sleeping Osawa, who lay flat on his back in the grass, his belly a gently moving mound, his eyes closed, and his mouth open to emit loud snores.

"Ho, you there," repeated Taira.

Osawa blinked, then jerked upright and stared.

"Who are you?" Taira wanted to know.

Osawa bristled and his face got red. "What business is it of yours, old man?" he snapped.

The black eyebrows beetled. "I am Taira. I asked you your name."

"Taira?" Osawa slowly climbed to his feet. "Lord Taira, the prince's tutor?"

"Yes."

Osawa bowed. "Begging your pardon, Excellency. This person has long wished to make Your Excellency's acquaintance, but has hitherto not had the pleasure. This person's humble name is Osawa, provincial inspector of taxes."

"Hah." Taira turned and craned his neck. This time he saw Akitada, who stared back at him stolidly. "You there," commanded Taira. "Come here."

Irritated by the man's manner, Akitada strolled up slowly. They measured each other. On closer inspection Taira looked not only old but frail. His back was curved and bony shoulders poked up under his robe. No wonder he traveled by sedan chair, and this one was large enough for two. Only the black eyes under those remarkable eyebrows burned with life. "Who are you?" Taira demanded.

"Er," interrupted Osawa, who had come up, not to be ignored. "Actually, he's a convict, temporarily assigned to me as my clerk. Can I be of some assistance, Excellency?"

"No," snapped Taira without taking his eyes off Akitada. After another uncomfortable moment, he said, "Move on!" to the bearers. They stopped grinning, shouldered their load, and left, falling easily into their trot and rhythmic "Eisassa" again.

Osawa stared after them. "What a rude person," he muttered. "He's an exile, of course, even if he's a lord. Ought to be more polite to someone in authority. Come to think of it, the prince used to live in Tsukahara. Wonder where Taira's been."

Akitada could have answered that, but instead he brought up Osawa's horse.

"Let's go slowly," Osawa said, as he climbed into the saddle. "I don't want to catch up with him. A dreadful old man. They say he went mad when his pupil died. It seems to be true."

"Has he always lived with the prince?"

"Oh, yes. Thought of himself as the prince's right hand, I suppose. They kept a regular court in exile. Taira would receive all visitors and instruct them about the proper respect due the prince. Complete prostration and withdrawing backwards on your hands and knees, I heard. Thank heaven, I never had to go there. Members of the emperor's family don't pay taxes. Hah! And both of them traitors." Osawa's good humor had evaporated.

Akitada also had no desire to encounter Taira. The old man's stare had been disconcerting, but he did not for a moment think the prince's tutor mad. He thought Taira had looked suspicious. On the whole, he wished they would speed up and pass the old man before he had a chance to warn Shunsei.

Fortunately, Osawa reached the same conclusion. "This is too slow," he said irritably. "Let's hurry up and get past Taira, so we'll reach Tsukahara before sunset."

It was not even close to sunset. In fact, since they had left the lake, the cool breeze had died away and now it was uncomfortably hot. They whipped up their horses and galloped past the trotting bearers and their burden in a cloud of dust.

Osawa was red-faced and sweating, but he kept up the pace, and they soon reached the foothills.

The pleasant small village of Tsukahara nestled against the mountains where the Ogura River came down and watered the rice paddies of the plain. Its two largest buildings were a shrine and the walled and gated manor of the Second Prince. The Temple of the True Lotus and its monastery were another mile up the mountain. Akitada would have liked a closer look at the prince's dwelling, but did not think it wise to be caught by Taira.

The dirt road dwindled to a track winding and climbing through the woods. It was wonderfully cool in the shade. Sometimes they heard the sound of water splashing down the mountainside.

When they reached the monastery, both riders and horses were tired. They found a small, rather humble temple compound, comprised of only seven buildings. The temple had neither gatehouse nor pagoda, and there were no walls to enclose it. Surrounded by forest trees, the halls were built of weather-darkened wood roofed with cedar bark and stood dispersed here and there among the trees wherever a piece of reasonably level ground had allowed construction. Paths and steps of flat stones connected the different levels; the approach to the main Buddha hall was a very long and wide flight of steps flanked by two enormous cedars.

It was peaceful here, and the air was fragrant with the smell of cedar and pine. Ferns and mosses grew between the stones, under the trees, and in the cedar bark of the roofs. Birds sang in the trees and monks chanted somewhere. A sense of calm descended on Akitada.

They left their horses and the mule with a shy young monk, and followed an older one to the abbot's quarters, a house so small and simple it resembled a hut. The abbot was an old man with pale, leathery skin drawn tightly over his face and shaven skull. Osawa was known to him from previous inspections, and they exchanged friendly greetings. Osawa introduced Akitada and presented the customary gift, a carefully wrapped donation of money. Then they were shown to their quarters, two small cells at the end of the monks' dormitory, and offered a bath in a small forest pond.

Osawa wrinkled his nose at the idea of bathing in a pond, but Akitada accepted eagerly. The ride had been hot and, while the air was cooler under the trees, he felt gritty and his clothes clung unpleasantly to his skin. He took a change of underclothing from his bag and walked down to the pool.

A mountain stream had been diverted to fill a small pool with constantly changing clear water. Two naked boys were already there—novices by their shaven heads. They squatted on the rocks which edged the pond, engaged in washing piles of monastic laundry. Akitada introduced himself, was told their names, that they were thirteen and fifteen years, respectively, and that he was the first visitor from the faraway capital they had ever met.

Their progress in the discipline had not yet cured them of avid curiosity about the life of the great and powerful. They chattered eagerly while Akitada stripped and plunged into the dark, clear waters of the pool. It was deliciously cool and soft on his heated body, and he splashed and swam about under the fascinated eyes of the two youngsters.

When he emerged, they expressed amazement that he could swim. He laughed and washed out his shirt and loincloth, draping them over a shrub to dry in the sunlight. Looking curiously at his lean body, they asked about his scars, and he told them—matter-of-factly, he thought—about each. To his dismay, their eyes began to shine with notions of martial adventure.

Dressed again in clean clothes and feeling a little guilty for tempting these half-trained youngsters from their peaceful life, he entertained them instead with descriptions of the religious festivals in the capital. They were grateful and trusting and readily answered his questions about their life in the monastery. Working Shunsei into this chat was not really difficult. From reminiscences about life at court it was only a short step to a casual remark about the Second Prince by one of the novices, and he was soon informed that Shunsei, who had been so signally marked by the prince's attention, was in deep mourning for his benefactor.

To do them justice, the two youngsters seemed to be completely innocent about the precise nature of the prince's attentions to Shunsei and talked away happily about their distinguished colleague.

"He stays by himself, eats nothing, and prays day and night in front of the Buddha to be transported to the Pure Land. He's very holy," confided one.

Akitada expressed a desire to meet this exemplary monk and was told that he might do so by walking a little ways up the mountain to the Hall of the Three Jewels. It seemed this had been donated to the temple by the Second Prince, who had also overseen its design and construction and had often stayed there. Shunsei apparently now lived there by himself, fasting and praying, practicing spiritual purification in an effort to approach Buddhahood. "He doesn't sleep or eat the food we take him and only drinks water," repeated the boy. "We think he'll die, but the reverend abbot says he has found enlightenment and will join the prince in the land of bliss."

Akitada refrained from snorting. The fellow, he decided, must either be demented or an arch-hypocrite. But Shunsei's isolation from the others made his own plans much easier. Had Shunsei remained a part of the monks' community, it would have been difficult to speak to him alone.

He returned to his cell and found a bowl of millet and beans and some fresh plums waiting. He ate, quenched his thirst from the water jug, and then went to Osawa. The temple collected the local taxes, and they were to examine the accounts. For Akitada this was, of course, primarily a pretext to meet Shunsei, but he had to maintain the deception a little while longer.

The newly betrothed Osawa was in no mood to look at accounts. He referred Akitada to the monk bursar and told him to take care of the matter. "Nothing to it," he assured him. "Couldn't possibly suspect the good brothers of shortchanging us. Ha, ha, ha."

As Akitada wandered about the temple grounds, peering into its halls and asking for the monk bursar, he passed a cemetery with moss-covered stone markers. The sun was setting. Its light gilded moss and stone and turned the trunks of the pine trees a tawny gold. Akitada stopped, struck by the beauty and peacefulness of the scene. Death almost seemed attractive in such a setting. Of course, monks practiced detachment from the pleasures of life and might be said to prepare themselves for the end. Was Shunsei about to join those who had gone before him because he had been too attached to a life that had become unbearably empty? Akitada shook off a shiver of panic and left the place quickly.

He found the bursar in the small library adjoining a meditation hall. A perpetually smiling man, he was eager to demonstrate the neatness of his bookkeeping, and it took Akitada a while to get rid of him so he could glance through the documents and take a few notes. His mind was not on business and he had to make an effort to give Osawa what he wanted. Fortunately, Osawa had been right and it turned out to be a simple matter.

He walked back through rapidly falling dusk and reported to the inspector, who was drinking the rest of Takao's wine and softly singing love songs. Then he set out in search of the Hall of the Three Jewels and Shunsei, unable to rid himself of an unnerving sense of urgency to be gone from Sadoshima.

The sky was still a pale lavender between the thick branches of the trees, but the forest was already plunged into darkness. Only a few glowworms glimmered in the ferns. The Hall of the Three Jewels stood on a small promontory overlooking the great central plain of Sadoshima. As the last daylight was fading, the moon rose in the eastern sky, and he could see details quite well. Though small, the hall was newer and far more elegant than any of the other monastery buildings. It was the kind of personal hermitage in which any great court noble could have felt comfortable. The mountains around the capital had many private religious retreats like this. As Akitada now knew, this one was also the love nest of the late prince.

From the forest behind him a temple bell sounded, but all was silent here; the building seemed deserted. Akitada called out Shunsei's name several times before one of the carved doors opened and a slender figure in black appeared on the threshold.

Shunsei came as something of a surprise. Akitada had expected a handsome, pampered minion, but this was an ascetic. He was small-boned, pale, and thin, his eyes overlarge in a face of childlike innocence.

"Yes?" he asked in a soft voice. "Are you lost?"

"No. My name is Taketsuna and I came to speak to you."

"I don't know you." It was a statement of fact without surprise or curiosity. Shunsei seemed indifferent rather than hostile or impatient about strange visitors.

"We have never met. I came to talk about the Second Prince. May I come in?"

Shunsei stepped aside, waited for Akitada to remove his sandals, and then led the way into a single spacious room inside. It was dark, and the young monk lit one of the tall candles in the middle of the room. By its light, Akitada saw that thick grass mats bound in fine silk covered the floor, and the built-in cabinets along the wall were decorated with ink paintings of mountain scenes. There was an altar on another wall, and against the third a shelf with books and papers. A fine desk stood in front of the fourth wall. Doors were open to a veranda overlooking a picturesque ravine that plunged down to the central plain. Beyond were the distant mountains of northern Sadoshima. The peaks stood dark against the translucent sky, and the pale moon hung above them like a large paper lantern. The view was magnificent; the occupant of this quiet retreat surveyed the world from godlike heights. Akitada reminded himself that it was the room of a dead man.

Shunsei's place in this luxurious retreat appeared to be confined to his small prayer mat before the altar. As Akitada stood gazing, the monk lit some candles there also. Suddenly glorious colors sprang to life in a room which otherwise completely lacked them. Behind a small exquisite carving of the Buddha hung a large mandala of Roshana, the Buddha of Absolute Wisdom. The painting's dominant color was a deep and brilliant vermilion, but there were contrasting areas of black and gold, as well as touches of emerald, cobalt, white, and copper. The mandala shone and gleamed in the candlelight with an unearthly beauty and was surely a treasure the temple would have been proud to display in its Buddha Hall. But here it was, the private object of worship of a prince and his lover.

The symbolic connection between the Buddha and Okisada, once emperor-designate, was instantly clear to Akitada. On the mandala, the Buddha occupied the very center and was surrounded by concentric rings of petals of the lotus flower, representing an enormous spiritual hierarchy; each petal contained a figure, from the Buddha's own representations to hundreds of increasingly smaller saints, each representing multiple worlds. The court had always perceived an analogy between this Buddha and the emperor who, surrounded by his great ministers, each in charge of his own department of lesser officials, ruled the lives of the people down to the least significant persons in the realm. When the emperor was a descendant of gods, the religious hierarchy validated the secular one. Okisada had certainly not lost his delusions of godlike majesty in exile.

But what of Shunsei? Apparently the young monk now spent his days and nights in front of the mandala. Praying? Grieving for his lover? Meditating in an effort to achieve enlightenment? Or atoning for a mortal sin?

The monk stood, waiting passively, patiently, his eyes lowered and his hands folded in the sleeves of his black robe. Up close, he was older than Akitada had at first thought. He must be well into his thirties, no boy but a mature man. He also looked frail and ill, as if the childish flesh had fallen away, the soft skin had lost its healthy glow, and the rounded contours of cheek and chin had disappeared to leave behind the finely drawn features of total abstinence. Startlingly, the very large, soft, and long-lashed eyes and the softly curving lips were still there and powerfully sensual in the pale, thin face.

Shunsei raised those tender liquid eyes to Akitada's. "Would you like to sit down?" he asked in the same soft voice. "I have only water to offer you."

"Thank you. I need nothing." Akitada seated himself on the mat and gestured toward the mandala. "I have never seen a more beautiful painting of Roshana," he said.

"He sent for it when he built this hall. Now I pray to him. Perhaps, someday soon, he will allow me to join him."

Somehow this strange statement made sense. Shunsei's identification of the Buddha with the late prince might have been the result of excessive grief, but Akitada suspected that Okisada had planted the seed of worship in the young monk's mind a long time ago. For the first time he wondered about Okisada's physical appearance. He must have been old enough to be Shunsei's father. Of course, Shunsei himself looked deceptively young because of his small size and dainty shape. The only imperial princes Akitada had met had been portly men of undistinguished appearance. How, then, had Okisada attracted such deep devotion in his lover unless it was through linking physical lust to spiritual worship? The thought was disturbing, and Akitada glanced away from those soft eyes and curving lips to the Roshana Buddha.

"What do you wish to know?" the soft voice asked.

Akitada pulled his thoughts together. He had a murder to solve and a conspiracy to prevent. "Tell me about him," he begged.

"Why?"

Akitada phrased his response carefully. "I have been sent here. In the capital his death will raise questions. I have already spoken to the high constable and Professor Sakamoto and I have listened to Lord Taira and the prince's physician, but still some of the answers escape me."

It was surprising how easily these half-truths came to his tongue, and amazing how this simple monk accepted them without question. He even smiled a little. "Yes, they all loved him," he said with a nod, "but not the same as I. We, he and I, became as one when we were together. When he entered the dark path, I wished to join him but couldn't. Not then, but soon now." He nodded again and looked lovingly at the altar.

"Will you tell me about it?"

"Yes. It is good that they should know in the capital. That his family should know, and the whole world. You see, he knew the great transformation was approaching. At first he thought it was just an indisposition. He called his doctor in and took medicine, and when the pains got very bad he would come to me, and I would chant as I rubbed his back and his aching belly."

Akitada stared at Shunsei. He had a strange sense that the floor beneath him had lost its solidity and there was nothing to hold on to. "The prince was ill?" he asked.

"At first that was what we thought, he and I. I gave him relief, he said, but now I know the great transformation had already begun. The pain came more and more often, until he wished for release from this world. I thought my weak prayers had failed, and lost my faith." He hung his head and looked down at his hands, which rested in his lap.

Dazedly Akitada followed his glance. Beautiful hands, he thought, long-fingered and shapely, covered with the same translucent skin as his face. Curled together, they lay passively where once, no doubt, the dead lover's hands had roamed, where Shunsei and Okisada had found the center of their universe together. The thought was disturbingly erotic, and Akitada felt hot and ashamed. He shifted to look back at the mandala. Death, religious ecstasy, and sexual arousal were perhaps not far apart. The thought would be rejected as blasphemous by most, but here was at least one man who, in the simplicity of his faith and because of repressed desires, had equated physical lovemaking with spiritual worship. How could you judge a man's faith?

Was this the secret the others had wanted to hide at all cost? That the prince had died from a severe and protracted illness? That would destroy the case against Mutobe and his son.

But what of the poisoned dog? Or had there been a dog? Perhaps that was a lie, too. Or the dog had been poisoned as an afterthought. And then another, more terrible thought entered Akitada's mind. What if Okisada had become ill because someone had administered poison to him over a period of time? Shunsei's account of Okisada's "transformation" could describe the effects of systematic poisoning, and his death in the pavilion would have marked the final dose. That would also clear young Mutobe, who could not have had the opportunity to administer all the prior doses. But why kill Okisada, whose return to imperial power had been the object of the plot? Was there someone else who wished Okisada dead? Akitada shook his head in confusion.

Shunsei's soft sigh brought him back. The monk said gravely, "Do not doubt the miracle, as I did. He achieved what we had both prayed for, a state of blessedness, a cessation of pain. I know, for he has come and told me so."

Akitada looked at Shunsei's deep-set, feverish eyes and felt a great pity. This man was dying himself, by his own choice, and in the final stages of starvation and meditation he must have been hallucinating.

Kumo, Taira, and Sakamoto need not worry about his testimony. Shunsei would not live long enough to travel to Mano. Of course, there was still Nakatomi. They had wanted the physician to testify only to the cause of death, and not touch on the prince's prior state of health. They had known of his illness. But Akitada's eavesdropping had convinced him that his death had shocked and surprised them. Sakamoto in particular had complained bitterly about it. Only one fact was certain: they all wanted the governor's son convicted of murder as soon as possible.

Shunsei still sat quietly looking down at his hands.

"You knew he would die?" Akitada asked.

The monk raised his eyes and smiled sweetly. "Oh, yes. Only not so soon."

"And young Mutobe? Is he to die also?"

The smile faded to sadness. "If it is his karma. We all must die."

Akitada gritted his teeth. A moment ago he thought he had his answer, but Shunsei seemed to have changed his mind again. Perhaps he was dealing with a madman after all. He looked long into Shunsei's eyes. Impossible to tell. The large black orbs gazed back calmly.

"But you do not believe that he murdered the prince?" Akitada finally asked bluntly.

Shunsei smiled again. "He assisted in the transformation," he corrected.

"What? How?"

"He helped him achieve nirvana more quickly."

Akitada staggered to his feet. He had failed. Shunsei, who had been present, truly believed that young Mutobe had poisoned Okisada. "Thank you," he muttered, and bowed.

Shunsei also rose. He swayed a little as if light-headed. "Thank you for coming," he said politely. "Please tell them what I said. His memory will be sacred forever."

Blindly, Akitada walked to the door, followed by Shunsei. On the steps, he turned one more time to look back at the other man, who stood on the veranda, supporting himself against a column. The moon cast an eerie whiteness over his face, sharpening the angles of the underlying skull and turning the eyes into fathomless pools of darkness.

On some strange impulse, Akitada said, "I was told the prince enjoyed *fugu*. Did he, by any chance, eat some the day he died?"

This time, Shunsei's smile broke the spell of strangeness and made him almost human again. "Oh, yes. The blowfish. He sent me to the fisherman's wife for it. He was not well and wished to be strong for the meeting. He always enjoyed *fugu*, but since his illness he also derived relief from it."

Akitada reached for the railing. "But . . . no *fugu* was served to the others."

"Oh, no. He prepared it himself in his room and carried a small dose with him. He was very familiar with the preparation." Shunsei pressed his palms together and bowed. Then he disappeared back into the room, extinguishing the lights until all was plunged into darkness again.

Akitada groped his way back to the monks' dormitory, his mind as murky as the darkness of the forest around him. Had Okisada died by accidentally poisoning himself?

Or had he committed suicide to escape the torment of his pain?

CHAPTER THIRTEEN

LIEUTENANT WADA

Akitada woke. At first he was not certain what had disturbed his sleep because all was dark and silent. He turned over, but the memories of the previous day began to crowd in. It was finally over and soon he would be home. The prince had taken the poison himself. Okisada might have mistaken the dosage or, in the knowledge of a slow and increasingly painful death, decided to end it quickly, but ultimately it did not matter. He was dead, all danger of his leading another rebellion was over, and the conspiracy against the governor would fall apart as soon as the fact was known. True, Shunsei's condition was worrisome, but there was at least one other person who knew that the prince had eaten blowfish: his regular supplier, Haru.

He sat up and stretched. Hearing soft noises next door in Osawa's room, he got up, opened the door, and peered out. It was still night in the forest, but the sky above the trees was already turning the deep blue-black which precedes dawn, and a few birds chirped sleepily.

It was unusual for Osawa to rise this early, but he, too, now had someone to rush back to. Akitada smiled, yawned, and took a few deep breaths of the pine-scented air. It was deliciously cool and he hated to leave the woods for the hot plain again, but tonight they would be back in Mano.

Akitada looked at Osawa's closed door and decided to get dressed. If Osawa was in such a hurry, he was not going to delay him. The sooner he could settle this affair and leave Sadoshima, the better. He longed for his family with an almost painful intensity.

After lighting the oil lamp, he reached for the blue robe he had been wearing for days. It looked and smelled the worse for the hard wear. In his bag was still his own robe of plain brown silk, the one he had arrived in and which had been stained and torn during those first appalling days. He shook his head at the memory of the misery suffered by convicts.

He rolled up the blue robe and shook out the brown one after removing the flute from its folds. Surely Osawa would not mind if he put on clean clothes for the trip back. They had no more official calls to make on the way.

The silk robe was a little creased, but it looked and smelled a great deal better than the blue one. He slipped it on and fastened the black sash about his waist. Reaching up to adjust the collar, he touched the stiffness of the documents between the layers of fabric. They, too, would soon no longer be needed. He thought guiltily of Masako, who had not only nursed him back to health, but had washed and mended his clothes. He was ashamed of having rejected her affection so harshly. Tonight he would speak to her, explain his situation, and offer her . . . what? He thought he would know once he knew her real feelings for him.

Smoothing down the familiar cool silk, he felt relief that it was over. The judge, once informed of the facts, would know what questions to ask. If Shunsei was too weak to travel, he could sign an affidavit. Taira would be called to testify, and Haru. Nakatomi would be forced to speak about Okisada's illness. Finally, Sakamoto would be confronted with the mass of evidence, and he would break and reveal the plot to build a murder case against the governor's son. Yes, it should all unravel nicely, even without Shunsei's presence.

He used his fingers to comb his beard and hair, retied his topknot, and checked the neck of his robe again. It bulged a bit, refused to lie down flat. He patted the fabric down firmly, but it still buckled. With his index finger he checked the seam where he had inserted the documents and found it torn.

His heart pounding, Akitada fished out the papers and unfolded them. For a long time he stared in disbelief at the blank sheets of ordinary paper.

He turned them this way and that, wondering foolishly if the august words had somehow faded, not wanting to believe the obvious, that someone had stolen his imperial orders and the governor's safe conduct, and with them his identity.

Sweat broke out on his forehead. He tried to remember when he had last seen the documents. They had still been there after he left Mano, after Masako had found them without realizing what they were.

Or perhaps she had realized only too well! For the documents to have been stolen from such a hiding place, the thief must have known what to look for and where. Had Masako revealed his secret, perhaps unintentionally?

If so, he had been allowed to leave Mano with the documents. Yes, the papers had still been in his robe on the road to Kumo's manor. Later he had worn his blue clerk's robe and, foolishly, he had only checked the documents by touch, and not often that. Where had the theft happened? At Kumo's manor or in Minato? He had slept with the saddlebags under his head in the groom's room and also later in Takao's kitchen, but there had been many times when his saddlebags had lain somewhere while he was doing Osawa's bidding. He had worried more about the flute than the documents.

Anyone could have removed the papers anywhere between Minato and here, but surely the most likely thief was Genzo.

Seimei would say, "Spilled water does not return to its pail." It was more important to think about what would happen next.

He could not raise an outcry. What could Osawa do, even if he believed him? No, he must return to Mano as quickly as possible. Thank heaven Mutobe had seen the papers and could vouch for him.

Akitada packed the blue robe, the flute, and his other belongings into his saddlebags and walked through the waking forest to the monastery stable to saddle the horses. But there a second shock awaited him.

A distraught Osawa was getting in the saddle, while a red-cheeked novice was holding the reins and listening to Osawa's agitated instructions with an expression of blank confusion on his young face.

"Why the rush, Master Osawa?" Akitada called out.

Osawa turned. "Oh, there you are. Good. I have no time. I'm off to Minato this instant. Takao's had an accident. Very bad. You must go on to Mano. There"—he flung a hand toward a small pile of boxes and bundles—"are the records. All of them. Also my letter of resignation. Make my excuses to the governor." He pulled the reins from the novice's hand and dug his heels in the horse's flank.

"Wait . . ." cried Akitada, but Osawa was already cantering down the forest path at breakneck speed, the skirts of his gown fluttering behind him as he disappeared around the first bend of the track.

Akitada and the novice looked at each other. The novice shrugged and smiled.

"What happened?" Akitada asked.

"Not sure. I couldn't understand the gentleman too well. He came rushing up to the stable, shouting for his horse. I didn't know which one, and he was jumping up and down, crying it was a matter of life and death. I finally found the right horse, and he had all these instructions. For you, I suppose. I didn't really understand them at all."

"But how . . . ? Did a messenger arrive for him?"

The novice nodded. "A man came on a horse and asked the way to the gentleman's room. I took his horse and showed him."

"His name?"

The youngster looked blank again. "I didn't ask. He was short and had a nose like a beak."

Akitada stared down the path Osawa had taken. So the bird-faced man had reappeared. He wished Osawa had knocked on his door or at least discussed the matter before taking off so precipitously.

"Get my horse," he told the novice, then changed his mind. "Never mind. I'll do it." He ran to the stable. Dropping his saddlebags on the ground beside the mule, he threw blanket and saddle on his horse, which sensed his agitation and sidestepped nervously. The young monk came to lend a hand. Leading the horse out, Akitada told him, "I'll be back. Load the mule in the meantime!" Then he swung himself into the saddle and kicked his heels into the animal's flanks.

He plunged down the path after Osawa, bent forward, his eye on the path, worried that his mount might stumble and hurt itself but almost hoping that Osawa, not the best rider, had been thrown. No such luck. The ground leveled, and Tsukahara lay ahead, and beyond stretched the empty road. Akitada reined in and turned back. He could not catch up with Osawa without injuring his animal, and he needed it to get to Mano as quickly as possible.

He worried briefly about what the unsuspecting Osawa might be running into, hoping it had nothing to do with the theft of his papers. But he did not believe in coincidence and knew better. In any case, the urgency of reaching Mano had just increased a hundredfold. The message to Osawa was almost certainly a fabrication, Takao's accident trumped up to send Osawa back to Minato, leaving Akitada unaccompanied and without papers. For a prisoner to be caught without proper documentation while in possession of an official's property was enough to subject him at the very least to the most severe and painful interrogation. His only safety lay in reaching provincial headquarters before he was stopped.

Back at the monastery stables, the young monk had the mule ready, and Akitada asked directions to Mano. He would have to go down the mountain to Tsukahara again, he was told, and from there take a road southwestward along the foot of the mountains. "Not far!" the novice said with a cheerful smile. "Only a day by horse."

Only a day!

Akitada left the monastery, convinced he was riding into an ambush. Saving his horse and the laden mule, he descended the mountain much more slowly this time. His eyes roamed ahead constantly, and he worried about every bend in the road, keeping his ears alert for the sound of weapons and armor, knowing that he had nothing with which to defend himself.

He reached the valley safely, but Tsukahara, the home of Lord Taira, was the next danger spot. He passed through the village quickly, keeping a wary eye out, suspecting even a harmless group of poor farmers who had gathered before the shrine. But they merely turned and stared at him in the way of country people who see few strangers. When Akitada found the crossroads to Mano, he left Tsukahara behind, breathing more easily.

If he had been familiar with the island, he would have tried to find a less obvious route. He could not rid himself of the conviction that, after the unnatural calm of the past days, his enemies were about to act. Whoever had arranged to steal his papers and send Osawa back to Minato knew very well who Taketsuna really was and why he was in Sadoshima. He or they would hardly let him live. The most frustrating thing was that he still did not know exactly with whom he was dealing.

Toward noon of a tense but uneventful journey, Akitada became aware of hunger. In his rush, he had left the monastery without eating or taking provisions for the day. Though he still had a few coppers, he did not dare use them. But when the road crossed a stream, he broke his journey. He took some of the baggage off the mule—an astonishingly well behaved creature—and led both animals, one after the other, down to the water.

Then he searched the saddlebags for food and came up with Osawa's silk pouch full of coins and a stale and misshapen rice dumpling left over from some earlier picnic. The money he put back, shaking his head. Osawa had been truly upset, to go off without his funds. Having eaten the dumpling and drunk his fill from the stream, he loaded the mule again and returned to the road.

By now he was puzzled that he had been allowed to get this far. There were few other travelers on the road, and none gave him a second glance on the final stretch to Mano. When the road turned westward, the sun sank blindingly low and horse and mule showed the first signs of fatigue. But he passed over the last hillock and saw Sawata Bay spread before him, a sheet of molten gold. The huddle of brown roofs that was Mano was little more than a mile away. He had done it. Possibly there was some slight danger still as he passed through town, but by then he would be too close to provincial headquarters to suffer more than a minor delay until Mutobe was notified.

Blinking against the brightness of sun and sea, he tried to increase his speed to a canter, but the mule finally balked. He pulled on its lead; it snorted and shook its head and tried to dig in its hooves.

Preoccupied with the recalcitrant beast, Akitada did not see the men stepping from the trees up ahead. When he did, his stomach lurched. Still blinded by the sun, he squinted at them. There were six, all brawny men with hard faces and some sort of weapon in their hands. Highway robbers? Pirates on a landfall? Akitada stopped his horse and peered at them. Their clothes looked rough but serviceable, too good for robbers or pirates. And there was a certain uniformity about them. All wore brown jackets with leather belts about their middle and a chain wrapped about that. Constables?

Then a familiar red-coated figure stepped out into the road to wait, legs apart and arms folded, in front of the six men in brown. He was armed with sword and long bow. Wada. The law. He would be arrested and escorted to the provincial jail. Akitada almost smiled with relief.

Urging his horse forward, he stopped before Wada. His relief faded a little when he saw the man's face.

An unpleasant smile twitched the lieutenant's thin mustache. "Ah," he said, "what have we here? A convict, and in possession of a horse and a mule. We met only recently, I believe, and already I find you a runaway?"

"I did not run away, Lieutenant. I've been on an assignment for the governor and am on my way back." Akitada glanced over his shoulder and added, "I would be glad of an escort, though. Someone may be trying to kill me."

Wada guffawed and turned to his constables, who grinned. "Did you hear that? Someone's trying to kill him! He's funny, this one. Says he's on official business and wants a police escort, what?"

They burst into laughter.

"Silence!" barked Wada.

The laughter stopped abruptly. The way they looked at him reminded Akitada of a pack of hungry dogs who had found a helpless rabbit.

Wada seemed to be enjoying himself. "The fun's over. Who would send a convict on a trip with a horse and a mule and all sorts of valuable equipment?" he sneered, then waved his men forward. "Search him and the saddlebags."

The constables jumped into action. In a moment, Akitada was pulled from his horse and pushed into the dirt. Two men knelt on him, pulling his arms behind his back and wrapping a thin chain around both wrists. It was standard procedure in the apprehension of criminals, but he had never realized how painful tightly wrapped chain could be and gritted his teeth to keep from crying out. He had to remain calm at all cost. Wada, no matter how ruthless he was in his treatment of convicts and how stupid he might be in this instance, was still an official, and one who had been appointed to his present position by someone in authority. He was doing his duty in arresting the supposed escapee. The problem could be worked out later. The important thing was to be cooperative and not give the man an excuse for more physical abuse.

They pulled him to his feet and searched him. The imperial documents being lost, along with Mutobe's safe-conduct, Akitada submitted meekly, which did not prevent them from pummeling and kicking him a few times.

They found nothing, but the mule's burden caused an outcry. "Papers," cried one of the searchers. "A flute," cried another, tossing Ribata's precious instrument to Wada. Akitada winced, but Wada caught it, glanced at it incuriously, and tossed it back. This time the flute fell between the mule's hooves, and Akitada instinctively moved to rescue it. He was jerked back instantly and painfully.

Wada cried, "Wait. It must be valuable. Pick it up. What else is there?"

"This, Lieutenant," cried a man triumphantly, holding up Osawa's silk pouch and jingling it. "He's a thief, all right." Akitada silently cursed Osawa's forgetfulness.

Wada rushed over. He opened the pouch, shook out and counted the silver and copper, and then extracted some papers. "Belongs to a man called Osawa," he said. "A provincial inspector of taxes." He almost purred when he asked Akitada, "What did you do with him?"

"Nothing. Osawa had to go back to Minato and sent me on by myself." Akitada knew how this must sound, but was shocked by the viciousness of Wada's reaction. Wada snatched one of the short whips from a constable's leather belt and lashed him across the face with it. The pain was much sharper than he could have imagined. Tears blinded his eyes, and he heard Wada sneer, "I warned you that the fun is over. You don't listen well, do you?"

Akitada was seized by an unreasoning fury. The insult was too much. He would kill the man, but not now, not while Wada had the upper hand. Focusing was difficult. He blinked away the tears. His face was bleeding, and he licked the salty drops from his lips. "Lieutenant," he forced himself to beg, "please take me to the governor. He'll explain."

"The governor?" Wada's eyes grew round with pretended shock. "You want me to trouble the governor with this? You think he likes me to bring him every robber, thief, and killer we catch?"

"I did not rob, steal, or kill anyone," Akitada began again, but it was useless.

"Enough chatter!" snapped Wada. "Take him into those woods over there. We'll soon sort out what he's done with the body of this Osawa."

It was getting out of hand. Once the sadistic Wada and his thugs got him out of sight of passersby, it would be too late to remonstrate. "Lieutenant," Akitada said, drawing himself up as much as he could under the circumstances. "You are making a mistake. I am not a convict, but a government official. I demand that you take me to Governor Mutobe this instant."

Wada chuckled. "You've got to give it to him. He's pretty good," he said to his men, who guffawed again. "All right. Let's show him some fun!" He marched ahead toward a cluster of trees, and Akitada's guards obliged with some well-placed kicks to his lower back which sent him staggering after Wada.

Dear heaven, he thought, as he stumbled toward the woods, let me get out of this alive and I'll never be off my guard again. He recalled vividly the battered face and body of little Jisei. Staring at Wada's swaggering back, he tried to think of some way to talk himself out of this. Then he glanced at the constable who held his chain, wondering about an evasive action he could take to escape. At least his legs were not tied. Maybe he could pull the chain out of his guard's hand and run. Wada had a bow and arrows. Still, it was worth a try if nothing else offered.

"Lieutenant," he called out, "if you will stop this nonsense, I'll explain before it is too late. There are matters you're not aware of, and they will be easy enough to verify."

Wada did not stop.

They passed into the trees, and the constables moved in more closely until they reached a clearing, and Akitada saw their horses and a small pile of wooden cudgels near a tree. Cudgels? The moment he realized they had been prepared for him, he exploded into action. Kicking out at the constable on his right, he flung himself forward, feeling the chain bite his wrists and his arms jerking up under the strain. His shoulders were almost wrenched from their sockets, but he pulled away with all his strength, knowing that if he did not get free, much worse awaited him.

And he almost made it. In the confused shouting and angry cries, he felt the chain slacken and took off, twisting past one of the constables to loop back toward the road, dodging another man, and thinking of Wada, who was probably placing an arrow into the groove of his bow even then. He dodged again, a tree this time, and then the chain caught on something, and he fell forward, his face slamming into a tree root.

After that, he had no more chances. They took him back to the clearing and lashed the chain around a large cedar. A cut he had suffered in the fall was bleeding into his right eye, and his left eye was swelling shut because the constable he had kicked had returned the favor. But he glimpsed—and wished he had not—the neat pile of sticks and cudgels and the constables arming themselves before they formed a circle around him. They were going to have their fun.

His chain was loose enough to allow him some minimal dodging. Wada stood off to the side, his face avid with anticipation.

"So," he said, stroking his skimpy mustache with a finger. "Let's get started. Where is the body of the man you killed?"

Akitada saw no need to reply. He kept his eyes on the constables.

"Very well," said Wada, and the first man stepped forward and swung.

Akitada dodged, and the end of the stick merely brushed his hip. Not too bad, he thought.

Wada shook his head. "Go on. All of you. At this rate we'll be here till midnight."

What followed was systematic and practiced. As one man stepped forward and swung, Akitada dodged and was met by the full force of the cudgel of the man at the other end. The blows landed everywhere on his body, but for some reason they avoided his head, which he could not in any case have protected. The pain of each blow registered belatedly. The full sensation was blocked by his concentration on dodging the next one, but this did not last long. He had never been so totally at the mercy of an enemy. The experience was simultaneously humbling and infuriating. It became vital not to disgrace himself. In an effort to distance himself from his pain, he thought of playing his flute. Concentrating on a passage which always gave him trouble, he played it in his mind, allowing his body to move by instinct.

Time passed. Perhaps not much, perhaps a long time. Eventually one of the sticks broke, and once Akitada stumbled and fell to his knees. He ducked in time, or the swinging cudgel might have hit his head. Somehow he got back on his feet, and once he even landed a kick to the groin of one of the men who had strayed a bit too close. But he was quickly wearing out, and his mental flute-playing disintegrated in hot flashes of agony. Parts of him had gone numb. One arm was on fire with pain that ran all the way from his shoulder to his hand. Then one of the cudgels connected with his right knee, and he forgot the other pains and his pride. He screamed and fell.

Mercifully they stopped then—though there was no mercy about it, really. Wada walked over and kicked him in the ribs. "Get up!"

"I can't," muttered Akitada through clenched teeth.

They jerked him upright. He screamed again as he put weight on his injured knee and both knees buckled.

"Silence!"

Wada was listening toward the road. At a sign from him, his men dropped Akitada. This time they left him lying there as they walked away. Through waves of torment he heard someone leaving on a horse but did not care.

The grass under Akitada's face became sticky with the blood from his cut and clung to his skin, but his mind was on his knee. Compared with that even the multiple bruises on the rest of his body, which had combined to form a solid robe of pain, paled. He wondered if his knee was broken and tried to move his leg. The effort was inconclusive. All feeling seemed to have left it. He turned the ankle, and was successful this time, but feeling returned with a vengeance, running all the way from the knee down to his foot. He held his breath, waiting for the spasm to pass.

As the agony in the knee ebbed away slowly, he checked the damage to the rest of his body. His fingers moved, though the skin on his wrists felt raw. Never mind! That was nothing. His shoulders? Painful, but mobile. Ribs and back? He attempted a stretch and managed it without suffering the kinds of spasm a broken rib produces. The knee remained the problem. He could not stand or walk, and that made eventual flight impossible.

Having got that far, he considered Wada and his thugs. Were they planning to kill him? Since they had brutalized him in this manner, they would not let him live if they feared him. He was glad now that he had not told Wada his name. As long as the man believed he was an escaped convict, he had a chance. He heard the horseman returning and twisted his head to look. Wada dismounted. He was giving orders, speaking to the constables separately until each man nodded. Akitada tried to guess where he had been and what these orders were by reading expressions and gestures. The faces were mostly glum. Wada looked determined, but his men were not happy with whatever they were to do. Akitada took courage from this.

After a while, four of the constables left on foot, leading the mule. Wada was busy talking to the two men who were left. Their faces got longer and longer, and they cast angry looks in

Akitada's direction. Finally they walked off also, and Wada came toward him alone.

The short police officer paused beside him and looked down with an unreadable expression. Panic seized Akitada. He croaked, "Let me go. I won't report you. If anybody asks, you can claim you had provocation because I tried to escape."

Wada chuckled. It was a very unpleasant sound. "No," he said. "You are to disappear. Mind you, if it had been my choice, you'd have disappeared permanently here today, but . . ." He used his foot to roll Akitada on his back. "Sit up!"

Akitada struggled into a sitting position, and his knee promptly went into another spasm. He doubled over with the pain and gasped.

Wada bent down and roughly straightened the injured leg. When Akitada turned a scream into a groan, Wada laughed. "You pampered nobles are all alike, Sugawara," he said, probing the knee with pleasure in the torment he caused his prisoner. "You turn into whimpering babes at the first little pain. This is nothing but a bruise, but I'm in a hurry, so you can ride."

Pain and humiliation registered first. Akitada clenched his jaws to keep from groaning as Wada poked, turned, and twisted. He would not give the bastard the satisfaction of mocking him again.

But then, sweat-drenched and dazed, he opened his eyes wide and stared up at Wada. "What . . . did you call me?"

Wada rose and looked down at his prisoner with smug triumph. "Sugawara? Yes, I know you're not the Yoshimine Taketsuna you pretended to be when you got off the ship. Oh, no. You're Sugawara Akitada, an official from Echigo, come to catch us fools at our misdeeds. Look who's the fool now!" He bent until his face was close to Akitada's. "This is Sadoshima, my lord, not the capital. You made a bad mistake when you became a convict and put yourself into our hands."

So. The charade was over.

"Since you know who I am and why I am here," Akitada snapped coldly, "you also know that continuing this will cost you your life."

Wada threw back his head and laughed. "You still don't get it," he cried, pointing an exulting finger at Akitada. "It's not my life, but yours that's lost. Quick or slow, you'll die. Have no doubt about that. We'll take you to a place you won't leave alive and where it won't matter how loudly you proclaim your name, your rank, and your former position, for nobody will come to your rescue." Still laughing and shaking his head, he walked away.

Surprisingly, Akitada's only reaction was relief that he no longer needed to pretend. While he had not precisely disliked the convict Taketsuna, Taketsuna had been a man who had humbled himself with a cheerfulness which had cost Akitada such effort that he had become both foolish and careless about other matters. No wonder a creature like Wada sneered.

He considered his next step. Of course, there was no longer any doubt that Wada was part of the conspiracy. Akitada had not missed Wada's use of the word "we" when he had talked about his prisoner's future. Whoever had arrived and given Wada his orders had, for some reason, decided that a slow death was preferable to a quick demise. That was interesting in itself, but more immediately it meant he had gained precious time. Had Wada continued the beating, he could not have saved himself. Now, however unpleasant the immediate future, he might get another chance to escape.

Apparently he would be moved soon, and far enough to make riding necessary. He looked at his swollen knee. The pain was fading a little. Wada's manipulation had not necessarily reassured him that nothing was broken, though. He must try to move it as little as possible. At the moment, when even the smallest jolt caused shooting pains all the way up his thigh and down his leg, he was not tempted. He wriggled his wrists again. Was the chain looser than before?

They were coming back, Wada and two constables, each leading a saddled horse. Wada got in his saddle and watched as the two men untied Akitada's chain from the tree and then led a horse over. Three horses and four men? Was one of the constables expected to run alongside?

On the whole, while they looked sullen, their treatment of him on this occasion showed a marked improvement. They lifted him into the saddle, a process which was only moderately painful because they allowed him to clutch his knee until he could prop his foot into the stirrup. Their consideration made him wonder what he was being saved for. Once he was in the saddle, they briefly freed his wrists to rechain them in front so he could hold the reins.

To all of this Akitada submitted passively and without comment. He felt as weak as a newborn. All his strength was focused on protecting the injured knee. He realized that, even supported by the stirrup, his leg would respond to every step of the horse, and that the journey, possibly a long one, might make him reconsider the option of a quick death.

But before they could start, there was another shout from the road. Wada stiffened. "Keep an eye on him," he snapped, and cantered off.

Two thoughts occurred to Akitada: Someone, foe or friend, was on the road. And the two constables were not as watchful as they should be, because they took the opportunity of Wada's absence to get into a bitter argument about who was riding the third horse. He would not get another chance like this.

Kicking the horse as hard as he could with his good leg, he took off after Wada. His knee spasmed, behind him the constables shouted, before him branches whipped at his face, but he burst into the open at a full gallop. Wada was on the road, talking to another rider. He turned, his mouth sagging open in surprise. Then he flung about his horse to intercept him.

But Akitada's eyes had already moved to the other man. Kumo. He made a desperate attempt to wheel away, but his injured leg refused to cooperate. The horse, confused by mixed signals, stopped and danced, and Wada kept coming. In an instant they faced each other. Wada, his sword raised, looked murderous. At the last moment, Akitada raised his chained hands to catch the descending blade in the loop of chain between them. The force of the strike jerked him forward and sideways. Miraculously, he caught the reins and clung on as his horse reared and shot forward. Then another horse closed in, they collided, and both animals reared wildly.

This time, he was flung off backward, and landed hard. For a single breath, he looked up at the blue sky, tried to hold back the darkness that blotted out the day, tried to deny the pain, the fear of dying, and then he fell into oblivion.

CHAPTER FOURTEEN

TORA

Almost a month after the arrival of Yoshimine Taketsuna on Sado Island, another ship from Echigo brought a young man in military garb. Under the watchful eyes of several people, the new arrival made his way from the ship to a small wine shop overlooking Mano Harbor. He was a handsome fellow with white teeth under a trim mustache, and he wore his shiny new half armor and sword with a slight swagger. A scruffy individual in loincloth and tattered shirt limped behind him with his bundle of belongings.

The rank insignia on the visitor's breastplate marked him as a lieutenant of the provincial guard. Both the iron helmet with its small knobs and the leather-covered breastplate shone with careful waxing. Full white cotton trousers tucked into black boots and a loose black jacket covered his broad shoulders.

He took a seat on one of the benches outside the shop and removed his helmet, mopping it and his sweaty brow with a bright green cloth square he carried in his sleeve. Then he pounded his fist on the rough table. His bearer limped over and squatted down on the ground beside him.

"Hey," growled the officer, "you can't sit here. Go over there where I don't have to smell you."

Obediently the man got up and moved.

"Miserable wretches don't know what respect is," grumbled the new arrival, and eyed the bearer's bony frame with a frown. Surely the man was over forty, he thought, too old for hard physical labor. Besides, he was crippled. One of his legs was shorter than the other. Worse, the fellow looked starved, with every rib and bone trying to work its way through the leathery skin.

He turned impatiently and pounded the table again. A fat, dirty man in a short gown and stained apron appeared in the doorway and glared into the sun. Seeing the helmet and sword, he rushed forward to bow and offer greetings to the honorable officer.

"Never mind all that," said his guest. "Bring me some wine and give that bearer over there something to eat and some water to drink. If I don't feed him, he'll collapse with my bundle."

The officer was Tora, normally in charge of the constables at the provincial headquarters of Echigo, but now on a mission to find his master.

Glancing about him, he rubbed absentmindedly at the red line the heavy helmet had left on his forehead. Made of thick iron and lined with leather, even half armor was heavy and uncomfortable, but his was new and he was still inordinately proud of it.

The owner of the wine shop returned with the order. He set a flask and cup down on the table and turned to take a chipped bowl filled with some reeking substance to the bearer, when Tora clamped an iron fist around his arm.

"What is that stinking slop?" he demanded.

"Er, fish soup, sir."

Tora sniffed. "It stinks," he announced, and jerked the man's arm, spilling the soup in a wide arc into the street. Immediately seagulls swooped down with raucous cries to fight over the scattered morsels. He growled, "Get fresh food or I'll put my fist into that loose mouth of yours."

"Yes, sir, right away, sir," gasped the man, rubbing his wrist and backing away. From a safe distance, he pleaded, "But he's only a beggar. Lucky to get anything. I wouldn't have charged much."

"What?" roared Tora, rising to his feet. The man fled, and quickly reappeared with a fresh bowl, which he presented to Tora, who first smelled and then tasted it. Satisfied, he nodded.

The squatting servant received the food with many bows and toothless grins toward his benefactor before raising it to his mouth and emptying it in one long swallow.

"Give him another," instructed Tora. "He likes it."

Having seen to the feeding of his bearer, Tora poured himself some wine and leaned back to look around.

He had spent the crossing planning his approach carefully. Tora was not much given to planning, but life with his master had taught him to respect danger. In the present situation, he knew he must restrain his anxiety and move cautiously to gather information without precipitating unfortunate developments. His master had used a disguise. Perhaps it had failed. Tora felt that nothing was to be gained by doing the same. Something had clearly gone wrong, or he would have returned or sent a message by now. As it was, they had waited well beyond the time of his master's expected return.

Though it was a beautiful late summer afternoon, with the sun glistening on the bay, seagulls wheeling against a blue sky, and colorful flags flying over the gate of a nearby palisade, Tora frowned. There was nothing cheerful about the people here.

Half-naked bearers were unloading bales and boxes from the ship. They were younger, stronger, and better fed than the pathetic creature guarding Tora's bundle, but their expressions were uniformly sullen or dejected. There was no talk. Neither jokes nor curses passed their lips as they crept, bent double under their loads, along the beach toward piles of goods stockpiling under the eyes of bored guards.

Tora considered the cripple. Their host had referred to him as a beggar, but the ragged creature had offered his services as a bearer. On second thought, the man could not have handled anything much heavier than Tora's bundle, which contained little more than a change of clothes.

The man bowed and grinned. At least four of his front teeth were gone, he had a flattened nose, and one ear was misshapen. Either he was incredibly foolhardy about getting into fights, or he had been beaten repeatedly. Tora thought the latter and beckoned the man over.

He rushed up with that lopsided limp of his and carefully positioned himself downwind. "Yes, your honor?"

"What's your name?"

"Taimai."

"Taimai? Turtle?"

The man nodded. "It's lucky."

"Hmm." Tora glanced at the skinny, twisted figure and disagreed. "Well, Turtle, would you know of a good cheap inn?"

"Yes, yes," Turtle crowed, jumping up and down in his eagerness. "Just around the corner. Very cheap and excellent accommodations."

Tora rose, dropping some coppers on the table. The host rushed out and scooped them up eagerly. He bowed several times. "Come again, your honor. Come again."

Paid the rascal too much, Tora thought as he put on his helmet and followed the limping Turtle into town.

"Just a moment!" said a high, sharp voice behind him.

Tora turned and recognized the red-coated police officer, also a lieutenant. He had come on board ship to check everybody's papers before they disembarked. Under normal circumstances, Tora would have struck up a conversation and proposed a friendly cup of wine, but there was something about the man that he did not like. He had passed his papers over silently, and the lieutenant had studied them silently, giving Tora a long measuring look from small mean eyes before returning them without comment.

Tora now narrowed his eyes and looked the other man over, from his meager mustache to his leather boots, and said, "Yes?"

"Where are you going with that piece of shit? I thought you had a dispatch for the governor."

Tora turned to glance at Turtle, who had shifted his small twisted body behind Tora's bulk and looked terrified. "Is there a local law against hiring someone to carry your baggage?"

"There's a law against associating with felons. You!" the policeman snapped, advancing on Turtle. "Out of here! Now!"

Turtle dropped Tora's bundle and scurried off.

"Stop!" roared Tora, and Turtle came to a wobbly halt. He glanced over his shoulder, his eyes wide with fear. "Stay there." Tora turned back to the policeman. "What is your name, Lieutenant?" he asked in a dangerously soft voice.

There was a pause while they stared at each other. Then the policeman said, "Wada," and added, "I'll get you another bearer. Hey, you! Over here! A job for you."

A big fellow with bulging muscles and the brutish expression of an animal trotted over.

"No," said Tora. "I like the one I picked. Now, if you don't mind, I have business to take care of. I wouldn't want to explain to your governor that I was detained by the local police." He turned his back on Wada, picked up the bundle, and took it over to the cripple. With a nervous glance at the policeman, Turtle accepted his burden again, and they continued on their way.

Wada's shrill voice sounded after them, "I'm warning you, bastard. The ship leaves in the morning. Make sure you're on it."

Tora froze.

"Don't, please! He's a bad man," whispered Turtle on his heels.

Tora threw up an arm in acknowledgment of Wada's words and started walking again. "He says you're a felon," he told Turtle.

"Huh?"

"A felon's someone who's committed a crime and been convicted," Tora explained.

"Then he told a lie," Turtle cried in a tone of outrage. "Him and his constables are always picking on me. I'm innocent as a newborn child. More so."

"Very funny."

It became obvious that the inn was not close by. They passed through most of Mano to a run-down area on the outskirts. The term "inn" could hardly be applied to the place. It was the worst sort of hostel Tora had ever seen, a small, dirty tenement which appeared to cater to the occasional whore and her customers.

Turtle bustled ahead and brought out a slatternly woman who was nursing a child and dragging along several toddlers clinging to her ragged skirt. Other children in various degrees of undress and filth peered out at them. This landlady, or brothel keeper if you wanted to split hairs, was grinning widely at the sight of a well-to-do customer. A missing tooth and a certain scrawniness suggested a family connection with Turtle. Sure enough, he introduced her as his sister. Tora glanced around, wrinkled his nose at the aroma of sweat and rancid food, sighed, and asked for a room and a bath.

The bath was to be had down the street in a very fine public establishment, Turtle offered cheerfully. Was ten coppers too much for the room? Tora looked at the skinny children and their mother's avid eyes and passed over a handful of coppers with a request for a hot meal in the evening. The woman bowed so deeply that the child at her breast let out a shrill cry.

Tora followed Turtle down a narrow, odorous hallway to a small dark room. It was hot and airless. Tora immediately threw open the shutters and looked out at a side yard where several rats scurried from a pile of garbage and a few rags dried on a broken bamboo fence.

Turtle had placed Tora's bundle in a corner and was dragging in an armful of grimy bedding.

"Never mind that," Tora said quickly. "I always sleep on the bare floor."

Turtle looked stricken. "It's very soft and nice," he urged anxiously. "And the nights get cold here. Besides, it's only a dirt floor."

Hard use and filth had smoothed and polished the ground until it could be taken for dark wood in the half-light. Tora had slept on the bare earth before, but usually in the open and in cleaner places than this. He weakened. "Well . . . just one quilt, then." He knew he would regret it, but the poor wretch looked relieved. Turning his back on the accommodations, he looked out over the neighboring tenements toward the curved roofs of the provincial headquarters on the hillside. Its flags fluttered in the breeze, and he was suddenly impatient.

He was halfway out the hostel's door when he heard Turtle shouting after him, "Wait, master. I'll come with you or you'll get lost. I know everything about Mano and can be very useful."

Before Tora could refuse, a small boy rushed in from the street and collided with him. Vegetables, salted fish, a small bag of rice, and a few copper coins in change spilled from his basket. His uncle fell to scolding him, and Tora realized that his money had bought a feast for a starving family.

"Very well, Turtle," he said, when the nephew had disappeared into the kitchen, "you can be my servant while I'm here. I'll pay you two coppers a day plus your food."

Turtle whooped, then fell to his knees and beat his head on the floor in gratitude. Tora turned away, embarrassed. "Hurry up," he growled. "We're going to see the governor."

"Yes, master. We're going to see the governor." Turtle was up and hopping away, chanting happily, "We're going to see the governor."

Tora caught up. "Stop that," he snapped. "I want to ask you something." Turtle was all attention. "Tell me about that police officer. What happened?"

The crippled man touched his nose and misshapen ear. "Wada is a bad man," he said again, shaking his head. "Very bad. Watch out. He doesn't like you." He glanced around to make sure they were alone and added in a whisper, "He kills people. Me, I just get beaten."

Tora frowned. "Why do you get beaten? Didn't you tell me that you're as innocent as a babe?"

Turtle shrugged. "I get in his way."

"That's no reason. You must've done something. He called you a fel . . . er, criminal."

Turtle drew himself up. "I'm an honest man," he said. "Besides, I'm not the only one that gets beaten up for nothing by the constables. Wada likes to watch. Just ask around."

"Why don't you complain? Ring the bell at the tribunal and lay a charge against him?"

"Hah," said Turtle. "There's a bell, all right, but nobody rings it. Especially not now. The governor has his own troubles."

Tora had been momentarily distracted from Turtle's chatter by a very pretty shop girl. He winked at her and was pleased when she blushed and smiled. "Troubles?" he asked absently, craning his neck for another glimpse of her trim waist and sparkling eyes.

"The governor's son poisoned the prince. Hadn't you heard? It was a bad affair. He was about to go before the judge, but he ran away from the prison here. People say the governor helped him and that he'll be recalled. So he's hardly going to listen to complaints from someone like me."

Turtle had Tora's full attention now. "The son escaped? When did that happen?"

Turtle frowned. "Seven—no, eight days ago. They couldn't find him in Mano or the other towns and villages, so they're searching the mountains now. I bet he's long gone on one of the pirate boats."

It made sense. Everybody knew about the pirates who plied their trade between the mainland and Sadoshima. If the Sadoshima governor's son had fled the island, he had headed either to Echigo or Awa Province. More likely the latter because of the unrest there. During troubled times, a man could disappear without a trace. The question was, did the escape have anything to do with the master's disappearance. Well, he was about to find out.

When they reached the gate of the provincial headquarters, Tora told his companion that he would probably have to wait outside, then identified himself and his errand to a guard engaged in lively repartee with several young women. The guard waved Tora through with barely a glance.

Shocking discipline, thought Tora. Not even a request for papers. In fact, the guard had only bothered to bar the way to the ragged Turtle.

Inside the compound, Tora saw more signs of slovenly standards. Off-duty guards were shooting dice with clerks, and trash blew across the graveled courtyards. He made his way to the governor's residence without being stopped. Nobody seemed to care who he was or where he was going.

Inside the residence, he found neither guards nor servants, nor the customary clerks and secretaries. Eventually he almost stumbled over a dozing servant and asked directions. The man yawned and pointed toward a door before turning over to resume his nap.

Expecting the door to lead to another hallway, Tora opened it and stepped through. To his dismay he had walked into a study occupied by two elderly gentlemen. One of them was clearly the governor.

Tora bowed deeply. “This insignificant person humbly apologizes. There was no guard outside the door.”

The two gentlemen did not seem surprised. The governor behind the desk was a thin, pale man in official black silk robe and hat, while a chubby individual in brown sat toward the side. Both looked drawn and dejected.

“Come in, whoever you are,” said the governor. His voice was so listless that Tora had trouble hearing him. “Close the door behind you if you have anything to say that you would rather not have overheard.”

Tora closed the door.

“I’m Mutobe and this is Superintendent Yamada. Why are you here?”

Yamada’s brown silk gown was stained and wrinkled, he was hatless, and his gray hair was carelessly tied. He also looked as though he had been weeping.

Tora saluted. “Lieutenant Tora from the provincial guard of Echigo. I carry a dispatch from my master to you, Excellency.”

“What?” The governor shot up and stretched out his hand eagerly. “Hand it over! Thank heaven he’s all right. What can have happened?”

The dispatch, as Tora knew very well, was from Seimei. They had all put their heads together to concoct a document that would look authentic without revealing the true purpose of Tora’s journey. Seimei had written it out in official style and affixed both the provincial seal and the Sugawara stamp.

The governor unrolled the paper, ran his eyes over it, and sank back down. Looking up at Tora, he said, "Lord Sugawara did not write or dictate this, I think."

Tora glanced at Yamada and cleared his throat. "I am to report back on a prisoner called Yoshimine Taketsuna. He left Echigo for Sadoshima a month ago. We expected to receive confirmation of his safe arrival. Instead there has been no news at all."

Superintendent Yamada cried, "Ah, Taketsuna. Poor fellow. Yes, he got here, all right. In fact, he was staying with me and my daughter for a while. We became very fond of him even in the short time he was with us. What a pity! What a pity!"

Tora turned cold. If his master was dead, what would he do? What could he tell the master's lady, left all alone in a cold northern land with a baby son? His fear and grief cut through the thin veneer of protocol he had acquired reluctantly. He took a few strides across the room until he towered over the two elderly men. "What happened?" he demanded harshly. "Why was no one informed?"

Tora's rude and disrespectful tone made Mutobe flinch, but his companion gave Tora a kindly look. "Ah, I don't blame you for being upset, my good fellow. You must have been fond of him, too." Tora did not like that "must have been." He glared at Yamada, who continued, "I don't quite understand the ins and outs of it myself, but Taketsuna wasn't his real name, apparently. Frankly, I never thought of him as anything but a gentleman, and Masako . . ." He paused and sighed. "Masako is my daughter. She's disappeared also. We're at the end of our ropes, the governor and I. Both of our children gone, heaven only knows where. And now here you are, asking about Taketsuna." He shook his head sadly.

Tora thought respect for his betters was all very well, but there were more important things at stake here. "Tell me what happened to . . . this Taketsuna," he demanded of Yamada.

"We don't know. He's gone," said Yamada. "In fact, he was the first to disappear."

Tora blinked. Gone? Perhaps not dead, then. "When, where, and how?" he asked.

"Wait, Yamada," said the governor. "We do not know how much this young man knows. You have already said too much."

Tora closed his eyes and clenched his fists. Patience, he reminded himself. He was on his own and he must not make a mistake. Looking at the governor, he said, "Sir—Excellency—do I take it that you have told Superintendent Yamada about Yoshimine Taketsuna? I thought nobody was to know besides you."

The governor flushed and looked away. "Yamada is perfectly safe," he said. "You don't understand my problems. After my son escaped with the superintendent's daughter, my people refused to follow orders. Superintendent Yamada was the only one with whom I could discuss the situation. He knows that . . . Taketsuna was sent here to investigate my enemies."

Tora felt more anger building inside him. "You shouldn't have done that, sir."

Mutobe blustered weakly, "Who are you to tell me what I can or cannot do, Lieutenant?"

Tora stiffened. "I'm Lord Sugawara's personal retainer and I'll gladly die for him and his family. I don't mind stepping on anyone's toes, provided I find him. So you'd better tell me what you know, and hope he's still alive. Your blabbing to everybody about this may have cost him his life. And if it did, I'll be back." His hand moved to the grip of his sword.

Mutobe paled. "I assure you . . . I had no occasion to tell until after the incident. And then I only told Yamada. No one else knows."

"What incident?"

"My son's escape." He bit his lip and glanced at Yamada. "Toshito is innocent and fled to save his life. I had no hand in it but was instantly accused of having helped him, and now—"

Tora interrupted, "Yes, never mind. What about my master?"

"Ten days ago, Lord Sugawara was on his way back from Tsukahara. I don't know if he was successful in solving the case. He never arrived. Of course I ordered a search, but we found no trace of him. They say he escaped or joined with bandits or pirates. With the trial just a day away, my son despaired and fled, and after that I could do nothing more. I live here like a prisoner now. The servants and the guards simply ignore my orders. I don't know if anyone is still looking for your master. I do know they are looking for Toshito and Masako. And that they'll kill them if they find them." He sagged and brushed a hand over his eyes. Yamada wept openly.

Tora let out a slow breath. "All right," he said. "I'll find him myself. Tell me everything he did up to the time he disappeared."

Mutobe began the tale, with Yamada supplying what he knew. The governor concluded, "That fool Osawa decided to get married and left your master to travel the last leg of the trip alone. Lord Sugawara disappeared on the road between Tsukahara and Mano."

"Or at that monastery," said Tora. He was no friend of Buddhist monasteries, remembering only too well a past encounter with murderous monks.

Mutobe protested. "Our monks are very gentle and devout. No, I know what must have happened. I'm convinced he was caught by Kumo and the others who tried to pin the murder of the prince on my son and me. I think he did solve the case and was on his way back to clear us when they stopped him."

"If that's true, then they knew his real identity."

"Not from me," said Mutobe sharply.

Tora chewed his lip. It was possible that something else had given the master away. He wished he could retrace his master's steps, but there was no time. "And you think this fellow Kumo's behind it?"

Mutobe nodded.

"Does he have soldiers?"

"No. That is not permitted. Kumo's family lost all its privileges. But he employs many people and is very wealthy. If he wished to rebel, he could raise a small army very quickly."

Tora wrestled with this for a moment. His background had made him regard the privileged classes with suspicion, and his instincts were on the side of men like Kumo who had risen in spite of the opposition they faced. "From what you say, he employs farmworkers, house servants, and the men who work his mine. I don't see any of those attacking my lord."

Mutobe looked at him bleakly. "Why not? You see the situation I'm in. Kumo controls all of Sadoshima, even my headquarters and staff."

Tora looked from Mutobe to Yamada. Yamada nodded his head mournfully. No help here, Tora decided, and got to his feet. "I'll need a pass to travel without being stopped. There's an obnoxious police officer in town who's been threatening me already." Suddenly it struck him that those threats were completely irrational unless Wada knew or suspected why Tora had come, and that must mean that he knew who Yoshimine Taketsuna really was. The job no longer looked so hopeless after all.

The governor wrote out a safe-conduct, inked his seal, and impressed it on the paper. Handing the pass to Tora, he said, "I doubt it will do you much good, considering my position, but you have my best wishes." He glanced at Tora's sword and smiled a little. "Normally my guards would have taken that from you, but it appears that I have become expendable. Be careful and hold on to your sword. You may need it."

Tora stiffened into a snappy salute. “Thank you, Excellency. If I come across news of your son or the young lady, I’ll let you know.”

◆

Turtle was huddling in the shade of the tribunal wall and jumped up when he saw Tora stepping through the gate. “Whereto now, master?” he cried.

Tora blinked at the westering sun. The brightness from the bay was blinding. Hmm,” he said. “It’s almost evening. How about something to drink, Turtle? You know a quiet place where one can have a good cup of wine without being bothered by police? Preferably a place not owned by one of your relatives?”

“Oh, yes, master. Follow me.” Turtle hobbled off, grinning happily.

Tora grinned, too. He liked being called master and he had a plan.

Turtle took him to a noodle shop in one of the alleys behind the market. This time of day, it was already crowded with farmers and market women snatching a quick bowl of soup before returning to their wares for the last sales of the day. Nobody paid any attention to them. There was a line in front of an immensely fat woman with a large iron kettle. She dipped out the soup with a bamboo ladle and took their money. Turtle whispered to her and she jerked her head toward the back.

They went to sit, Turtle at a little distance from Tora, and in a moment she came and brought two bowls of noodle soup, a large flask of wine, and two cups. Tora paid and poured for himself. Then he sampled the soup.

“A cup of wine would go well after sitting in the dust outside provincial headquarters,” Turtle hinted.

“No wine for you,” said Tora, smacking his lips. “Eat! I need your advice.”

Turtle's eyes opened a little wider. He gobbled the soup and moved closer. "Yes, master?"

Tora flinched away. "Why don't you take a bath more often?"

"Water wears down a person's skin, and then sickness gets in. What you should do is rub plenty of oil on yourself to keep your skin fat and thick. Ask me something else."

"Idiot. What I meant is, you stink so bad you ruin a man's appetite. I want you to take a bath today. I'll pay for it."

Turtle's face fell. "Please don't make me, master. It's my life I'm risking," he whined. "If you like, I'll stop using the oil."

"Oh, never mind. I'll hold my breath. Now, here's what I want to know. That Lieutenant Wada, do you know where he lives?"

Turtle nodded. "Inside the provincial headquarters."

"Not good. Too many guards and soldiers about. What does he do at night, after work?"

Turtle's eyes got bigger. He rubbed his hands and grinned. "You want to jump him in a dark alley, master? Beat him up good, eh?"

Tora glanced around. Nobody was near them. "No. I want to nab him."

Turtle's eyes almost popped out. "Oh, heavens! Oh, dear! Oh, Buddha! If you do that, you'll have to kill him or it'll be both our necks."

"I may kill him if I have to. Now, how can I get him alone?"

Turtle leaned closer and whispered.

He whispered so long that Tora's face turned red from holding his breath, but he started to smile, and reached for the flask to fill Turtle's cup.

CHAPTER FIFTEEN

THE MINE

Later Akitada guessed that he had been in his grave for weeks. Telling the days apart was impossible in a place where there was no daylight. He gauged the passage of time by the visits of the old crone with his food. Once a day she crept in with her lantern, blinding him by shining it on his face, put down full bowls of food and water, took up the empty ones, and left.

Before, he had existed blessedly somewhere between sleep and unconsciousness. With the return of reason came confusion, pain, fear, and panic. The total darkness made him think he was blind until the stench of the stagnant, fetid air brought the realization that he had been buried alive. And that discovery had driven him back into a semiconscious state which resembled dreams. Or in his case, nightmares.

The first time he thought his jailer was part of his hallucinations. As he passed in and out of consciousness in this utterly dark place, a distant clinking became the hammering of carpenters, or the clicking of the *gigcho* ball when hit with its stick, or the tapping of the bamboo ladle against the stone water basin in the shrine garden, each drawn from childhood memories which took on a frightening, mad life of their own in his dreams. Light and shadow also moved through his dreams, for neither consciousness nor sleep could deal with impenetrable darkness.

In the case of the old crone, a strange clanking and creaking preceded her appearance. Then the darkness split into thin lines of gold forming a rectangle which expanded suddenly into blinding brightness. He closed his eyes in fear. A sour smell reached his nose, and the sound of soft scraping his ears. Something clanked down dully beside him and an eerie voice squawked, "Eat."

He blinked then, cautiously, and there, not a foot from his nose, a horrible goblin face hung in the murk made by the flickering light reflected from black stonewalls. Long, shaggy, kinky hair surrounded a moonlike visage dominated by a broad nose, a wide mouth turned down at the corners, and small pale eyes disappearing in folds of orange skin pitted and covered with wens. She was female, he deduced from her voice only, and he was glad when she turned her scrutiny and the light of the lantern away and left him once again to the silence and darkness of his grave.

But the intrusion of the goblin had marked a return to awareness. After a while he overcame his nausea enough to feel around for the bowl. When he lifted it to his face, it stank, but the shaking weakness in his hands and wrists convinced him to eat. It tasted slightly better than it smelled, and it was best not to think about the gristly, slimy bits in the thick soup. He had managed about half of it before he vomited and fell back to doze off again.

He slept a lot. Lack of food or his injuries were responsible for that, and he was grateful for the oblivion because his waking moments were filled with terror. He was unbearably hot—feverish?—and his grave was indescribably filthy. The stench of urine and excrement mingled with the sour smell of vomit and sweat. Why did they bother to feed him?

Why did he bother to eat? Yet after each visit, he would raise himself on an elbow and make another effort. In time he managed to keep down some of the food. In time he slept less and was forced to take notice of his body, which remained stubbornly alive, adding periodically to the filth around him and protesting against each movement with sharp pain.

He charted the pain as if his body were unknown territory and he were taking gradual possession of it. Head and neck at first seemed the worst, especially the back of his head. He managed to turn it enough to avoid contact between the sorest area and the hard stone. But twisting his neck brought on new, lesser, but persistent pains. The other center of agony was his right leg. He could not bend it, and a steady dull ache radiated from hip to knee and from knee to ankle even when he was not moving it. The rest was uncomfortable but did not take his breath away at every move. As for his skin, apart from being covered with sweat, almost every part of him was painful to the touch, and there was an itching scab on his forehead.

At first he did not bother to think, to remember, to wonder what had brought him to this state. But pain is a great stimulator of thought. Pain will be recognized and acted upon. Pain has nothing to do with dying, and everything to do with being alive. You might wish you were dead, but pain fights blessed oblivion and forces you into some sort of action.

The blinding ache in his head and the swelling on his skull had no associations whatsoever, but when he thought about the leg, touching it and encountering a grossly enlarged knee, something clicked. A cudgel. Many cudgels in a forest clearing. Wada's constables. The mad escape attempt on the horse and

Wada with his sword raised high. Then nothing. Strange, he felt no sword wounds, smelled no blood.

But wait. Someone else had been there. Kumo!

With Kumo's image came the rest. So it had been Kumo all along! And that raised the question: why was he still alive?

The fact that there was no satisfactory answer exercised him for days, though he did more than think. During those days he managed to explore his grave by touch, a very slow process because of his weakness and injuries. He learned that it was carved from solid rock, moist, and hard under his fingers, that the rock floor was gritty and full of sharp bits of gravel. This fact jarred his memory about the distant hammering, which seemed to last for hours at a time. A stonemason might make such sounds. Somewhere nearby people were chipping their way into the rock.

He was in one of Kumo's silver mines. For no logical reason this discovery gave him new strength of will and curiosity. He could not stand, so he was uncertain of the height of his grave, but by careful rolling and shifting, he established that he occupied a square slightly larger than he was, perhaps six feet by six. Its only opening was barred by thick wooden planks, a door of some sort that was only opened by the female goblin with his food and water. The rock walls felt rough and were bare.

He moved away from the vomit and excrement to a clean corner and took off most of his filthy clothes, using them to clean himself with. The shirt he kept on. All of this took the best part of a day and required concentration and willpower, but afterward he felt marginally better.

At some point he had begun to count the visits of his wardress, but he soon became confused. He guessed she had come ten times since he had first seen her. But how much time had passed before, he did not know. He wondered if someone was looking for him. Surely Mutobe would have sent out search parties to comb the island from one end to the other. But they would scarcely look for him underground.

In his blackest moments he thought of Tamako, his wife. And of his baby son. Of old Seimei, who had been both father and mother to him. Of Tora, with his ready smile and his eagerness to be of service. Surely Tora would come to find him.

Dear heaven, where was this mine? Kumo's secretary had said the mines were in the northern mountains. Not too far from Mano, then. Two weeks, perhaps more, had passed. On a small island like Sadoshima that meant he was hidden too well to be found. Only his jailers knew he was still alive.

He forced his mind away from the present and thought of the conspiracy. Okisada, Taira, Sakamoto, Nakatomi, and Kumo. As unlikely a group of rebels as he had ever encountered. The prince, of course, had rebelled before, and Taira supported him. But Sakamoto, a fussy professor who spent his nights getting drunk in Haru's restaurant, was hardly a useful ally. Nor was Nakatomi, who had neither the rank nor the education of the others, though he appeared greedy enough for the spoils. At best, these two were minor players. Kumo was different. Though he was without ties to the capital, he had enough wealth and local power to make their grandiose plot feasible. He had been playing for control of Sadoshima, just as Mutobe had charged.

The plot failed when the prince had killed himself, yet the conspiracy had continued and was still continuing, or Akitada would not be here. The vengeful Genzo had provided Kumo with Akitada's papers, proving that his suspicions of the convict Taketsuna had been correct. Treason was punishable by death in one of its more painful forms, and that explained why Kumo had ordered Akitada captured. But it explained nothing else.

When Akitada was not thinking about Kumo, he exercised his body. He began by stretching his limbs and moving all but his injured leg regularly and repeatedly. The slop he ate, unappetizing though it was, gradually brought back some strength so that the enervating trembling stopped and he was less light-headed. The pain was still with him, but head and neck improved until he could sit up and lean against the rock. His right leg did not get better. He feared that he was permanently crippled, for however much he tried to bend his knee, he could not do it. Still he persisted, over and over again, gritting his teeth against the pain as he massaged the swollen flesh, and wondered why he bothered.

The day he pushed himself up against the wall and stood upright for the first time, the goblin caught him. He heard her at the plank door, but did not manage to get back down because of his stiff leg. When she saw him, she shrieked and disappeared, slamming the door behind her.

He took a deep breath and made himself slide along the rock toward the door. The right leg hurt abominably every time he put his weight on it, but he needed only a few steps. When his fingers touched wood, they were wet with sweat, and his eyes burned with perspiration. Still he pushed and pulled on the door. But it was locked. He felt all around and above it. The ceiling was barely a foot above his head at its highest point, but the door was much lower, so that he would have to bend to get out.

He was still leaning against the door when he heard them and saw the light again. In a panic, he tried to get away from the door too fast. Pain, hot like scalding water, shot up and down his right leg and he fell. The door, when it flew open, struck his foot, and Akitada writhed in agony.

They had no trouble at all with him after that. The three men made quick work of tying him up with a thick rope. The goblin held a burning torch for them, and later he was to remember the scene like something from a painting of hell, with himself the tortured soul about to be fed to the flames. Then the door clanked shut and he was alone again.

Things were immeasurably worse than before. His wrists were lashed together behind his back, and the rope continued to his ankles, which were also tied together. Not only did the rope restrict his circulation, but he was now in an arched position causing continuous pain to both his neck and injured leg.

He also could no longer feed himself. The goblin had left his soup and water within reach, but he was lying down and his hands were tied. Eventually ravenous hunger drove him to stretch enough so that he could lap like a dog, covering his face and beard with food, dirtying his water.

Why did they not just make an end of him? What was he being saved for?

After a while, he resorted again to taking his mind off his condition by concentrating on other things. He was not entirely successful in this, because the moment he cast his mind back to his family and pictured himself with his wife and child, or practicing stick-fighting with Tora, he would be seized by despair. Even the playing of an imaginary flute did not work any longer. Eventually he turned his thoughts again to the events in Sadoshima.

The trial must be long over by now, its outcome surely a guilty verdict without Akitada's information. Had Toshito been taken to the capital or quickly executed in Mano? And what about his father? Mutobe would hardly remain governor. Perhaps father and son had been taken off the island together. That would account for the lack of interest in the disappearance of the convict Taketsuna. And even if Mutobe reported in the capital, help would not reach Akitada in time.

All his thoughts tended to the same dismal conclusion. More time passed. Nothing happened, except that now when the goblin brought his food and water she was accompanied by a short, burly man with the same long matted hair and a long curly beard. The man carried a cudgel and wore some sort of fur. Once

Akitada tried to speak to them, begging to have the rope loosened a little, but he was ignored. They communicated only with each other in strange grunts and left again as soon as possible.

It came to him then that they must be Ezo. He had seen people of mixed Japanese and Ezo blood. But these were full-blooded Ezo. That accounted for their curly hair, their strange light eyes, the fur clothing, and their guttural language. If his guards knew that he was an official in the service of the emperor, they would have little pity for him.

He suddenly wondered if he was being kept alive because they planned to ransom him. Perhaps he would go home after all, home to hold his wife and child, home to breathe the clean air, home to become human again.

That hope brought such relief that he relaxed in spite of his miserable condition and fell into a deep, dreamless sleep.

But waking up in the same hot, stinking darkness cured him quickly of ridiculous hopes. He had forgotten Kumo, the man who had put him here, as well as the fact that no ransom payment would be made for him. His family certainly had nothing to trade for his life. And the imperial government would hardly raise a large amount of gold or trade territory for a junior official who had so signally failed in his assignment. Knowing how powerful his enemies at court were, and how little his superiors thought of his ability, he doubted they would even negotiate on his behalf. So it would only be a matter of time before either Kumo or the Ezo got rid of him.

When the goblin and her companion brought his food, he looked at them more closely. Both creatures looked brutish, but they seemed indifferent to him as a person. There was no particular animosity in the way they treated him, just caution and dull obedience to orders.

In spite of an overwhelming sense of hopelessness, he ate. Life was extraordinary. The more someone tried to crush it out of you, the harder you struggled to stay alive. There was neither honor nor pride in this persisting. Chained in the bowels of the earth, lying in your own filth, and lapping food from a bowl like a dog, you were nothing. Yet you clung to life.

One faculty distinguishes a man from a trapped animal: his reason. Akitada spent the waking hours thinking. What, for example, were Ezo doing working in this mine? They had been subjugated everywhere except in Hokkaido. Their presence lent some credence to the fears that had brought the imperial secretaries first to Sadoshima and then to him. Okisada and/or Kumo had formed some sort of alliance with the warlords of Dewa or Mutsu, strongholds of the subjugated Ezo. Their territories were only a short ship's journey away. Aided by a rebel Ezo army and funded by Kumo's wealth, the traitors could march on the capital to place their candidate Okisada on the throne. No doubt the Ezo lords had been promised whole provinces as reward for their help. Such an alliance had happened before when Koreharu had rebelled. It had taken decades to subdue the uprising.

But then the prince had died, and an extraordinary thing must have happened next. Kumo had apparently stepped into Okisada's place. With Mutobe out of the way, he would take over the government of Sadoshima and from there join the rebel army and attack the northern provinces of Japan. He could hardly claim the throne by birth, but other possibilities were terrible enough. Because of his carelessness Akitada had failed to stop him. Even if, by a miracle, he survived this ordeal, and even if Kumo's rebellion was crushed, there would be no future for him anywhere.

He fretted over his helplessness and became so discouraged that he stopped eating, and even the simple act of breathing seemed an intolerable burden.

It seemed particularly bad one night, or day, when he awoke, choking and gasping for air. After a moment he realized that he was breathing smoke, dense, acrid, throat-searing smoke. As if being buried alive were not enough, he was apparently about to be cremated alive.

But he was wrong. Just when he was about to give up the pointless struggle, they came for him.

They cut the ropes and dragged him out of his grave and back into fresh air, life, and time.

It was nighttime outside, a chill, wet mountain night with a slight drizzle falling. They dumped Akitada somewhere near a tree and ran back.

Akitada did not know this and, had he known, he could not have taken advantage of the perfect opportunity for escape. He wanted nothing but breath after breath of clean air. He lay on his belly on the wet ground, shaking with the sudden cold after weeks in his grave, and coughed in great wrenching spasms. The moisture in the air he gulped made him aware of a great thirst. He was breathing water, he thought. He was drowning in sweet-smelling water. Pressing his face and lips into the rain-drenched moss, he sucked up the moisture and wished he could stop shaking and coughing, and just let himself float in the moist, clean air.

His coughing stopped after a while. He rolled himself into a ball against the chill and opened his eyes. In the light of torches and lanterns, men darted back and forth, their shadows moving grotesquely against the cliff face. Others lay about, inert or barely moving. He thought belatedly of escape, but collapsed after the first attempt to rise. After that he sat, staring around him, thankful for the air—much cleaner than any he had breathed in weeks, dizzyingly clean—and enthralled by the visual spectacle after all the time spent in darkness.

A fire in a mine is deadly not because there is much to burn. Later Akitada was to learn that there were only the notched tree trunks the miners used to ascend and descend between shafts, and baskets and some straw and hemp rope to raise and lower the baskets, and the many small oil lamps and occasional torches with which they lit their way through the tunnels. A fire might start easily if oil was spilled on rope and somehow ignited, but it was the smoke that did the damage. The smoke had nowhere to go and seeped through the tunnels, choking the men.

Eventually Akitada thought of the filth caking his skin and took off the sodden rag of a shirt. Pressing it against the wet moss and then scrubbing himself with it was exhausting work, but he felt better afterward. Sitting there, stark naked in the chill mountain air, he looked around for something to cover himself with. No one paid attention to him. He crawled over to one of the still bodies. The man was dead, his eyes rolled back into his head and his face black with soot, but his clothes, a cotton shirt and a pair of short pants, were almost dry because he lay under a tree. Akitada managed to take the shirt and pants off the corpse and put them on himself. But the effort was all he could manage. He collapsed beside the dead man and fell into a brief sleep of exhaustion.

He woke when the goblin and her companion wrapped a chain around his waist and attached it to the tree. It was loose enough to allow short steps if he could have stood up. His hands were tied in front with rope, so that he was much more comfortable than in the mine. The corpse was gone, tossed on top of a couple others. Akitada spent the rest of that wet cold night leaning against the tree trunk, alternately shivering and dozing, too weak and tired to take notice of the dark figures milling about and the coarse shouts and cracks of whips.

The rain stopped at dawn when blessed light returned, a gray and filtered light here under the tree on a cloudy morning, but that, too, was a blessing, for his eyes were no longer used to sun. The goblin returned with a bowl of food. He ate it gratefully, sitting up and lifting the bowl to his mouth like a man instead of an animal. It took so little now to please him.

But the distinction between men and beasts began to blur again as he saw his surroundings. They were somewhere in the mountains, fairly high up. Before him was a wide, open space covered with rubble and stone dust and ragged creatures. Ahead rose a cliff perforated by many holes, some only large enough for a small animal to enter, some—like the one from which he had emerged and around which still hovered a slight smoky haze—large enough to drive an ox carriage through.

For a mine, it was a small operation. Akitada saw no more than fifty people. About a third were guards. Several of them were Ezo, bearded and wearing fur jackets, and all were armed with bows and swords or carried leather whips. Most of the miners wore few clothes, and chains hobbled their feet so they could only shuffle along. So much for Kumo's gentle treatment of his workers, Akitada thought. Though these men had been condemned to hard labor for violent crimes, the number of armed guards seemed excessive, particularly in view of the convicts' miserable and cowed behavior. Indeed, where would they run to on this island?

At the moment, they sat or lay on the ground, but already one of the guards was walking about, snapping a leather whip. One by one, the men stood, chains clinking, heads hanging, arms slack. A few glanced toward the corpses, but nobody spoke.

Some of the miners were half naked, and several of the smallest had rags wound around their knees and lower arms like little Jisei. Akitada glanced up at the holes in the cliff face. They must be the badger holes the doctor had talked about.

The guards rounded up the bigger convicts and marched them back into the smoking cave opening. They resisted briefly, protesting and gesturing, but the whip soon bit into their backs and bare calves and, one by one, they disappeared into the earth. One of the guards followed but returned quickly, gasping and coughing, to wave another guard in. They took turns this way, but the convicts only reappeared briefly, dragging charred timbers or carrying baskets of equipment. The cleanup had begun.

As the daylight grew stronger, he saw that his knee was still swollen and the tight skin was an ugly black and purplish red. But the cooling rain had soothed the throbbing, and after a while Akitada began to test his leg. He could move foot and ankle easily, but the knee was too stiff to bend more than a little. Still, he was encouraged that it would heal in time.

The remaining convicts were fed and put to their normal tasks. Half-naked, childlike figures with small baskets scrambled up the cliff and, one by one, disappeared into the badger holes, from which they reappeared after a while, bare buttocks first, dragging out baskets of chipped rock. The baskets were passed to the ground, where other convicts took them down the slope toward a curious wooden rig. This appeared to be some sort of a sluice carrying a stream of water down a gentle incline. Two men walked a treadmill that raised buckets of water from a stream to the top of the sluice.

Armed guards watched seated workers who used stone mallets to crush the rock chips into coarse sand before emptying that into the sluice. Now and then a worker would lift a traylike section of the wooden sluice to pick through the debris caught in it before reinserting it for the next batch of ground rock.

Akitada watched this, trying to account for the amount of effort expended on rock. He had never seen such a time-consuming and inefficient method of mining. No wonder the emperor saw so little silver from Kumo's operations.

Toward noon there was an unpleasant interruption. A horseman trotted to the center of the clearing, stared at the smoky cave opening, then shouted, "Katsu." One of the guards appeared from the mouth of the cave, ran forward, and bowed.

"The master's displeased," the rider barked. "This is the second time in one month. You are careless. How many this time?"

The guard bowed several times and stammered something, pointing to the corpses.

"Three? Well, you won't get any more. Put everybody to work. Guards, too. Your last take was disappointing."

"But we're running out of good rock. Just look. We had to make six new badger holes."

The horseman slid off his horse and together they went to the cliff and looked up. The new arrival was short and had a strange, uneven gait. They stood and watched as one of the miners backed out of his hole and lowered his basket to the ground. The newcomer reached in and inspected its contents, shaking his head.

Akitada could no longer hear what was said, but the horseman seemed familiar. He had heard that voice before. Then it came to him that it had been in Kumo's stable yard. This was Kita, the mine overseer who had arrived with bad news that night. Another fire.

But he was unprepared for what happened next: Kita turned his head and Akitada saw his profile. Kita was the bird-faced man who had followed him to Minato and later to the monastery. He would have recognized that beaky nose anywhere. Then the overseer turned fully his way, shading his eyes to see better, and asked a question. When the two men started purposefully toward him, Akitada knew that his troubles were far from over.

CHAPTER SIXTEEN

LITTLE FLOWER

When Tora and Turtle returned to his sister's hostel, they found several excited children waiting anxiously at the door. Apparently they looked forward to sharing the remnants of the dinner the generous guest had paid for.

Tora was no longer very hungry after the noodle soup but did not want to seem unappreciative of Turtle's sister, whose name was Oyoshi, and asked the whole family to join him. An amazing number of children appeared instantly. They all sat down on the torn and stained mats of the main room, the children in their gay, multicolored bits of clothing lined up on either side of their mother, three girls to one side, five boys to the other. She served Tora and her brother first, steaming bowls of rice covered with vegetables and chunks of fish. An appetizing smell filled the room. Tora sampled, while the children watched him fixedly, licking their lips. The food was quite tasty and he said so, inviting the others to join them. To his discomfort, Turtle's sister served only the little boys. She and the little girls had to wait until the men had eaten their fill.

Nevertheless, it was a cheerful gathering, with Turtle chattering away and the children giggling. But when Turtle mentioned their run-in with Wada earlier that day, his sister suddenly burst into such vicious invective that even he stared at her.

"Why, what'd he do to you?" he asked when she ran out of terms of abuse.

"Not me, you fool. Little Flower. She was near to dying on the street when I heard. I brought her here this morning."

Turtle's eyes grew large. "Amida. Not again! And just now. I should have known bad luck was coming when that crow cawed at me."

"Who's Little Flower?" Tora asked.

"She's the whore I told you about," said Turtle, looking apologetic. "Wada's girl. They call her that because she's sort of small and pretty. He likes them that way."

"Well, she's not feeling very pretty now," his sister snapped. "That bastard!"

"Damn," said the Turtle. "I didn't know. But if she's laid up, maybe he's got somebody else. I can find out."

"More fool she," muttered his sister, refilling a boy's bowl while three little girls watched hungrily. Only the baby, lashed to its mother's back, was uninterested in the food and stared with unblinking eyes at Tora over its mother's shoulder. He wondered where the children's father was. Having tended to her sons, Oyoshi looked sternly at her brother. "You stay out of it, Taimai. He'd kill you as soon as slap at a fly."

"Could I talk to this Little Flower?" asked Tora, pushing his half-filled bowl toward the little girls.

Their mother snatched it away and divided the contents among the boys. Men came first in her household. Having reestablished the sacred order, she turned a gap-toothed smile on Tora and said, "A strapping officer like you doesn't want a pitiful little flower. Let me fix you up with a real beauty for the night, Master Tora. Only fifty coppers, and you'll feel like you've been to paradise."

Her wheedling tone was familiar. Tora had heard such propositions before and was not too surprised that Turtle's sister also worked as a procuress. People did what they had to do in order to feed a large family. He grinned. "But I like them little and bruised," he teased.

Her smile faded. She had begun gathering the various leftovers for herself and the hungry girls, but now paused to look at Tora dubiously. "Well, she needs the money, but . . . you aren't planning to beat her? Because, I tell you, I won't have it. She can't take any more."

Tora flushed to the roots of his hair. "No. I was joking. I don't beat my women. I just want to talk to her, that's all."

"Just talk? Hmm," she muttered, frowning at him. "Well, I'll go and ask her." She left the little girls watching tearfully as one of the boys helped himself to several juicy bits of fish.

When their mother returned a moment later, Tora insisted that she let the girls eat now and watched as they fell on their food like small savages. Then he followed her to the back of the hostel. This part of the building looked worse than where Tora's room was. The walls leaned at odd angles, water had leaked in and stained them black, and doors did not shut properly or were missing entirely. Here and there whole boards were gone, put to use in other places. He glanced into empty rooms, each no more than a tiny cubicle, hardly large enough for two people to lie down together, and passed others, inadequately covered by ragged quilts pinned up in the doorway, where he heard the grunts and squeals of lovemaking. Oyoshi opened the last door and said to someone inside, "Here he is, dear. Mind you, you don't have to have him."

Tora ducked into a dark space. In the dim flicker from his hostess's oil lamp, he made out a cowering figure in one corner. "We'll need a candle," he said.

"I have no candles, Master Tora. Too much money," his hostess said sadly. "I can leave my lamp, but please bring it back. Oil's expensive, too." She closed the door behind him.

The oil also stank and smoked. He squatted on the floor, and they looked at each other by the fitful light. Tora thought at first that she was a little girl of ten or eleven. Little Flower was tiny and small-boned, and perhaps she had been pretty once, but now she looked sick and discontented; her eyes were ringed with dark circles, her lips pinched, and her thin cheeks unnaturally flushed. She gave him a nod and a tremulous smile.

He saw no obvious bruises on her and said, "I've been told that one of your customers has hurt you badly. Is that so?"

She trembled a bit then, and nodded again. "I can't lie down on my back, but I could be on top, if the gentleman liked. Or I could kneel and—" Her voice, soft and girlish, was breathless with desperate eagerness to please.

Tora interrupted quickly. "I didn't come for that."

"Oh." Her face fell. "I thought . . ."

Tora pulled a handful of coppers from his sash. "I'll pay for your time, of course. Whatever you would get from a customer."

The slender face lit up, and he thought that she had very pretty, soft eyes. "Thank you, sir," she said in her childlike voice. "Would ten coppers be too much?"

"Not at all." Tora counted out fifteen and pushed them toward her.

She did not touch the money. "I'm called Little Flower. Does the gentleman have a name?"

"Tora."

She smiled again, and Tora was glad that Wada had not touched her face.

"What shall I do for you, Master Tora?"

"Tell me about Wada."

Her eyes widened. She shook her head and pushed the fifteen coppers his way. "No. He'll kill me if he finds out."

Tora pushed the money back. "He won't find out. Can I see what he did to you?"

She hesitated. A flush spread from her cheeks to her ears and neck. It made her look prettier and healthier. She got to her feet, clumsily, supporting herself with one hand against the wall. Tora saw that she wore a wrinkled hemp gown dyed in a blue and white pattern of flowers. Around her tiny middle was a brown-and-black-striped sash. It was tied loosely, and when she undid the knot, it dropped to the floor and her gown fell open. Underneath, she was naked and, except for small, high breasts, entirely childlike, since she had shaved off all body hair. Tora's skin prickled unpleasantly. He was ashamed for staring.

Turning slowly, she let the gown fall from her shoulders.

Tora felt sick. Muttering a curse, he got to his feet and raised the oil lamp to look at her back and buttocks. The blood had dried, but the welts, and there were many of them crisscrossing each other from the nape of her neck to the back of her knees, looked swollen and inflamed. He could hardly imagine the pain she must endure at every move. And she had offered to service him anyway.

He picked up her gown and placed it very gently around her shoulders again. "Has a doctor treated you?"

She shook her head.

He opened the door and shouted for the landlady. She appeared at a trot, dragging two toddlers behind her.

"What's the matter?" she asked anxiously.

"Send for a doctor," he snapped. "I'll pay for it." Then he slammed the door in her face and turned back to Little Flower. She was tying her sash. Her head was lowered, but he could see the tears running down her face. "I'm sorry," he said. "Let me help you down."

She settled on the floor, carefully, and brushed away her tears, giving Tora a little smile. "I'll be all right," she murmured. "It'll heal."

He stared at her in helpless anger. His familiarity with the pleasure quarters of the capital had taught him that there were men who enjoyed sex only when they could inflict pain on their partner. But this? He asked harshly, "And next time? Will you let him beat you to death?"

She flinched a little at his tone. "Perhaps he won't want me anymore."

Tora ran his eye over her appraisingly. He liked his women well padded and lusty. But a man like that bastard Wada probably got his kicks out of abusing children, and she looked more childlike than ever, cowering there and wiping at her tears with the back of her hand. "What if he does?"

She looked away. "Life is hard. It's my karma because I did bad things in my previous life."

He said fiercely, "No. Wada is the evil one, and I'll make him pay for this."

She gave him a startled look, then leaned forward and put a small, somewhat dirty hand on his arm. "You're very kind, Master Tora," she said softly, "but please do not go near Master Wada. You're younger, stronger, and very much more handsome, but he'll kill you."

Tora threw back his head with a shout of laughter. "What? That little bug? Listen, Little Flower, you don't know me very well. If he weren't so repulsive, I'd chew him up and spit him out."

She started to weep again, covering her face and rocking back and forth.

"What's wrong? What did I say?"

"Oh," she said, her voice muffled, "you don't know him."

"Well, that's why I'm here. I was hoping you'd explain. See, I need some information from the bastard. I think he knows something about someone I'm trying to find."

She looked up then. A shadow passed over her face. "Is she someone . . . like me?"

He shook his head. "No. It's . . . a man. He came here about a month ago as a prisoner and has disappeared."

She brightened, but shook her head. "Then he's dead. Or in the mines, which is the same thing."

Tora clenched his fists. "I've got to make sure."

"Is it your father, or brother?"

"No. I can't tell you. Just talk to me about Wada. Whatever you know. His habits, the places he goes after dark, where he eats, his friends."

She gave a snort. "He's the head of the police. They have no friends. His constables are worse than the criminals. Everybody's afraid of them. Those who complain are dead a day later. So nobody complains ever."

Turtle had said the same thing. "Has it always been this way?"

She frowned. "It's worse now. Anyway, Master Wada's got no friends, unless you count the constables, and most of them hate him, too. He eats in the best places for free, compliments of the owners. I don't know about his habits, except for what he does to girls like me."

"He has other women?"

"Sometimes. But he likes me best." She said this almost proudly.

"Where were you when he did this to you?"

"At the Golden Phoenix. He sent word for me to come there. It's a restaurant near the harbor. There's a little cottage out back for private parties. He goes there so the other guests won't hear the girls scream."

Heavy, dragging steps approached their door, and someone belched grossly. Then the door slid back, and a fat, bald old man peered in, bringing with him the sour fumes of cheap wine.

"What do you want?" Tora snapped.

"I'm the doctor," the old man grunted, and squeezed his bulk in. He put down a medicine box and used his sleeve to wipe the sweat off his red face and scalp. His robe was dark, like a doctor's, but so filthy that it was difficult to guess its original color. Taking a couple of uncertain steps, he sat down heavily in front of Little Flower. More rancid wine fumes filled the small cubicle. Tora closed the door and stood against the wall. The man's body seemed to fill the space.

"Ah," the doctor said to the girl, "it's you again, is it? Same trouble?"

She nodded. "Yes, Dr. Ogata."

"Let's see, then."

She got to her feet and repeated the disrobing process, turning her lacerated back toward Ogata. He gave a soundless whistle.

"Girl," he said, "you won't survive the next one. I told you to come live with me."

At this Tora lost his patience. "You filthy old lecher," he growled. "Passing yourself off as a healer when you're a drunk. And then you want to get the poor girl in your bed before you've even treated her back. Get out of here. I'll send for a real doctor."

Little Flower cried out a protest, but the doctor just turned to stare at Tora. He chuckled. "Well, well, girl, that's more like it. A handsome fellow, and considerate. Not like that animal you've been consorting with. Take my advice and stick with this one."

Tora glared at the fat man, and Little Flower flushed scarlet and averted her face. She pulled the gown around her and murmured, "He just wanted information. Nothing else."

"Hmm." Ogata looked from one to the other, scratched his bald head, and grinned at Tora. "Sit down, young man, or step outside. You're making me nervous, hanging over me like a mountain. Now, as to my fee, you can pay me five coppers or two flasks of wine, whichever you prefer. You don't want the other doctor. He knows nothing about the way these girls must live and would make trouble for her." Turning back to Little Flower, he said, "All right. You know the routine. Lie down. It'll hurt this time, but you've waited too long and I must clean some of the poison out."

"What poison?" demanded Tora suspiciously, as Little Flower spread her robe and stretched out on it. "Did the bastard rub poison on her back after beating her half to death?"

"No, no." Ogata was peering closely at the welts, pressing them with his fingers from time to time. "Leeches," he muttered. "That's what we need. Well, I don't have any, but I'll do the best I can." He turned to Tora. "Don't you know anything? Miasma are all about us, in the air, on the ground, in our clothing, just waiting to enter our bodies. The dead rot because of the poisonous miasma about us. Sometimes even the living rot if the poison gets into their wounds. Miasma are why the gods warn against touching the dead and demand we cleanse our hands and mouths before addressing them in prayer. In her case, they've invaded some of the cuts and poisoned them. Leeches would suck out the poison, but there are other methods. Go fetch some warm water and two or three eggs."

Tora's skin itched. He retreated nervously. Miasma? Eggs? Afraid to show more ignorance, Tora did not ask. He found the landlady and relayed the doctor's instructions, then asked worriedly, "Are you sure that fellow's any good? He's drunk and looks filthy, quite apart from being old and not too healthy himself."

To his surprise, Oyoshi glared at him, "Around here people better watch what they say about the doctor. He may not look like much, but he's saved a lot of poor girls, and men, too. Often he doesn't charge them anything. Besides, he's the coroner, which means he's smart. The government pays him a salary for that and for treating the prisoners. Maybe if people had to see the things he does, they'd drink, too."

She left him standing in the hallway to get the water and eggs, still muttering to herself.

Tora was astonished at her outburst, but even more surprised that the fat drunk was the coroner. And he looked after sick prisoners. Forgetting all about noxious miasma, Tora turned on his heel and plunged back into the small room so suddenly that he bumped into Ogata's formidable backside. The physician had been standing bent over his medicine case and tumbled forward, causing Little Flower to cry out.

"Sorry," Tora cried. "I didn't hurt you, did I?"

"No. Please don't worry," Little Flower said with an adoring look. "You're very kind and generous, Master Tora."

"Speak for yourself, girl." Ogata straightened up, rubbing his posterior, when he caught her expression. He turned to look Tora over. "A soldier, eh? Not from around here, are you, son?"

Tora, the newly promoted lieutenant, considered this somewhat condescending from a drunken quack, but under the circumstances he swallowed his pride, and said, "No. On temporary assignment from Echigo."

"Echigo, eh? Been here long?"

"I arrived today."

"Really? Staying long?"

If it had not been for the fact that Tora had his own questions for the doctor, he would have balked, but he only said, "As long as it takes. Tell me something, please. How can you people let an animal like that Wada terrorize decent citizens? Where I come from, there are laws to protect people against bad officials."

The physician snorted. "So they say. And some have died proving it. You can't blame the rest of us for postponing the experiment a little while longer."

Oyoshi bustled in with a bucket of water and two eggs in a small bowl. "Sorry," she said, catching her breath. "Had to run across the street for the eggs. They cost a copper apiece."

Tora fished the coins from his sash and paid her. He wondered if he had paid for the doctor's snack, but Ogata took the eggs and sat down next to Little Flower. Tora and the landlady watched as he gently washed the lacerated skin, occasionally squeezing swollen areas, while Little Flower bit into the sleeve of her gown to keep from crying out. When he was satisfied that he had cleaned out most of the poison, he broke the eggs and dabbed egg white over the wounds.

"Lie still and let it dry," he told the girl.

"What's the egg for?" Tora wanted to know.

"Draws out the poison."

They sat and waited. Tora studied Ogata and finally said, "I hear you're the coroner."

Ogata nodded.

"So you know all about the murdered prince, I suppose?"

Ogata shifted a little to look at him. "That have anything to do with your business in Sadoshima?"

Blast the man. He answered questions with more questions. Tora said, "No. I was just curious."

"I did not see the body. The prince's own physician did that. You'll have to ask him."

"What happened at the hearing?"

Ogata cocked his head. "Sure you're not officially interested?"

Tora flushed. "I went to see the governor today. He mentioned that his son escaped."

Ogata nodded. "Yes. Smartest thing he could do. Took his girl along. Or maybe it was the other way around." He leaned forward and tested the drying egg white on Little Flower's back. Then he reached into his medicine case for a twist of paper and sprinkled some white powder over her back. "Since you're going to ask me anyway, this is powdered oyster shell. It dries out the wounds." He started to close his medicine box. "Well, girl," he said to his patient, "stay off your back for a few days and you should do all right. I'll look in again tomorrow."

Tora got up and fished more coins from his sash. "If your work's finished for the day," he said, handing over the fee, "I'd like to stand you that wine, too."

"A man with a generous heart," Ogata said cheerfully. They started to leave the room, when Little Flower called out to Tora.

She was kneeling, clutching her robe to herself. "Would you help me with this, please?"

Tora helped her up and took the robe from her. She was so pitifully thin, her small hands fluttering as she tried to cover her nakedness, that his heart contracted with pity. He placed the robe gently around her shoulders, then tucked each small arm into the full sleeve, when she reached up and pulled his face down to hers. "Please don't go," she whispered. "I feel quite well now."

He disentangled himself, flushing with embarrassment because he did not desire her. "Shame on you, Little Flower," he said lightly, bending for her sash. "You heard the doctor. You have to lie down now and get some rest."

Tears rose to her eyes and spilled over. She looked exactly like a forlorn little girl. He pulled her gown together, then draped the sash loosely about her small waist and tied it in a clumsy bow.

"Will you come back?" she pleaded. "It won't cost anything. Just come back, please?"

"I'll come back," he said, taking pity, and left quickly.

The wine shop was a few streets away and crowded with poor laborers and small tradesmen. Tora's military garb got him hostile stares instead of admiring glances. "You hang around with a low crowd," he told the doctor sourly.

Ogata ignored the comment and sat down near the wine barrels. He ordered a large flask of their best from the waiter who rushed up eagerly.

"Their best probably tastes like dog piss," grumbled Tora, but he asked the waiter to bring some pickled radish to go with the wine.

Ogata smiled with approval. Wine and radish appeared, and Tora paid, while the doctor poured himself a cup, gulped down the wine, refilled the cup, and emptied that also.

"Bad manners, I know," he said, pouring the next cup for Tora and passing it over, "but I needed that. That poor, miserable girl. I offered her a job as a maid, but I can't pay her what she makes as a whore, and she sends all her earnings to her mother and grandparents." He heaved a sigh. "Ah, well. That's better. Now, young man," he asked, "what is it that you want from me?"

Tora stared, then grinned. The shrewd old codger! "Well," he said, "I want information about Wada. And about the prisoners you may have seen lately. One called Taketsuna in particular."

Ogata raised his brows, then nodded. "Oh, Taketsuna. Yes, I remember him. I've wondered. He's disappeared, you know. So that's why you're here. And you think Wada is responsible for his disappearance?"

This was almost too easy. Tora leaned forward eagerly. "Yes, I do. I just don't know the reasons and the means, and what he's done with him. What can you tell me about Taketsuna?"

Ogata looked at him, then lowered his eyes to his empty cup and was silent for a long time. Finally he said, almost sadly, "I don't think I can help you, Tora. Take my advice and go home. If you go on with this, you'll come to harm. Like Taketsuna." He reached for the wine flask, but Tora clutched his hand hard. "Ouch. Let go! I need my hands."

Tora let go, but fear and anger overwhelmed him. The old crook was playing games with him. "Tell me what you know, you old drunk!" he shouted. "We had a deal. I paid up. Now it's your turn."

The room fell silent. Then there was a general shuffling as some of the guests got up and joined them.

"You need any help, Doctor?" asked a tall, broad-shouldered man with a scarred face.

"Yes," piped up a small man, "we'll teach him about respect, show him what's what." He stuck a scrawny fist in Tora's face.

Ogata raised his hands. "It's all right, friends. He got some bad news, that's all. Thanks, but go sit back down. It's a private conversation."

Tora watched the men shuffle off, muttering and casting suspicious glances over their shoulders. He was spoiling for a fight, but thought better of it. Turning to Ogata, he said fiercely, "I came here to find Taketsuna and I will do so or die. And if I find he's dead, I'll go after his killer. Neither you nor your friends can frighten me off."

Ogata refilled his cup and drank. "Better order another flask," he said. "All right, I saw Taketsuna the day after he arrived. The governor sent me to have a look at him. He was with some other prisoners in the harbor stockade and had a few bruises from the welcome Wada's constables had given him, but he was otherwise well. I could see he was no commoner, so I convinced the governor to take him on as a scribe. He was put to work in the archives and stayed with the prison superintendent Yamada and his daughter. Then one day he was gone. I know the Yamada family well, and the girl told me he had left with the tax inspector Osawa for an inspection tour. That's all I know. I never laid eyes on him again."

Tora was not satisfied. "Why do you think something bad happened to him?" he demanded. He could not bring himself to mention death.

The doctor sighed. "Young man, I do not know who you are, and I did not know who Taketsuna was, except that he was one of the good people and had no idea what he was getting into. Maybe he was a convict, but there was something about him that made me wonder. Just as I'm wondering about you now. You both look and act like men bound for trouble, and I think Taketsuna found it. Me, I avoid trouble at all cost." He started to rise.

"Wait!" Tora put a hand on the doctor's arm. "I think you told me the truth," he said. "But you're wrong. Trouble will find you wherever you are. You're a learned man and you get to talk to your governor. How can you keep on patching up that poor girl's back and do nothing about that animal Wada?"

Ogata suddenly looked very old. He said, "Because I'm more good to her and to others like her alive than dead. You know, your master asked the same sort of question." His watery eyes looked in the distance and he shook his head. "We were looking at a corpse. Beaten to death. A good example why a man should keep his nose out of trouble. But did your master heed it? No. Look where it got him. I expect he died for his convictions. And it probably was Wada who killed him. It's usually Wada who arranges deaths. A very efficient man who seems untroubled by the sort of scruples you and your master labor under."

Tora clenched his fists. "I don't believe you," he said. "I won't believe it till I see his body."

Ogata said nothing. He sat hunched, his many chins resting on his chest.

Tora frowned. "And what makes you call him my master?"

The doctor gave him a pitying glance and shook his head. "You're not his brother or his son. The only other relationship strong enough to send one man off to risk his life for another is that between a nobleman and his retainer. I think the man who claimed to be Taketsuna was taken to one of the mines. I expect by now his body is in an abandoned mine shaft, covered with a heap of rubble. You'll never find him. You're a good fellow, Tora, and I'm truly sorry about your master, but there's nothing you can do here except die. Go home. And take Little Flower with you. She's a nice girl who needs someone to look after her and she likes you."

This time Tora did not stop the physician, and Ogata staggered to his feet and departed, weaving an uncertain course among the guests who waved and called out to him or touched his hand as he passed.

CHAPTER SEVENTEEN

THE DARK TUNNEL

Kita, the mine supervisor, stood above Akitada, studying him with a frown of concentration. The small bright eyes moved from face to body, pausing at the injured knee, and then returned. They locked eyes. Kita's were cold and beady. The eyes of the predator, thought Akitada, the eyes of the *tengu* in the Minato shrine.

Akitada wondered if Kita also recognized him. Apparently not, for the supervisor grunted and said, "Not much to look at, is he? Thought he'd be younger, in better condition."

It was very unpleasant to be talked about as if one were no more than an animal, but Akitada kept his face stiff and waited for the guard's response.

The guard said, "He's been inside the whole time. Sick as a dog. Since the day the boss brought him."

Kita pursed his lips and came to a decision. "Put him to work in the mine."

Akitada's eyes flew to the mine entrance, where an exhausted and choking creature dumped his load and crept back in when a guard's whip was raised. He felt such a violent revulsion against returning to the darkness in the bowels of the earth that he thought he would rather die here and now than go back.

"He can't walk yet," said the guard dubiously.

"Then put him to work over there till he can," Kita said, pointing to the men who were pulverizing rock near the sluice.

And that was where they dragged him. He was given a small mallet and told to break up the chunks of rock someone dumped in front of him. In his relief that he had been spared the mine, Akitada worked away at this chore with goodwill. He was far from strong, but the activity required little strength, just patience and mindless repetition. When he finished one batch, a worker would remove the dust and gravel and replace them with more rock chunks. He saw no silver veins in any of the chunks he broke up. There were some small yellow spots from time to time, but he was too preoccupied with his body to wonder much at this.

He ate and slept where he worked. His legs were hobbled at the ankles even though he was unable to walk. When he wished to relieve himself, he dragged himself behind some bushes and then crawled back. On the next day, a guard forced him to stand. To Akitada's surprise, he could put a little weight on his right leg again and, when poked painfully in the small of his back, he took the couple of staggering steps to the shrubs without screaming. All that was left from his injury was a stiff, slightly swollen, and bruised knee and an ache whenever he attempted to bend it.

They allowed him another day in the sunlight and fresh air before they sent him into the mountain. It was not a good moment for heroics. He was surrounded by hard-eyed guards, variously armed with whips, swords, and bows, and marched to the cave entrance, where they slung an empty basket over his shoulders by its rope and pushed him forward. In front of him and behind him shuffled other miserable creatures, each with a basket on his back. A break from the line was impossible.

The darkness received him eagerly. Air currents pushed and pulled as he shuffled in near-blindness in a line of about ten men following a guard with a lantern. They went down a steep incline, past gaping side passages, turning this way and that until he lost all sense of direction or distance. The rock walls closed in on him, and the tunnels became so narrow that he brushed the stone with his shoulders, and so low that he had to bend.

Panic curled in his belly like a live snake, swelling and choking the breath out of him until he wanted to turn and run screaming out of that place, fighting his way past the men behind him, climbing over their bodies if need be, clawing his way back to the surface, because any sort of death was better than this.

But he did not. And after a while, he could hear the hammering again, and then the tunnel opened to a small room where by the light of small oil lamps other miners chipped pieces of rock from the walls with hammers and chisels. He stood there staring around blankly, his body shaking as if in a fever. The empty basket was jerked from his back, and a full one put in its place. Its weight pulled him backward so sharply that his legs buckled and he sat down hard. A guard muttered a curse and kicked him in the side. Someone gave him a hand, and he scrambled to his feet. His bad knee almost buckled again. He sucked in his breath at the sudden pain. One of the other prisoners turned him about, and he started the return journey.

They carried the broken chunks of ore to the surface, where others dealt with them while they plunged back into the bowels of the mountain for another load. Kumo, for whatever reason, had spared his life to condemn him to a more ignominious and much slower end. As he trudged back and forth, he thought that he, Sugawara Akitada, descendant of the great Michizane and an imperial official, would finish his life as a human beast of burden, performing mindlessly the lowest form of labor, the dangerous and unhealthy work the drunken doctor had tried to spare him, and he knew now he would not survive it for long.

Two facts eased his panic. The smoke from the earlier fire had cleared and the air was relatively wholesome. The mine also seemed a great deal cooler than he remembered from the weeks he had spent in his grave. The other fact concerned his right leg. He still limped and felt pain in his knee, especially when he put strain on it carrying his load uphill, but the swelling was gone and he had almost normal movement in it again. In fact, activity seemed to be good for it.

But he was still very weak and the rocks in the basket were abysmally heavy. The rag-wrapped rope, which passed in front of his neck and over his shoulders, cut into his flesh, and he had to walk bent forward to balance the load. This, added to the steep climb back out, strained his weakened muscles to the utmost. The first trip was not too bad, because he was desperate to get back to the surface, but on the second one he fell. To his surprise, the man in front of him turned back to help him up, telling him brusquely to grab hold of his basket. In this manner, the other man half dragged him up the rest of the way into the daylight.

When Akitada had unloaded and looked to see who his benefactor was, he was startled to recognize him. The man's name escaped him for the moment, but he knew he was one of the prisoners from the stockade in Mano, the silent man with the scarred back. Their eyes met, and Akitada thanked him. The other man shook his head with a warning glance at the guards and started back into the tunnel. Akitada followed him.

He would not have lasted the first day if the man with the scarred back had not pulled him up on every trip to the surface. Even so, Akitada sank to the ground after his last trip. He was too exhausted to notice that the sun had set and it was dusk. His companion pulled him up, saying gruffly, "Come on. It's over. Time to rest."

Akitada nodded and staggered to his feet, heading toward the trees where he had spent the past nights. But the guard gave him a push and pointed his whip after the others who went back into the mine. So he was to spend even his nights underground again. Akitada almost wept.

They gathered in the larger cave by the light of a single smoking oil lamp. The prisoners sat and lay wherever there was room. Akitada found a place beside his benefactor. Someone passed food and water around. He drank thirstily, but his stomach rebelled at the sight and smell of food.

"Better eat," said the man with the scarred back.

Akitada shook his head. Then he said, "Haseo. Your name is Haseo, isn't it?"

The other man nodded.

"I'm sorry you ended up here."

Haseo lowered his bowl and looked at him. "So did you. Almost didn't recognize you."

"My own fault. I was careless."

An understatement. He had made many careless errors, had thrown caution to the wind, had followed every whim, thoughtless and mindless of obligations and prudence. His punishment was terrible, but he had brought it upon himself.

The other man gave a barking laugh. "I suppose that's true of all of us."

Akitada looked at the others, so intent on their food that few of them talked. They were here because they had been careless of the law, of the rights of their fellow men, and of their loved ones. He had not broken any laws, but he, too, had failed. He thought of Tamako. She would never know that he had betrayed his promises to her with Masako, but he knew and was being punished for it. If his mind had not been preoccupied with his affair, he would surely not have made the foolish mistakes that led to his capture. He had known that Genzo was treacherous, yet he had left his precious identity papers and orders unattended for hours, no, days, all the while congratulating himself for having so cleverly eavesdropped on the conspirators.

"What's funny?" asked Haseo.

Akitada started. He must have been smiling—bitterly—at his own foolishness. "I was thinking of my carelessness," he said. Most of the prisoners were already settling down to sleep, and the single guard was arranging himself across the tunnel that led to the outside in case anyone attempted to run away during the night. Then he blew out the oil lamp and plunged them all into utter darkness.

Akitada tensed against the terror. His fingers closed convulsively around sharp bits of gravel. Any moment, he knew, he must scream or suffocate. Then he felt a hand on his shoulder, giving it a reassuring squeeze. "Sleep," Haseo whispered.

Akitada took a long, shuddering breath. "Is there any chance of getting out of here?" he whispered back.

Haseo sighed. "Whereto?"

"It doesn't matter. I have to get out of this mine."

"They'll catch you fast enough and you'll be ten times worse off then," Haseo hissed.

Akitada thought of the man's horribly scarred back. "It's a chance I'll take. There's nothing here but certain death."

Haseo said nothing for a long time. Then he muttered, "Go to sleep. You'll need your strength tomorrow. I can't drag you behind forever." He turned his back to Akitada and lay down.

Akitada sighed and closed his eyes.

The next morning began badly, because Akitada's body, unused to the previous day's labors, rebelled against movement of any sort. He had to grit his teeth to get up and make his way to the outside. He was determined not to be a burden to Haseo again.

But every step eased the stiffness, and for the first time he felt ravenously hungry. They ate with the others at the mouth of the mine. Akitada looked his fill at the blue sky and the tips of trees gilded by the rising sun, listened to the sound of birds and of water running down the sluice, and drew in the clean sharp scent of the forest.

The goblin brought his food, staring at him intently. He nodded his thanks and smiled. To his surprise, her fierce coloring deepened to a more fiery red and she scurried away with a giggle. He was too hungry to wonder at her behavior, especially when he saw that his portion was unusually large and contained several generous chunks of fish.

Work was no easier this day, especially since he took care not to burden Haseo again, but he managed to get through it, and that night he decided to ask Haseo more questions.

"Have you been here long?" he began as they settled down to their evening meal.

"Came right after we met."

It struck Akitada that Haseo, though still taciturn, spoke rather well for a common criminal. "What sort of life did you lead before they sentenced you?"

The bearded face contorted suddenly. "Amida, how can you ask a man that? How about you? Did you leave a wife and children to starve? This"—he waved a hand around to encompass mine, prisoners, sleepy guard, and empty food bowls—"is hell, but it's nothing compared to the fear for those you leave behind. They took my land and drove my family into the streets."

"I am sorry for you and for them." Akitada felt vaguely guilty. He was an official himself, and had on occasion pronounced sentences like Haseo's. His crime must have been very serious to warrant not only exile at hard labor, but confiscation of his property. To judge by the man's speech he was no commoner, and the confiscation of his land implied that he belonged to the gentry. Hoping not to offend again, he probed cautiously, "Sometimes a man's allegiances may be held against him."

"Sometimes a man's greed may cause him to take another man's property." Haseo gave a bitter laugh. "If I had known what I know now, I would have left my land with my family before it came to this."

"What happened?"

Haseo snorted. "You wouldn't believe it. Forget it."

Akitada whispered urgently, "Don't you want to escape?"

Haseo merely looked at him.

Akitada looked around the room. Nobody paid attention to them. The guard was busy arranging a bed for himself. Moving closer to Haseo, Akitada whispered, "I know there are problems, but once we are out of this mine, I believe I can get us off the island. What I need to know is if there is another way out of this place. You've been here longer than I and you seem an intelligent man."

Haseo glanced at the figure of the guard who lay across the tunnel opening again and was about to blow out the lamp. Akitada caught a speculative look on Haseo's face before they were plunged into the dark. "There might be," Haseo breathed in his ear.

"How?" Akitada breathed back.

"Old tunnels. The ones they stopped working. Nobody goes in them anymore. There's one where air is blowing in through the planks that board it up. Fresh air!"

Akitada had noticed that the smoke had cleared out of the mine rather quickly, and that cool air currents passed through the tunnel all day and night, but he had not thought why this should be so. Now he realized that the air came from the outside and moved back to the outside, and that meant there were other openings in this mine.

"Of course!" he said, and sat up, causing the chains around his ankles to rattle.

The guard in the tunnel entrance growled sleepily, "Quiet there, filth, or I'll put you on night shift."

Total silence fell. Even the snorers held their breaths.

There was no chance of further talk that night or during the following day, but Akitada was alert to the air currents as he made his way back and forth with his basket. He found the place Haseo had mentioned, and the next time they passed the boarded-up section, he caught up to him and gave his basket a small nudge. Haseo paused for the space of a breath, then, without looking back, he nodded his head.

The opening was slightly smaller than the tunnel they were in. They would have to crawl, but it was not as tiny as the badger holes and might even widen out later. The boarding-up had been done in a makeshift manner, more to mark this as an abandoned working and to keep people from getting lost than to prevent entrance.

Akitada spent the rest of the day memorizing the location and trying to picture the direction of the abandoned tunnel in relation to the cliff and the rest of the mountain they were working. He thought it likely that somehow one of the workings of a vein of silver ore had led from the interior of the mountain back to its surface. Each time he passed the blocked tunnel, he sniffed the air, and imagined that he could detect a faint tang of pine trees and cedars.

That night he waited impatiently for the guard to go to sleep, then murmured very softly to Haseo, "Are you willing to try?"

There was no answer. He opened his mouth to repeat his question more loudly, when a callused hand fell across his lips.

Haseo whispered, "When?" The hand was lifted, and Akitada breathed, "Tomorrow night?"

There was a very soft snort, almost a chuckle, and, "You're a fool!"

Akitada was not sure what that meant. He spent most of the night considering how they might accomplish such a mad endeavor. And mad it surely was, for no one knew if they would really find a way out. But what did they have to lose? And staying here longer while he slowly regained his strength was even more foolhardy, for Kumo's order to put him to death might arrive any moment.

He was methodical about his planning. Their only chance of getting away was at night. Only one guard stayed with them and, certain that the prisoners were too exhausted to attempt anything, he slept. To be sure, he slept with his body blocking their only way out, secure in the knowledge that the chains on their feet would warn him of any improper movements. The guard was the first obstacle, but not an insurmountable one.

Next Akitada considered whether they should invite the other prisoners to join them. He rejected the thought—reluctantly, because help was useful. The abandoned tunnel might contain obstructions, and Akitada was not really strong enough yet for what might await them inside. He suppressed a shudder at the thought of becoming lost and dying a slow death of starvation in utter darkness. There was also safety in numbers, because the guards would have a much harder time chasing down twenty men than two. But the trouble with taking the others was that they would make too much noise and slow them down. Besides, the cowed creatures he had observed might well give the alarm and draw the guards after them.

So it had best be just the two of them. After overcoming the sleeping guard, they would make their way up the main tunnel to the boarded section. They would need a few tools.

Fortunately, the workers left their hammers and chisels lying about. They would also need an oil lamp and some flint.

And they would need a lot of luck. A great deal depended on whether the boarded-up tunnel led out of the mine, preferably without emerging near the front. Akitada whispered some of this to Haseo, who responded merely by squeezing his shoulder.

The next morning there was little chance for communication with Haseo except through eye contact. Among the discarded debris were rags and remnants of frayed rope. Akitada cast a meaningful glance at one such pile and bent to touch his chained ankle. Then, in passing, he scooped up a handful of the torn material, tucking it inside his shirt. He noticed that Haseo did the same later. They dropped their gatherings near their sleeping places, where they attracted no notice because the floor was already covered with all sorts of litter. At one point, Haseo surreptitiously slipped a chisel under their small hoard, and before the light was extinguished, Akitada marked a place where several hammers had been left.

That night they ate what might be their last meal for a long time, perhaps forever. Then they waited. They did not talk. There was nothing to talk about, and they could not afford to attract attention.

When he judged that the snoring around them had achieved its usual fullness and rhythm, Akitada began passing rags and rope bits to Haseo. They wrapped the fabric carefully around their chains to muffle them.

When the moment came, it was Haseo who gave the signal and Haseo who moved first. Akitada had wanted to get to the guard himself to silence him because he feared that Haseo would simply kill the man. But it was too late to worry about it. Too much—their lives—hung in the balance, and this guard was one of the more cruel Ezo males.

Akitada crept toward the tools, felt for two hammers and a second chisel, and tucked them into his belt. Then he crept back to the tunnel opening. By now his heart was pounding so violently that it interfered with his hearing. Where was Haseo? At one point Akitada put his hand on a sleeper's leg and froze, but the man merely mumbled and turned over. He was still crouching there, trying to remember the layout of the room, when Haseo's hand fell on his shoulder. He heard him breathe, "Follow me," and took his hand.

Moving soundlessly, they came to the guard, now unconscious or dead, and, feeling their way, stepped over his body. The room behind them remained quiet. Holding their breaths, they shuffled up the dark tunnel as quickly and silently as they could. Akitada expected to hear an outcry at any moment, but nothing happened.

When they reached the boarded-up tunnel, he passed one of the hammers to Haseo, whispering, "What did you do to the guard?"

Haseo must have rescued his chisel, for he was already loosening the boards. "What do you think?" he hissed as something creaked and splintered.

"Careful," whispered Akitada. "Someone might hear." He reached for his own chisel and felt along the edge of the top board. Haseo had loosened it so that it could be pulled outward. Other boards were nailed to it. "Can we just shift it enough to creep through and close it behind us? It would give us time when they start searching."

Instead of answering, Haseo bent to loosen the lower edge while Akitada pulled. Working by touch alone was difficult. Akitada had forgotten to bring a light, and had had no opportunity to steal a flint anyway. The thought of creeping into an unfamiliar tunnel in utter darkness momentarily made his stomach heave. He reminded himself that showing a light would have been too dangerous anyway.

The makeshift doorway eventually gaped far enough to let them slip through. They pulled it back into place after them, hoping that their prying chisels had not left noticeable scars.

Starting forward slowly, they felt their way by moving along one of the walls with one hand stretched out in front to keep from running into sudden projections. They had progressed for some distance along the winding tunnel when Haseo stopped. Akitada heard the sound of a flint, and then the rough tunnel walls lit up around them.

Taking a deep breath of relief, Akitada said, “Thank heaven for that. How did you manage both lamp and flint?”

But Haseo was already moving on. “Took them off the guard, of course. It’ll make it harder for them to get out in the morning.”

Seeing their surroundings was not reassuring, however. Cracked timber supports and large chunks of rock fallen from above marked this as a dangerously unstable section, and when the tunnel eventually widened and the ceiling rose so that they could walk upright, they found numerous branch tunnels, some of which they explored until they ran out. The air remained fresh and sweet, however. They spoke little, and then tersely and in low voices about their desperate undertaking.

“There are too many tunnels,” Akitada said after a while. “We cannot waste time with all of them, and how do we know we’re in the right one?”

“Don’t know. Have to follow the air current.”

Some tunnels were too small to consider. With the rest they checked the air flow, but could not always be certain, and in the end, they chose to stay in the largest tunnel.

“How far have we come?” Haseo asked at one point.

Akitada had attempted to count steps, short ones since their chains still hobbled them. He told Haseo, who muttered, "Got to move faster. Damn these chains," and took such a large step forward that he fell flat on his face. The oil lamp flew from his hand and broke with a small clatter. Instant darkness enveloped them. Haseo cursed. When Akitada had helped him up, he said, "Well, we'll have to feel our way like blind men. But let's take off these chains."

"We have no light. It will be time enough when we get out."

Haseo protested, "But we need to get to the outside while it's still dark and then run like demons. I tell you, this place'll swarm with guards and soldiers as soon as it's daylight."

"What did you do to the guard?" Akitada asked again.

"Hit him with a piece of rock."

"Did you kill him?"

"Maybe."

They continued. The tunnel climbed upward, making several turns but still promising escape. It was nerve-racking work in the utter darkness. They groped their way, taking turns at going first, feet testing the ground, and hands stretched out to meet obstacles. Their inability to see seemed to magnify sounds, and small rocks kicked by their feet made them stop to listen, reminded of the constant danger of rock falls. The darkness raised vivid images of being crushed or, worse, becoming walled in alive. Each caught in his own nightmare, they stopped talking.

And then the tunnel ended.

Akitada had been in front for a while, moving more quickly in his impatience. He suddenly stubbed his toe, stumbled, and fell forward onto a pile of rocks.

"What are you doing?" Haseo asked. He came up and felt for Akitada.

"It's a rock pile," muttered Akitada, scrambling up it with some difficulty, because the rubble kept shifting under his feet and he kept slipping back down, causing small rock slides.

"Move aside." Haseo passed him, having better luck.

"How much is there, do you think?" Akitada asked from below. He jumped aside when a low rumble announced another rock slide. When it stopped, he said, "Be careful or you'll bring the whole mountain down on us."

Haseo did not answer. Akitada could hear him sliding all the way down. "It's the end," Haseo said tonelessly, stopping beside him. "It goes all the way to the ceiling. If this tunnel ever led to the outside, the rock fall has filled it. Maybe that's why they stopped working it."

Akitada sat down next to him. He was very tired. "We must think," he said.

Haseo gave a bark of bitter laughter. "You're a fool. I told you so last night. We'll die here."

"We won't die here. And if you thought it was so foolish, why did you come?"

Haseo did not answer that. Instead he said, "You're right. Let's think."

"We could go back and try the other tunnels. One or two seemed promising."

But they did not have the heart for it. They had been so sure. Perhaps an hour passed while they rested, dozed, tried to gather their strength for the next attempt. Akitada was the first to stand up.

"Come on. There's not much time. We must try another way."

Haseo staggered to his feet. "All right." He started back, but Akitada caught his sleeve.

"Wait," he said. "Do you hear something?"

Haseo listened. "No. Nothing. Just the air."

"Yes, the air. The current is still there. And it makes a whistling sound we did not hear before. Like the sound a flute makes when you blow it. Do you know what that means?"

"Forget it! You can't go by air flow. See where it got us."

"But the sound comes from the rock pile. Somewhere up there is a narrow opening letting in the air and that is why it whistles."

Haseo pondered this. "Surely you don't plan to move the whole rock pile?" he finally said.

"We've carried rocks before. Why not now when it may mean our freedom?"

"The whole thing may come loose and crush us."

"Yes. But perhaps not."

Haseo grunted and then climbed back up to the top, Akitada at his heels. He could hear him scrabbling about, and then a large piece of rock slid his way. He caught it barely before it would have crushed his fingers, and slid back down with it.

They worked on like this for what seemed like hours, sweat and stone dust crusting on their skin. Haseo grunted, cursed, and muttered, "Waste of time," and "Stupid" under his breath, but he continued loosening rocks and passing them down by feel alone. Akitada was tiring. His excitement had carried him this far, but now his weakened body rebelled. After each stone he deposited below, it was a little harder to climb back up the few steps to where Haseo had made a foothold for himself. He was working much faster than Akitada could carry the rocks down.

Eventually Haseo was surrounded by a wall of rocks and stopped. "It's no good," he said. "There are too many for us to move. Let's go back before we wall ourselves in."

Akitada listened. "The whistling has stopped," he said.

Haseo listened also and started groping around again. "Wish we had a light. I can feel the air in my hair. Wait a minute." There was clatter, then the rocks beneath them seemed to come alive and shift.

"Watch out," cried Akitada as he fell on his back and was carried downward. Haseo began to curse amid the rumble of falling rocks. When the noise stopped, Akitada cried, "Haseo? Are you all right?"

"Yes. I think so." Haseo's voice came from somewhere beyond the rock pile.

"Where are you?"

"You were right. We're through. The tunnel goes on from here. Come on, but watch your feet. I got a nasty cut on my ankle."

"Stand back in case it shifts again." Akitada groped his way to the top of the pile carefully, found that he could wiggle through beneath the roof of the tunnel, then sat and slowly slid down on the other side.

Their success gave them new hope and they moved forward again. But soon the tunnel narrowed sharply and the ceiling dipped until they had to crawl again. It looked as though they were coming to the end of the lode. Haseo was in front, and when Akitada got down on his hands and knees, he felt something wet on the ground. He raised his hand to his nose and sniffed. Blood.

"Wait, you're bleeding," he cried.

Haseo gave a snort—"I know"—and kept crawling.

"It must be bad. We should stop and tie up the wound," said Akitada.

"There's not enough room," grunted Haseo. Then he stopped and said, "Amida. I don't believe it."

"What?"

"I can see the stars. Either that or I'm dying."

Since Haseo's body blocked the crawl space almost completely, Akitada could not see, but his heart started hammering. "Can you get out?"

A muffled "Yes, oh, yes" came back on what sounded like a sob. Then Haseo slid away from him and there, barely lighter than the tunnel, was a patch of night sky.

Akitada crawled forward like a man in a dream. His hands touched the moist coolness of grass and he felt his shoulders brush past the mouth of the tunnel as he slipped through, then rolled down a steep slope and came to rest in a batch of bracken, breathing the scent of pine and clover and looking up at a starry sky.

CHAPTER EIGHTEEN

THE GOLDEN PHOENIX

Little Flower asked to see Tora the next morning. He had just finished his bowl of watery rice gruel without complaint—he did not mind sharing with Oyoshi's large brood—when the request came. His hopes that Little Flower might have some new information about Wada to impart were quickly crushed by the landlady's knowing wink.

"I'm pretty busy this morning," he hedged, scratching one of the flea bites he had picked up overnight.

She grinned her gap-toothed smile and slapped his back with a cheerful, "Go on, handsome!" Tora, conscious of his new rank, thought her manner overly familiar, especially when she added, "You're the first man Little Flower has lost her heart to. She deserves something nice for a change."

He reached for his helmet and edged toward the door. "I'll look in later," he lied.

"It'll just take a moment." Oyoshi firmly took his arm and led him to the back of the hostel.

She flung back Little Flower's door and pushed him in, slamming it behind him with a giggle.

Little Flower had taken pains with her toilet. She wore a garishly printed robe, covered mostly with red and pink peonies and brilliantly green leaves, and had tied a yellow sash about her tiny waist. Her face was powdered, the eyebrows black smudges painted on her forehead, the eyes ringed with charcoal, and her lips rouged into a tiny rosebud. Someone, perhaps Oyoshi, had brushed her hair and draped it artfully over her thin shoulders. On either side of her painted face, a portion of hair had been whacked off in the style that little girls wore. These small black wings framed her face, making it appear incongruously young.

Tora, still scratching, simply stared at her.

She smiled—carefully, so as not to disturb the thick layer of powder—and revealed black teeth. "Do you like it, Master Tora?" she asked. "I wanted to show you that I can be quite pretty when I'm not sick. I'm much better today."

Tora swallowed. "I'm glad."

She sat down and patted a cushion beside her invitingly. "Why don't you keep me company for a little while?"

"I . . . I have things to do."

Her eyes grew large with hurt. "You don't like me like this? The hair? I should have pinned it up. Or perhaps you prefer less paint? Master Wada doesn't like me to paint. He wants me to look like a child, but I thought you . . . you would be used to the women in the cities . . . very elegant and beautiful . . . oh, I shouldn't have bothered." Forgetting the thick white paint, she hid her face in the peony sleeves and wept.

Tora muttered a curse and knelt beside her. "Don't do that, Little Flower," he said gruffly. "You are really very pretty just as you are. You shouldn't try to please that animal Wada or me. You should go home to your family and find some other kind of work where you don't get hurt by men."

But it did no good. She sat there, weeping sadly into her finery, and after a while, he got up and left.

For once Turtle was nowhere to be found, and Tora walked to the harbor alone. The day was overcast and a chill wind whipped up the incoming tide so that the fishing boats bobbed like chaff among the whitecaps and dirty yellow foam covered the shore. Gulls swooped with raucous cries, diving for the small creatures the sea had thrown up on land and which scrambled madly to return to the safety of the ocean. This land was inhospitable to man and beast. The scene filled Tora with more gloom and a sense of urgency.

A few bearers were moving remnants of the previous day's cargo, but no new ships from the mainland had arrived, and the harbor was without its usual staff of constables. Tora strolled along the street of ramshackle wine shops, warehouses, and port offices toward the end where some trees and more substantial roofs signaled better accommodations. He passed the wine shop where he had first stopped after disembarking. It was empty, but then it was still early in the day.

The grove of trees was behind a building that bore the sign "The Golden Phoenix." Tora stopped and looked the place over. So this was where Wada had met Little Flower. Somewhere in back must be the place where he had almost beaten her to death. He wondered how often a man like that needed to repeat this sort of experience. There seemed no shortage of poor women willing to take their chances with such men, but how sharp were Wada's appetites? Did he indulge them once a month, every week, or more often? He wished he could send Turtle to ask some questions for him. Where was the rascal when he was needed?

It was much too early for business, and no one seemed about. Tora decided to play the curious visitor and take a stroll about the premises. He put his head in the main house first. It was filled with the smells of such establishments: stale wine, food, perfume, sweat, and, faintly, sex. Apparently none of the employees had returned yet to clean up and ready the place for another night of debauch. But Tora did not think that even in lax Sadoshima a house would be left wide open to casual thieves, and he continued his reconnaissance with a stroll around the main building and into its back gardens. These were surprisingly well kept. When he turned to look back at the house, he saw why. Most of the rooms of the Golden Phoenix overlooked the gardens. Very nice.

But the gardens were only trimmed neatly near the main house. Farther off, dense shrubs and trees had been allowed to close off the view to the small building whose roof just showed above them.

A narrow path, lined with stones, led to the far corner of the property. Here a small cottage or summerhouse stood close to the woven bamboo fencing separating the grounds of the Golden Phoenix from a wooded shrine area beyond. The door to the cottage was open, and he saw that it contained only a single room, occupied at the moment by a small elderly woman on her hands and knees, scrubbing the grass mats and muttering to herself.

Tora had approached silently on the smooth stones of the path. She jumped a little when he cleared his throat.

"Good morning, auntie," he greeted her. "Up so early after a late night?"

She took in his uniform, then stood painfully and bowed. "Good morning, sir. We're not open yet, but please to return later this evening. The Golden Phoenix offers the most elegant entertainments, the finest wine, and the most delicious foods. Can I be of some service to the officer?"

Apparently the polite phrases had been drummed into her head. As a potential customer of the Golden Phoenix, Tora must be encouraged to spend his money. He sat down on the veranda steps and smiled at her. "I was taking a stroll out near the harbor, but it's a bit windy, so I came inside. Nice garden, this. Do you mind if I rest here for a while?"

She bowed again. "Please make yourself at home, sir. Can I fetch you some wine?"

"No, don't trouble. Go on with your work. I'll just sit here." The infernal bites started to itch again, and Tora scratched as he watched her.

She got back on her knees and started scrubbing again. Bloodstains? Yes, Tora thought the water had a pinkish tinge. "Some of your guests spilled their wine?" he called out to her.

"Not wine." She made a face.

Pretending idle curiosity, Tora got up to take a closer look. "Oh," he said in a startled tone, "it's blood. Somebody got hurt. A drunken brawl?"

She sat back on her heels and looked around at the many small dark red splatters which dotted the mats in all directions. Tora pictured the nude childlike body of Little Flower flung face down on the floor while that bastard Wada stood over her with a leather whip. The picture sickened him. Would she have been tied down? He glanced around the small room. Two smooth wooden pillars supported the wooden ceiling. The floor was also wood under the grass mats. Against the back wall stood a screen with badly painted willow trees and two lacquered trunks for bedding. There was no sign of any whips. Wada probably carried his own.

The elderly woman followed his eyes and shook her head. "Just a customer and his companion."

"What did they do?"

"Some men enjoy hurting the girls," she said, her face stiff with disapproval.

"That sounds nasty." Tora pretended shocked interest. "Does it happen a lot?"

"No, thank heaven. The Willow Cottage costs extra." She bent to her scrubbing again.

"It should. These men, what do they do to the women?"

She paused in her scrubbing, but did not turn around. For a moment, Tora thought she would tell him, but she just shook her head and continued with her work.

"If the owner knows," said Tora, "why does he allow such customers here?"

"Money."

"Oh." Tora sat back down. "You'd think the police would take an interest in such things."

"Hah," she snorted.

"What do you mean?"

She turned around and gave him a pitying look. "You being a stranger here, Officer, all I can say is, stay away from the police."

Tora tried to get more from her, but she clamped her mouth shut and shook her head stubbornly.

"You must expect the customer back tonight," he said.

"I hope not." She got up and gathered her rags and bucket of water, muttering, "I doubt the poor thing's in any shape for it."

And that was that. Tora thanked her for the rest and took his leave. He walked away glumly. Turtle's suggestion had been to catch Wada here during one of his private nights of pleasure with Little Flower. It would have been perfect. The cottage was secluded, and even if they made any noise grabbing him, nobody would pay attention. Now, with Little Flower too injured to service the depraved lust of the police lieutenant, there was no chance to catch him alone, and Wada knew what had happened.

Tora turned at the next corner and passed the shrine. Beyond its gateway the trees clustered thickly, hiding both the shrine building and the adjoining Golden Phoenix. He walked into the grounds, looked around, and then resumed his stroll about Mano. The main street took him all the way to the end of town without revealing much of interest. People were going about their daily business, glancing his way, but averting their faces as soon as he looked at them. No doubt recent events in Sadoshima had made them suspicious of soldiers.

Eventually, the houses thinned and straggled into open country. The road split, one arm leading north toward the mountains, and the other east. A dilapidated set of stables marked the crossroads. Tora put his head in the open door. A one-eyed groom who had several fingers missing—there seemed to be a lot of cripples in Mano—was tossing a small amount of stinking hay into a trough where three thin horses gobbled it eagerly.

"How much to rent a horse?" Tora shouted.

The man spat and mentioned an exorbitant amount.

"What? And where do you keep the magnificent beasts worth that much silver?"

He got an ugly squint from the remaining eye and a thumb pointing at the three nags.

"Them? You're joking. I guess you don't do much business at those rates."

"Take it or leave it. Most people walk. Horse fodder costs as much as food."

Tora told the fellow he would think about it and walked back to the hostel. Oyoshi greeted him so eagerly that he was afraid she would try to lock him into Little Flower's room, but she only wanted to know if he wished to buy another dinner for that evening. Half her brood were gathered about her to hear his answer, their eyes glued on him with such fixed intensity that they might have been praying to the Buddha.

"Why not?" he said, smiling at the children and pulling out the money. Back in his room, he kicked the vermin-ridden bedding out the door and checked his money. Feeding a family the size of Oyoshi's and taking care of the injuries of local whores was rapidly depleting the funds his mistress had carefully counted out. He decided against a visit to the bathhouse to get some relief for his itching body. If he did not catch Wada tonight, his chances would rapidly disappear.

Turtle made his appearance late in the day, about the time when appetizing smells wafted from Oyoshi's cooking pots. Since Tora planned to visit every low dive in town and thought his fine new uniform too good for what might happen, he was changing into a plain dark robe when Turtle appeared in his door.

"Where have you been?" Tora demanded. "I thought you were going to be my servant."

"Sorry, master. I was working for you all morning. Had to advance my own money to get some information."

Tora looked at him suspiciously. "What information?"

"Nobody has seen Master Wada anywhere."

Tora grabbed Turtle by the neck and shook him. "You crook," he cried. "You think I'll pay for that kind of news? You're fired." He pushed the small man away in disgust.

"No, no. Wait. There's more. Today he sent a message to old Motoko."

"Who's old Motoko?"

"She keeps whores and makes assignations."

"Ah." Tora felt a thrill of satisfaction. "So the bastard is at it again. Do you know what he plans to do?"

Turtle shook his head regretfully. "Motoko won't talk to me. We're competition."

"Well, I was going to look for him tonight anyway. I'll stop by the Golden Phoenix again. Maybe this new girl is as big a fool as Little Flower."

"I can find out for you," wheedled Turtle.

"Can you? Good. Do it."

Turtle's face fell. "You mean now? Before I eat? And aren't you going to pay me what you owe?"

"If you're quick about it, there'll be some food left. What do I owe you?"

Turtle mentioned a reasonable amount, and Tora paid. Turtle looked at the coppers in his hand thoughtfully and said, "You know, sometimes it costs more. For example, the Golden Phoenix is very expensive."

Tora snapped, "I don't expect you to go there as a paying customer. If you have any brains, you should be able to ask one of the waiters or servants if the Willow Cottage is still available."

Before leaving his room, Tora gave his half armor, the helmet, and the long sword a longing glance, but he settled for his short sword, tucked out of sight under the loose jacket.

As before, he sat down to dinner with Oyoshi's family. Turtle was not back, but his sister had laid a cushion for him. There was, however, another guest tonight. Little Flower, dressed more modestly and without paint on her face, knelt next to Oyoshi, ostensibly to help with the children.

Tora saw her with a slight panic, but approved of her appearance and told her so. She blushed and smiled shyly. He was struck by how much she resembled the young women with whom he usually flirted and he smiled at her.

"You look very handsome also," she murmured, encouraged by his compliment. "Why are you not wearing your uniform tonight?"

Her question reminded Tora of his failed efforts with Wada and he became glum again. "I don't know what I'll get into tonight," he said grimly. "Better not ruin the uniform. Some people have no respect for an honest military man."

Instantly she looked alarmed. "What are you going to do?"

Tora was touched by her concern, but thought it best to sound manly and determined. "I'm going to get that bastard Wada tonight. If I have to, I'll fight him, his constables, and the local guard to find my master."

"Oh, no! You'll get yourself killed," she moaned, turning quite pale.

"Well," he snapped, hurt by her lack of confidence, "since you're in no shape to set the bastard up for me, I'll have to get him any way I can."

Little Flower gave a small sob and ran from the room.

Oyoshi said reprovingly, "You shouldn't tease her so. She's fallen in love with you."

Tora stared at her. "She hardly knows me. Why would she do a stupid thing like that?"

"Oh, you men!" Oyoshi refilled his bowl with large chunks of some excellent grilled fish and topped this off with stewed eggplant and mushrooms. "Little Flower has never met a man like you before." She gave him an appraising look as she passed the food across. "She says you're as handsome as Genji, as strong and brave as Fudo, and as loving and kind as the goddess Kannon herself."

"Nonsense." Tora blushed and turned his attention to his food and to joking with Oyoshi's children.

Turtle returned, out of breath and with an anxious eye to the leftovers. He announced, "Nobody's reserved the Golden Phoenix's cottage tonight or tomorrow night." He snatched the bowl his sister had filled from her hand and fell to.

"I hope you had the brains to ask if Wada ever comes as a regular customer," Tora growled.

"Never," mumbled Turtle through a mouthful of food. "The food's no good and the charge too high. He eats and drinks in the Crane Grove or at Tomoe's restaurant."

"Hmm. We'll start with them first. You can come along as soon as you've stuffed your belly." He stretched and readjusted the sword under his sash.

Turtle's eyes widened. He lowered his bowl, his face shocked. "You're going to make trouble. Somebody's going to get hurt. I think I'll stay home."

Tora gave him a look of disgust. "Nonsense. I may need you. But you can wait outside for me. Just be there when I come out."

They left soon after. It was almost dark and the wind still blew sharp from the sea, signaling the end of summer. The streets were nearly empty. People had gone home to eat their rice, or to one of the wine shops whose lights winked invitingly up and down the main street of Mano.

When they did not find Wada at either of the establishments Turtle had mentioned, Tora began a systematic search of all the restaurants and low dives, looking grimmer by the minute.

He did not see Wada but had another kind of success. In one crowded wine shop, a burly guest rose when he heard Tora's question and walked over. "Who wants to know where the lieutenant is?" he demanded in a belligerent tone.

Tora's hopes lifted marginally. "The name's Akaishi. Who are you?"

"Ikugoro. Sergeant of constables. So what's your business with the lieutenant?"

"I have a few questions. Maybe you'll do." Tora gestured with his thumb toward a quiet corner.

The other man's small eyes narrowed even further. "What makes you think I'll talk to you?"

Tora looked around. He did not want to pay for wine for one of Wada's thugs, but a brawl would get him nowhere and cause people to get hurt. The three men Ikugoro had been sitting with were watching. Inspiration came to his assistance. He dug his faked dispatch with its official seals from his sash and held it before Ikugoro's face. The light was bad and he didn't think the sergeant could read in any case. "I shouldn't be showing you this," he said in a low voice, "but since you're his second in command, I'll let you in on a little secret. As you see"—he pointed to the first line of writing—"I'm an inspector for the imperial police in the capital. It's my duty to visit different provinces to check up on our appointees." Looking around in case someone was listening, he quickly put his document away again.

Ikugoro's face had fallen almost comically. "B-but what do you want with our lieutenant? Is anything wrong?"

"No, no." Tora chuckled. "On the contrary. He's applied for promotion and transfer to the capital and it looks like it'll be approved. I'm to clear up a few details before they act on it. To tell you the truth, I'm a bit behind schedule already and need to grab the next boat back to the mainland."

Ikugoro's eyes had grown round. Belatedly he came to attention and tried to salute.

Tora snatched his arm down. "Don't be a fool. I'm incognito, of course."

"Oh, sorry, sir. It's just . . . the surprise. Lieutenant Wada never mentioned to me that he wanted to leave."

"No. He wouldn't. It's one of the rules. He'd be disqualified if he let it get out that he planned to leave. You can see why."

Ikugoro nodded slowly. "Right. All hell would break loose. But . . ." He frowned. "You say his promotion is pretty certain? And then he'll leave here? And someone else will come to take his place?"

Tora could see that such a change and its impact on him troubled the sergeant deeply. He leaned closer. "You're his number two man," he whispered. "Most likely you'd be the one."

Ikugoro's small eyes widened again. Casting a nervous glance toward his companions, he said, "We'll talk over there in the corner, sir. I'll just tell my men it's private business."

When he returned, Ikugoro ordered the best wine in the house and paid for it. "The lieutenant was supposed to stop by tonight," he said, "but something must've come up." He winked and touched his crotch.

Tora emptied his cup, smacking his lips. "A ladies' man, eh? He'll be glad to get back to the big city, then. I bet he's running out of fresh fare by now."

Ikugoro laughed. "The lieutenant's got plenty of money. He buys what he wants." He leaned across to refill Tora's cup. "So tell me, sir, how likely is it that I'll get his job?"

"Provided I get my information and his application is approved, it depends on him."

"It does?"

"Will he speak up for you? You know, praise your brains, hard work, organizational skills, devotion to law enforcement, and honesty?" Ikugoro's face lengthened. "If he puts in a really good word, it'll save the government sending a new man all the way from the capital."

Ikugoro pondered this; then his face lit up. "Hah," he laughed. "It's done, then. He'd better write all that if he knows what's good for him."

"How do you mean?"

But Ikugoro apparently decided it was wiser not to mention certain details of their relationship that made him sure Wada would oblige. Instead he said, "Suppose my men and I start looking for him and send him to you? Where are you staying?"

Thinking quickly, Tora gave the name of an inn they had passed earlier. It was in a quiet part of town. He thought he could lie in wait for Wada and jump him when he came hotfoot to check out the news. He added, "Don't mention that I told you about his application. Just say an inspector from the capital wants to discuss his reassignment." They parted on friendly terms, and Tora rejoined Turtle outside. He found him in agitated conversation with his eldest nephew.

"What are you doing out on the streets this time of night?" Tora asked the boy.

"Mom sent me. I've been looking for you for hours. She says to come home right away. Little Flower's in some sort of trouble."

Tora cursed roundly. "Go tell your mother I haven't got time to go chasing all over town because of some stupid woman."

Turtle looked shocked. He said, "Oyoshi won't like it. She's taken to that girl. We'd better go see what happened. It's not far."

Tora gritted his teeth, but gave in. He hoped Ikugoro would not find Wada right away.

They found Oyoshi pacing up and down by a cold hearth to keep herself warm in the frigid drafts that whistled through the cracks. "There you are," she cried when she saw Tora. "Where have you been? I've been going out of my mind with worry. It's been hours. He's probably killed her by now."

"What did she do?" asked Tora, glowering.

Oyoshi wrung her hands. "Oh, the stupid girl. But it's all your fault. Men!"

Tora clenched his fists to keep from strangling her. Turtle gave him a worried glance and told his sister, "The officer is an honored guest in your house, sister. You should not speak to him this way."

Oyoshi flushed and bowed. "Oh, sorry. It's the worry. Please forgive what I said, sir. It was very improper. Especially when you have been so generous."

"Forget it and get on with the story," Tora ground out.

"After you and my brother left, Little Flower came to me, all dressed up for work. She said she was going to the Golden

Phoenix to meet that bastard Wada and to tell you so you could catch him. Oh, dear. It was such a long time ago. You must go immediately. The fool! She wanted to help you."

Tora turned on his heel and headed out the door, his face grim and his hand on the hilt of his sword. "Come on," he flung over his shoulder to Turtle. But on the street, he came to a halt. "No. Go back in and get my things," he said. Digging in his sash, he passed a handful of money to Turtle. "Then run to the post station outside town and hire three horses. Bring the horses to the shrine behind the Golden Phoenix and wait for me."

A party was in full swing at the Golden Phoenix. Lights blazed in the main house, ribald songs and shrill laughter of women came from inside, and a drunk vomited into the gutter near the entrance. Tora, grateful that his clothes were dark, slipped past him into the garden. Someone had thoughtfully lit an oil lamp in a stone lantern marking the path to the cottage.

It was occupied. Dim lights glimmered behind the closed shutters.

Taking off his boots, Tora climbed the steps in his bare feet, testing each before he put his weight on it. Outside the door he paused and listened. At first he thought nothing had happened yet, but then he heard a soft moan, followed by a male murmur and a rich chuckle that sent chills down his spine. He stretched out his hand to fling open the door, when common sense reminded him that a woman's moan might denote pleasure as well as pain, and that someone else might have rented the cottage after all. He could hardly burst in on a pair of strangers without causing trouble.

He crept toward the nearest shuttered window, crouched down, and peered through a chink. A narrow field of vision showed only the naked leg and bare buttock of a man standing upright. Just beyond the muscular leg was another, paler, and more slender leg of a woman. But the legs might belong to anyone.

There was another moan. What were they doing? Making love standing up? Why not? He had done it himself.

Tora was about to rise a little to look for another chink when he saw a thin red line creeping down the woman's leg. A second joined it before he realized that what he saw was blood.

He freed his sword and was at the door in an instant. It was locked. With a roar of rage and frustration, he stepped back and threw himself at it. The wood splintered and gave with a crash, and Tora burst into the room.

He took in the scene at a glance. Wada, also with a short sword in his hand, pulled away from Little Flower, who was leaning against one of the pillars. Both were naked and their bodies were crimson with blood.

A second glance showed why. Wada had been cutting Little Flower's breasts and belly with the sharp blade of his sword. She was covered with crisscrossing cuts, not deep enough to kill but enough to cover her and Wada with blood. When she saw Tora, she gave a little sob and sagged against the ropes that tied her wrists behind the pillar.

Wada cursed viciously, his face distorted with fury, and came for Tora with his bloody sword.

Tora, tall and athletic, had been rigorously active all of his life. Wada was shorter, older, and had gone soft about the middle from too much good living and debauchery. It should have been easy. Tora stepped aside, thinking to disarm the man in one swift, smooth movement. But Wada, for all his years of bad living, had one advantage. Unlike Tora, he had been trained by a master in the military arts, and his use of the sword had become instinctive.

Thus Wada corrected instantly and slashed at Tora's belly so quickly that only Tora's alertness and youth allowed him to twist aside in time. He bit his lip and concentrated on blocking Wada's blade, which seemed to come at him from all directions.

The man's technique was far superior to his own, and he could only count on the fact that Wada's fury would cause him to make a mistake sooner or later. And even then, he could not kill the man. Everything depended on his taking Wada alive.

In the end, it was neither Wada's superior swordsmanship nor Tora's cool deliberation that ended the fight. Part of the broken door separated from its frame and fell; Wada dodged, stepped into some of Little Flower's blood, and slipped, sinking momentarily to one knee. Tora moved forward instantly, hitting Wada's sword arm hard with the flat side of his blade and disarming him.

Wada's sword skittered into a corner, and Wada clutched his arm, doubling up in pain. Tora dropped his sword, then bent and raised Wada's head by its topknot. "You're finished, bastard," he hissed, and struck him full in the face with his fist. Blood spurted from Wada's nose and mouth and he passed out.

Taking up his sword again, Tora went to Little Flower and cut her loose. She collapsed into his arms, whimpering softly. "That was a stupid thing to do," he scolded. "He might've killed you."

She gulped and mumbled, "I thought you'd never come. He started cutting deep when I told him about you."

She was clinging to him, and he thought he felt blood seeping through his robe. "Why did you tell him?" he asked.

"I was afraid. When he used his sword on me, I thought he'd kill me, so I told him I left a message for someone. He wanted to know who and kept cutting me until I told him. Then he got really angry. He called me a cheating whore and said he'd watch me bleed to death and . . . and . . ." She sagged abruptly and Tora laid her down on the mat, so recently cleaned by the old woman and now covered with gore beyond repair. Little Flower had many cuts, all of them bleeding, but two or three looked ugly. He snatched her thin undergown from the pile of clothing and, tearing it, pressed the fabric to the worst wounds, wondering what to do next. He could hardly call for help with Wada lying there unconscious.

He was still crouching over the unconscious Little Flower, both hands pressing fabric to her wounds, when he heard steps outside. Heavy male boots, and at least three pairs.

He twisted around just in time to see Wada on all fours crawling toward his sword. Then the broken door flew back and the brawny figures of Wada's constables appeared on the threshold, Sergeant Ikugoro in the lead and evidently bent on delivering Tora's message.

It was an awkward moment, and Tora had no time to consider his strategy.

He abandoned Little Flower and plunged for Wada, putting his foot so hard on Wada's outstretched hand that he could hear a bone snap. Wada screamed. Tora turned his head toward Ikugoro and said, "Good work, Sergeant. Just in time to help me tie up the prisoner."

Ikugoro's eyes bulged and his jaw dropped. "Wha . . . what's going on here?" he managed. Wada moaned and twisted on the floor, his hand still under Tora's foot. For a moment, the outcome hung in a delicate balance.

"Well?" growled Tora. "What are you waiting for? I thought you were a man of decision."

"Kill him, you fools," screamed Wada. "Kill him now!"

Ikugoro stepped forward. "Er, yes, sir," he mumbled, looking uneasily from Wada to Tora, "but what happened? Why are you arresting Lieutenant Wada, Inspector?"

"Look around you. Attempted murder—mine and hers—for a start. Now let me see if you have the qualities to uphold the law in Sadoshima."

Wada shouted, "You idiot. Don't listen to him."

Ikugoro glanced at Little Flower, sprawled naked and bleeding on the floor, and made up his mind. "Yes, sir. All right, men. Tie him up!"

The constables stepped forward, unwound the thin chains they carried around their waists to secure prisoners, and glanced doubtfully from Tora to Wada. "Which one, Sergeant?" asked the bravest one finally.

"The lieutenant, you fool. You heard the inspector. The lieutenant's been at it again, and this time he's killed the whore. Better put some clothes on him first, though. Knock him out, if you have to."

Tora took his foot off Wada's hand and left him to the constables. They actually grinned as they pulled up their cursing, screaming, and kicking commander, put his clothes back on him, and tied his wrists and ankles. Wada's hand was turning dark and swelling to twice its size. He squealed like a wounded animal at their rough handling. Ikugoro watched the struggle impatiently, then snapped, "I told you to knock him out."

"Sorry, Sergeant," grunted the big constable, and slapped Wada so hard that his head bounced off the wall and he crumpled to the floor.

Ikugoro shook his head. "They never liked the lieutenant much," he informed Tora.

"I see. Thank you, Sergeant. Well done. I'll see this gets mentioned in my report. Now we'd better get a doctor to see to the girl."

Ikugoro walked over to Little Flower and bent down. Straightening up, he said, "Not required, sir. She's dead."

It was true. Little Flower had lost too much blood, and the already weakened body had been unable to deal with the deep wounds Wada had inflicted. Rage filled Tora, rage against the man who had tormented her and finally killed her as he had promised to do, rage against himself for having come too late. He snatched up his sword and swung around. Ikugoro and his constables watched him uneasily.

Tora took a shuddering breath. "Yes," he said, and slowly tucked his sword back into his sash. "Well. We have a crime scene here, Sergeant. Send one of your men ahead to the coroner. The other two can get a ladder or plank to put the body on and take it to the tribunal. You, Sergeant, will help me here and then transport the prisoner to jail."

Ikugoro did not question the voice of authority, even if the orders were questionable in the present circumstances. He sent the constables about their duties and then helped Tora go through the motions of observing the evidence of what had happened here. Wada looked much the worse for wear when they turned their attention to him. His lip was split, his nose was purple and bloody, and both eyes were nearly swollen shut. When they asked him questions, he mumbled unintelligibly. Together they dragged him out into the garden. Tora cast a glance toward the back fence. Beyond lay the densely wooded shrine precinct. He hoped Turtle was waiting with the horses.

"Tell you what, Sergeant," he said. "We don't want to attract too much attention. You've got to make sure the coast is clear. Go out front to wait for your men and post one of them at the gate. Then come back."

As soon as Ikugoro had trotted off, Tora slung Wada over his shoulder and headed for the back fence. Dropping Wada over like a big bag of rice, he vaulted after, and dragged him off into the shrubbery.

CHAPTER NINETEEN

ESCAPE

Akitada lay among the bracken and looked at the tops of gently swaying trees and at the winking stars until he was dizzy. The world was filled with the scent of grass and clover, the clear chirruping of waking birds, the touch of a cool, dew-laden breeze. He had no wish for more.

But Haseo did. "The chains," he said softly, creeping up. "We've got to get the chains off. Do you still have your chisel or hammer?"

Akitada knew he did not, but he sat up and felt his clothing. "I lost them somewhere inside." He looked at the dark form of his companion and felt ashamed and irresponsible. "I'm sorry. That was careless," he said humbly. "I should have remembered." All that work and now they would be caught because the chains would keep them from getting away from the search parties which would soon start combing the mountainsides. He glanced at the sky again. There was a faint but perceptible lightening toward their left. The east. As far as he could make out, they were on the far side of the mountain, well above and to the back of the cliff with the badger holes. This was good, because they could not be seen or heard from the work site.

Haseo sighed. "Never mind. I lost mine, too. Look, maybe you'd better tie up my leg. I'm getting a bit faint. Here. Tear up my shirt."

Akitada could not see much of Haseo, but he felt the fabric thrust at him and groped for Haseo's leg. His fingers touched blood, lots of it, warm and slick under his touch. He ripped the shirt into strips, folded a part of the fabric, and told Haseo to press it over the wound, then tied it into place as firmly as he could.

"Stay here," he told Haseo, "while I look for a rock to work on those chains."

After much trial and failure, they found that draping the chain over a rock outcropping and then hammering away at it with a loose stone would eventually break a link. The small chinking noise terrified them in case someone should hear, and they paused many times to listen. All remained quiet, and they decided finally that they were too far from the mine entrance to be heard. But they were both exhausted by the time they had freed themselves.

And it was no longer night. The light had changed to a translucent gray, and the mountainside around them was filled with ominous dark shapes and obscure forms. They were far from safe, for with daylight their pursuers would find them gone. All around rose other peaks, wooded and rocky. Night still hung over the west, or they might have seen the sea. They would have to make their way down this mountain and get as far away from the mine as possible. The trouble was that neither knew exactly where they were. Haseo explained apologetically that he had not thought of escape when he was brought here, and Akitada had been unconscious.

Akitada looked curiously at Haseo in the growing light. He noticed for the first time how much thinner he had become since they had met inside the harbor palisade. Haseo was looking him over also and smiled. No doubt, thought Akitada, I look a great deal worse than he, even without a blood-soaked bandage around my leg. Two less likely creatures to make a successful escape from the top of a mountain guarded by Kumo's men could hardly be imagined. But they were free and had a chance, and that was wonderful. He chuckled.

"Why do you laugh?" Haseo asked.

"We look terrible, but by heaven, we will make it," said Akitada, and raised a grin on Haseo's drawn face. "Your leg still bleeds. Can you walk?"

Haseo got up and took a few steps to look down the mountainside. "Come on," he said. "This way. It'll stop bleeding, and if it doesn't, I'll at least put some distance between myself and those bastards before I collapse."

As the sun slowly rose over the mountains, they scrambled through gorse, brambles, and shrubs, sliding part of the way on their backsides, until they reached a small stream. It bubbled and splashed downhill, making its way around rocks and over them until it reached a small basin, where it pooled, clear as air, before washing over a rock outcropping in a small waterfall. Here they drank thirstily and then washed themselves. The water was cold, but it removed layers of dust, sweat, and dirt and made both of them feel nearly human.

It was such a pleasant place, and so peaceful—the only sign of life a rabbit, which scampered off—that they paused to tend to their injuries. Akitada tore up his shirt and replaced the blood-soaked bandage on Haseo's leg. The bleeding seemed to have lessened, but Haseo was pale and shivered even though the day was warming and they were sitting in the sun.

"I'm going to slow you down," Haseo said, when he got to his feet.

"Don't be ridiculous. I'm limping myself." Akitada's knee had not taken well to the hurried descent. It was painful, and Akitada feared it would swell again.

Haseo glanced at it and chuckled weakly. "Two cripples."

They smiled at each other, though there was little to smile about, and followed the stream downhill. Akitada liked Haseo's cheerfulness. The silent, glowering prisoner in the stockade had been a different man. This Haseo had both courage and a sense of humor. And he spoke like an educated man.

"Why weren't you speaking when we first met?" Akitada asked after a while. "I thought you hated us."

Haseo's face darkened. "I did. I found that when the constables and guards heard me speak, they were quite likely to use the whip on me. Mind you, it took me a while to work this out. I used to think that a man with my background might make a difference in the way the prisoners were treated. But my suggestions and comments were not well received by either the guards or my fellow prisoners. When one of the other prisoners ratted to the soldiers that I planned to complain about their brutality to the next official I encountered, I learned my lesson. My back's a constant reminder not to trust anyone. So I stopped talking altogether."

"But you spoke to me in the mine."

Haseo smiled crookedly. "By then I knew you were like me. Too clever to know when to shut up. Who are you, by the way?"

"Sugawara Akitada. I'm an official on temporary assignment in Sadoshima."

"Sugawara?" Haseo raised his brows and whistled. "And an imperial official! But you mean you used to be. What crime did you commit?"

"None. I'm neither a prisoner nor an exile. I'm a free man."

Haseo fell back into the grass and burst into helpless laughter. Akitada stopped and chuckled.

"Well," he corrected himself, "I'm theoretically a free man. The problem is getting back to provincial headquarters in Mano to establish my identity. And the gods only know what will await us there."

Haseo stopped laughing and sat up slowly. "You are serious? But what happened?"

Akitada bent to give Haseo a hand and winced at the pain in his knee. "It's too long a story. Let's keep moving and I'll try to tell you some of it on the way."

But when he turned, his eyes caught some movement on the other side of the stream. A large furry animal of some sort? Perhaps, but he did not think so.

"Take cover," he whispered to Haseo, and crossed the stream. His knee hurt, but he had to find out if they had been seen.

He caught sight of the squat brown figure almost immediately. Resembling some lumbering bear with a curly mane from this distance, the goblin was hurrying uphill with two buckets of water. Akitada scanned the area. Could they be that close to the mining camp? The hillside was empty, but evidently the stream was where the goblin got the water to cook with. Dear heaven, what if she had seen them? He could not take that chance.

The Ezo woman was not particularly agile at the best of times, and the full buckets hampered her. When she stopped to look back, Akitada was certain. He made a dash and seized her shoulders to swing her around. Water splashed from the buckets, and she gave a little cry.

Now that he had caught the woman, Akitada did not know what to do with her. Prudence suggested killing her, or at least tying her up to gain them a little more time, but he remembered the extra food she had brought him and could not bring himself to do either.

She looked up at him with an expression that was part fear and part joy. He dropped his hands, and she set down the buckets and smiled the familiar gap-toothed grin. "You safe," she said, nodding her head. "Good! You go quick now." A dirty brown hand gestured downhill. When he did not move, she said, "They looking in mountain." Her arm swept upward and waved a circle around the mountain looming above to indicate that the search had not progressed from the mine yet.

Haseo came up behind him. "We cannot let her go," he said softly.

Akitada swung around and hissed, "No. She won't tell." He wished he were as certain as he sounded. Her words had implied that she would not, but what if she had lied to save her neck? It was a terrible risk to take, and he was risking Haseo's life also.

Haseo shook his head. "Don't be a fool. She's the enemy. I'll do it, if it bothers you too much." He brought his hand forward and Akitada saw that he was clutching a large rock.

He stepped between Haseo and the woman. "No. She saved me from the fire and was kind to me. I cannot repay her by letting you murder her."

They spoke in low voices while she watched nervously. Someone shouted in the distance, and she cocked her head. "You go now. Quick or they kill!" she said urgently, gesturing toward the valley.

Akitada put his finger to his lips, and she nodded. He turned and took Haseo's arm and pulled him back into the trees.

Haseo dropped the rock. "That was foolish. They'll be after us faster than you can blink an eye. You should have left her to me. I would have made sure of her."

Akitada just shook his head.

They struggled on, following the stream down the mountain as fast as their legs could carry them while listening for sounds of pursuit. Fearful of being seen from above, they stayed under the cover of trees, though it slowed them down.

But all remained quiet, and eventually, out of breath and unable to run anymore, they reached the valley. The stream had widened and the mountains receded on either side of them. They saw the first signs of human habitation, small rice paddies or vegetable patches tucked on narrow plateaus. Haseo helped himself to a large radish and a half-ripe melon at one of these, and they stopped briefly to devour the food and wash it down with water.

Later they skirted a few small farms, cautious about being seen, even when the buildings looked like abandoned shacks. Akitada feared that the peasants were loyal to Kumo and would report to him the sighting of escaped miners. Walking became more and more difficult. They needed rest, but fear of their pursuers kept them plodding on doggedly.

The sun was setting when they staggered down yet another hill and found a road.

"I cannot go any farther," said Akitada, dropping down under a fir tree, one of a small copse, and rubbing his painfully swollen knee. "How is your leg?"

Haseo stood swaying. He looked terribly pale. "Bleeding again, I think," he mumbled. "Don't really want to know." Then he collapsed into the deep grass.

Akitada waited for him to sit back up, but Haseo had either fallen asleep or passed out. He crawled over and checked. The bandage was soaked with fresh blood. But Haseo was breathing normally, his mouth slack with exhaustion. He needed rest and a doctor's care.

A small stream passed nearby, and Akitada slid down to it. Pulling up some moss, he soaked it in the cold water and held it to his knee. He was faint with hunger and worried about Haseo. He had no idea where they were, but assumed the road in front of them led eventually to Mano. Moving southward should bring them to the sea. But roads were traveled by people, and they would attract attention. It struck him for the first time that they had a choice between risking recapture or dying from their injuries or lack of food in the wilderness.

When his knee felt a little better, he gathered more moss and wetted it, then crawled back to where he had left Haseo.

But Haseo was no longer alone.

Peering down at his sleeping figure stood a youngster of about ten who had a load of kindling tied to his back. He wore only a ragged shirt and did not look much better than they. Perhaps that was why he did not run away when Akitada approached.

"What's wrong with him?" he asked, pointing to Haseo's bloody bandage.

"He got hurt coming down the mountain," said Akitada, busying himself with undoing the bandage and packing the wound with the wet moss instead. "Do you live around here?"

"In the village. If he's hurt, you should take him to Ribata."

Akitada stopped what he was doing. "Ribata? The nun Ribata?" he asked the boy, dumbfounded. "Do you know her?"

The youngster made a face at such stupidity. "Of course. She lives here, doesn't she?"

Akitada stood up and looked around. "Here? Where?"

The boy pointed up the mountain on the other side of the road. "Up there. You can see the smoke. That means she's home. Sometimes she goes away."

Akitada regarded the child dubiously. Why would the nun live here on a mountain? Yet the more he thought about it, the more he was inclined to believe. He squinted at the thin spiral of smoke rising above the tall cedars halfway up the mountainside. Both nuns and priests withdrew to lonely mountain dwellings to spend their days in prayer and meditation. And they were probably not far from Mano. He asked the boy, "How far is it to Mano?"

The youngster pursed his lips and looked at the sun. "You might get there by night, maybe, but you'd better have her look at your friend first. She set my arm after I broke it last year."

In the distance a temple bell rang thinly. The boy straightened his load. "I've got to go," he said, and trotted away.

Akitada looked at the sleeping Haseo and decided to move him a few feet into some shrubbery out of sight from the road. Then he crossed the road and a field of tall grasses and began his climb through the forest toward Ribata's hermitage. He found a footpath after a while, but it was steep and when he finally emerged from the forest path into the small clearing, he was drenched in sweat and could not control the trembling in his legs.

A tiny wooden house, covered with morning glory vines and surrounded by a small vegetable plot, stood in the clearing. Below lay the grassy valley and beyond rose another wooded mountainside. A few feet from him was an open cooking fire with a large kettle suspended from a bamboo tripod. An appetizing smell drifted his way. Ribata's hermitage was simple but adequate and resembled many such places in the mountains around the capital. Only an abundance of flowers, the blue morning glories which covered its roof, the golden bells of day lilies, yellow rape, and purple asters, suggested that the hermit was a woman of refined tastes. The small place was so well hidden among the trees and vines that only those who knew of its existence would find it.

Greatly cheered by all of this, Akitada approached the hut and called out, "Is anyone home?"

It was indeed Ribata who appeared in the doorway, looking as slender and aristocratic in her white robe and veil as he remembered her. He bowed. "Forgive this intrusion, reverend lady, but a boy from the village directed me here. I have a friend who is wounded."

She shaded her eyes, then came down the steps to peer at him more closely. Half naked, dirty, and with his hair and beard grown wildly about his face, he imagined he was hardly a welcome visitor, but she recognized him. "Taketsuna? Praise to the all-merciful Buddha," she murmured. "Is it really you? We had almost given you up."

Akitada had not thought of himself as Taketsuna for such a long time that her mistake made him laugh. Or perhaps it was finally seeing a friendly face, being greeted with pleasure, being made welcome—all of this signaling his return to safety, to a world he knew, having crossed the threshold between a living death and life. He found it hard to stop laughing, but then his legs started shaking again, and he stumbled to the small porch and sat down. "We escaped from one of Kumo's mines," he explained. "But can you come with me to help my friend? He has lost a lot of blood from a leg wound. We must get to provincial headquarters in Mano as fast as possible."

She asked no questions. Saying, "Rest while I get ready," she disappeared into the hut. Akitada leaned against one of the beams supporting the roof and basked in the warmth of the sun, unaware that tears gathered in his eyes and slowly spilled. Bees swarmed in the morning glories above him. Doves cooed in the branches of a cedar, and far above a kite rode the breeze in leisurely circles. He closed his eyes.

"Masako? Toshito?"

Akitada jerked awake, not quite sure where he was for a moment. Then his surroundings took shape and meaning, and he saw that Ribata had come out of her hut. She held a bundle and was looking toward the forest. Akitada stumbled to his feet. "Masako? Masako is here? And Toshito? Mutobe's son Toshito? I thought he was in prison in Mano."

"They are both here." Ribata scanned the trees. "When you did not return before the trial, the children decided to escape. Masako helped Toshito by putting a sleeping powder in the guards' soup. They came to me and have been here ever since. I cannot imagine where they are. We will need their help."

Akitada tried to make sense of this. Ribata had made it sound quite natural that Masako should be with Mutobe's son. Whatever one might think of a young lady helping an accused murderer escape from his jail cell by drugging his guards, their coming here to hide had been smart. Perhaps the nun had suggested it herself on one of her visits to the young man. Perhaps she had even supplied Masako with the correct herbs to mix into the guards' food. Ribata seemed to have a knack for appearing in interesting situations. But Masako here? Akitada wondered what he would say to the girl when they met. He had not thought of their lovemaking in many weeks. That time seemed incredibly remote, though he found that her involvement with Toshito did not sit too well with him.

"I must go back to my friend," he said, moving toward the path down the mountain. "He is beside the road near a small stream and a stand of firs. If I go ahead, can you follow?"

She nodded. "I know the place."

He limped down the mountain, crossed the field and the empty road, and found Haseo still fast asleep in the grass where he had left him. Shaking his shoulder gently, he waited until his companion sat up groggily, then said, "Good news. I've found some shelter for us with someone I know. It's quite safe. And there is a good chance that Kumo has not taken over the island yet."

Haseo tried to stagger to his feet and failed. "How do you know it's safe?" he demanded, looking around anxiously.

"My friends are also hiding. It's too long a story to tell now, but there is a nun who has healing skills. Her hermitage is up on that mountain. She will see to your wound." Akitada's eyes searched the line of trees on the other side of the road. There was no sign of Ribata and the others yet. He was becoming impatient and worried that they were too close to the highway. "Come, lean on me. We will walk across to the forest and wait there."

Haseo's eyes followed his. "Sorry," he said. "You'll have to go without me. I can stay here."

"No. Just hold on to me. If I have to, I'll carry you on my back. You pulled me behind you in the mine, and this is nothing compared to that."

Haseo submitted with a weak chuckle, and they made their way across the road, and from there through the field of tall waving grasses toward the steep, wooded mountainside.

But Haseo sat down abruptly in the middle of the field. "It's no good," he gasped. "I have no strength left."

He looked dreadfully pale and, to Akitada's dismay, blood was seeping from his makeshift bandage again. They had nothing left that could be turned into bandages and regarded each other helplessly. Haseo grinned a little. "You know, for an official and nobleman you're a remarkably generous and patient man, Akitada. I was right to trust you."

It was the first time Haseo had used his personal name. Akitada felt touched and honored. "We put our reliance in each other," he said, squeezing the other man's shoulder. "When we reach provincial headquarters, I'll see what can be done about your case, though I'm afraid that I have no influence with the government in Heian-kyo."

"Never mind. I have some friends," Haseo said. "Perhaps now, after what has happened to me, they will try their utmost. There is a chance now where there was none before."

"Good." Akitada shaded his eyes against the setting sun and peered toward the mountainside. There they were finally. Three figures emerged from the trees, two women and a man.

Toshito reached them first. Akitada almost did not recognize him. The slender, pale young man he had last seen in the prison cell had become a sturdy bearded peasant. Toshito seemed to have the same problem; his eyes searched their faces, before he nodded to Akitada. But there was nothing friendly or grateful about his welcome.

"Who's your friend?" he asked bluntly.

"A fellow prisoner. We escaped from Kumo's mine."

The women joined them then. Ribata gave Haseo a very sweet smile and bowed, her hands folded. "Thanks to all-merciful Buddha you are both safe."

Akitada made the introductions, adding somewhat stiffly, "It is very good of you to come to our assistance. I'm afraid my friend is too weak to walk up the mountain."

When Ribata knelt beside Haseo to check his wound, Akitada's eyes went to Masako.

Like Toshito, she wore rough peasant clothing and her long hair was tied up in a scarf. She blushed charmingly when their eyes met, and he found that her beauty touched him as strongly as it always had.

"How are you, Masako?" he asked, his voice soft with their remembered friendship.

She flushed more deeply and took a step closer to Ribata. "I'm well, thank you, my lord. And very glad to see you alive and w . . ." Her voice trailed off. He guessed that she had meant to say "well," but that he looked too shocking for that word. Her manner puzzled him, and her address proved that she knew his identity. Had she told the others? Well, it did not matter any longer.

"I see you know who I am," he said. "Did you read the documents hidden in the lining of my robe?"

She looked uncomfortable but nodded. "I felt paper. Since water would have ruined it, I undid the stitches. I saw the imperial seal—just like one in the governor's office—but I put everything back after I had washed your gown."

"I know. Thank you." He wanted to pursue the matter, but decided to wait and instead ask about her relationship with the hostile Toshito. Glancing across to him, he said, "Ribata tells me that you helped the governor's son escape. That was brave and generous, but surely not very wise. Your father must be frantic with worry about your safety and reputation."

The young man had caught his last words and came over now, his face dark with anger. Putting his arm around Masako's shoulders, he said sharply, "My wife is under my protection and her reputation is above reproach, so I'd advise you to watch both your tongue and your manners in the future."

Akitada was taken aback—literally. He stepped away from them, his eyes on Masako for confirmation. "Your wife?"

She buried her face in Toshito's shoulder. It was answer enough. Akitada met the smoldering anger in the other man's eyes and bowed. "My sincere felicitations," he said lightly. "I had no idea." Then he turned his back on both of them.

Haseo was explaining his injury to Ribata. "It's been bleeding all day and part of the night or I'd be as strong as an ox," he said apologetically.

Ribata nodded. "Yes. I see. Putting moss on the wound was good. Few people know that it stanches bleeding and cools the fever in the wound."

Haseo smiled up at Akitada. "My friend's idea."

Toshito, still glowering, joined them. "We could put him on some branches and drag him up to the hermitage, but it will take two strong men to do it, and Lord Sugawara does not look very fit."

"Oh, no, I'll walk," cried Haseo, shocked.

"I'm perfectly capable," snapped Akitada.

They solved the impasse by Toshito and Akitada supporting Haseo between them. It was an unpleasant collaboration, as their arms touched behind Haseo's back. For Akitada the journey turned into torment, especially after they began their climb up the mountain. His pride did not allow him to ask for rest periods. Instead he forced himself to keep step with the younger and much healthier Toshito. Somehow they dragged Haseo to the narrow wooden veranda and set him down.

Ribata and Masako disappeared inside, and an awkward silence fell. Haseo was dozing, much as Akitada had earlier. Toshito stood glowering. Finally Akitada could not bear it any longer. "So you and Masako came here to hide out?" he asked, though the answer was obvious.

Toshito's lips twisted and he did not bother to answer. There was nothing conciliatory in his manner. Akitada wondered if Masako had told him of their indiscretion. Surely not. But his earlier remarks could not account for this much antagonism. Could Toshito be blaming Akitada for not having arrived in time to clear him? Whatever the reason, their stay here would be more than uncomfortable if this continued. Akitada swallowed his resentment and tried again.

"I did my best for you and succeeded in getting the information that will clear you," he said. "I was on my way back when your enemies stopped me."

"I did not ask for your help and I had nothing to do with what happened to you," snapped Toshito, and stalked away.

"Hmm," murmured Haseo, opening his eyes. "That's a very angry young man. What did you do to him?"

Akitada flushed. "Don't pay any attention to him," he said evasively. "He's a moody fellow who has been accused of a murder he did not commit. Perhaps he worries that we will draw our pursuers here."

But Akitada knew there was more to Toshito's hostility than mere resentment that he and Haseo had intruded into their safe haven. He recalled that Toshito used to bristle at him even when he thought of him as the prisoner Taketsuna. No, surely the problem was jealousy. Toshito either suspected or knew of his affair with Masako.

The tangled relationships between the men and women in the hermitage complicated matters. He tried to gauge the situation later, when Ribata cleaned Haseo's wound and applied powdered herbs and various ointments, wrapping his leg again in some clean hemp bandages. When Haseo left to lie down, she asked to see Akitada's knee.

"So. You have sought out trouble and found it, my lord," she murmured, probing his leg.

Though she had addressed him as Taketsuna earlier, she knew very well who he was and that he had been trying to clear the governor's son. Almost her first words to him had shown it, but he had been too shocked at the news that Masako and Toshito were with her to think clearly. He wondered how long she had known, and remembered her friendship with the Kumo family, but he only said, "Yes. And I'm afraid I have lost your flute."

She looked up then and smiled. "Never mind. It is your life which matters." Then she glanced through the door of the hut to where Masako was cooking over the open fire while her husband watched. "And that matters not only to you, but to your loved ones."

Was Ribata reminding him that his duty lay elsewhere? Of course, Masako's marriage solved his problem. There was now no need to take her into his household. He should have been glad, but was perversely irritated and hurt that she had preferred the immature, ungracious, and inept Toshito. In fairness, Toshito was probably only a few years younger, and yet had already achieved an official position which was both more secure and better paid than Akitada's. But it rankled.

In his resentment he reminded himself that her background, though upper-class, was severely lacking in proper upbringing and that her manners had never been ladylike. In that sense she certainly matched her new husband perfectly. Akitada looked at her figure critically, trying to find fault. She was attractive, but no more so than his wife or other women he had had. There was a certain coarseness about her. All those muscles, while useful, were certainly not feminine. Yet, as much as he tried to soothe his hurt pride, the memory of how she had clung to him in her father's room came unbidden, the way she had pulled him down to her and taken him passionately, hungrily into her embrace. Had she truly felt nothing at all?

A sudden sharp spasm in his knee recalled him.

"There," said Ribata, vigorously massaging a palmful of ointment into his sore joint. "That should help. Go get some rest now. We'll wake you when the food is ready."

Haseo had stretched out under a pine and was asleep already. Akitada suddenly felt drained of strength, but he walked over to Toshito, who greeted him with a scowl.

"You probably want to know what I learned about the prince's death," Akitada said.

Toshito looked toward Masako, who shot an anxious glance their way. "Not particularly," he said.

Akitada raised his brows. The fellow's manners were insufferable. But he had no intention in wasting any more time on the puppy, so he said, "There was no murder. Okisada either died accidentally or committed suicide by eating *fugu* poison."

Toshito turned a contemptuous face toward him. "Ridiculous," he snapped. "I was there, remember? No one ate *fugu* fish, least of all Okisada. And why would he kill himself when he intended to claim the throne?"

Akitada felt like knocking the smug fool to the ground. Turning away abruptly, he said, "Nevertheless, he did," and walked away to join Haseo.

The weather had remained dry and pleasant in the daytime but grew much cooler at night. Here in the mountains it was chilly in the shade and they had no clothes except their ragged pants. Akitada shivered and worried about Haseo, who looked flushed in spite of the cold. He found a sunny, sheltered hollow for himself, where he slept fitfully until Masako's touch on his shoulder returned him to consciousness.

"The food is ready," she said aloud, then whispered, "What did you say to Toshito?"

Akitada sat up. Tempting smells came from the large pot over the fire, and he felt ravenous. "Nothing to worry you. I told him that the prince committed suicide. He scoffed."

"Oh." She was going to say something else, but Toshito called to her.

Haseo looked better. He was less flushed and more inclined to take notice of the others. "Those two are in love," he told Akitada with a nod toward the young couple.

They were standing close together, and as Akitada met Toshito's eyes, the young man put a possessive hand on the girl's hip.

"He doesn't like you," Haseo said. "Must be the jealous type. Though why he should worry about a pathetic scarecrow like you, I cannot fathom."

Akitada, for his part, could not fathom Masako. After their meal, he found an opportunity to talk alone with her. She was washing their bowls in a stream that ran behind the hermitage. Toshito had gone to gather more firewood.

"Why did you make love to me, Masako?" he asked.

He had startled her and she dropped one of the wooden bowls into the water and had to scramble after it. The delay gave her time to gather her wits. In her typical fashion, she, too, was blunt. "When I found out why you had come and what power you had, I knew you could help us. That is, help both Toshito and Father. I was desperate. But the papers were secret and I could not ask you, so I tried to win your regard . . . by other means."

He flinched as though she had slapped him. "So you seduced me, and I was fool enough to allow myself to be seduced," he said bitterly.

She nodded.

Akitada turned away, angry and shamed. There were many kinds of love. Their relationship had been only lust on his part after all, but something altogether different on hers. He had at least felt a strong attraction to her, but she had merely manipulated him to gain her ends. And she had done what she did for another man, for Toshito. It struck him as abominable that some women, like Masako, strong, independent, and unconventional, would not hesitate to give their bodies to another man to save their husbands or lovers. He thought of Tamako. He would gladly sacrifice his life for her and his new son, and believed she would do the same for him, but he hoped she would never sleep with another man for any reason. The very thought made him sick.

Masako whispered, "Don't tell Toshito, please. He's jealous of you."

"Of course I won't tell. But I hope you don't think I helped your father because you slept with me."

"I shall always be grateful," she said softly.

He glared at her. "I'm sorry we met."

She hugged herself and began to cry.

"Twice," he said. "You lay with me twice, and all the time you only wanted to place me under obligation to you?"

She gulped and sniffled, but said nothing in her own defense or to salvage some of his pride. After a long silence, Akitada said bitterly, "So be it. I wish you both well." Then he turned and limped away.

Haseo watched him coming back. "Why in such a temper?" he asked lightly. "Did the pretty flower slap your face?"

Akitada managed a laugh as he sat down beside him. "Of course not. She is married now and I'm a married man also. And you? Do you have a wife and children?"

"Three wives and six children, two of them sons." Haseo sounded both proud and sad. "I hope they have gone to my first wife's parents. She comes from a wealthy family. My other wives were quite poor. And you?"

"One wife and one son. He's only six months."

"You must miss them."

"Yes. Very much." His need for Tamako suddenly twisted his heart. He had been a fool to desire another woman.

"Only one wife for a man of your station?" Haseo marveled. "She must be exceptional."

Akitada nodded. "She is." And he wished for her with every part of his being.

The rest of the evening both Toshito and Masako avoided him. After their meal—a vegetable stew thickened with millet—they disappeared into the forest together. Akitada watched them with a certain detachment and put his mind to other matters. Now that he was rested and fed, and his knee was no longer so painful, he was becoming increasingly nervous about their safety. His eyes kept scanning the highway in the darkening valley below. He could not be certain that the goblin had kept their secret, and even if she had, Kumo would have been notified of his escape by now and would extend the search to the surrounding areas soon enough. He could not afford to let Akitada escape. Ribata's vine-covered hermitage was not visible from below, but Akitada recalled the tracks they had made through the tall grasses of the valley.

The trouble was, they had neither weapons nor horses. If Kumo sent armed men after them, as he must surely do, they would either die here or be taken back to the mine to face a worse fate.

He was glad when night fell, and the possibility of an attack became remote. Candles and lamps were extinguished early and they prepared for sleep. The women stayed in the hut, but Ribata came out with blankets for her guests and spoke briefly to Toshito, who nodded and disappeared on some errand.

In spite of his blanket, Akitada awoke, shivering, long before dawn. He got up and started moving his body vigorously to warm his sluggish blood. His knee felt much better. Haseo still slept, and there was no sign of Toshito. Eventually, as the night sky slowly paled, he decided to make himself useful and gathered sticks for the fire. When it was burning, he squatted beside it and rubbed his chilled arms.

A touch on his shoulder made him jump. Masako held out his blanket. "Put it around you until the sun comes up." He did and watched her heating water for rice gruel, regretting his anger of the day before.

"How far is it to Mano?" he asked.

"Half a day's walk with a shortcut. The road passes on the other side of this mountain." She left to go back into the hut.

Only a few hours' walk? Akitada felt fit enough. Surely Haseo could manage a short journey, one that would become easy once they reached the road. After that—well, they would deal with whatever came.

Masako returned. "Ribata wants you," she said.

When he ducked into the shadowy room, he found the nun at prayer. She sat in the center of the small square space, perfectly straight and still. Dark wooden beads passed through her thin fingers like beans falling through the ribs of a bamboo strainer. He could not see her face clearly, but her lips moved, and now and then he caught a word or cadence from a sutra.

He sat down across from her, quietly waiting, wondering again about this strange, aristocratic woman who seemed content to lead a simple, religious life so far from court. Good manners and respect for her present status forbade his asking questions. Once he reached Mano and the governor and started an investigation into Kumo's activities, and those of his fellow conspirators, he hoped that the tangled relationships between the Kumo family, the late prince, and Ribata would also unravel.

As if she knew what he was thinking, Ribata said, "You should both be able to travel in another day. Then the governor will reconvene the court and Toshito's name will be cleared." She sighed and folded her hands around her beads. "Life is filled with pain. But the young people can settle down and raise their family. And you, too, will be eager to return to wife and child."

Akitada nodded. He thought of the baby son he had left behind. Children often sickened and died during their first year.

"Place your trust in the Buddha and all will be well," said the nun.

"Yes."

He suspected that she was steering his thoughts to his family and smiled in the darkness because she had succeeded. His heart swelled with love and gratitude for the slender girl he had left behind among strangers, far from her home and family. He remembered how she had stood in the doorway, holding their son in her arms. Smiling bravely, she had faced their separation without complaint, certainly without self-pity, her back straight and her voice strong when she called out, "We will be waiting when you return."

The sun was rising outside and the first ray crept through the door. It touched Ribata's sleeve and shoulder, then lit up her pale drawn face. She moved out of its light and looked at him. Her eyes were extraordinarily bright for a woman her age.

"I am happy for you," she said. Then she reached into her sleeve and held out a flute to him. "And I am returning this to you. I hoped that you would come for it someday."

He took it, uncertain, raised it into the sunlight, and saw that it was Plover's Cry, the flute she had given him in Kumo's garden, the flute taken from him by Wada.

"But how did you get it back?" he asked, shocked.

"Sanetomo returned it to me. It seems the regrettable Wada had it in his possession. Sanetomo recognized it, of course."

Sanetomo?

Then Akitada remembered the name, and drew in his breath sharply. Kumo Sanetomo had returned the flute to its owner. She must have known what had happened to him all along, he thought, his mind racing at the implications. And Ribata had sent Toshito away the night before. The knowledge of what his errand must be came too late; the damage was surely done by now. In his anger and despair Akitada almost broke the flute in his hands.

CHAPTER TWENTY

KUMO

Akitada slowly laid the flute on the floor between them. Hot fury at the betrayal churned in his belly and pounded his temples. With an effort he kept his hands from shaking; with another effort he controlled his voice. "Where is Toshito?"

There was a moment's silence, then she said vaguely, "He'll be back soon."

Imagining what this might mean, Akitada clenched his hands. Then he gestured to the flute. "I cannot accept your generous gift after all." When her eyes met his, puzzled, he added harshly, "And I am not beaten yet." Rising abruptly, he inclined his head, saw with satisfaction that he had shocked her, and left the hut.

Outside, the early sun made golden patterns on the ground, and birds were singing, but the valley below still lay hidden in white mist. Masako was stirring the morning gruel in the kettle. Akitada looked at her suspiciously. He had met with more female duplicity lately than in his entire previous life. It seemed likely now that she had told Ribata of his mission, and that Ribata had alerted Kumo.

Haseo was up. He stood at a spot overlooking the valley and shaded his eyes against the sun. High in the translucent sky circled the first kite. The world was dew-fresh and very beautiful. Akitada had too recently emerged from continuous night not to feel an almost dizzying fear of losing his fragile freedom again.

"Haseo," he called out. "We must leave."

Haseo did not turn. Instead he motioned to Akitada, who repeated, more urgently, "We must leave immediately. I think we have been betrayed."

"Ah." Haseo nodded without surprise and pointed to the foot of the mountain on the far side of the valley. Where the sunlight had melted away a narrow patch of fog, gray rocks and towering cedars floated like a small island in the sea of white which filled the rest of the valley.

And there, among the firs and pines, something sparkled and moved. As insignificant as ants at that distance, a small contingent of horsemen wove in and out between the trees and, one by one, disappeared into the misty sea. The scene was surreal, and they would have missed it, if the sun had not caught the shining helmet of the leader and then drawn the eyes to the rider who followed, a colored standard attached to the back of his armor. There had been fewer than ten horsemen, but more might follow.

Akitada felt certain that the man in the gilded helmet was Kumo himself, eager to make an end of their cat-and-mouse game. He turned to look back at the hut, its drapery of morning glories an intense blue in the sun. Ribata had come out on the veranda, a small and frail figure in her grayish white nun's habit. Masako was looking from Ribata to them, a frown on her pretty face. No doubt Toshito was among the horsemen in the valley below, showing Kumo the way to the hermitage, certain that the women would keep their prey distracted.

Ribata called out, "What is the matter, my lord? Is something wrong?"

Ignoring her, Akitada turned back to Haseo and said in a low voice, "They will have to leave their horses below and climb up on foot. It gives us a little time. Kumo counts on surprising us, on finding two invalids taking shelter. We must go down the other side of this mountain. Masako said the road to Mano passes there. It's not far."

Haseo nodded. It was like him not to argue or ask questions. Instead he said with a regretful grin, "A pity! They're a mere handful apiece. What I wouldn't give if we had a couple of swords!"

As they ran past the hermitage toward the forest, Ribata stepped in their way. "Stop! Where are you going?" she cried, her eyes anxious. "What is happening?" Akitada pushed her aside without answering.

The forest was still dark and gloomy, but the ground was soft with pine needles and dry leaf mold and they ran quickly, talking in short bursts.

"How are you today?" Akitada asked.

"Much better. I suppose that nun was healing me for whoever's coming after us?"

"Yes. Kumo. A relative. I saw a golden helmet. Only Kumo's rich enough for one of those." Haseo was moving well, but Akitada suddenly felt guilty. He said, "It's my fault. I brought you into this. Kumo's after me."

Haseo snorted. "You're wrong. Anyone in the mine might've found out. He's been stealing gold for years."

"What?" Akitada almost stumbled over a tree root. "What do you mean?"

Haseo looked back over his shoulder, missed a step, and slid down the slope. He got back up and continued. "Don't you know? You were chipping away at those rocks for two days."

Of course, Akitada thought. How could he have missed it? All those badger holes and baskets of rock with little or no silver in them! They had been after those tiny bits of yellow metal. That was why he had pulverized the rocks, and why they had washed the gravel on that sluice. That was why there had been so many guards. Kumo was not mining silver for the emperor, but gold for himself. "Jisei!" Akitada cried. "I forgot to ask you about Jisei."

Haseo stopped. "The little fellow in the stockade? What about him?"

"Someone killed him the night they took me to see the governor. Did you see anything?"

Haseo cursed softly. "Yes. I was sleeping, but he must've cried out. Those two pirates were having some argument with him. By the time I guessed what was happening and got to my feet, he was on the ground and the guards came. They took the two bastards away and put the little fellow on a litter. I thought he was only hurt."

"They called it a fight between prisoners, but I think he was murdered. He knew about the gold and was blackmailing someone. That's why he was so sure he was going home."

Haseo turned away. "Too late now! We've got to save our own tails. Come on!"

Yes, this time Kumo would make certain by killing them. A helpless rage filled Akitada as he plunged down the slope after Haseo. He would make Kumo pay for what he had done to him and to Jisei, make him fight for his gold, but not here. Not in this murky forest where you could find no firm foothold and where he would lie forgotten among the roots of giant cedars while spiders built their webs between his bones.

Halfway down the mountain, they found a barely noticeable track. Perhaps charcoal burners had come this way and had marked the easiest and most direct path down to the valley. They were glad, for the rapid descent over the roughest parts had taken its toll. Going down a hill is faster than climbing it, but not necessarily less tiring for two men weakened by illness and blood loss and hampered by leg injuries. Only the knowledge that, in spite of their bravado, they had little chance against heavily armed men speeded their descent, and they emerged from the dim forest into almost blinding sunlight a scant hour later.

The view extended southward, across thinly forested lower slopes down to a sun-bright sea where Sawata Bay merged into the infinite expanse of ocean and sky. The highway beyond the foothills skirted the edge of the bay like a pearl-gray ribbon joining two pieces of fabric, one glistening silver, the other deep green. They could see the brown roofs of a town some distance away, and beyond that, farther along the vast bow of the shore, another, larger town—Mano. Fishing boats worked the shimmering bay and a large sailing ship lay at anchor nearby. Above stretched an immense pale blue sky streaked with streamers of thin clouds and dotted with black crows and white seagulls, circling and rising, swooping and plunging into the waves.

"The road's empty," said Haseo. "Maybe we'll make it."

They trotted down the slope, skirting stunted pines and sending nesting birds aflutter, but Akitada knew that they could not keep up the pace much longer. Both of them limped and gasped for breath, and now, in the warm sun, sweat poured down their faces and bodies. It had been cooler in the forest, but the hard exercise had heated their blood. They chased a lone hare through the dry gorse down the hill, its white tail bobbing up and down before them, mocking their slow pursuit. When they crested one low hill, they found another. They glanced over their shoulders and slapped at stinging gnats, and eventually they reached the road and started walking.

Apparently there was not much travel between the northern mountains and Mano, for they saw only one farmer, driving an ox with a load of firewood, and three women on their way to tend their fields. They attracted curious glances, but their greetings were returned and the peasants hurried on to their chores. Then three horsemen came from the south.

Haseo stopped. "What now? Soldiers? Maybe we'd better hide."

"Yes." They crouched down behind some low shrubs on the embankment. Akitada narrowed his eyes. Only one of the horsemen was armed. The other two seemed to be peasants, unused to riding, because they sagged in their saddles. And the horses, all three of them, were mere nags. They could not be Kumo's men. He touched Haseo's shoulder. "Get ready. We need those horses. We won't have a chance on foot."

Haseo began to laugh. "Wonderful! Look, the guy in front even has a sword. What luck!"

Only Haseo would consider this a fortunate circumstance. Akitada was less sanguine. He had not formed any cogent idea how two half-naked scarecrows would convince a fully armed soldier to give up his weapons and horses to them. At least the soldier's companions looked negligible. One seemed sick; his body not only slumped but swayed in the saddle. Someone had tied him to the horse to keep him from tumbling off. The other man was frail and no longer young. He clutched his horse's mane and slipped at every bounce. Neither had any weapons that Akitada could see.

No, the only dangerous man was the one in the lead. Tall, a good horseman, and young, judging by his straight back and easy movements with the stride of his horse, he wore his helmet pulled forward against the sun, a breastplate, and a long sword. He was still too far away for them to guess his military rank, but possibly he also carried a second, shorter sword in his belt.

Then Akitada's heart started beating wildly with a sudden hope. There was something very familiar about the set of those shoulders, the tilt of the head. "Dear heaven," he muttered. "Tora?"

Haseo turned to look at him. "What?"

Akitada gave a laugh. "Come on," he cried, rising from behind the shrub, "I know that soldier." He started into a stumbling run down the embankment, hardly thinking of his knee now.

The horseman saw them and reined in his horse. After a moment, he urged it forward again, but now his hand was on the hilt of his sword.

Akitada stopped and waited, grinning foolishly, chuckling from time to time, until Haseo shook his elbow. "Are you all right? Are you sure you know those people?"

"Only one of them, and yes, I'm sure."

The three horsemen approached at a slow pace. The two in back seemed to take little interest in them, but the young soldier stared, frowned, and stared again.

He came to a halt before them. "What do you want?" he asked, not unkindly. "I've no money to give you, but we can share a bit of food."

"Thank you, Tora," said Akitada. "That is very kind of you. We missed our morning rice."

"Amida! Oh, dear heaven! Can that be you, sir? Is it really, really you?" Tora bounded out of the saddle and ran up to Akitada, seized him around the waist, lifted him, and crushed him to his chest. He laughed, while tears ran down his face. When he finally put the weakly chuckling Akitada back down, he said, "Sorry, sir. I was on my way to Kumo's mine to look for you, and here you are. They said you were dead, and I'd started believing it." He wiped his face with his sleeve.

"Never mind. An easy mistake. There was a time when I thought I was. This is my friend Haseo. We're both on the run from Kumo's men."

It was said casually, as if they had just met on the street, old friends exchanging broad smiles and trivial news, but Tora was sobered instantly. "You look terrible," he said. "I'll kill the bastards." This seemed to remind him of his companions. He turned, his face grim, and pulling his short sword, went to the man on the second horse. Akitada saw the bloodied, blackened, swollen face, the eyes so puffy that it was a wonder the man could see, and he heard the man's high scream of fear, before he realized that he was looking at Wada and that Tora meant to kill him right here in the middle of the road to Mano.

"Wait!"

Tora turned, and Akitada saw the deadly determination in his eyes. "He dies," Tora said, his voice flat. "He would've died yesterday, but I kept him around to show us the way."

"Not here and not now," Akitada said. "I don't want to remember our meeting this way."

Tora reluctantly put back his sword. He came to Akitada and took him into another bear hug.

"Thank you, my friend," Akitada said when they finally released each other. "And who is your other companion?"

Tora grinned. "That's Turtle. A bit of a coward, but his heart's good. He's my servant."

Akitada raised his brows. "I see you've risen in the world. Congratulations on the new armor. You do look like a man in need of a servant."

Tora had the grace to blush and looked at Haseo, who had sat down beside the road to adjust the bandage on his leg. "Your friend's hurt?"

Haseo made Tora a slight bow. "It's just a cut which likes to bleed. We're anxious to get to Mano before Kumo catches up with us, and I've already caused too many delays with my infernal leg."

"Never mind, Haseo," said Akitada. "We can ride now. I see no reason to transport the despicable Wada. Let him run alongside. And Tora's servant can walk, too."

Turtle slid from his horse and rubbed his behind. "Glad to," he said cheerfully. "He's not a very comfortable horse."

Tora unpacked his saddlebag and passed his spare trousers and robe to Akitada. To Haseo he gave the wide-sleeved jacket he wore over his armor. Then he frowned at their callused, scarred feet. "How did you walk like that?" he asked Akitada, taking off his boots.

Akitada said, "Thank you, but your boots won't fit. And my feet have become accustomed to worse than road gravel."

"Uh-oh!" Haseo grabbed his arm. He was looking up the road toward the north. Where the road disappeared around the foot of the mountain, a dust cloud had appeared. It moved rapidly their way.

"Kumo," cried Akitada, and swung himself on Turtle's horse. "Come on. We'll try to outrun them."

Tora cut loose a whimpering Wada, who tumbled heavily onto the road, where Tora kicked him out of the way, and called to Haseo, "Here, get on!" before running to his own horse.

Turtle stood, staring at them with frightened eyes. "What's happening?" he cried. "Who's coming? Please, take me with you, master!"

Tora was in the saddle. "Sorry, Turtle. No time. Hide in some bush. If I can, I'll come back for you."

"Tora, your sword," cried Akitada, bringing his horse alongside Tora's. After the merest moment of hesitation, Tora passed over his long sword and offered his helmet, but this Akitada refused. Then they cantered off after Haseo.

The nags were not up to a chase. Having spent all their miserable lives in post stables, fed on small rations of rotting rice straw or trotting back and forth between the two coasts, carrying fat merchants or visitors on leisurely trips, they had never galloped. Now, beaten and kicked into a burst of speed, they lathered up, started wheezing and heaving, and eventually slowed to an agonized trot. Behind, the dust cloud came on rapidly, already revealing horses, men, and the flying banner.

Haseo shouted to Akitada, "We'll have to make a stand. Are you any good with that sword?"

"Adequate," Akitada shouted back. He had kept up his practice with Tora, and he was not about to give up the sword. "Sorry."

Haseo nodded. He eyed Tora's short sword, but evidently decided against asking an officer in robust health to render up his only weapon to an invalid.

Looking about for a suitable place to face their pursuers, Akitada knew their chances of winning were slim. They were badly outnumbered and lacked weapons. Tora, with his short sword, would have to dismount, because a horseman had the reach on him with a long sword. His only chance was to fight on foot, slashing at the horses' bellies or legs, and then killing the riders when they were tossed.

They approached the small town, a collection of fishermen's huts strung along the bay, with farmhouses, a couple of manors, and a small temple set back on higher ground. The road skirted the bay with its hard shingle beach. On the other side were muddy rice paddies like irregular patches of dingy hemp cloth sewn on a ragged green gown.

"Stop at those first houses," Akitada called to the others. "The road narrows there, and we'll use the house walls to cover our backs."

"Like cornered rats," Haseo shouted back, but he grinned.

Kumo was nearly on top of them. They had been seen a long way back, and their pursuers had whipped their horses into a gallop. Now they came, banner flapping, and raucous shouts of victory mingling with the pounding of hooves. Akitada, Haseo, and Tora spurred their own nags into a last short burst of speed.

The first farm consisted of several independent buildings. The main house with its steep thatched roof fronted the road, but barns, kitchens, and other low buildings clustered around and behind it. Narrow passages and small fenced gardens linked the buildings. There was no one in sight. The men were probably in the fields, and the women had gone into hiding when trouble arrived.

Haseo tumbled down before his horse had stopped. Half running, half limping, he went to a side yard where the farmer's wife had pushed several tall bamboo poles in the ground to support her drying laundry. He pulled up one of the sturdier poles, letting the rest of the rig topple into the dirt, and weighed it in his hand. With a grunt of satisfaction, he joined the others.

Tora had also dismounted, his short sword drawn. Only Akitada remained in the saddle, blocking the road, Tora's long sword in his hand as their pursuers halted in a cloud of yellow dust.

Kumo's helmet was brilliant in the sun, his armor, trimmed with green silk, also shone with gold, and a golden war fan flashed in his raised hand. The banner bore the insignia of the high constable. Kumo's men were all armed, their armor polished, their bows over their shoulders, and their swords drawn. Bright red silk tassels swung from the horses' bridles. Their faces were avid with excitement, with the hunger for blood. Only Kumo looked utterly detached, his lips thin and his forehead furrowed in a frown of distaste.

Akitada waited to see what Kumo would do. He no longer felt the pain in his knee, or weariness, or even fear. He wanted to meet this man sword to sword. He wanted to kill him more than he had ever wanted anything in his life.

Kumo shouted across, "Give yourselves up, in the name of the emperor."

In the name of the emperor? Akitada laughed.

Scowling, Kumo brought his horse a little closer. "I am the high constable. You're escaped convicts and under arrest."

Akitada shouted back, "You know who I am, Kumo. Sugawara Akitada, imperial envoy. You're under arrest for treason. Tell your men to lay down their swords."

Kumo's people burst into laughter in their turn, but Kumo raised his golden fan, and they fell quiet. "You're outnumbered," he shouted. "If you don't give up, you'll be cut down like dogs."

"Try it, you bastards!" shouted Haseo, stepping forward and swinging his bamboo pole. Akitada hoped he was as skilled at stick-fighting as Tora.

"If you want a fight, Kumo," he shouted back, "let it be between the two of us."

Kumo was heavily armed and sat on one of his magnificent horses, while Akitada wore nothing but Tora's trousers and robe and rode a worn-out nag which stood wide-legged, its head hanging in exhaustion. Akitada was also becoming conscious of the weight of Tora's sword. He was much weaker than he had thought. But his anger kept him there. This man had done his best to kill him slowly and horribly and had failed. Now Akitada wanted a quick and clean kill of his own. He could taste the sweetness of such a victory, knew he could not lose, and gloried in the moment.

But Kumo gave him a look of contempt, then turned his horse and rode up the embankment. There he stopped and waited for his bannerman. It dawned on Akitada that he had refused single combat and would conduct this like a battle, as a general from a safe distance.

A battle? Stunned by this ridiculous turn of events, the fury at the insult still gripping his belly like a burning vise, Akitada bellowed after him, "Stand and fight, you coward!"

Kumo ignored him. The great man would not fight a mere convict. He raised his fan and pointed it at Akitada, and his men burst into raucous cries, spurred their horses, and came at him, swords flashing in the sun, the horses' flying hooves splattering gravel.

Later Akitada could not remember how he had met their charge, what had given him the strength to grip his horse between his legs and force it to the side of the road so the attackers had to pass on his right. The animal was stolid enough, but with a sudden onrush of so many riders, it kept backing and sinking onto its hindquarters, its eyes rolling in its head with fear. Because the road was narrow, they came single file. Soldier after soldier passed, each one slashing down or across with his sword, in an almost comical imitation of a parade-ground drill, except that he was the bale of rice straw they practiced on. He parried, hacked, slashed, and swung the heavy sword, felt each jarring contact with steel, the impact traveling up his arm like fire; but he feared making body cuts more, because the blade could get caught in the other man's armor and there would be no time to free it. Below him, on either side, Haseo and Tora slashed and swung their weapons, but he was hardly aware of them because the enemy came so fast.

And then they were past.

Two riderless horses galloped off, and two groaning men rolled on the ground, their blood soaking into the hot earth. A wounded horse screamed dreadfully, its legs flailing in the air as it rolled on the body of its rider. Tora grinned up at him, his sword dripping blood.

"That's three of the bastards," he called.

Akitada nodded. Kumo had foolishly given them the advantage by sending his men singly at them. True, the road was narrow, but if he had ordered his men to use their bows and arrows, or to dismount and attack on foot, their numbers would have made short work of three weak adversaries. He glanced up the road where the remaining five soldiers gathered for a return sweep, and then at Kumo, who was watching impassively from his embankment.

Haseo's bamboo pole lay broken, but he helped himself to the sword of the dead man under the wounded horse, then stepped forward and quickly cut the suffering beast's throat. Its blood drenched him, but he returned to the others, swinging the sword triumphantly, his face exultant.

Up on his embankment, Kumo raised his fan, and here they came again, hooves thundering on the roadway, frenzied shouts ringing, long, curved blades slashing and hissing through the air. Akitada attempted to turn his horse, but this time the abused nag had had enough. With a frenzied whinny, it reared, unseating Akitada, and took off down the empty roadway ahead of the attackers, legs flying.

Akitada fell onto the road, but managed to roll out of the way of the pounding hooves. Slashing swords missed him by inches. When they were past, he tried to get up, staggered, then saw one horseman turning back, bent low over his horse's neck, his sword ready. Akitada was still swaying when a strong hand grasped the back of his robe and pulled him out of the way.

Haseo.

Muttering his thanks, Akitada rubbed dust from his eyes and shook his head to clear it. Somehow he still gripped his sword. The horseman reined in, turned, and charged again, scattering loose stones and screaming hoarsely. Tora was now beside Akitada, crouched low, his short sword ready. Akitada caught only a glimpse of Haseo's face; he was grinning, his eyes bright with the joy of battle. Then the rider was upon them and they jumped clear, slashing at his horse's legs. They heard the animal scream, saw the man fall, and then the other horsemen came, and they slashed and swung some more, and thrust at horses, at the legs of men, ducking and parrying the swords of their attackers. This time, they wounded two horses and killed one man, but Haseo was bleeding from a cut to his shoulder, and Tora's sword was broken.

"Back," gasped Akitada. "We've got to get back to the buildings where they can't ride us down. We'll force them to meet us on foot." A strange exhilaration had seized him. He wanted to taste victory and savor its sweetness.

He and Haseo ran to the narrow passageway between the farm and an outbuilding. Up on the ridge, Kumo was shouting orders again. His bannerman now joined the remaining soldiers. Only five left? No time to count.

Tora, swordless, was slowly backing away from a horseman who had been thrown by his wounded horse and attacked on foot. Tora crouched, dodged, and jumped out of the way of the furious sweeps of the other man's sword. Akitada rushed forward, swung down hard, and severed the man's sword hand at the wrist. The wounded man was still staring stupidly at the stump when Tora snatched up the fallen sword and ran it through the man's throat. The body arched back, the man's eyes already glassy in death. When Tora jerked free the blade, the wound vomited forth a stream of blood like a second mouth. The man fell forward, convulsed, and lay still.

On the road the four other soldiers had dismounted and were coming toward them, slowly now, swords in hand, in a half crouch. Kumo had finally realized his mistake.

But still the high constable kept his distance, alone and aloof on his magnificent horse, waiting and watching.

They faced the oncoming enemy side by side, the wall of the farmhouse to their right, and the fence of the drying yard to the left. There was not enough room for the attackers to get past and come at them from the back, but if Kumo's men remembered their training, they could easily overcome them by working together. It is impossible to parry two swords simultaneously if one slices from above and the other thrusts from below at the belly.

Akitada warily watched as two men came for him. When they decided to move, one raised himself on his toes with an earsplitting shriek and rushed Akitada, his sword held above his head with both hands. He clearly hoped that Akitada would back away and he could bring his sword down to split Akitada's head. Fortunately, this dramatic attack caused the second man to hesitate, and Akitada, instead of backing away, crouched and lunged, his sword held in front with its blade pointing upward. His attacker impaled himself with such force that the sword penetrated to the hilt, and Akitada had to put his foot against the body to pull it free in time to meet the belated attack of the second man.

Whether this one had learned from his mate's mistake or was afraid for his life, he circled back and forth without making a move. Akitada could hear the clanging of steel against steel, the thumps and grunts, as Haseo and Tora dealt with their opponents, but he did not take his eyes off this man, for a lapse in attention could cost him his life.

In the end it was the other man who glanced away to see how his companions were faring, and Akitada quickly slipped under his guard and killed him.

He stood, rubbing his sore right arm, looking around him in a daze, and saw that they had survived and their attackers had not. Four bodies lay in the farmhouse passageway, some still, some twitching, one vomiting blood. Tora looked unhurt, and at first glance Haseo also, but then Akitada saw the hand pressed against the abdomen, the fixed smile, the defiant wide-legged stance, and knew something was terribly wrong.

"Haseo?"

"The bastard got me from below, I'm afraid," said Haseo through stiff lips.

"How bad is it?"

"Bad. I'm afraid to take my hand away, but it went in pretty far. I think I'd better sit down."

They helped Haseo, leaned him against the fence. Akitada looked at Haseo's hand, pressed hard against his waist, and saw the blood seeping through the fingers. His heart contracted in pity.

"Sir!" Tora pulled his arm and pointed.

Kumo was finally coming down from his embankment. At the farmhouse, he dismounted, tying up his horse, and walked toward them. Akitada rose and seized his sword.

Kumo stopped about ten feet away. Close up, he still looked magnificent, tall and slender, with his golden helmet and his gold-trimmed armor laced in green silk. But the handsome face was pale and covered with perspiration.

"So," he said, his right hand clasping his sword, its hilt also gold but its blade gleaming blue steel, "you have left me no choice."

"You have that backward, Kumo. You chose this way. It's too late now to complain because you have chosen death."

Kumo laughed bitterly. "You fool! I could have killed you many times myself. I could have had you killed by my men. But I did not. Now you force me to commit the ultimate sin, the sin which will cost me eternity."

What nonsense was this? In any case, the slow death Kumo had condemned him to in his mine would have been much worse than any quick strike of the sword. Then Akitada caught a glimmer of sense in what Kumo had said. He gestured at the farmyard and the road, both covered with the corpses of men and horses, the stench of their blood filling the hot midday air and attracting the first buzz of flies. "This is your handiwork, Kumo. You are the bringer of death, as guilty as if you had shed their blood yourself."

"No!" Kumo flushed with anger. "I never touched them. My hands are clean. I never killed man or beast." He stared at Akitada, at Tora and Haseo behind him, then back at Akitada. "Now you force me to kill you and your companions. The great undertaking must not be jeopardized. I am sacrificing my Buddhahood for my emperor." He made a deep bow toward the sea; then the hand with the sword came forward.

Akitada stood, his sword loose in his hand, its point downward. He thought of the difference between them: Kumo rested and fully armed, both his body and head protected by that extraordinary suit of armor, with a superb blade on his sword—he, in Tora's blue robe and pants, both now blood-spattered, neither his head nor his body protected, exhausted, favoring an injured leg, and fighting with an ordinary sword borrowed from Tora. He put these thoughts aside quickly in the knowledge that, nevertheless, he would not, could not lose this fight. He knew nothing of Kumo's swordsmanship, though his men had been trained if inexperienced, but that did not matter. Kumo would die, here, and by his hand.

But Kumo said a strange thing, and Akitada's confidence fled "Come on and fight," Kumo said. "You enjoy killing. I watched you and I can see it in your eyes now."

Akitada lowered his sword and stepped back; he wanted to deny the charge but knew that there was truth in it and that the truth was profoundly disturbing. He tried in vain to put it from his mind.

Kumo used this moment of weakness to attack. Akitada parried instinctively. Then their blades met again and again, sharply, steel against steel, each parry a painful tremor in Akitada's arm, and Akitada realized that Kumo's way of fighting was done by rote, that he had memorized moves and practiced them, but that, like his men, he had never fought a real opponent. And as he became aware of this, he also recognized the fear in Kumo's eyes. Kumo was stronger and quicker than he was, but his clumsy handling of his sword made his end certain and quick.

Akitada lunged for Kumo's wrist, pierced his sword guard, and twisted sharply. Kumo cried out, releasing his grip, and Akitada flung Kumo's sword in a wide arc through the air. It struck point down in the dirt, the golden hilt vibrating in the sun.

Their eyes met. This was the moment for Kumo to surrender, and Akitada was so certain he would that he lowered his sword. But the man surprised him by snatching a short sword from his sash. When he attacked, Akitada's long sword came up. Kumo met its point below his right arm where neither shoulder guard nor body armor protected him. It was one of the few places an experienced fighter aimed for when confronted by a fully armed enemy, but there had been no design in Akitada's action. He felt the impact along the blade of his sword, the brief halt as the point met bone, then heard the bone part, and the blade plunged deeply into Kumo's body.

When Akitada stepped back, bringing the sword with him, Kumo stood swaying, a look of surprise on his face. Then the short sword fell from his hand, he opened his mouth as if to speak, but blood poured forth and ran down his beautiful armor. His knees buckled and he sank slowly to the ground.

Akitada looked from his dead enemy to the bodies of men and horses and at the dying Haseo tended by Tora. The scene blurred, and he sat down, bending his head in exhaustion and relief.

It was not yet midday.

CHAPTER TWENTY-ONE

FUGU FISH

When Akitada opened his eyes, he looked again at the slain Kumo. The golden helmet had fallen off, and his face looked younger in death. The eyes were closed and the lips had relaxed as if he had merely fallen asleep. Akitada got up to make certain he was dead and disturbed the first fly on the bloody armor. Akitada felt neither triumph nor regret, only immeasurable exhaustion.

Staying on his feet took all the strength he could muster. He stumbled over to where Tora sat with Haseo. Tora had fashioned some sort of pad for Haseo's belly wound. When Akitada gave him a questioning look, he shook his head. Belly wounds were fatal. Always. They were also agonizingly painful. Haseo's eyes were closed, his lips compressed.

Akitada sat down on his other side. "How are you, my friend?" He took the big man's callused hand in his.

Haseo's eyes flicked open. He managed a smile. Akitada would always remember Haseo smiling. "A great fight," Haseo murmured. He paused and added, almost inaudibly, "Wonderful!"

Akitada felt helpless. "Yes," he said, glancing around with rising sickness at the scattered bodies and noticing for the first time that some of the peasants were timidly peering around corners and from windows. Life would go on.

But not for Haseo.

Tora said to Haseo, "I saw you fighting two of the bastards at the same time. People say it can't be done, but you did it. I meant to ask you to teach me."

Haseo smiled. "Thanks. You'll learn. You're not bad yourself."

Akitada had been too hard-pressed to see him fight, but he remembered how Haseo had wished for a sword on the mountain and later longed for Tora's weapon, and he wondered about his background. "I never asked your name," he said. There was a long pause, and he repeated his question. "What is your family name, Haseo?"

Haseo unclenched his bloody hand long enough to make a dismissive gesture. "Gone. Taken away. Sentence."

So they had not only sentenced him to exile, but stripped his family of their ancestral name. "What was it?" Akitada persisted.

At first it seemed that Haseo would not answer. But then he whispered, "Utsunomiya."

"Utsunomiya. I'll find your family and try to clear your name. Your sons will want to know of your courage."

Haseo opened his eyes then and looked at him. "It is too much to ask," he whispered.

Akitada shook his head. "Not among friends." He was about to ask more questions but there were shouts in the distance. Someone was coming. Tora jumped up and ran to the road, while Akitada struggled to his feet and seized his sword. What now? More of Kumo's soldiers? He had no strength left.

But Tora, shading his eyes, was looking toward the south. He waved to Akitada to come. The distance suddenly seemed very great; Akitada shuffled like an old man, with small uncertain steps.

"It's the governor, I think," said Tora when Akitada reached him. Akitada shaded his own eyes. Yes, he could make out the banner flying in front of the cortege. "I thought he'd lost his power," Tora remarked in a tone of surprise. "Wonder how he got anyone to come with him."

They were on foot, probably some forty men, foot soldiers with halberds and bearers carrying the governor's sedan chair. And now that they approached a town, they began to chant the traditional warning, "Make way for His Excellency, the governor! Make way!" Slowly the local people gathered by the roadside and knelt as the banner and sedan chair passed them.

The soldiers' shouts became more urgent when neither Tora nor Akitada would step aside. Then they caught sight of the bodies of men and horses and lowered their lances.

Akitada raised his hand. "Halt! We have business with His Excellency."

The column faltered and stopped. The woven curtain of the sedan chair parted and Mutobe stuck out his head.

"What's going on?" he shouted. "What do these people want?"

"Governor?" Akitada started toward the sedan chair, but a small forest of sharp halberds immediately barred his way.

"Who are you?" asked Mutobe.

"Sugawara."

Mutobe's jaw dropped. "Good heavens!" Then he cried, "Put me down! Put me down, you fools." The sedan chair was lowered and opened. Mutobe climbed out and came to Akitada with outstretched hands. The halberds parted and the soldiers stepped back. Mutobe's steps faltered. "Is that really you, Sugawara?" he asked uncertainly. "All that blood. Are you hurt?" Belatedly his eyes fell on the carcass of a dead horse, then on human bodies. "What has happened here?" he asked, his eyes wide and his voice hoarse.

"Kumo caught up with us. May I introduce Lieutenant Tora? If he had not found me in time, we would not be speaking to each other now."

Mutobe looked at Tora, turned a little green at the amount of gore on Tora, and nodded. "Yes. We met. Are you telling me that you two killed all these men?" His eyes counted. "Four mounted soldiers? All by yourselves?"

"No, there were three of us. My friend was wounded. He is dying." Akitada led the way to the farmyard, where Mutobe counted more bodies, pausing in astonishment beside the corpse of the late high constable.

"It's Kumo," he said, picking up the golden helmet. "You killed Kumo. Wonderful! It's a miracle. Finally we are free of the monster. Oh, we will celebrate this day!" He clapped his hands together like a small child.

Akitada did not feel like celebrating. He knelt beside Haseo. Mutobe came to lean over him. "Who is he?"

"Utsunomiya Haseo. My friend."

"Don't know him. How did you meet?"

"He was a prisoner as I was. In Kumo's mine."

"Oh, a convict. He looks dead."

Akitada was holding Haseo's hand, willing him to open his eyes, to smile. Tora joined them. He reached down and felt Haseo's neck. "Gone," he said bluntly. "Better this way."

"Yes," said Akitada dismally, tears blurring his eyes. "But I had so much to ask him still."

"Well." Mutobe straightened up and looked about. "The locals will take care of him and the others. Cheer up. He's only a convict. Would have been executed anyway for escaping."

Akitada felt like striking the man. Even if it had been some other convict and not Haseo, he would have flared up in righteous anger. Mutobe had not confronted Kumo to stop the abuse of prisoners and mine workers. He had been engaged in a miserable private struggle to solidify his and his son's authority against the increasingly powerful high constable. But Akitada was too exhausted to be able to say more than, "No. He will return with us for an honorable burial in Mano. Whatever he was, he fought bravely in an honorable cause."

Mutobe was distracted. "Oh, very well. Whatever. But where are the ladies?"

"The ladies?" Akitada put Haseo's hand back on his chest and got to his feet. He saw now that they had been joined by two other men. One was Yamada, looking shocked and anxious, the other the governor's son. "Toshito?" Akitada gasped. "What are *you* doing here? I thought you were with Kumo."

"With Kumo?" Yamada and his son-in-law cried in unison.

"Why would my son be with Kumo?" the governor asked. "He ran most of the way from Ribata's hermitage to tell me of your escape and to ask me to bring help in case Kumo came after you. He took quite a risk. I'm sorry we did not get here sooner, but my men were reluctant to obey me."

Akitada said quickly, "Never mind. I'm grateful you're here." He glanced toward the governor's soldiers. An elderly officer was directing his men to collect the bodies and clear the road of dead horses. Mutobe must have had an impossible task. It was a miracle he had appeared with such numbers. And Akitada had been wrong about Toshito and owed the obnoxious fellow an apology. There were more important matters in life than a moment's humility. Bowing to the governor's son, he said awkwardly, "I beg your pardon for my mistake, Toshito. I thought when you left last night . . . Ribata is close to Kumo's family and you were very hostile. When we woke up and saw Kumo and his men coming, there seemed to be only one explanation."

"Damn you to hell!" Toshito spat. "How dare you call me a traitor? You ran like the coward you are, leaving two helpless women to the attentions of . . . soldiers, low creatures without principle." He waved at the bodies which still lay about the courtyard and had attracted a small crowd of jabbering villagers.

Akitada bit his lip and said again, "I am sorry. It was a mistake."

Mutobe stepped between them. "Toshito," he said sharply, "you forget yourself. Lord Sugawara is under imperial orders and has done us a great service. Apologize."

His son compressed his lips and glared.

Yamada asked, "Do you really think they hurt the women?"

Suddenly Akitada had had enough. He told Mutobe coldly, "Tell your son to take the sedan chair and some of the men to bring the ladies here. Meanwhile, there are other matters to discuss. Inside. It is hot out here and stinks of blood."

The farmer, his wife, and several female relatives or maids prostrated themselves when they entered the house. Mutobe demanded use of their main room, and a place for them to wash themselves. Akitada was grateful for the last, for the clothes he had borrowed from Tora were stiff with drying blood, and his skin and scalp itched under layers of sweat and filth.

One of the women brought a large bowl of water and hemp cloth for drying, but he asked for the well. There he stripped and poured bucket after bucket of clean water over himself, scrubbing his face, beard, hair, and body until he felt clean again. Someone brought him a silk robe—one of the governor's, to judge by its quality and size—and he ran his fingers through his hair and twisted it up into a topknot. When he went back into the house, Mutobe and Yamada both looked relieved at his changed appearance.

"Have some of this wine," offered Mutobe. "It is only ordinary, but it will give you some strength."

Strength. Yes, he could use that. The cold water had temporarily dispelled his exhaustion, but now he sank down on the wooden planks of the farmer's best room and gulped the rough wine gratefully.

Yamada and Mutobe watched him expectantly, too polite to burst into excited questions, but clearly hopeful that the wine would loosen his tongue.

Akitada's first thought was Haseo. "What has been done about my friend's body?"

"He will be taken back to Mano," said Mutobe quickly. "My men are building a stretcher. I hope that is satisfactory?"

Akitada nodded. "Where is Tora?"

"Your lieutenant suddenly recalled having left some people behind. He took horses to get them."

Akitada had forgotten the wretched Wada and the strange little man with the crippled leg. "One of the men he left behind is the police official Wada," he told the governor. "I assume you know him?"

Mutobe made a face. "Er. Yes. Not perhaps what one could wish. There have been some complaints."

"You have, of course, investigated them?" Akitada asked.

Mutobe flushed. "Why? Even if they proved true, what would you have me do about it?"

Akitada snapped, "Well, he could receive a reprimand and warning. Or he could be arrested and tried and sent to jail. Or he could be sent back to the capital as unsuitable. I gather you took none of these options. Wada was working for Kumo when he waylaid me. He had me beaten half to death by his constables, and when Kumo interfered he took me to a gold mine where I was left to die."

The two men stared at him.

"A gold mine?" asked Mutobe.

"My mistake. I meant to say silver mine."

"Terrible," cried Yamada. "My dear Taketsuna, I wish I had known. Oh, dear! Forgive me. Lord Sugawara, I mean. You will have to do something about that man, Governor."

Mutobe stiffened his back. "Certainly. I will have him arrested immediately. I had no idea. Up until now there were just a few concerns about his rough treatment of criminals and vagrants or prostitutes. . . ." Seeing Akitada's expression, he flushed again. "Well. I tried to discipline him, but Kumo stepped in to stop me. Then this business with Toshito happened." He faltered miserably. An uncomfortable silence fell. Mutobe asked diffidently, "I trust we can settle my son's affairs once and for all now, my lord? It was suicide, not murder?"

Akitada did not think much of the way Mutobe had carried out his duties, but there were extenuating circumstances. At least now that his son's name would be cleared, the man should have the time to tend to business, and Akitada needed his cooperation. He started to explain Okisada's death when he had second thoughts.

From what everyone had said about *fugu* poison, such a death was painful. Would a spoiled prince like Okisada really choose this method to end his life? Especially when his reason was to avoid the pain of a stomach disorder? How ill had Okisada really been? He had been well enough to travel and attend the gathering at Professor Sakamoto's house. And had not his fellow conspirators, with the exception of the alcoholic professor, been rather complacent about his death and the failure of their enterprise? Only the professor had been truly upset. And perhaps Shunsei. The monk's faith in his beloved's achieving Buddhahood might have overcome his grief. But Kumo, Taira, and the physician had only been concerned with getting young Mutobe convicted.

And then there were Kumo's strange final words. Something about making a sacrifice for his emperor.

Mutobe cleared his throat. "May I ask, my lord, what it is that you found out?"

Akitada was spared an answer. From outside came the sound of voices, and then the door flew open and revealed one of Mutobe's men trying to bar Tora's way.

"Let him in!" Akitada snapped.

Mutobe gave him a reproachful glance and nodded to his guard. The small incident reminded Akitada of his awkward position. He no longer had his imperial orders and had to depend on Mutobe's cooperation.

Tora looked slightly shaken. He bowed to them, then addressed Akitada. "I went back for Turtle and that swine Wada."

Akitada nodded. "I hope you tied up Wada. He is under arrest."

Tora shook his head. "He's dead, sir."

Akitada gave him a sharp look. "How?"

Tora hesitated. "Er, it wasn't me, sir. I found him dead when I got there, sir. Turtle claims the soldiers did it."

"Nonsense! We would have seen them stop. Kumo was in such a hurry to catch up with us that he did not bother to slow down." Akitada frowned. And that was strange. Wada must have been dead already or unconscious, or he would surely have cried out to Kumo. Getting to his feet, he said, "Excuse me, gentlemen. I think I'll have a word with my lieutenant's servant. Come, Tora."

Outside, he found a grinning and whistling Turtle holding the reins of the three horses. One of them had the corpse of Wada slung over its saddle. Blood dripped slowly into the dust. Akitada lifted the dead man's head and saw that his throat had been slit. It did not look like a sword wound, and his eyes went to the servant's waist. There was a bulge under his jacket.

"Show me your knife!" he ordered.

The smug expression on the small cripple's face changed to unease. After a moment, he reached into his jacket and produced a small, sharp knife.

Akitada inspected it. The blade was clean, but traces of blood still clung to the joint between blade and hilt. "Did he give you trouble?" he asked mildly, gesturing toward the corpse.

A nod and a small cringing wiggle were his answer.

"You thought he might alert the soldiers?"

Akitada was rewarded with a more energetic nod and a tentative grin.

"That took courage. The soldiers might have caught you."

Turtle cried, "I was quick, your honor. He was sitting up and looking at the soldiers coming toward us. I could tell he was glad to see them. I pulled my knife and reached around him like so." He gestured vividly. "Then I jumped behind a bush like my master told me to." Turtle straightened his shoulders proudly and gave Tora a wide smile. When Tora remained impassive, Turtle turned back to Akitada. "I did right, didn't I, your honor?"

"You did right." Akitada returned the knife. "Put Wada with the other corpses, Tora. I'm glad your servant spared you the trouble."

Tora growled. "He deprived me of the satisfaction. The bastard should've died before he was born." And with that peculiar logic, Tora slung the corpse of Wada, once the most feared man on Sadoshima, over his shoulder and walked away.

Akitada looked after him with affection and then retraced his steps to the passage where he had fought Kumo. The body was gone, though large bloodstains still marked where it and the other slain men had lain. How quickly it had been over! All those weeks in the mine he had thought of what he would say and do to Kumo when they finally met face to face. It had turned out very differently. They had exchanged few words, and those had been mostly Kumo's, accusing Akitada of bloodlust. He knew now that Kumo had been wrong, that a man may feel a certain exhilaration in fighting for his life or for a righteous cause, but that he would never kill for mere pleasure.

Surely Kumo must have known that he might die. He had simply not been a sword fighter. Akitada did not pride himself on special expertise and he had been exhausted, yet he had known immediately and with astonishing disappointment that the man was not much of an adversary. Kumo had talked about sacrifice and bowed with great reverence—as if he were about to carry out a sacred duty. Strange! The puzzle nagged at him.

Akitada went where Kumo had stood. As he recalled, the man had turned slightly toward his right. All that could be seen in that direction were two of the farm buildings and between them a narrow slice of the sparkling bay. No temple. No small shrine. No flying banners. Just a bit of water with a few fishing boats, some gulls, and that ship at anchor.

It was odd that there should be such a large ship outside a fishing harbor. What was it doing here? Why was it not at Mano?

He walked back up to the highway and looked across the houses of this small town. There was nothing of any significance on the waterfront. All the more substantial buildings—a temple and a few large farms like this one—were on higher ground. He shook his head in confusion and decided that he did not want to talk to Mutobe yet, not until he settled some of his uncertainties, some of the niggling suspicions in the back of his mind. And so he started walking along the road.

Something about the way Okisada had died still dissatisfied him. Shunsei had told him that Okisada habitually consumed *fugu* and had done so the night of the dinner because he had claimed to get relief from his constant pain by eating a small amount of the poison. It was Shunsei's testimony which had convinced Akitada that the prince had died by his own hand.

Sakamoto had also thought that Okisada poisoned himself and that he had done so in order to throw suspicion on Toshito. But Sakamoto had not been in the others' confidence. No, Akitada was convinced the true conspirators were Kumo, Taira, and Nakatomi.

According to Haru, the expert in matters pertaining both to *fugu* and to men, the poison could make a man feel as though he had entered heaven and give him back his sexual strength. What was more likely than that the self-indulgent Okisada had also become an expert in those properties of the *fugu* poison? Would such a man kill himself with it, intentionally or accidentally?

Akitada became transfixed in the middle of the roadway, much to the consternation of a group of peasants who had to pass him in order to visit the site of the battle. They eyed him with fear, this bearded, gaunt creature in silk robe and trousers but with bare feet and a scowl on his face. Wondering perhaps if he was some supernatural creature, they kept to the shoulder of the road, bobbing deep bows as they edged past him.

Akitada had been seized by an awful suspicion. He swung around suddenly to look past the peasants to the ship in the harbor and cried, "Hah, they think they have been clever, the scoundrels. But by heaven, they shall not get away with it!"

The peasants squawked and took off running.

Akitada walked back to the farmhouse, turning matters over in his mind before speaking to Mutobe. Nakatomi's role had been crucial. And Taira had had a very good reason to refuse visitors at the manor. But he could not make out Shunsei. The monk had seemed too simpleminded for such an enormous deception. Amazingly, the clever plot had almost worked.

And then another thought came. Kumo and his men had worn their finest armor and ridden silk-trimmed horses. Their bows and arrows had been purely ceremonial. They had never been meant to be used in combat. Kumo was not chasing a couple of convicts, even if one of them was an imperial official. He had come here to serve "his" emperor and had only attacked because Akitada got in his way. That was why Kumo had faced battle with Akitada, claiming that he was sacrificing his Buddhahood for his emperor. He had been willing to kill Akitada even though that would prevent his salvation.

Whatever the true state of affairs, no time was to be lost. Mutobe must board the ship immediately. They must search the town. Akitada glanced again at the substantial roofs of the temple. That was where he would start.

Full of purpose again, he strode into the farmhouse and confronted the others with his suspicions.

"You cannot be serious!" gasped the governor, turning pale. "But how is this possible? And after all that time!" He rose and paced. "What will I do if it is as you say? How can I arrest him? What do I charge him with? I have no such authority. And you have lost your documents." He stopped and stared accusingly at Akitada. "What will we do? This is a very delicate matter."

"Delicate?" Mutobe's continuing self-interest appalled Akitada. Did the man not know that there were duties he could not shirk? It was obvious that he could not expect much help from the man. But Mutobe was quite right about one thing. Without his papers, Akitada had no authority whatsoever and was dependent on Mutobe's support. He took a deep breath. A shouting match would solve nothing. "It seems the ship in the harbor is a pirate craft. If you will board it and arrest the captain and crew, I will do the rest. I will need a few of your men. Please instruct them to obey Tora's commands."

Mutobe nodded reluctantly. "You will take the responsibility, then?"

"Yes."

Mutobe still looked unhappy, but he agreed. "Very well. Let us go and get it over with."

Akitada took eight of the soldiers and Mutobe the rest. Then they set off, Mutobe with his banner carried before him, Akitada without such marks of authority, though he pushed Kumo's gilded sword through the silken sash of Mutobe's spare robe, and smoothed his hair a little. Tora put on a little show of snapping commands at his troops, and they were off, followed by a gaggle of curious peasants.

The temple was a very modest one. It had no pagoda and only one main hall and some low buildings to house the local priest and visiting monks. An old man was sweeping the courtyard, but otherwise the scene was peaceful. Doubts began to stir in Akitada's mind. How Toshito would mock if it turned out that Akitada was wrong again. And he could offer nothing but a far-fetched argument based on a fishwife's tale! Sending a detailed report about Akitada's activities to the emperor would be the perfect revenge for the governor's son.

The old man stopped his sweeping, stared at them, then bowed. Perhaps he thought they were expected. Akitada took it for a hopeful sign. He made straight for the hall and took the stairs to the double doors, Tora and the soldiers at his heels. Throwing wide the doors on empty space, he shouted, "Is anyone here?"

The light was dim inside. Across from him was a long dais, and on the dais rested a Buddha figure. Behind the statue a lath screen extended across the hall. Lights flickered beyond and a shadow moved behind the screen.

His heart pounding, Akitada quickly crossed the hall and passed around the end of the screen. Here grass mats had been spread and more screens placed to create a series of smaller chambers. The first of these was empty, though a candle burned in a tall holder. Two silken cushions still held imprints. Akitada flung aside a flimsy screen, saw that the next enclosure was also empty, and rushed across it to tear aside the final screen.

Two old men huddled in the center of this room, their arms about each other and their eyes looking fearfully his way. Tora and the soldiers quickly surrounded them.

One of the two was Taira of the snow-white hair and beetling black eyebrows.

"Who are you? What do you want?" he quavered, hugging the other man to him.

Akitada's eyes were on his companion. At first glance this man had appeared as senile as Taira, but Akitada now saw that he was only slightly past middle age. He looked much older because his skull was shaven, he was fat, and he had the unhealthy pallor of a sick person. He had changed greatly with the years, but there was no doubt in Akitada's mind that this was Okisada, the Second Prince, formerly crown prince and heir to the imperial throne. Not dead, but very much alive.

He had the round face, small nose, and thick lips of his imperial and Fujiwara relatives, and once, years ago, on the occasion of an imperial procession, Akitada had seen him ride past in all the pomp and glory of his former exalted position. His present condition made a shocking change from those happier times, but Akitada had never forgotten his face.

He bowed deeply. "Your Highness," he said, "My name is Sugawara Akitada. I regret extremely to find you under such circumstances. I am afraid that it is my duty to place you and Lord Taira under arrest for attempted treason."

Okisada said nothing. His lower lip trembled and he clutched convulsively at Taira. Taira detached himself gently and said, "Let us resume our seats, Highness, and hear what this person has to say in explanation of such outrageous charges."

Passing Akitada and the staring soldiers, he led his master back to the cushions in the first room. The soldiers put up the screen again. On a gesture from Akitada, they remained. A brazier full of glowing coals made the area hot and stuffy on this late summer day. Nobody invited Akitada to sit. He knelt formally, found that his knee hurt abominably, and sat back on his heels.

He addressed Okisada. "I have no doubt that you already know who I am and why I am here on Sadoshima, but to observe the formalities, I serve as temporary imperial envoy with powers to inquire into certain irregularities among the exiles here. More specifically I was sent to investigate Your Highness's alleged murder. Would you care to explain why you performed this extraordinary charade?"

Okisada's lower lip began to quiver again. Taira put his thin hand on his arm and said angrily to Akitada, "How dare you address His Imperial Highness in such a tone and with such words? Where are your credentials?"

"My lord, I believe you know very well where they are. Besides, since both of you are exiles here, I do not owe you any explanations. We are wasting time. I suppose you expect the arrival of the rebel Kumo before leaving on the ship at anchor in the harbor? I regret to inform you that Kumo is dead, and that Governor Mutobe is at this moment boarding the ship to arrest its captain and men. Your supporters will shortly be rounded up and tried for their involvement in this plot."

Okisada cried out and clutched at Taira again. Taira turned very pale. He snapped, "You lie."

Akitada removed the gilded sword from his sash and placed it on the mat before Taira. "I told you the truth," he said. "I killed Kumo myself and took his sword off his body not an hour ago."

They both looked at the sword in horror. Taira bit his lip, then his eyes searched Akitada's face. Okisada began to weep.

"All for nothing," the prince blubbered. "It was all for nothing. Poor Shunsei starved to death, and all my suffering wasted. Oh, why is this world so cruel to me?"

Taira murmured something soothing and stroked the prince's back.

So Okisada's lover had died, expecting to join his beloved in another world. Akitada sighed. There was little pleasure in confronting this man with his guilt. He was weak, spoiled, and self-centered, but he had been raised expecting to be emperor. The disappointment apparently had destroyed whatever good qualities the prince might once have had. He said, "I think you took a carefully measured amount of the *fugu* poison during the professor's dinner in order to induce a deathlike trance. You did this to cause the governor's son to be arrested for your murder and to cover preparations for your return to imperial power. Your charade worked because neither Sakamoto nor Mutobe's son were familiar with this particular effect of the poison."

"What you are pleased to call a charade, Lord Sugawara," said Taira in a tired voice, "was no more than an accident. We all thought His Highness dead. It was his physician, Nakatomi, who discovered that the prince had fallen into a state approximating nirvana. He remained like that for days. We thought it a miracle when he returned to life, and we were, of course, overjoyed, but . . ." He paused, searching for words.

Akitada snapped, "In that case, why did you pursue the murder charge against young Mutobe? And why allow the monk Shunsei to die of grief?"

Okisada buried his face in a sleeve and sobbed.

Taira sighed. "You don't understand. We had hoped for better treatment from the authorities here. Instead Mutobe and his son began a systematic campaign of persecution against us and our sole protector, the high constable. Don't forget that you are in the presence of the rightful emperor. Our lives are dedicated to returning him to the throne."

"And so you would have let young Mutobe die for a murder which did not happen?"

Taira raised his brows. "Certainly not. Exile is the worst that could happen to him. He is an irritating young man. A period of military service in the north might make a man of him."

Akitada found himself agreeing with that. Having wronged Toshito by misjudging him had worsened his dislike for the young man. There was something about Toshito that made him the perfect target for false accusations. But it would not do to let Taira know of his feelings. He said coldly, "I do not believe you. Many people have spoken of the prince's fondness for *fugu*. I expect he knew the effects of the poison very well indeed. But Sakamoto, Shunsei, and young Mutobe all thought the prince had died. You had the presumed corpse taken to Nakatomi, who pronounced death by poison. Then you staged a cremation and afterwards you, my lord, left for your mansion with the prince hidden in your sedan chair. There you and the prince waited until Toshito would be found guilty and Mutobe would be recalled. But two events interrupted your plans. First I arrived on the scene, and then Toshito escaped from prison."

Taira growled, "Kumo always was too devout. He should have killed you."

"Yes. I wondered why I was buried alive in his mine. I take it that the thief Genzo brought you my papers?"

Taira did not answer.

"Well, as I said, Toshito's unexpected escape from prison caused another delay, and that is why you are still here now. With your ship at anchor in the harbor."

The prince whimpered. Taira was very pale, but his black eyes burned. "Prove it! We have done nothing."

"The proof is waiting. The governor is about to arrest the ship's captain and crew. Then we will question Nakatomi. I doubt they will hesitate to speak under the circumstances. And with Kumo dead, your connections to the mainland and ties with the Ezo rebels are broken. Your contacts there will also be arrested. It is pointless to persist, my lord."

There was a long silence. Then Taira said, "I wish to see Kumo's corpse."

Akitada dispatched Tora with four of the soldiers to bring the body. Then he turned to Okisada. "You must have been afraid of dying, Highness."

Okisada sat up a little and dabbed the tears from his face. "Nonsense," he muttered. "I was very careful. There is not another person in the world who knows as much about the fish as I do."

Akitada heard the boast and believed it. But he still thought Okisada had been lucky. Or perhaps not. For what would happen next was in the hands of the emperor and his advisors, and it would hardly be as pleasant as Okisada's exile on Sadoshima. As for Taira, a second attempt at rebellion meant the death penalty.

More to the point, Okisada had just admitted his guilt, though he would not think of himself as being either culpable or foolish. Taira compressed his lips, but did not chide his master.

"I have been wondering how you smuggled the *fugu* fish to the dinner," Akitada went on. "Everyone said that you ate only Toshito's stew and the dishes served by Sakamoto's servants."

"I have been in the habit of preparing my own *fugu* for years. It has certain properties which ease pain and produce a pleasant sense of well-being. That evening I brought a small amount of the so-called poison with me in my sleeve. Nobody noticed my adding it to the stew."

Heavy steps sounded in the hall beyond the screen, then a dull thump. After a moment Tora appeared and asked, "Where do you want him?"

Before Akitada could answer there was a shout, and then a slight figure in fluttering white robes slipped past Tora. Ribata. A few steps into the dim room she stopped uncertainly. Her eyes found Okisada. She cried, "Cousin! It is true. You are alive. A miracle! Oh, praise the Buddha!" She went to him, knelt, bowed deeply, and then raised her shining face, taking his hands in hers. "Oh, my dear. How happy I am to find you alive after all! I was lonely for you, my almost-brother."

Ribata's being another member of the imperial family was no complete surprise to Akitada. After all, Kumo's grandmother, the senile Lady Saisho, had addressed her as Naka no Kimi, Princess. But if anything, Ribata's imperial blood made her presence on this island of exiles an even greater mystery.

Okisada leaned forward to embrace Ribata. "Dearest cousin. It is not a happy occasion, I am afraid. Is it true that Kumo is dead?"

Ribata's face lost some of its joy. "Yes. His body is outside. The soldiers said you wished to pay your last respects."

With her help, Okisada struggled to his feet. Together they walked to the front of the hall, followed by Akitada, Taira, and Tora.

Kumo had been dropped carelessly on the wooden planks, one arm flung over his face and a leg bent awkwardly at the knee. Ribata knelt and gently rearranged the body. Dark blood disfigured his brilliant armor, but he was handsome in death.

Okisada made a face, then bent to peer at him. When he straightened, he said, "A pity. He was a great man. And he could have been an even greater one under my rule." Taira also took a long look and nodded. They stood for a moment in silence. Then Okisada reached into his fine robe and handed Akitada something before turning to take Taira's arm. Together they went back to the room they had left.

Akitada looked down at what he had been given and saw that the prince had returned his imperial mandate. It had been done without explanation or apology for the theft. Of course, as the present emperor's brother and, in his own opinion, the rightful emperor himself, he probably felt that he had a right to the documents. But Okisada's voluntary surrender of the papers meant that he had accepted defeat. He had allowed Akitada to complete his assignment. He heaved a deep breath and turned to Tora. "Stay with them. They are to see or speak to no one without my permission."

Ribata still knelt beside Kumo's corpse. She was praying, her beads moving through her thin fingers with soft clicks. Akitada waited. When she finished and rose, he said, "Forgive me for troubling you, but I gather that you, too, are a member of the imperial family."

She bowed her head. After a moment, she said, "Only a handful of people know why I am here. I ask that you keep my secret."

Akitada hesitated. "It may become relevant to the case against your cousin."

"No. I swear to you, it has nothing to do with poor Okisada's case. It is my story alone. Nothing but tragedy will come to innocent people if it becomes known in the capital that I am here."

"Very well. If what you say is true, I promise to keep your secret."

"Thank you." She sighed. "I am . . . was the third daughter of Emperor Kazan. He died when I was only eight. Okisada's mother and mine were sisters, married to different emperors. My cousin and I grew up together until my marriage to a high court noble was being arranged. But I was sixteen and in love with a low-ranking officer of the guards. We were found out, and he was sent here into exile. I followed him, disguised as a nun." She fell silent, as if that explained all.

Perhaps it did, but Akitada was not content. After a moment's silence, he said, "You must both have loved very deeply to give up so much. And Toshito?"

Now she smiled. "How very perceptive of you, my lord. I suppose you saw the resemblance?"

"Yes. And your . . . husband?"

The sadness returned. "There was no future for us. They would have killed him if I had become his wife. After my son's birth, I shaved my head and took the nun's habit for good. Toshito was formally adopted by Mutobe."

So Mutobe had been the lover? It explained his permanent appointment. No doubt the emperor who had sent him to Sadoshima had made him its governor on condition he stay there. And she had become a nun rather than bring down the wrath of the emperor on the man she loved. Young Toshito probably knew or suspected that she was his mother. No wonder his bearing was haughty. The imperial lineage was in his blood, though it would hardly make him welcome at court.

"Thank you, Princess. Your confidence honors me," said Akitada, bowing deeply. And, even though he still had his doubts about her, he added, "I ask your pardon for having suspected you of supporting Kumo."

She gave him a very sweet smile. "Call me Ribata. I am an old woman now and a nun. And you were wise to be suspicious." She turned to look down at Kumo's corpse. "I knew him when he was a mere boy. In those days I could not visit my own son, and Sanetomo became like my own. We used to talk about his love for the Buddha's teachings and for all who suffered injustice in this life. I loved him dearly, but even then I feared and distrusted him. He was . . . too passionate. I often wonder if this place makes some men pursue grand schemes because their world has become as small as a grain of sand." She turned back to Akitada. "You are a good man and a man of honor. May you find happiness in the small things."

Akitada bowed deeply. As he left the hall and the temple compound to walk back to the farmhouse, he thought about Okisada, Kumo, and even Mutobe. All three were weak men, and all three had become obsessed with dreams of power. Even little Jisei had bargained his life for an impossible dream. Akitada suddenly felt a great need to be with Haseo, who had been his friend and protector. Without him he would not have survived. He remembered his face again, shining with the happiness of being free—for too short a time. Haseo had fought joyfully against their enemies and been a better man than any Akitada had met on Sadoshima.

The sky was clouding up a little, and the brightness of the afternoon sun had become like light shining through gossamer silk. The sea, instead of brilliant silver and blue, now stretched before him faintly green, pale celadon fading to the color of wisteria. He looked at the softened greens of the mountains, themselves turning to a bluish lavender, and at the russet houses below, and found the world both sadder and more beautiful than before.

EPILOGUE

The return voyage was swift and unexpectedly pleasant. Neither storms nor seasickness spoiled Akitada's homecoming. The skies were as clear as they sometimes are in autumn, a limpid blue which swept from Sawata Bay past the headlands of Sadoshima all the way to the shore of Echigo. A brisk wind carried them smoothly toward the mainland.

Akitada stood at the bow, watching the approach of the long rugged coastline that protected a green plain and distant snow-covered mountains, and was filled with an astonishing affection for the place. He resolved to make the best of his future there, for he was going home to his family, the firm center of his turbulent life.

His deep joy in being alive was increased by Tora's cheerful presence and, to a lesser extent, by the exuberant spirits of

Turtle, who had decided to follow his new master. Killing Wada, a man who had tormented him repeatedly in Mano, had given Turtle self-confidence and an altogether more optimistic outlook on life. Even his limp seemed less noticeable, perhaps because it was modified by a distinct swagger. Turtle had become "somebody" in his own eyes by ridding his fellow drudges of a cruel and petty tyrant. Turtle was now a man to be respected, even feared, by other men, and so he had offered his talents and services to Tora and Akitada.

But the ship carried far more important travelers. Okisada was returning to the capital under heavy guard. Akitada had twice visited the prince in his cabin and doubted that Okisada would survive the overland journey to Heian-kyo. Soft living and repeated doses of *fugu* poison had undermined his health to such a degree that he was in constant pain and frequently vomited the little food he consumed.

Akitada had not escaped unscathed, either. He still limped, and his knee ached when he walked too much or the weather changed. Spending long hours sitting cross-legged on the dais during the court hearings in Mano had not helped.

Three officials had been present for the hearing which had cleared young Mutobe of the murder charge. The judge, a frightened rabbit of a man, expected ignominious dismissal for having ordered the governor's son jailed in the first place. He kept looking to the governor and Akitada for approval.

The third man on the dais was so far above the judge that he did not dare look at him. He was the imperial advisor who had sent Akitada to Sadoshima. It was widely assumed that he was there to protect Prince Okisada's interests, but this was not quite true. He had come to take the prince back to Heian-kyo to face the punishment chosen by the emperor. Unlike his shorter, more irascible assistant, he had not returned to the capital, but remained in Echigo to await the results of Akitada's mission. He had taken ship when the news of Kumo's death and Okisada's arrest had reached the mainland.

After lengthy deliberations and many nervous recitations from his legal codes, the judge had found Taira and Nakatomi guilty of laying false charges against the governor's son. He was not, of course, competent to deal with Okisada's treasonable intentions. That would be judged by a higher court in the capital. However, the sovereign's advisor, along with the governor and Akitada, had extracted private confessions from all three conspirators. Afterward Taira had requested a sword. When this was naturally refused, he had broken a sharp sliver of bamboo from a writing table in his cell, forced this into the large vein in his throat, and died during the night. The physician Nakatomi, on hearing the news, hanged himself the next night by his silk sash from the bars in his cell door. Only Okisada, protected by his imperial blood from public execution, seemed apathetic to his fate.

That left Sakamoto. Akitada had long since decided that the poor and elderly professor had been duped by Taira and Kumo. They had not trusted him with their real plans or the details of the plot but had played on his adulation of Okisada to use his home for their meetings and his good name to cover their activities. Not unlike Shunsei, though the relationship had been different, Sakamoto had been the victim of his own foolish sentiment. The thin gentleman from the emperor's office had, once he had spoken to Sakamoto, agreed. Sakamoto was left with a warning that he faced arrest if he returned to the capital. It amounted to unofficial exile, much like that imposed on Mutobe many years earlier, but since Sakamoto had no wish to leave, he expressed tearful gratitude.

Kumo's mines were confiscated and closed, and their workers were dispersed among other public projects. Osawa, newly wed and in rotund health, had provided useful testimony that the mines had not produced enough silver to justify their continued operation. Akitada wrestled with his conscience about the gold. Gold was vitally important to the nation, but more intensive mining and abuse of prisoners were sure to follow if the government heard of the gold deposits. Eventually he told the emperor's advisor. The thin man asked some searching questions and had Kita, Kumo's bird-faced mine supervisor, brought in. Kita saved his life by making a full report, which caused the thin gentleman to remark that the distance from the capital and the difficulty of transport made it highly unlikely that His Majesty would be interested.

And so Akitada was returning home, a man so changed that he felt like a stranger to his former self. As he strained his eyes for the shore, he was seized by a dizzying sense of unreality. For a man who had lived like a common criminal, subjected to vicious beatings and backbreaking labor, who had been buried alive and barely survived against all odds a battle to the death, this uneventful and untroubled homecoming seemed more dreamlike than the nightmares that had plagued his feverish brain underground.

To steady himself, he searched for his wife and son among the people waiting on shore. The shoreline began to swim before his eyes, and the snow-covered peaks fractured into green and white patches floating against the blue of the sky. As he reached up to brush the tears from his eyes, the thin gentleman interposed his tall frame between Akitada and the view.

"Not long now," the emperor's advisor said in his dry voice, averting his eyes quickly from Akitada's face. "You will wish to be with your family after we land, so I shall make my farewells here."

"Thank you, Excellency." Akitada managed to choke out the words. To cover the awkwardness of the moment, he asked, "You have been to see His Highness? How is he?"

"Not well. He may survive the journey, but his mind is weakening rapidly. I doubt that he will be able to say much in his defense. He seems to be under the impression that he is to assume the throne."

Akitada said, "I am sorry." It was the strongest expression of sympathy he could find. He thought of the dying Haseo and found difficulty in adjudging proper levels of regret to the tragic lives of the men he had met. What, for example, of the little thief Jisei? Would his soul rest more happily knowing that the two pirates who had beaten him to death had been captured on Okisada's ship? Akitada had identified them in the provincial jail and brought murder charges against them, based on Haseo's account. Ironically, they, like Akitada, had been in the stockade under false pretenses. They were there to deal with Jisei if he decided to make trouble about the gold. And, of course, he had done just that, hoping to buy himself freedom with his knowledge.

"I wished to thank *you*," the thin man continued more cordially, "for your help and your loyalty. Without your brilliant exposure of the prince's clever sham, all of our efforts would have been in vain. You have certainly confirmed the high opinion your friends have of you. If it had not been for your determination and courage, we would be involved in a major war by now."

Akitada bowed. "I have done nothing," he murmured. It was the polite response to a compliment, but he knew it was painfully true. There was little to be proud of in the way he had handled his assignment, and he had almost paid with his life for his careless mistakes.

The thin gentleman said, "I do not need to tell you that you have made enemies in the capital. Your requests to return to your former position in the ministry have been blocked by your superior, for example."

Akitada glanced at the other man's profile. Soga's dislike was no news to him, but he had not known that the minister hated him so much that he would condemn him and his young family to permanent misery in Echigo. He turned his eyes back to the approaching land. Green and golden, the shoreline stretched before him until it faded into a misty horizon. Those waiting on shore were waving now. And there, in front, he now saw a slender figure of a young woman holding a child. Tamako and Yori. He raised his arm to wave, and saw Tamako lift up Yori in response. Warm, joyous gratitude flooded over him. Whatever the hardship, he still had his work and his small family. Injustice flourished everywhere, in Sadoshima, Echigo, the capital, and also in the place where Haseo had lived. Akitada had survived, and that was all that mattered.

But his companion still waited for a comment. "Thank you for telling me," Akitada said. "I shall have to be patient and work harder to win the regard of my superiors, that's all."

The thin man smiled and put his hand on Akitada's shoulder. "Courage! You may have enemies in the capital," he said, "but you also have a new friend."

HISTORICAL NOTE

During the Heian Period (794–1185) the Japanese government loosely followed the Tang China pattern of an elaborate and powerful bureaucracy. The junior official Sugawara Akitada is a fictional character, but his ancestor, Sugawara Michizane (845–903), was very real. His life exemplified the dangers faced by even the most brilliant and dedicated officials who made enemies at court. Michizane, a superb administrator and great poet, rose to preside over the sovereign's private office but ended his life in miserable exile.

By the time of the present novel, two hundred years after Michizane, the administrative power is almost exclusively in the hands of the Fujiwara family, whose daughters had consistently been empresses. The Fujiwara women had borne emperors who tried to rule briefly before resigning under pressure from their in-laws in favor of sons who were often too young to interfere in Fujiwara policy. The tale of the Second Prince illustrates the political uncertainties inherent in the imperial succession and the numerous incidents of rebellion by claimants to the throne or to the position of prime minister. The real power, the prime minister, was almost always a senior Fujiwara and he headed, assisted by brothers, cousins, and uncles, an enormous central government located in Heian-kyo (Kyoto). They controlled more or less successfully the rest of the country through provincial governors, men of rank and birth with university training and Fujiwara support. A governor's duties encompassed overseeing tax collection, law enforcement, and civic improvements in his province. He normally served four years but might choose to serve longer or absent himself altogether while his duties were carried out by a junior official. Akitada is such a substitute, while Mutobe has taken permanent residence. Their provinces, Echigo and Sadoshima, are so remote from the capital, and life there is so dangerous for officials that more favored individuals considered such assignments not only undesirable but punitive.

Sadoshima, or Sado Island, is located in the Sea of Japan, about thirty-five kilometers from Echigo (modern Niigata) Province. In the eleventh century, it was an independent province with provincial headquarters, several towns, and Buddhist temples. It was also a place where people were sent into exile for serious offenses, and where gold was discovered fairly early. Though there was no government mining of gold until 1601, panning for gold in rivers and streams had been known for centuries. Kumo's secret mining operation described in the novel is fictional. The descriptions are based on other early gold mining practices and on the pictures of the Sado mine in a contemporary scroll (*Sado Kozan Emaki*). According to the scroll, both silver and gold were taken from the same mine. In the absence of Japanese historical sources, I am indebted to Angus Waycott's *Sado: Japan's Island in Exile*, a charming journal of his eight-day hike around the island, in which he describes the local geography, flora, and fauna, and gives brief accounts of the island's history.

Provincial law enforcement was carried out by three distinct authorities: the local imperial police—present in Sadoshima since 878; a high constable, usually a local landowner with manpower at his disposal, who was appointed or confirmed by the central government; and the governor, who appointed and supervised local judges. Because of Buddhist opposition to the taking of life, the death penalty was rarely imposed. Exile, often with extreme deprivation and hard labor, was the punishment of choice for serious offenses. This was, as in the case of Haseo, commonly accompanied by confiscation of property and dispersal of the rest of the family.

In addition to the practice of Buddhism, the other state religion recognized in Heian Japan was Shinto. Shinto is native to the Japanese islands and involves Japanese gods and agricultural rituals. Buddhism, which entered Japan from China via Korea, exerted a powerful influence over the aristocracy and the government. It was common for emperors and their relatives to shave their heads and become monks and nuns in their later lives. The Buddhist prohibition against taking a life accounts for Kumo's strange behavior. The shrines mentioned in the novel, along with the *tengu* sculpture, belong to the animistic Shinto faith which was more closely tied to peasant life.

Intellectual life reached a high point during the eleventh century. The sons of upper-class families (the "good people") were trained in Chinese and Japanese studies at local schools and at the universities in the capital. Their sisters wrote generally only in Japanese, but they produced exquisite poetry, diaries, and the first novel anywhere. In the other social classes, education probably ranged from illiteracy to the partial acquisition of useful skills, especially that of writing with ink and brush not only in Chinese characters but also in Japanese script. Akitada, with his university training, would have been adept at both, in addition to having a very good knowledge of the Chinese language, while the *shijo* Yutaka would associate characters only with their Japanese meaning. The emphasis of education was on supporting an efficient bureaucracy run by the "good people."

A brief reference to the Ezo (modern Ainu), a people distinct in origin and custom from the Japanese, may explain the very real danger of Okisada and Kumo's plan. Considered barbaric by the Japanese, the Ezo had been pushed northward for centuries until, by the tenth century, they were more or less pacified in Dewa and Mutsu, the northernmost provinces of Honshu. The pacification process had been achieved by allowing Ezo chieftains to become Japanese lords, often with the title of high constable of their territory. But in 939 the Dewa Ezo rebelled and in 1056 the Nine-Years War erupted when the Abe family, who had Ezo origins, rose against the governor of Mutsu. Thus the warrior lords in the unstable northern provinces close to Echigo and Sadoshima would have been obvious allies for Kumo and Okisada.

Finally, the story of the fake silver bars was suggested by an early Chinese legal case (# 9A) in Robert van Gulik's translation of the *'Tang-Yin-Pi-Shi*.